MURDER
OFF THE RECORD

by
Marnie L. Schulenburg

A Write Way Publishing Book

FIC

SCHULENBU
M

Bardo, Robert
Killed TV actress Rebecca Schaeffer
"When I think about her I feel that I want to become famous and impress her."

Booth, John Wilkes
Abraham Lincoln's assassin
"What a glorious opportunity for a man to immortalize himself by killing Abraham Lincoln ... I must have fame, fame!"

Bremer, Arthur
Shot, wounded Governor George Wallace
"If I survive the plot, I hope to become rich by giving my story to *Time-Life* or the *New York Times* people."

Chapman, Mark David
Killed John Lennon
"I wished someone would write a book about me."

For my hero,
Lois Lindsay Schulenburg

CHAPTER ONE

A siren moaned low under the rumble of the crowd shuffling into the concert hall. It didn't register on Peg Lindsay; she was looking forward to slipping out of her shoes. Beside her, Matthew Drum paused, put a hand to his hip and disengaged a beeper. He tilted it toward the lobby light to read the number and drew Peg to him with his other hand.

"It's the paper," Drum said. "I'll need to call—"

His voice was drowned out by the siren bark of a police car as it braked in front of the Riverview Civic Center. The marble floor of the lobby throbbed pink from the lights of more squad cars and emergency vehicles. People near the back of the hall twisted in their seats and jumped up to follow Matthew Drum and Peg Lindsay across the lobby to the glass doors.

Across the street and two buildings down, the police were cordoning off Bogies, a video rental store. That was odd: it looked to Peg as if the store was closed.

Channel 7's Action News van sped up the street and stopped in front of the Civic Center. The doors split and people spilled out—Peg counted five of them—their faces alight with excitement.

"What do you suppose?" she said.

"You stay here," Matthew told her and shouldered open the door.

Maybe he was being gallant but Peg Lindsay didn't appreciate the tone and had no choice in the matter, anyway. She was roughly thrust outside by the first wave of the black-tie and sequined mob behind her. Someone's ankle tangled up with hers and Peg's arthritic hip slammed into the brick wall of the Civic Center. She stayed pinned for a moment, catching her breath.

Bodies surged against the sawhorses and yellow tape the police were hurriedly cobbling together. Peg eased toward the curb and rose on her toes to find Matthew. He stood inside the taped zone with the police chief, Sterling Opel. Sterling's profile, a dead ringer for the old TV silhouette of Alfred Hitchcock, was unmistakable. Opel gestured broadly and then hollered through cupped hands into Matthew's ear.

Peg looked back to the Action News van. A young woman was adjusting switches on the back of a camera, supporting it on one raised knee. It was Marsha Sanger! She had been in Peg's Girl Scout troop nearly 20 years ago.

"Marsha?" Peg pulled harder at the denim vest. "Marsha!"

Marsha's irritation washed away. "Mrs. Lindsay. Hi. Gee, how *are* you?"

"Marsha, I'm in your way here, but can you tell me, what in the world?"

Marsha Sanger hooked her long hair behind one ear and hoisted the camera to her shoulder. "It's a hostage deal in Bogies, can you believe it?"

"But the store is all dark."

"That's paint. He's painted the windows black from the inside." Marsha glanced to her left and gestured with her head at a young man in baggy jeans and a sport coat who stood close to their van, concentrating with a frenzied manner on a small spiral notebook, his lips moving. It was Johnny Rangel, the station's news anchor and the closest thing to a celebrity in Riverview. Hundreds of schoolgirl hearts had been broken the year before when he got married.

"The shooter is demanding to talk to us," Marsha said. "Johnny and I are going in, if Chief Opel okays it."

"The shooter?" Peg asked. "You mean he'll kill someone if he doesn't get what he wants?"

"He already has. The threat is, he'll do it again."

Peg Lindsay pressed both hands over her heart. "Oh, heavens no. Who?"

"Who did he kill, you mean?" Marsha shrugged as she unsnapped a gadget from her belt and held it toward the light. "No idea."

The poor girl was trying to play it cool but the tremor in her hands blurred the dial she was trying to read and she pulled it close to her waist, using her body to steady it. Peg laid a hand on her arm. "Nobody would blame you if you didn't go in there."

"Oh, Mrs. Lindsay," Marsha laughed gaily, "that's sweet. But you don't understand, see, this guy needs us. He's hardly going to take *us* out."

Peg shook her head. If this was her daughter, if this was Sabina, she'd drag her by the hair to get her away from there. Of course, Sabina would slap her away and do what she wanted to, anyway. Peg turned in time to see Matthew Drum hurrying back toward the concert hall. They met up at the doors. "It's all right," she said, pre-empting him. "I'm not so nuts about Mahler anyway."

On the drive home to the Bluffs, Matthew was with her in body only. "I wonder who was killed," Peg said at one point. His response, after a long pause, was to curse the absence of a cellular phone in the car he was leasing. When they rolled into her driveway, Drum shifted into reverse, his foot tapping the brake pedal. "Don't bother walking me up, Matthew," she said mockingly. That seemed to restore him to the present, but Peg repeated herself, meaning it. She started up her walk, wobbling a little in her new navy heels.

Matthew leaned across the car seat and called to her through the open window. "I'm sorry about this."

Peg turned around, drawing her shawl tighter around her shoulders. "You've got a story to cover," she told him.

"Or not to cover," he said. "Sabina talked to you about it?"

"About what?" Peg said quickly and, she hoped, convincingly. Her daughter had told her of Ed Fountain's idea for some kind of crime news moratorium, but the girl was a touch nervous about this new careers of hers, and more than a touch sensitive about how she got the job. Peg thought it safer to play dumb.

"Never mind," Drum said. "Do me a favor?"

"Certainly."

"Call Sabina. Tell her what's happened, that I could really use her at an emergency meeting at the paper. Right away."

Peg Lindsay shook her head, smiling. "You don't know Sabina very well yet, do you? She's there already, or on the way. I'd lay odds on it."

CHAPTER TWO

The heavy steel door of the camera-plate room clanged shut. Sabina Shaw looked over her shoulder to see a redhead in leather vest and pants threading her way through the jumbled monochrome beige of the Riverview *Times* newsroom. Sabina braced herself. With every newcomer, Phelps Pascal, the city editor, had been introducing her in two parts. The first part: "This is Sabina Shaw, our new ... ah ... consultant." Something about the word consultant, she had noticed, made people stammer. The second part, by way of explanation for why anyone would hire a consultant, much less Sabina: "Her mother is dating Mr. Drum."

Oh, well, that explained it. Only way she could get the job, don't you know.

Sabina was leaning against a steel column, also beige, at the fringes of a subdued group watching the Bogies story unfold on a ceiling-mounted TV. Phelps Pascal was perched on the edge of a desk in front of her. Sabina tapped him on the shoulder and gestured for him to follow her. When they were a safe distance from the others, she faced him.

"Phelps. I like to think I got this job because I owned my own company, and I've done downsizing and acquisitions, and strategic planning big and small for fifteen years, you know? So maybe I heard about it because of my mother, but do you really think someone like Matthew Drum is going to hire me because he's trying to get my mother to, um ... like him better?"

"Oh, gee, Sabina, I'm sorry." Phelps Pascal had the cadaveric body of a long-distance runner and skin so literally thin that the flush ran up his neck and face like a prairie fire. "*Geez*, I'm sorry. Is that how I sounded?" He spread out his hands, palms up. "My wife is always telling me ... well, it's just that you don't, you know ... *look* like a heavyweight kind of *advice* giver."

She grinned at him. "I should be, let's say, fifty-eight years old, male, stand-up white crewcut, laser blue eyes"—she streaked her fingers from hairline to eyebrows—"lightning-bolt creases in my forehead, indicating deep, deep thought—"

Phelps caught on. She was describing Matthew Drum, the new boss, to a T. "I get it," he chuckled. "*Mea culpa, mea culpa*." He held out his hand good-naturedly and she shook it, relieved not to have made an enemy. She could see already that management consulting wasn't like being president of your own company. In this job, you didn't give orders; you listened, persuaded. Sabina wasn't convinced she had the patience for it.

Johnny Rangel was still dominating the TV screen, but the camera had pulled back to show Bogies' awning and front door. The door opened inward and a bare arm was visible, waving something white. Then a woman stood unsteadily in the doorway. She reached behind her and pulled a young girl to her side. Leaning into each other, they walked slowly to freedom, followed by another hostage, and another and another. All except the one who had been killed, and it took another five minutes or so to learn who that was. When the young man didn't come out of Bogies, his mother began a drawn-out, keening cry. The cameras had only to follow the sound.

Negotiations had been resolved by fiat minutes before another Bogies' patron was scheduled for execution. The corpse was collected from the back door, the hostages released, and the Action News team moved in to grant the murderer his wish: an unedited interview fed to their 10 PM newscast and from there, Sabina was sure, to national feeds.

There was a delay of some forty minutes while Channel 7 set up a technically sound environment inside Bogies. In that time, various reporters patched together sketchy information on the victim.

Peter Klassen had simply been after some videos for his prom party. He walked into Bogies at 6 PM and was dead by 6:30. The other hostages said Peter Klassen laughed, or made some sound too close to a laugh. The gunman bound Klassen's hands and feet together with shipping tape, then forced him to hop behind the service counter, drop to his knees, drop to his stomach, and die from a bullet in the back of his head. From TV, viewers knew what Peter Klassen looked like: a graduation photo showed jug ears, big curious eyes and a black shock of hair shaved at the sides. They knew his mother loved him: there was her agonized face.

Then it was showtime, and the viewing audience learned more about the killer, Burton W. Warflin—everything he wanted them to know.

As the madman on the screen jabbered on, Sabina Shaw's attention was drawn irresistibly to Ed Fountain. The editor of the Riverview *Times* sat cross-legged on a desktop, his head tipped to the TV monitor, his pale features gradually contorting. She was reminded of the universal baby game, where hands pass across a face like curtains between performances of shifting expressions. Except this was a painfully slow curtain call and the mask, savage. A baby would not gurgle with delight; a baby would scream.

A few of the others cut glances at Ed Fountain as well, and if they were talking, their words fell away. Sabina was impressed by the respect they showed for him, and perhaps the slimmest measure of relief that fate's grim finger had not branded them quite so enduringly. For thirty-five years, until this day, nothing more violent than a fist-sized bite of tenderloin had done in a citizen of Riverview, Wisconsin ... unless you counted Ed Fountain's daughter, Casey. She was murdered on the other side of the state, in Milwaukee, but she was born and raised in Riverview, and her death was certainly violent.

The interview with the Bogies' murderer lasted twelve long minutes. Ed Fountain opened his eyes at its close and, to a perfectly still room, he said: "Perfect."

Only Phelps Pascal and Sabina Shaw knew what Fountain meant by that pronouncement: a perfect story *not* to cover. And Pascal hadn't fully bought into the idea.

"We didn't really get a green light yet, Ed," Pascal said. "Did we? From Wiley, or from Mr. Drum?"

Fountain unwound his legs and shifted to the edge of the desk. "We glorify that criminal," he said evenly, "over my dead body."

A sound from a back corner of the newsroom startled them. Sabina turned to see Matthew Drum standing in the shadows behind the break table, spinning an ashtray on its metal surface. "I sincerely doubt that will be necessary," he responded to Fountain. "But we have work to do. I'll need you, Ed. And Phelps. Sabina, if you could stay? Frank is on his way. And the Martinelli woman, if she can get a babysitter. Ten minutes. Conference room." He gave the ashtray a final spin and strode off.

That broke the crowd apart. Ed Fountain patted his top shirt pocket, the classic gesture of a non-smoking smoker, and leveled a gaze at his city editor that was the equivalent of a line in the sand.

"Call in the troops, Phelps," Fountain said. "They've got enough to run with. Tell them"—a long pause—"tell them not a single quote from this Warflin asshole. Not one."

Pascal wagged his head from side to side once, his last quiet run at rebellion. "Okay, Ed. I'll help them see the light."

Fountain lowered his head, fixed on Pascal's belt buckle for a moment, and shambled away.

"The poor guy," Pascal said, rubbing a thumb along his jaw line and watching as Fountain turned into his office.

"Do you think he's going to be okay?" Sabina said.

"Will he be *okay*?" He mocked the word, and maybe her as well. He walked to the TV monitor and slapped his palm against the power control. The screen went quiet and blank.

"There's some ways," Pascal said, softly, "that I think Ed won't ever be okay again. He's got enough brains for three guys, but"—he turned his eyes to hers—"just between us, Sabina?"

She nodded.

"Well, he can work." He smiled and shook his head. "Ed can *always* work. And he's started kidding around again, some, but he's, like, permanently distracted. You know? Some part of Ed just isn't *here* anymore."

Sabina had an idea what he meant. On first meeting Ed Fountain a week earlier, she had been struck by his reserve. Yet he was also a man on a mission. He opened up to her because he needed help.

Earlier in the Spring, Peg Lindsay had offhandedly mentioned to her daughter that the head of DEI—Drum Enterprises, Inc.–had moved in next door after buying the *Times*. Peg welcomed Matthew Drum to the neighborhood with a fresh-baked lemon meringue pie. In the next couple of months, there followed fleeting references to art exhibits and plays, which Sabina assumed her mother was attending with her usual set of friends. Until Peg's comical, defensive phone call to Sabina on a night late in May, two hours after Peg's usual 9:30 bedtime.

Her mother barely waited out Sabina's "Hello" before rushing into her prepared speech. "Darling," Peg said, "you should know I've been seeing someone. It's my neighbor, Mr. Drum. I know he's younger, but if he doesn't mind, I don't. Now I don't want any objections from you. I've been in the fridge for too long, what with your father's illness before he died, and now it's been seven years and, well, by God, I'm going to have some fun!"

It turned out Peg Lindsay had been bragging to Matthew Drum about her daughter the entrepreneur, and when Sabina hung out her consulting shingle, Peg told him that, too, and learned Drum was looking to hire someone locally to help with a business plan.

So Sabina faxed a résumé to Matthew Drum on her new SABINA SHAW, MANAGEMENT CONSULTANT letterhead, then spent all of ten minutes with him on the phone. His questions let her know he had already checked her out thoroughly and he as much as said the job was hers if she wanted it. Drum was flying to his Boston headquarters that night and wanted Sabina to meet the next day with the newspaper's editor, Ed Fountain.

Her mother filled her in on the details. Having lived all her sixty-two years in Riverview, there wasn't much that got by Peg Lindsay. Fountain's marriage was shaky even before Casey died, and she had been their only child. Ed coped by working around the clock.

"Casey was apparently very much her father's girl," Peg told Sabina. "Exacting. Funny. Cynical. The perfect reporter."

"I can't remember, this all happened when?"

"A year ago ... my goodness! A year ago tomorrow, it was. I've been president of the garden club one year exactly. I remember thinking, the way one does with these things, that just as I was giving my little speech to the club, that's when Casey was killed."

So it was Sabina Shaw's bad luck to meet Ed Fountain on the anniversary of his daughter's murder.

Sabina had no trouble finding a parking spot directly in front of the building. The Riverview *Times* was housed in a tired, three-story brick structure that squatted at the corner of Water and Edison on the fringes of a struggling industrial sector nicknamed Teedee Valley, after tool-and-die businesses that once dominated the area.

Sabina and her husband, Jacob, moved back to Wisconsin, and to Sabina's hometown five years ago, when they were still married and still partner-owners of Linshaw Bicycle Works. They wanted to be closer to Sabina's mother, and the move also gave them a good price on commercial property for building a new plant. Riverview hadn't changed much since Sabina left for college. The population was still hanging around thirty-three thousand and the economy still hanging on by its fingernails. Most of the wealth was old money, from its manufacturing days. Sabina liked the city best from an airplane, looking down at its rolling perch on cliffs overlooking the Mississippi. Up close, some neighborhoods had gone on the skids, houses run-down or unoccupied and a snaky kind of watch-your-back feel to them.

The Riverview *Times* seemed the only operating business remaining in the 900 block of Water Street. Once a rich yellow cream, the bricks were pockmarked gray from slurping up six decades of truck exhaust and fumes from a coal-burning power plant. But commercial life was slowly returning to the area: a seed catalog company one block south, a plastic tubing plant occupying the shell of a former tool-and-die plant, and Theo's Bar & Grill right across the street.

Sabina assumed the "grill" part because the pink neon sign, missing one letter, read Theo's Bar & G ill. For some reason, the paper's editor, Ed Fountain, asked to meet her there. It was one of those blackboard menu restaurants and smelled of corned beef and a gardenia-spiked cleaner. From a back booth, a man in an open-necked white business shirt half-stood and waved her over. She crossed the sagging pine floor, feeling his unsmiling scrutiny, and reached out her hand. Fountain continued to stare at her a moment too long, a shade too clinically.

"Mrs. Shaw," he said, and took her hand. "Do you mind if I call you ... how do you pronounce your first name? Sabeena?"

"Sabina," she corrected him with an inward sigh. "Rhymes with Carolina."

Or she could say it rhymed with vagina, a discovery that some jerkface in fifth grade leapt upon and ran around chanting at recess. Her classmates had loved it and took it up *en masse*, gleefully calling her 'Sappy Vagina'—Sappy Vee if their parents were around. Sabina's grandmother and namesake would have drowned herself from the shame of it. Since coming back to Riverview, Sabina had run into a few of the 38-year-old "kids" from the old days and could see in their faces the twitches of Sappy Vee memory surfacing.

This was hardly the time to test Ed Fountain's sense of humor. Something was distracting him and Sabina thought it was her, under the microscope of his sleepy green eyes.

Peg Lindsay told her daughter that thirty-five pounds

had flushed off Fountain's frame in the months following his daughter's death, and Sabina couldn't see that he had put any of it back on. His watch was so loose on his wrist he had to chase it down with his other hand and rotate it to read the dial.

After they placed their orders—apple juice for him and a Reuben sandwich for Sabina—Fountain got right to business.

"I've got a time problem today, Sabina."

"I can see that."

He blinked.

"You've checked your watch twice," she explained.

There it was again, the inscrutable assessing look. "My city editor, Phelps, is out having a baby—he's the cheerleader, his wife is the pusher. There's an editorial meet I've got to cover for him. Leaves me an hour with you. I should spend it filling you in so this planning thing comes off. We've got ourselves a few morale problems."

She nodded. "Unusual if you didn't. The buy-out and all."

"Right," he said, dismissively. "But there's a little something else I need to talk to you about."

Then he clammed up. After what this man had been through, Sabina looked in vain for bitterness to have scored his face. Pale complexion, straight brown hair dusting his collar, a sharp nose. And smudgy eyebrows that lent his face the emotionless receptivity of a robin, cocking its head to hear the earthworm. If he was angry, it was buried deep.

"Sabina, have you ever had a premonition?" Fountain grimaced, self-conscious. "I'm aware how loopy that sounds ... but have you?"

"I'm not the type. There was this hypnotist when I was a kid, and I was the only one he couldn't put under."

Fountain was nodding, smiling a little. "I'm as skeptical as they come, but ... well, look. I don't know if you heard about what happened to my daughter Casey?"

She wondered if it was too late to say she was sorry. Who knew the etiquette for murder? "I think I remember it being on the news."

"There's an understatement," Ed said, darkly. "That's, uh, germane to what I want to tell you."

He fell silent again and Sabina could only wait, a little curious and a lot uncomfortable about where this was heading. His juice and her Reuben arrived. The sandwich looked great, bulging and greasy, but she was losing her appetite.

He fiddled with his glass, rocking it from side to side.

"What happened, happened a year ago," Fountain said at last. "Today, in fact. Also, my birthday." He put up a halt-sign hand and added quickly, "I have a reason for telling you that. I'm usually the guy who goes by the facts. But you starting up with us today, of all days ..." He shrugged, his eyes still downcast. "There's something I want to do. Today being the anniversary and all."

He wasn't drinking his juice, just sloshing the liquid close to the lip of the glass and rocking it gently in the crescent puddle of its evaporation. There was another uncomfortable pause and then Ed Fountain stopped talking in jerks and starts.

"Casey knew I had this weakness for turtle sundaes and it was a broiler of a day. We had just loaded up the car to bring her home from school. So. We stopped on the way out of town to get some ice cream at this outdoor stand. This guy started shooting up the place, he crawled on top of his car and lay on his belly. Someone grabbed his ankles and pulled him off, but he got away, holed up in his car and stuck the gun in his mouth. Blew his brains out.

"Just before it happened, I had this ... sense of danger. Something tugging at me. If I had turned to where Casey was standing in line, if I had ..." His voice turned to acid. "Well, fuck. Never mind."

Sabina hadn't a word to offer him. She stared at his hands.

"They found a videotape in the car and it got played on TV there, and then hit the big time, on the news all over." Fountain started to lift his glass to his mouth, but put it down again. "He called it 'The Last Documentary.' Nobody could figure what it was about, except that he hated his stepfather and the world, in that order. He had been shopping the thing around Hollywood, but no one would talk to him. So he moved back home to his folks, the poor bastards, and saw a way to get his documentary aired.

"The killer got his coverage, big time, and Casey, hardly a mention. I decided that was good, that I wouldn't hand them her life, to be used that way. But still."

The front door of Theo's slammed and someone called a greeting to Ed. He kept his head down and the other guy stayed put.

Fountain finally tossed the juice down his throat in two gulps. "I've talked to a few other parents about this, who've also ... and they feel the same. First you do the guilt. Then, you don't want them to have died for nothing."

He sat up straighter and looked at me. "That's where you come in."

"Me?"

"Yeah. I have an idea I can do something about this. *We* can." Now Sabina understood why she had been under his microscope: would she cooperate?

"You're here to do us a strategic plan, and our new CEO, Drum, he tells me that includes ideas for how to distinguish ourselves from TV and other forms of competition. Right?"

She agreed, cautiously.

"One thing we can do is take an editorial position that we won't participate in the media celebration of killers. We put a moratorium, a news blackout, on certain kinds of fame-seeking murderers."

Ed leaned into it, arms stiff on the table and fingers spread wide. His voice had never been softer, but that subterranean wrath Sabina had guessed at was visible now, just. "No immortality, no soapbox for the fucking cowards. That could make a difference, Sabina, if every paper, every radio and TV network did that."

"But ... well, is that realistic? That the other media—"

"No. Of course not," Fountain said reasonably. "We can only be responsible for ourselves, can't we?" He leaned back, lifted an eyebrow.

That such a shapeless eyebrow could send such an unequivocal message. He acknowledged her doubt; he didn't accede to it.

"But Ed, you don't need me. I'm not even in the business! I'm just here to facilitate the planning process, keep things on track. Why me?"

Fountain had concluded that Matthew Drum was a bottom-line executive who would regard Ed's idea as either social welfare nonsense or not worth the potential loss of readers and advertisers, should circulation numbers fall. The editor explained certain financial facts: It had been three years since the paper had turned a profit, good people from the editorial and business side were deserting the ship, and the publisher, Frank Wiley, was incapable of turning things around.

Fountain spread his hands. "So who's the new CEO going to listen to? One of us? I mean, Sabina, it's a matter of presentation. What we want, the shlumps already working here ... what we think should be done gets nowhere with these CEO types. He's Harvard. That's why they hire consultants. Organize our ideas, pretty 'em up, feed 'em back, looks smart, he buys it."

She was taken aback. Was that how he regarded her? "I'm not Ivy League," she told him, and bit back just in time the newsflash that the *Times* was her first client.

"No offense," Ed said. "Generic. But couldn't you do that? Couldn't you think about it, put the potential benefits of a moratorium into consulting buzzwords"—his mouth twisted in a smile—"excuse me, I mean, sound business and marketing terms. The *potential* benefits, I'm saying. We won't get up from meeting one with this being a done deal, understand. There's logistics gotta be worked out. I'm not asking you to manufacture anything. It would have to make sense to you or you wouldn't be convincing. Why couldn't you do that?"

Sabina didn't enjoy being pushed. She hadn't even taken the job yet, or met Matthew Drum, her real client and Ed Fountain's boss. On the other hand, it was hard not to feel something for Ed. Sympathy, at least.

"I'll think about it, Ed."

He reached for something on the bench next to him and passed her a bulging manila file folder. "Here's a little background," he said, slightly shamefaced. "There's a lot of newspapers and broadcast media doing this kind of civic journalism. And stuff in there on copycat crimes. Save you time." He got to his feet and threw some crumpled dollar bills on the table.

They walked across Water Street to the *Times* building and Ed led the way through Editorial, a confusion of computers and huge dump bins and stabs at personalizing bland cubicles. In his office, he parked Sabina in a nicked-up oak chair and excused himself to use the men's room.

The chair sat on wheels over a plastic mat. She heelwalked it in a half-circle one way, then the other. Whenever Sabina was alone lately, time was the enemy. It seemed to her as if Ed had been gone long enough to tile the bathroom. She crossed her ankles and arms, slid forward and rested her head against the chair back. She had been holding depression at bay just fine; surely, she thought, she could make it a little longer. This job was important to her. Not the money, particularly: the working.

"Hello?"

Sabina pushed herself upright. A Partonesque blond hesitated in the doorway, then crossed the carpeted floor, a little wobbly on three-inch heels, to Ed Fountain's desk. She was palming a small, gift-wrapped package. Papers and files and diskettes covered the desk in slippery mounds; the woman put the package on Fountain's chair.

"Hi, honey," she said, turning a broad smile on Sabina. "I'm Ella Martinelli. Don't think I've seen you around?"

Sabina got to her feet and extended her hand. "Sabina Shaw. I'm a ... management consultant. I'll be working here for a while, on business planning."

"Is that right," Martinelli said, startled either by the news or the offer to shake hands. Sabina had her by four inches even in flat shoes and the woman's hand poked at Sabina's palm, crushable as a bird skeleton. Martinelli's nails matched her lips, bright red, and faint evidence of acne scarred her cheeks.

"You're waiting for Ed?" she asked.

Sabina nodded and resumed her seat.

"Do me a favor, honey?" the woman said. "Don't ask him if it's his birthday or anything, okay? I mean, maybe it is and maybe it isn't, it's just that ..." She rubbed some hair ends between a finger and thumb, frowning. "Well, the gift and all, I thought you might get the idea ... and it would be better if you didn't."

Sabina didn't feel like having a long chat with someone who called her honey. "Then I won't," she said, shortly. She watched Martinelli leave. Wide hips, criminy what a pair of boobs, big hair and somehow, despite all the tacky parts, attractive. In a flashy kind of way.

Ed Fountain had a brusque air about him when he returned. The sleeves of his white oxford shirt, buttoned before, were pushed above his elbows. His whole demeanor said, let's get on with it. He barely paused at the sight of the demurely-wrapped present on his chair, just opened a drawer and placed it inside.

Sabina was vaguely dismayed to learn from Ed that this Ella Martinelli was a member of the management team. Director of Advertising and Circulation. They would be seeing plenty of each other.

He ran through thumbnail sketches of the other managers Sabina would be working with most closely. There weren't many. Besides Martinelli and Matthew Drum, there was just the publisher, Frank Wiley, whose family had sold the paper to DEI, and a new position of Marketing Director that had been filled by the CEO's only son, Kendall Drum.

"To know the father is not to know the son," Fountain said, enigmatically. "I don't know much about him myself yet, except that he's thirty-six and he hasn't worked at a paper before, which is ... quaint. Anyway, his father's got him on a crash course and today he's traveling around with one of our sales guys so you can't meet him until our first planning session, whenever that is."

"Monday morning," Sabina told him. "Assuming Mr. Drum hires me, that's when he told me he wants our first session. If that's okay with your schedule?"

That earned a flash of humor from Fountain, but she had to be quick to catch it. It was more a sleight of lips: a smile inferred. "The new boss wants to plan our future," Fountain said, "I think I can arrange to be there."

He got to his feet with a goodbye attitude. Sabina gathered her purse and briefcase. It was at the tip of her tongue to wish him a Happy Birthday when she remembered the Martinelli woman's discomfort. Martinelli had been trying to do just that: warn her off a standard expression that could only bring him pain.

"So you've decided to take us on?" Fountain asked as he walked her to the door.

"I've got to meet Mr. Drum first. I think."

They both laughed politely and Sabina understood the subtext to be that Matthew Drum, this new CEO from out East, was an equally unknown quantity to Ed Fountain.

"May I ask you something, Ed? About your moratorium idea."

He looked back at her, alert.

"Are you going to introduce it regardless? Push for it with or without me?"

He nodded, his eyes going hard. "I'd like your help. But I don't really give a flip if I keep this job or not. So yes. You could say I'm going to push for it."

Well, well. This consulting business, Sabina thought, was shaping up to be pretty interesting.

CHAPTER THREE

Sabina paid attention to her first face-to-face with Matthew Drum. She ironed a blouse; set her alarm—hardly necessary, since she hadn't slept past six a single morning since Jacob moved out; and she researched the man, aware that she was investigating not just her first client, but this force in her mother's life that had Peg Lindsay sounding exhilarated in a way Sabina didn't much like. Community activist of sorts: fine. Mother and grandmother: of course, fine. But Peg Lindsay, woman in love? There was not much room in Sabina's imagination for that.

She learned that Matthew Drum was twice divorced and turned paper into gold. Before buying out DEI and growing it into an international chain of seventy-five publications, Drum made his financial reputation in Wall Street investment firms as a principal negotiator for several of the early 1980s more controversial debt-financed mergers and take-over battles—including a bitter fight for his own father's meatpacking business in Kansas City. In Matthew vs. Ambrose Drum, Matthew won.

As CEO of the newspaper and magazine chain, Matthew Drum's MO was to move to the locale of his latest acquisition, link himself electronically to DEI headquarters in Boston and run the new operation until he was satisfied his profit goals could be met. Fortunately for the *Times* employees, their new owner did not have a reputation for ruthless downsizing. Some reorganization and business planning was inevitable, however, and that's where Sabina came in.

When she walked into the *Times* building that Monday morning, she thought she was fully prepared to meet Matthew Drum. She was not.

There was the dissonance of what he should have looked like. Sabina had pictured a comfortable paunch, laugh lines, a pipe ... she had pictured her father. Matthew Drum wore European dress shirts that tapered to a fat-free waistline. Teeth too unblemished to have gripped a pipe. His crisp white crewcut stood erect, hand-combed, and even the wrinkles in his forehead had presence.

Power and success, she had expected. His far-flung business, DEI, was worth nearly a billion dollars and that kind of money didn't accumulate behind fools or dreamers. Sabina expected to be engaged intellectually. What she didn't expect from the man who took her hand in both of his, was that her skin would tingle from his touch and she would experience what her old friend Sonny called the "moist click" of sexual response.

It was appalling. This was her mother's boyfriend. It threw her off her game plan momentarily and she babbled like a consultant textbook, telling the CEO that the only way she could work was in a team process. When she heard herself talking about a "dynamic, organic strategic process," she snapped her mouth shut.

After a beat, Matthew Drum took over smoothly. "Great," he said. "Whatever you say."

Unlikely, Sabina thought. This was a man well used to calling the shots.

Drum ushered her out of his office and down a dark hallway filled with the broken-down clanking of an air-conditioner doing its first work of the season. She was feeling off-center, lonely—not the least prepared to lead a group of strangers through hours of strategic planning.

The management team was settled around a banged-up conference table in a room draped with electrical, phone and computer cords. The CEO took a seat anchoring one end of the oval table and Sabina had the other. She gave a non-threatening "I'm-just-here-to-guide-the-process" speech. Having guided her old company through plenty of plans, she knew it worked best if she gave them some sense of action, so she paced around the room between a blackboard and two flip charts, making lists, using colored grease pencils, trying to engage everyone in the discussion.

Ed Fountain was deceptively mild. He bided his time until two hours into the meeting, when he saw his chance. The CEO and his son, Kendall, were both unaware of Casey Fountain's death and Ed had to run through it again in advancing his moratorium proposal. Ella Martinelli, the flashy Director of Advertising and Circulation, was seated alongside the Editor. She was just too good; he had to have prepped her. Her eyes misted and she reached over to press Fountain's arm.

"We won't take any slams on the advertising side," Martinelli volunteered. "I know, like, five companies that are talking about PC kinds of marketing moves."

Phelps Pascal, the city editor, warned that the reporters would resent it. "You're actually suggesting we not cover certain murders?" he asked. "Legitimate news?"

"Not a total blackout," Fountain said. "Just a moratorium on the killer's 'life story' and whatever message he tries to send, including, I would hope, the speeches in court." Fountain sounded neutral, a disinterested bystander. "Remember,

Phelps, we're talking about muffling wire service mostly. The first suitable story that comes down the wire, we use it to announce the moratorium. How long since someone's been murdered in Riverview? We'd have to distinguish between all the different kinds of ... of slaughter, and be confident we were applying this to, oh ...." He trailed off for a second, lost in some thought. "To the right class of killer."

"But that side-line material," Frank Wiley said. "That's what we do best."

Frank Wiley, publisher of the *Times*, was a distinguished-looking man in his early sixties with sleek, styled, jet black hair—most certainly dyed—and a head the shape of a speeding bullet, the cartoon kind that elongates and sports a mad grin on its point.

Wiley looked around the table for confirmation. "Am I right? That's how we complement TV." He turned an apologetic face to Fountain. "With all due respect, Ed, many of our readers subscribe to one newspaper only. This one. If we don't do it, who's going to give them all the background details of these ... events, and the killers, etcetera?"

Sabina had Fountain's sleepy act figured out. When he was most impatient he looked closest to nodding off. At this moment, his eyes were slits. "Well, Frank," he said, "that's the point, isn't it?"

Fountain went on so softly they had to strain to hear him. He fixed his eyes on a cigarette burn on the table, tracing it with his index finger. "I think you could call me a student of the psychotic personality," he said. "I've studied the profile. And I tell you, these guys are empty personalities. They have no identity. We give them one. We fill them up."

Silence. Either no one wanted to shoot the idea down in front of Fountain, the tragic father, or they didn't want to be the first to endorse it if it flunked the CEO test.

Sabina cleared her throat. "It's up to you, of course, but if I can offer an outsider's opinion? This might be a smart move." Heads swung her way.

Pretending to consider the moratorium for the first time, she faced the flip charts filled with the product of their brainstorming and began ticking off points on her fingers. "It's a clean differentiation from the broadcast media. It fits the trend you talked about today toward activist, civic journalism. It's a leadership position over your competition. Remember all the hoopla with the *New York Times* and the Unabomber threat? You'd probably get some free publicity."

"Nationally," Matthew Drum said, thoughtfully.

"Probably. It doesn't appear to cost you resources and if you did lose some readers you might gain more in good will. It was also—"

"That's right!" Frank Wiley was struck by the thought. "The Chamber of Commerce will love this! Rotary, the Junior League ... etcetera."

Sabina gestured to Ed Fountain and rushed along. "It was also pointed out that you'd have to define—how did you put it, Ed?—the right class of killer. You could free up a body to do research, or I'd be glad to help. Dig up relevant incidents, talk to criminologists, psychologists. Then come up with some recommendations on what types of crimes and criminals would qualify and how far to extend the moratorium. We could get back together in a week or two."

"One week from today," Matthew Drum said firmly.

Kendall Drum actually waved his hand in the air. He hadn't peeped all morning.

"This isn't high school, Kenny," snapped his father.

Kendall flushed and fixed his eyes on the table. At 36, Kendall was nearly Sabina's age, but looked more boy than man. Amber doe eyes as round as pancakes. A little overweight, a little short. His face was ruddy, puffy, free of wrinkles—arrested innocence under thick, shiny brown, bowl-cut hair.

His voice was unexpected: a voice for a politician, deep and strong. "It's just ... won't the radio, and TV, and the weekly, probably the Twin Cities and other papers ... won't they all carry the killers' stories anyway?"

In other words, what was the point? Kendall looked to Sabina. She raised an eyebrow in Fountain's direction. But it was the publisher who boomed his blessing.

"Rome wasn't built in a day, dear boy," Frank Wiley said and got to his feet, signaling the meeting was over.

No one else budged until Matthew Drum flattened his hands on the table and pushed back.

Sabina's mood was fairly up as she turned onto Melody Lane and neared home. The bungalow Jacob and she had bought was a step down from where Sabina grew up in the Bluffs ... more like a whole staircase. But she liked it, it was manageable and solid. Also pink. She found that unbearable until she discovered sunglasses of a certain tint would transform the squat structure to a chic melon shade and were lots cheaper than paint. After dark, she had no objection. The pink lent the house a kind of inner glow, like a mastodon eating its nightlight.

The lawn looked great to Sabina. Tootie must have been over to mow it, and she'd bet he'd already spent his pay. They had an honor system: She stuffed cash into a toy pail under the porch and he took out what was owed him.

Catch her trusting his father that far. Daddy Jerk stepped out his front door across the street—no coincidence of timing. The man spent most days reclining in his living room, picture-window drapes drawn wide, monitoring the neighborhood and hogging the TV remote. Karl Jergensen's chin stubble was visible from a block away. He slow-motion stooped and groped for *that morning's* newspaper. If the world turned at Karl's pace, everything not rooted would be sucked into space.

And there was Karl's '74 Buick: pale green body bit by rust, tireless wheels planted with sequoia permanence in the moist earth. The warmer it grew outside, the hotter Sabina's irritation at Karl and his junk-yard car.

She overturned the wheel and the jeep bounded up and over the curb. She climbed out, balancing briefcase, purse and coffee cup and aware too late of her skirt hiked to mid-thigh. Karl ate it up.

"Gotta learn to take it slow, girl!"

Jerk. She stretched her lips into a keep-the-peace smile and ran the gauntlet into the house.

To think that Tootie, her favorite ten-year-old, actually sprang from that front-porch pervert. Toot's real name was Olaf, which he detested. His mother Cindy was a worn-out thirty-year-old who spent her days making telemarketing calls from the basement, and her nights avoiding Karl. So Toot really needed Jacob and Sabina. What else did she have? One husband, gone. One company, gone. Jacob hadn't wanted a baby—he'd even proposed they rent furniture. She didn't own a dog or a parakeet or a goiter-eyed goldfish. All but one of her friends had been sacrificed to her workaholic life and that friend, Sonny Ashendorf, lived in Wyoming with her succession of slim-hipped cowboys, three kids and a herd of Appaloosa. Sabina's three brothers lived out of state, too, and had a combined seven children to keep them busy.

She walked straight back to the first-floor bedroom, meaning to change clothes but finding herself on the edge of the bed, her hand on the phone. Jacob would want to hear how Toot was doing, surely? Or about her weird dream that morning?

It had been early, not yet six. One of those hours when friends never call friends without an emergency as an excuse. Sabina had surfaced slowly, trailing night fingers across the specter of a fireman who transformed into an octopus, and the octopus, on rubber plunger legs, scaled a mound of mashed potatoes ... no, it was a melting vanilla sundae the size of the Sears Tower, her at the top, arms flung to the skies.

It was an excuse, not an emergency, but it would do. She punched the speed dial number for Jacob's new place in Minneapolis.

"Hello?"

Sabina fell back on the bed. "I've got a symbolically-rich dream for you. Want to help me figure it out?"

"Sabina." His voice was low, intimate.

He knew who it was, he just liked to say her name.

They had a little problem.

The paperwork said their life together had ended, but they missed each other. She thought of them as two wild hares in the woods, attracted and scared, frozen in place. Nobody had said the "regret" word yet. Sabina was trying to contain herself during this aberrant phase of desire (Sonny called it the "not got hots") and come out the other side with a cooler head for weighing her emotions against some pretty sour memories.

She wasn't adjusting well to life as a single. One reason was that at thirty-eight years old, supposedly one year shy of her sexual peak, she felt cheated. These talks with Jacob had begun taking a quirky backwards dip. They occasionally managed to turn the clock back to two horny teenagers scrambling into the back seat.

"How are you doing?" Jacob said. "I called a couple of nights ago, about nine o'clock."

"Friday, you mean?" She shifted her hips and leg to the left, where they would have found his. "That was a big day. I got my first client, Jake. Red letter day. So I was ... oh, I remember, Toot and I took our walk late that night."

"Tell me, Sabina, do you do that to make me feel like a heel or an outcast? Which effect are you going for?"

No back seat revival this day. "Oh, for pete's sake." She jerked her leg back to her side of the bed. "Neither. You're not banished. You told Toot you'd come back—"

"Right," Jacob broke in. "What would you know about this working for someone else? I'm on the road all the time."

He blamed her for that? She heard running water. He must be standing at a sink she'd never seen, turning on the taps. "I'm putting you down for a minute," he said.

It had become a ritual, since Toot was old enough, for the three of them to walk down the tracks and back after dinner. Toot was probably the closest Sabina would ever come to a child of her own. Their real baby, Jacob's and hers, was the business. Sabina Lindsay and Jacob Shaw, the precocious entrepreneurs who started Linshaw Bicycle Works in a college apartment and grew it over seventeen years into a nice little business. The year they issued shares in the corporation, they got married.

Suddenly, it was all gone—torn into pieces and resurrected as cash by the courts. Big chunks of money landed on Sabina and the shareholders, which included her mother. Their thirty-two employees came away with nothing but severance pay and a resolve never to speak to either of them again. The divorce was Sabina's idea and so was a plan for an employee buy-out of the business. Jacob wanted to hold onto the business and her—in that order, or so she thought. Since he couldn't budge her on the divorce action, he fought the buy-out, hauling in valuation experts and lawyers to the point where she had to back down or they would have chewed up so many assets nothing would be left for the employees to own.

Five of the people who stuck with them through the years

were close friends: past tense. Sabina thought she would never forgive Jacob for that, until the night some weeks back when he admitted, in tears, that he would never forgive himself.

Now her bearded, brilliantly temperamental ex-husband worked in Minneapolis as a sales manager for a cosmetics company. They were hinting, he told her, that shaving his beard would be "not an undesirable career enhancement decision." He had money enough to walk if he wanted, but deep down, Jacob had always been uncomfortable with risk.

Poor man. From mountain bikes to mascara; from boss to employee. A slippery slide. He saw her at the top, palms out.

Was he wrong?

"What are you thinking?" His voice was low and intimate again, and oddly hollow.

"I'm thinking ... that we are where we are because of me, too. No company. No marriage. No friends." She closed her eyes and willed herself to say it, to stop protecting herself and show him something real. "I think I quit our marriage because I couldn't bear waiting around for you to prove you didn't want me anymore."

Whoa. She had barely faced that herself—neither the rejection part nor the quitting part. She curled on her side and drew up her knees. Sabina didn't like to think of herself as a quitter. Her parents were bulldogs: with their own marriage, their long-time friends, their community involvement. Scott Lindsay had worked for only two companies his whole life. The three-starred flag of Loyalty and Integrity and Discipline flew above their home.

Jacob was surprised into silence. She heard him breathing and thought of how that breath in her ear could raise goosebumps down to her toes. "Oh, kiddo," he said. "I appreciate that. Let's not even get into it now."

"Jacob, what *is* it with your voice? You sound like you're in an echo chamber."

One sentence and she knew he was lying; he lied so ineptly.
"It must be the portable phone."

"You're in the shower." She was surprised but certain of
it. She laughed at him. "Jacob, for heaven's sake ..." And then
her overactive imagination added the missing piece. "You're
crouched in the shower because there's someone in your bed."
It came out calmly.

This had been one of their problems. She stopped fighting with Jacob. She'd argue, yes, but corporately, reasonably.

Jacob hadn't changed, either. He screamed at her. Through
a megaphone it came: "We're divorced! Remember? Goddamn
you, Sabina!" Then the sound of the shower door sliding
open, a woman's voice, a dial tone.

Sabina lay still, watching the second hand tick, giving
herself two full minutes to wallow in it, to dwell on images of
Jacob performing his often exquisite moves on someone else.
At six PM on a weekday? She must be some kind of hot. Guillotined
those thoughts. Told herself to get up and eat something. Get
changed, go for a ride, move.

Loyalty and Integrity and Discipline. He had failed all
three, divorce or no divorce, so to hell with him.

On the way to the kitchen, the living room couch stopped
her, the solution of it. She would give up sleeping in their
bed. The couch was deep, sloping, comfortable. It had its own
memories, but one thing it didn't have was a phone within
easy reach. The nearest one sat in the front hall on an old-
fashioned pedestal that had belonged to her grandparents.
She could still see Grampa reluctantly accepting a call, holding the receiver away from his ear like a rancid sausage. He'd
finish his business, slam it down and get back to real life.

Back to real life. Under the illusion she had compartmen-
talized her desire for her ex-husband, Sabina opened the refrigerator door, closed it, and was back at the phone, dialing
the Pizza Parlor.

CHAPTER FOUR

Someone had corralled the conference room chairs into the corner farthest from the door—Matthew Drum, presumably. Sabina walked in behind Phelps Pascal and Ed Fountain for the post-Bogies emergency meeting a little after 10:30 PM. Drum was bent over some paperwork from a standing position at the head of the table. He was resplendent in a charcoal suit, white shirt and turquoise tie. Frank Wiley looked as if he had been interrupted mid-martini in the 19th hole at his country club. He wore a spotless hot pink golf shirt and was striding back and forth, frowning at the carpet. Kendall Drum was propped against one wall, arms crossed over his chest.

"Damn shame," Frank Wiley said to no one in particular, and kept pacing.

Matthew waited until Fountain, Pascal and Sabina circled the table and awkwardly spaced themselves roughly equidistant from each other, in front of the ghost chairs.

"Your assessment, Ed?" the CEO asked. "Do we pay overtime, or no?"

The *Times* was a morning paper and went to press at 11 PM. Since Editorial wasn't unionized, Drum was referring to overtime for the printers.

Ed Fountain rested one hip on the table. "Yeah, but it won't be too bad. We've got two reporters on it. One hostage already unloaded on the record, the rest is first-hand observation and whatever facts the police are releasing." He twisted his head to Pascal. "They can write it up before midnight. Right, Phelps?"

Phelps frowned at his watch. "Should be able to, right."

Conspicuous by its absence was any discussion about digging into the killer's background—the cops found identification in his pockets with a Cleveland address—and no suggestion at all that the *Times* devote space to the killer's broadcast statements. Matthew Drum smiled slightly, lifted his chin and looked from Fountain to Phelps to Sabina, measuring. "I see. All the news that's fit to print, right?"

In the pocket of silence, a snuffling and light tip-tap of a woman's heels came from the hallway. Ella Martinelli turned into the conference room, carrying a child diagonally across her chest. One sunburned arm swung free and the little girl, her eyes peacefully closed, had a thumb in her mouth and was working it over vigorously.

Martinelli took in the stand-up conference in one surprised sweep of her huge blue eyes and then appealed to Ed: "I can't help it. My stupid ex won't take her because she still wets. She'll be fine, she sleeps like a dead soldier."

"Why don't you take her over there," Matthew Drum said, tipping his head at the chairs. Kendall came alive: He trotted over to them and untangled one for her. Ella dimpled for him and sat down, rearranging the child.

The moratorium was apparently a done deal. Matthew Drum asked if Fountain could have an editorial ready for Sunday's front page.

Ed blinked slowly. "No problem. But my research is on the old side, and wasn't exactly systematic." He turned to Sabina, expectantly.

She smiled at him. "Lucky for you I'm a workaholic. I found some good stuff on-line, and a criminologist at UW is feeding me profiles on psychotics and anti-socials. There's still plenty to do, though."

"Our library's not half bad, you know," Phelps Pascal said. "Let's put some people on it tomorrow."

"Check," Matthew Drum said, closing the discussion. He had a way of using that word with a winner's finality, its meaning closer to "checkmate," that was probably cultivated through years of being agreed with and anticipated at every turn.

"I'd like you to prepare the editorial for my signature," Matthew Drum said to Fountain. "You're too close to the subject to be accepted as unbiased."

"Unbiased!" Ella Martinelli blurted, full voice. Her child didn't even twitch. Ella swayed forward in her chair. "Unbiased? Isn't that the point? And who better to write it, I mean, it was his daughter, if you want unbiased, why don't you—" She tumbled to a stop. Sabina watched her recognize how far she had overstepped the line; in particular, by implying what they were all thinking: *Why don't you write it yourself?*

Drum's head tipped inquiringly. "Yes, Mrs. Martinelli?" Icy elegance coated his prompt, the same brand of courtesy as the guy who asks, Do you want a blindfold.

Frank Wiley cleared his throat. "People. If I may change the topic? I'm disturbed about one other thing here." He turned to Fountain. "That profile business on psychopaths and anti-socials, etcetera—the lunatic fringe? How do we find out all that about some schmuck in time to decide if our moratorium should apply?"

"We watch the behavior surrounding the crime," Ed Fountain said. "Did the killer make an attempt to send a 'message' to society."

"But how about political deals?" Phelps Pascal asked.

"Like how would we have handled the massacre in Israel, remember—"

"Or the Oklahoma City bombing," Wiley put in.

The CEO cut off discussion. "We won't be diverting this meeting into a case-by-case," he said. "I've decided we need help with each decision, in the form of an expert advisory board. We find the experts, big names, pay them. They front each case. That's our PR buffer for Monday morning quarterbacks."

They broke for home. Sabina passed up the couch and went directly to her computer. With minimal sleep, she was back at the *Times* before 8 AM the next morning, Saturday. On the news side, her role was to feed relevant research to Fountain for the front page editorial, and to Phelps Pascal, who was directing development of related sidebars and stories to fill at least a week's worth of newspapers. On the business side, Matthew Drum asked for her help in patching together the advisory board they hoped to name in Sunday's paper, though she hadn't a clue what her value could be.

Working with Ed Fountain was chaos plucked from disaster by his intellect and easy-going, dry sense of humor. Papers hit the floor as he cleared a corner of his desk for Sabina to work on her laptop. He'd scratch his stomach and half-close his eyes at her one minute and the next, he was an intellectual cougar. He kept reaching over, grabbing whatever she was reading to him and then weaving it into his editorial, tapping madly away as he lofted new questions at her.

"That Arthur Bremer quote," he asked, plunging his hand into an open desk drawer looking for God knows what, "was that original research? Where'd you get it?"

"That's my 'scum' file," Sabina muttered. She scrolled, looking for the file, when he hit her with another.

"What have you got on gun injuries? Did you find something recent?"

"That's right in front of you," she said. She crossed behind him and leaned over his shoulder to peer at his screen. It was gone. "I just *gave* you that, pull it up, here—"

"Saw it, no good, I need dollars. But right now I really need that quote source." Tap, tap, tap.

"Okay." Sabina began to seethe. She never made it back to her chair.

"What time does the library close, you're the research expert, couldn't you call, maybe they've got that speech of the President's last month, he'd have the gun injuries in dollars."

She glared down at him. "Saw that speech. No good. Research not original."

That's when she understood, from his muffled delight, that he was deliberately driving her crazy. It was a test the paper's reporters had been goaded through. As an outsider, she was honored.

"Sabina? Ed?" Phelps Pascal stood in Fountain's doorway, crisply dressed in a starched pink shirt, college tie, creased pants, loafers, dress socks. He looked a lot prettier than Sabina. She had barely taken time to brush her teeth and catch her hair back in a rubber band.

"I think we need a snappy kind of sidebar," Pascal said. "A fast way to prove there really is a link between the crime and the publicizing of it. Up front and easy, we need a way—"

"I get it," Ed broke in. "You're absolutely right." He turned to Sabina. "Ideas?"

"Yes!"

Ed smiled. "Don't sound so surprised, Sabina. We'll think it's the first idea you've ever had."

"Har-har," she said, distracted. She hit a key to bring up her directory and searched it. "We were just talking about it. My Scum file? It's my dumping ground for quotes ... here. Look at this, you guys. Won't this do?"

Pascal and Fountain came around behind her and started reading.

"Man, oh, man," Pascal breathed after a minute. "There're so many you've got 'em alphabetical?"

"One thing that would help the story," Fountain said evenly. "There should be some unknowns in the piece. Quotes from people who killed non-celebrities; have you got those, too?"

"A few. You want to see?"

"I'll take your word for it," Ed said. He walked back around to his desk chair and threw himself into it. "There's your sidebar, Phelps."

Sabina copied it onto a diskette and handed it to Pascal. He left with a spring in his step, saying, "We'll call it 'Their Own Words.' Yes!"

She watched him dive back into it. The newsroom was jumping, boom-boxes playing, the TV cranked up loud.

"Is this his usual workday?" Sabina asked Fountain. "He's so duded up."

"A young man on the fast track." Fountain spun his chair around and rested his feet on the credenza. A corner of his mouth twitched: humor alert. "He's backing the wrong horse now. Phelps'll have to get himself some blue shirts."

Matthew Drum wore a lot of blue, to go with his eyes, Sabina supposed. Pascal seemed to be affecting a country club look ... "Frank Wiley?" she guessed.

"Bingo." Ed was giving her his half-mast once-over. "I wonder why I trust you," he said. "Flies against the conventional wisdom."

"About consultants, you mean? Well, true confessions. This is my first consulting job."

The eyebrow. "So when you've got, say, ten or so under your belt, you'll be pond scum?"

She laughed. "I intend to upgrade the profession."

"You're making a good start on it."

The sudden sincerity embarrassed her, and him, too. His feet thumped back on the floor and he concentrated on his computer screen.

"Okay," he said, rubbing his forehead. "Now we need to go over the psychological profile bit. You ticked off some stuff that was new to me. Why don't you do that again."

It was on top in her briefcase, a hodge-podge list of the documented personality and behavior traits exhibited by all manner of murderers–stalkers, serial killers, assassins, revenge in the workplace.

She reminded Fountain of that fact. "If a profile exists that's exclusive to killers who are hot to get attention," she cautioned, "I haven't found it yet."

"Read," he said, his hands poised over his keyboard.

"Okay. Let's see ... poor self-esteem. Dysfunctional family of origin. Intense interest in the media. Outward calm, even passive."

"Slow down."

Sabina resumed, dispassionately reading her grocery list for a sociopath. Homemade killer, oven to table, just mix and bake. "Often shy. Well-behaved. Loners. Histories of depression or paranoia. Diminished by a powerful parent. There can be a lot of gun buying. Some of them move around from city to city. Love junk food. Lead fantasy lives to get away from what the shrinks call 'intolerably unpleasant emotions.' Usually white males. Male-female ratio, nine to one. Problems expressing themselves or letting out feelings."

"And weren't there some caveats? You called them 'good' antisocials, or something like that."

"Right here. I'll read the quote, it's a psychiatrist the FBI uses. 'If they're not psychotic, antisocial personalities can be very hard to identify. They exhibit superb masking abilities, even after multiple therapy sessions.'"

Sabina looked up. "That's it."

"Gawd." Ed groped in his top shirt pocket and came up empty. "I thought I had this together in my head," he said, looking grim, "but it'll take me every minute until press time."

"We're through here, aren't we, Ed? I'm due in Drum's office."

Ed's mind had already traveled back to the editorial. The more intense his thinking, the blanker his face. She doubted he noticed her leave.

Walking from Fountain's office into the CEO's suite was like whisking from a laundry hamper into a dry-cleaning bag. In his crisp, stark office, where even the corner philodendron had its leaves polished weekly, Drum and Sabina manned three phones. Her role was pure secretarial: a scripted introduction to make it past a gatekeeper; then pass the call to Drum. In fact, his secretary, Rose Malwicki, would have been better at it.

Still, as it neared nine PM, Sabina was surprised at their progress. For nominal pay, they had an advisory board that surpassed credible: many of them were renowned in their fields. Kudos, really, to Drum's considerable connections. He was either directly acquainted with, or one contact removed from, the presidents of Harvard, Princeton, Yale, UCLA, Berkeley, and other prestigious universities.

She tried joking with him during one of the downtime periods that fell as they waited for callbacks. "I guess you don't need the name of my old sociology professor at State, huh?"

Matthew Drum smiled, dimly. Sabina felt a little sorry for him. Despite his considerable networking quilt, it didn't seem, from the side of the conversations she overheard, as if any of these men or women were his friends.

"You've moved around a lot, haven't you?" she asked him. "Do you have a family? I mean, other than Kendall."

Sabina sat on the thick gray carpet, her back against a leather couch and a phone in her lap. Drum lounged behind his glass-top desk. Lounging was an attitude difficult to strike, as the thing was so spare and clean it looked like a window turned on its side. Sabina was seeing the "casual" Drum for the first time. Even in jeans and an old sweat shirt, he was way above average. It was getting old, this conjuring up an image of Drum naked with her mother and then prudently banishing it before the details locked in. This could, after all, be her future stepfather.

Something must have shown on her face because Drum's answer was unresponsive to the question. "There's no father, and your brothers don't live around here, so it's up to you, is that it?" He raised his chin in that you-are-a-specimen way he had, but also wore an easy smile.

"What does that mean?"

"You're asking what my intentions are toward your mother."

"Not at all." But she felt the lie and smiled ruefully. "Well, I might have gotten there. It's not my business, really. I was just curious. I know you're a Harvard grad, but nothing else about you that the financial pages haven't run."

"So you know I usually win the game," he said, matter-of-factly. He swiveled his chair to face the window and tipped back in it, locking his hands behind his head. "Good businessman. Lousy father. Like my father was a lousy father. My parents don't talk to each other and Ambrose—that's my father—doesn't talk to me." Drum's voice took on a sneering quality. "The 'meatpacking king' of Kansas City. Hasn't talked to me since I made him rich."

From her research into Matthew's career, Sabina assumed he was talking about the sale of Drum Meatpacking back in 1987. Matthew glossed over a minor detail: The business had been in the Drum family for generations and his father, Ambrose Drum, had fought the buy-out bitterly.

"Two wives," Drum went on. "Excuse me, ex-wives. I had an older brother. He bought the farm in Korea. Where he had no business being. Kendall."

Sabina fiddled with the phone, hoping it would ring. She didn't know if 'Kendall' had been his brother's name or if he meant his son and was concluding the harsh inventory of his family. The spaces he dropped between sentences were more leaden than the words themselves.

"Peg," he said, with sudden warmth, "is a good listener, too. Like her daughter. But you and I were going to stick to business. Besides," now he was actually teasing her, "this isn't sporting. I already know all about you."

Oh great, Mom. Sabina was only too aware of what a picture of her thrilling life would look like: empty shelves. One husband, one job, both gone. Responsible and predictable and sick of both.

The phone trilled on his desk. He picked it up, studying her, then seguing smoothly into a conversation with the re-tired New York City Chief of Police, turning the room a little blue and shrugging for Sabina's benefit, charmingly apologetic. He could sound like Harvard and he could sound like an ex-cop or street-raised kid himself.

Was he both, or neither? It was high time Sabina pumped her mother for some real information on this guy. Since the woman was such a good listener; such a good talker.

It was nearly midnight when the first edition of Sunday's Riverview *Times* snaked overhead, carried by a conveyor belt that wound from the press to the mailroom. Bundles of folded papers thumped at the feet of a small group of people. Sabina hung at the fringes again, a little too self-conscious to be included. No one spoke; an aura of ceremony surrounded them. A woman with a pen stuck behind both ears stepped forward, bent over the first stack of twenty papers, and used a rusty jackknife to slit the yellow cord, sawing at it. She tugged at the bottom paper until it gave. Then she walked it to Ed Fountain and placed it across his outstretched arms. Fountain's mouth twisted awkwardly. He left abruptly, using the cement steps on the loading dock that led to the street. Sabina grabbed a paper and followed in time to see Fountain turn into the parking lot, still carrying the Riverview *Times* like a living thing across his upturned forearms.

She was holding a couple thousand words wrenched from Ed's soul. Perhaps because she was tired, all that registered was a profound cynicism. Two thousand words: so what? Put that up against, what had she read, about twenty thousand people killed last year, and just by handguns? Good luck. A BB-sized ping in the armor of senseless death.

In the light of a streetlamp, Sabina looked down at the paper. The headline was just two words, in the biggest typeface she had ever seen.

BANG BANG.

Now I've got your attention. This is a story about killing, so I know you're reading. If that sounds cynical, it's because I am. If this sounds personal, it's because it is.

I'm cynical because Friday's murder of Peter Klassen drew more attention to the murderer than to the victim. So do they all, and so do we all make it possible.

It's personal because when we cower behind locked doors, when mothers put their children to bed in the porcelain security system of a bathtub to keep them safe from stray bullets, when we fear solitary walks on moon-lit nights in this mid-sized mid-America town ... the power of a few to terrorize the many has gone way too far.

This is a story about too much killing and too much fascination with it. A picture of someone else's pain is gradually losing its power to evoke our sympathy, yet gaining power to fascinate.

What have we substituted for compassion? America's new secular religion: fame. In a divided and isolated America, fame is the new religion. The emptiest among us seek fame as a tragic shortcut in the search for meaning. They search with the efficient weapons of violence at their ready disposal and their search is one that leads only to more isolation and more violence. Though the search is rewarded. They gain attention, sometimes money ... and always, instant reincarnation from deserved obscurity to the bright, if not warm, beam of society's attention.

The killer as celebrity ...

CHAPTER FIVE

JR sat rigidly erect in a deep armchair, Sunday's paper open on his lap. CNN was broadcasting a story about floods south of Riverview, but JR was deaf to it. As he read the front page a second time, his finger found a burn hole in the upholstery under his leg. He dug into it, rimming its frayed edges, plucking at the stuffing and flicking it to the floor.

He folded the paper and placed it at his feet. Then JR maintained a soldierly stillness through two cycles of CNN's Sunday morning coverage.

Around noon, he got up to use the toilet, order a pizza, and fish a pair of scissors from a kitchen drawer. JR neatly snipped Matthew Drum's editorial from the surrounding copy. He tore a piece of masking tape from its roll and affixed the editorial to the base of his computer monitor. He dialed up the brightness of his screen, tapped in his password, and then ... nothing. Only the beat of deep anger, filling his head. JR's fingers curled uselessly into his palms. He read the offending words, yet again.

> Over the next two weeks we will, instead, be publishing research and opinion-leader articles proving that certain kinds of murderers kill to get attention, to earn a platform

denied them in ordinary life because they are dysfunctional cowards who need a weapon to speak for them.

Remember Charles Whitman, the "father" of mass murder after his Texas Tower "statement"? He got his page of history, this wife-beating, mentally-ill schizophrenic whose real beef was with his father but he couldn't face him, so instead he bayoneted his wife, stabbed his mother, and shot to death 13 people in a matter of minutes.

The pizza delivery girl smiled at the man who opened the door. He gaped at her. "You did call for a pizza?" she asked.

"A long time ago," the guy said, still blank-faced.

Was he gonna stiff her? She lifted the carton to read the receipt stapled to the side. "I'm sorry, Mister. It says here it was less than an hour ago you called it in?"

The customer gave her a kinda sweet smile. "I guess it depends how hungry you are. Reversely perverse."

She bobbled her head agreeably but hadn't a clue. She peered at the receipt again; this hallway was dark. "It's twelve-ninety you owe," she told him but he was already thrusting a handful of bills at her.

"Keep the change," he said.

She had trotted halfway back down the hall before she counted up the dollars. She turned around and he was still in the doorway, looking after her and smiling.

"Geez, mister, thanks!" He gave a little bow and backed into his apartment. As she waited for the elevator she smoothed out the bills. What a nice guy. Five whole dollars! That was the best she'd see today. Why was it was always the ones that looked like they couldn't afford it, gave the best tips?

JR popped a beer and resumed his seat at the screen, dropping the pizza unopened on the carpet. He tipped his head back and a trickle of beer coursed down his chin and wet his neck. He dabbed at it with a napkin and stared at the screen. For one hour he had labored over an article to post in his crime newsgroup. The cursor blinked, blinked, blinked. Made his head ache with its fucking demanding pulse-pulse-pulse.

"This is shit," he breathed. Delete. Now there was just his message ID and the hypnotizing eye of the cursor:

<1997Jun8.787763.1389.2205@jr.frat.org>

His hand reached for the beer. Sparks jumped from his fingertips! Distinct bolts, leaping the distance between his fingertips and the can of beer.

A baptism of comprehension washed over him. He had been allowing his life source to be drained away in details. He stiffened in his chair. This USENET group was a detail. It was not for this that he had been born special. The words were not flowing, because the Fraternity was locking him out. JR closed his eyes, placed his soft fingertips on the keys, and willed his Father to speak.

His fingers moved. His eyes opened. A single word behind the cursor: *Action.* The words would come after the action. He'd earn them. But first ... pure, poetic action.

"The right to write!" JR laughed open-mouthed into the rush of beer as he drained the entire can. And then another.

He sent his mind to the kitchen where it considered the knives. Into the bedroom, where he had two more choices: The Raven lay tucked between T-shirts in his underwear drawer and his Charter Arms Special was stuffed in a snakeskin boot.

JR decided: No. He would use his hands. They ached to serve.

He waited for night to fall, drinking slowly, steadily. He pulled on a navy windbreaker and changed his hard-soled shoes for sneakers. Outside his apartment, he turned downhill, toward the river, to the Flats.

He passed a trailer park. He coughed once. He held onto

the post of a mailbox and bent over. A stream of vomit burned through his chest and throat. A dog tied under a nearby trailer barked.

JR continued on his way, his legs weak. Blindly, he turned into the next dirt driveway, walked up three metal steps to the side door of a trailer and twisted the door handle. It was locked. He pulled at it, desperately, and a man's voice came from inside: "Who the hell is that?" JR heard a thumping from inside and hurriedly backed down the steps, running into the darkness.

He was losing his sense of destiny. His shoes were weighted down, caked with mud. In an act of pure will, he pressed his hands flat against his thighs, closed his eyes and summoned his brothers. A miracle: one came, one in particular, and touched his heart with courage. When JR opened his eyes his mind had quieted.

He turned his head. He was looking at a row of colorless single-story buildings. He walked toward them. In the weak light from a crescent moon and a dim single globe down the road, he could make out a hand-painted sign that said APT. MANAGER over an arrow pointing left. JR went left, obediently. Leaning against the shingled wall next to a pair of patio doors was a long-handled garden spade. Ted's way! He was supposed to do it Ted's way. He took up his instrument. There was a door leading into the building a few steps away. It was open. He went through it. The first apartment door was lighted. It said OFFICE. SINGLETON ARMS TOWNHOUSE. C. WASHINGTON, MANAGER. He knocked. A woman's voice told him to come in. Of course. He entered, obediently. She was turning around. A dark face. A yellow robe. She went down instantly. His blow was powerful. He was not acting alone.

He left the building. The sound of gravel crunching came to him, dimly. He turned right, onto a dirt road, and the sound stopped.

As JR neared his apartment building, the stillness in his

head broke. Words overpowered him. He ran inside. By the time he sat again in front of his computer, it was a roar, a roar of his brothers' voices. Rhymes crowded behind his eyes like a dream of the perfect army: disciplined and creative. His hands shook in the fever to get it down, to hear the Fraternity as a chorus, and to do it justice.

> For the powerLESS to be powerFULL
> We deliver our Word through a gun barRELL
> or knife, bare hands, club ... and good THINKing
> to show Society the ways it is SINKing.
>
> Whitman, Chapman, Sirhan and Speck.
> These are the MEN who lead us!
> Berkowitz, DeSalvo, Bianchi and Buono.
> Down the path of JUSTice!
>
> Oswald, Ferri, Gilmore and Bundy.
> They live and walk aMONG us!
> Manson, Bremer and J.W. Booth
> and GOD, who killed his SON for us!
>
> We're the Poets of PAIN riding quiet and low
> But the LIARS are louder and in conTROL.
> The FRATERNITY will act as the final WORD.
> We'll speak and speak unTIL we're HEARD.

JR worked on his poem until he could do no more. Eyes fixed on the screen, he groped for the carton at his feet, opened the lid and gobbled down cold pizza with both hands. He hit PRINT, rinsed his hands, addressed an envelope, inserted his poem, sealed it, stamped it.

"Wait wait wait!" JR said. "Shit!" He tore open the envelope. He had forgotten to make his demand! He picked up his pen and scrawled hugely across the bottom: APOLOGIZE. Then he thought some more, bent over the paper, and wrote in very tiny script.

He'd show Matthew Drum who was the dysfunctional coward. To Matthew Drum, CEO of Nothing, Nothing Street, Nothing USA. Dear Mr. Drum: We'll see who has the power to lay down the last word.

On Wednesday morning, Rose Malwicki stood frowning over her steel-rimmed bifocals at the mushrooming stack of unopened mail on Matthew Drum's desk. Rose had been hired from outside the *Times* organization, or so Mr. Drum had said, for two reasons: her efficiency and her regard for confidentiality. Mr. Drum had phoned all of her references (*personally*, that was a surprise) and she knew he had liked what he heard. Here she was, after all, with a promise of lifetime employment after he moved on. His condition was that she be, in his words, "scrupulous about confidentiality."

Rose had initially taken umbrage. No one had to buy her high standards. Then she thought it over. For over thirty years, her systematic and, some would say, compulsive approach to her work had satisfied seven bosses in three companies. But her bank statements didn't mirror their gratitude so she thought, why not? And made the last job change of her life.

For as long as Mr. Drum remained in town, this office was the center of the entire Drum Enterprises Incorporated, not just the Riverview *Times*. If he would only allow her to triage the important letters. She had always done so.

"Hi, Rose."

She hadn't heard him come in. As he circled his desk, Rose spoke firmly. "Mr. Drum. I wonder how you think I can do my job if you will not tend to your mail promptly." She laid her palm over the pile of correspondence.

"Of course, you're right, Rose." But he didn't mean for her to assume control. He leaned forward and scraped the lot toward him, sinking into his chair. "I'll get through it in ten minutes."

She didn't move. "Time me," he said to her, and smiled engagingly.

Rose left him alone and sure enough, eight minutes later, he buzzed her in and loaded her up. Most of the mail was unopened. A few letters were marked with his square backhand directions in one corner.

A few minutes later, Drum buzzed her again. "Rose, would you get Brakken and Farley for me, please?" As Rose was dialing, she heard Drum's door close.

Matthew Drum leaned on a corner of his desk, waiting for Duncan Farley's voice over the speaker phone. He re-read the curious postscript. "P.S. This one's for Ted." When the call was put through, he plucked the phone from its cradle and paced, enduring Farley's pleasantries.

"What I called about, Duncan. I've got a strange situation here. I want you to research legal precedents, fast. A First Amendment issue with a twist ... the right *not* to print something." Pause. "I know we do, technically, but I want to know what kind of pressure to expect, legal or otherwise, how it's going to come at me, from where and who, and what our options are in defending ourselves. Like that."

He listened to his attorney's question. Answered it. Listened to another one and answered that.

"Is it credible?" Drum repeated. He raised the folded letter and scratched his forehead with its edge. "God, Duncan, who can say? Probably just some impotent dickhead."

Long pause: Duncan Farley had entered his lecture mode. As Matthew Drum listened, he idly folded the letter into a small square and slipped it into a back pocket of his briefcase.

CHAPTER SIX

In the years since Scotty died, Peg Lindsay's friends had begun accusing her of turning into a "social grouch." It was true she despised big parties. She found herself lonelier at the end of the evening than before she made the effort to gussy up. The constant smiling when you weren't amused and the "air smooching," as Scotty used to call it.

Tonight was different. First, a neighbor of Peg's was the hostess, just three blocks away in the Bluffs. Second, it was a fund-raiser for a good cause, reforestation and soil conserva-tion at the headwaters of the Mississippi, which would also give her something to talk *about*. And then, of course, there was Matthew Drum and the new blue dress she wanted to wear for him.

She and Matthew shared another reason for accepting the invitation, a secret mission. He wanted to meet money, and Peg was making the introductions.

Matthew hadn't asked for her help; in fact, he resisted at first. It pleased Peg to remember the look in his eyes when he said: "Let's keep our relationship personal." He had only mentioned to Peg that he was in search of a buyer for one of his properties and Peg told him not to underestimate the retirees and widows with untapped disposable incomes right there in town. When he confided it was the Riverview *Times* he wanted to unload, Peg was shocked. Why, she asked him, would DEI sell a newspaper they had just bought three months before? Matthew responded impatiently and, Peg thought, with a shade of embarrassment. He said the DEI board knew nothing about it; his reasons were personal and would not affect the value of the business. If they could round up a local investor group, he promised to spell it all out then.

Peg was thinking of becoming a principal investor. She had a fat little nest egg going nowhere in treasury bonds too conservative for her portfolio—that's what her broker was always telling her. Well, now was her chance to do some good with it and maybe earn a reasonable return. If not for her, then for the children.

The hunt for a buyer was all on the hush-hush. That was the best reason Peg could think of to keep Carole Forbes-Gwynne out of the investor pool: The woman had a mouth on her. Unfortunately, she was also just so darn rich.

Matthew had just complimented Peg, telling her she was a bloom of color in a field of crows, when Carole swept up to them, wearing a flowing black number studded with gold and turning her leathery cheek for Peg to kiss while she ravished Matthew with her eyes.

"Peggy, what a beautiful shawl, you look stunning!" Carole Forbes-Gwynne smacked a kiss near Peg's ear, followed by a whisper that Matthew could hear perfectly. "He's gorgeous! I'm jealous!"

Peg managed a wan smile. "Then I'm probably making a mistake introducing you, aren't I? Matthew, this is Mrs. Forbes-Gwynne."

"Oh, call me Carole!"

"And this is Matthew Drum," Peg continued. "He's the new owner of the paper, as you've probably—"

"And much more, I've heard!" The heavy bracelets on her arm collided, jangling over the buzz of the party as she presented her hand to Matthew. "A communications empire, I believe?"

Matthew paused too long before taking her hand, smiled too thinly, and answered too cryptically. Peg could see the signals register on Carole's face—she may be a bore, but she wasn't stupid—and saw her decide to blaze on, forgiving him.

Besides the Mahler symphony so tragically interrupted by the incident in Bogies, this was the largest social event Peg had attended with Matthew, and they were getting plenty of attention as she steered him from group to group. Not many Fortune 500 heavyweights made their home in Riverview. By noon tomorrow, Peg expected her phone to be jumping. That would be good for Matthew, of course, but she couldn't help a twinge of regret. She liked the private Matthew better than the public one.

The evening was cut short when Matthew was paged; some kind of DEI crisis back in Boston, and he had to run into the office.

"It won't take long, Peg," Matthew said at her front door. He kissed the tip of her nose. "Maybe a nightcap when I get back?"

On the face it, Sabina was the dutiful daughter making a regular delivery of water-conditioner salt to her widowed mother. After ten at night, the façade slipped a bit. Sabina's real motives were prurient. If she could catch Matthew Drum with her mother, at that hour, then something surely was up between them.

The jeep climbed steadily higher on the old Bluff Road, where the houses were bigger, the lawns denser, the power and phone lines all tucked respectably underground. Even the air in the Bluffs, some two hundred feet above the Mississippi, had a richer bite to it.

The house Sabina grew up in was a 90-year-old Cape Cod with extra dormers, shaded by mammoth silver maples and white pine. She loved the place. She leaned solidly on the bell, her signature ring so her mother would know it was okay to open up. They both ignored the fact that Peg never locked it anyway. That was last year's argument.

The frosted windows on either side of the front door were cranked open and Sabina heard Peg's brisk step across the tile. Even her footsteps, Sabina thought, sounded happier these days.

"Sweetheart!"

Her mother wore another new outfit, the top a blue swirly pattern that deepened the blue of her eyes. This was a woman who used to climb into bed with popcorn and a good book at 9:30, yet there she was, looking chic and expectant. They hugged each other. Sabina's chin fit neatly over her mother's head and she smelled hair spray, felt its stickiness in her mother's hair. Aha.

Sabina trotted to the basement with the bag of salt and upended it into the conditioner bin. She rejoined her mother in the kitchen and accepted Peg's offer of a glass of wine. Sabina strolled with it to the window over the desk that faced Matthew Drum's house. All dark.

She panicked and swung back to face her mother. "Say, Mom, I should have asked: you don't have company do you?"

"Oh, yes," Peg answered gravely. "He's hiding under the bed."

There was a giveaway flush on her face. "But you're *expecting* someone, aren't you?" Sabina pressed.

"And who anointed you the social police, young lady?"

"Oh, cripes, you're right," Sabina said, acting chagrined.

She nosed around in the refrigerator, stalling, and recognized the Tupperware her mother used for leftover chicken. They settled around the old round table and talked while Sabina finished her wine and chewed on a drumstick. The oven clock DINGed and Peg stooped to check on her bread. That must explain why her mother was still up, Sabina thought: an urge to bake. Three fragrant mounds rose under dish-cloths so old she could see the tear where her brother Stewart had lost a tooth playing bullfight.

Lights brushed the back wall of the kitchen, followed by the muffled drone of an expensive engine. Sabina rose half-way out of her chair to see a car pull into Matthew Drum's driveway. Had to be Drum himself, at this hour, and since he lived alone.

"Well," she said, briskly. A sneak look at her mother's face told her all she needed to know. "I guess I'd better get on home, I've got all this reading to do."

And sure enough, no objections. Sabina moved rapidly to the front door, reached out to open it and found a thigh bone in her hand.

She thrust it at her mother. "Here."

Peg was laughing. "Darling, he'll wait until your car is gone, I'm sure." She lifted her glasses and wiped at the corners of her eyes. She was always tearing up unexpectedly, amusement or sorrow close to her surface. It threw the children, she knew that, but she couldn't help it. She gave Sabina a teasing smile. "He's just coming by for one drink and then I'll send him right home."

"Which you always do?"

"Now, look," Peg replied, testily.

"Right," Sabina said. "Not my business."

Peg put out a hand and touched her daughter's arm, her lips pressed tight. "Sabina."

"That's me."

Peg drew a deep breath. "You've been working with Matthew for weeks, surely you have an opinion? You haven't said a word. What is it? What don't you like about him?"

"I never said I didn't like him, Mom." Sabina paused, but she could see a fence-riding answer would not go over. "I mean it. I don't have a bad opinion of him and I can't say I have a good one. He's reserved. Probably because I'm your daughter."

Her mother relaxed and smiled appealingly. "That could be. He's really a very interesting man, honey. And I'm happy."

"It's just ... I was wondering if you thought you two were alike."

"Is that so important?"

"Well, he's a demanding man, or appears to be." Sabina ran her finger over the door molding. "The way he treats his kid, for example. Kendall."

"People are complex beings, dear. They usually have reasons." Peg crossed her arms. "Anything else?"

Yes, Sabina thought. *He could be boinking someone half your age.* And he seemed the type to do it. So why wasn't he? What did Drum see in her mother, four years older, financially sound but no match for his fortune?

"It's just that I worry about you, Mom."

"Well of course, dear, and I worry about you. We're supposed to."

After Peg shut the door behind her, Sabina wound a hand through the open side window and waggled her fingers. "Get screens for these windows, okay?"

"Yes, dear," came the patient reply. "And you try to drive carefully."

Trotting to her car, Sabina marveled at the old tapes. The mother would forever see the daughter as the speeding teenager she once was, and the daughter would never consider the mother safe enough, living alone.

You're living alone now, Sabina. Does that mean you're not safe?

She understood why she was thinking that way. It was the Washington woman, the manager of the apartments down in The Flats. The word was her husband had killed her, but it did make you check the shadows.

Sabina hopped in the jeep. The digital clock read 10:31. Letterman hour. She tried to picture them doing that, Peg Lindsay and Matthew Drum, in separate wing chairs, watching David Letterman together.

The TV was chalked over with dust at the back of the workbench but Julie Oleson was only listening to it while she cleaned up some tools. Letterman had just gotten a big laugh when she thought she heard the door, but couldn't be sure. The buzzer her Dad had rigged for the front of the service station was an on-and-off-again deal, anyway. Like the rest of this operation, she thought: just gettin' by.

"Someone out there?" she called.

After a beat, she heard a man's voice in a drawn-out "Hello?"

Shit, Julie thought. She could see from the shadows in the short hallway between the front office and the garage that her father had turned out the lights, but he must have forgotten to lock up.

"Just a sec!" Julie called. She hung up the wrench, threw her rag on the hood of a Saab with a screwed-up fuel system, and was just turning the corner when he came around it and whammed into her, nearly knocking her glasses off.

"Whoa, mister," Julie said, steadying herself by gripping his arm. "Make a sound or something, okay?"

"Hey, I'm sorry," the man said. They were about the same height, but he looked all-over smaller to her, his body lost in an oversized denim jacket. She backed into the garage, squinting at him in the light from two blinking fluorescent tracks.

"Do you remember me?" he asked.

Julie Oleson put an index finger on the bridge of her nose, staring at him. "Oh, yeah," she said. "Not your name, but you're the green Audi. That's how I slot the customers."

"That makes sense," he said, smiling. "Say, I'm sorry to bust in on you like this, but it broke down again. A few blocks from here, so I thought—"

"Really?" Julie Oleson was distressed. The guy was forgettable but he had a sweet old car, an '84, and she was sure she had it running fine. "Not the distributor?"

The way the guy shrugged politely and looked away made it clear he thought it was the same problem. Julie sighed.

"I'll get the keys," she said. "Tow you in here." She eased past him and around the Saab to the corner of the garage. She crouched in front of a set of red metal drawers, opened the top one where the keys should be and, of course, weren't. Her father had it out last; they could be anywhere.

"Where'd you say the car was?" she asked, pulling open the second drawer.

"I think ... about the three hundred block of Dewey."

His voice was right behind her. She looked up over her shoulder at him. "Jesus, mister, you and your feet don't make much noise, do you? Get your Scout badge for sneaking up on people?"

"Sorry," he said. His hands were clasped behind him like some kid being chastised by the teacher.

When she turned away again, JR took her from behind. He looped the flaccid inner tube from a bicycle tire around her neck, snapped it tight and twisted. Julie Oleson reached back with both hands, scrabbling at the rubber uselessly and then digging her fingers into his thighs. He held on. Her body thrashed from side to side. She rammed him with the back of her head. JR drove his foot into her lower spine, wrestled her sideways to the cement and knelt on her ribs, torquing his rubber noose until her face turned a muddy blue and the only breathing in the cold garage was his own.

She was a big one. He straightened under her weight as best he could, then staggered over to the Saab and eased her onto the hood. He arranged her carefully and stepped back. Something was wrong. He felt around on the floor until he found her glasses, one lens broken. He tucked them behind his note in the top pocket of her coveralls, over her breast, where her name was stitched in red thread: Julie. He pulled the corner of his note up high, so they'd see it right off.

JR was careful this time, and professional in every detail. He wrote the note first. He used a different printer, from work. No handwriting. He wore gloves. He did not violate her body, for this was a sacramental act. He wanted no mistaking the purpose. It wasn't for his pleasure. It was for Albert, for the entire Fraternity. Drum the Almighty could not ignore this one.

CHAPTER SEVEN

A shiny-eyed Rose Malwicki burst into the planning meeting wearing the puffed-up pigeon look of someone bearing
Very Big News. She showed her boss, Matthew Drum, what
appeared to be someone's business card and tilted her head
towards the door of the conference room. Drum gestured to
the publisher, Frank Wiley, and they followed Malwicki out.
From the hallway came a mingling of male voices.

When the CEO and the publisher returned, they were
trailed by two guys in cheap suits. To be fair, Sabina thought,
a lot of men would look shabbily dressed next to country-
club Wiley and Matthew Drum.

One of the men was pushing a vast piece of hard, round
real estate in front of him, pants tucked below it and a paisley
tie foreshortened above. His brown suitjacket gaped hugely.
Sabina recognized him from the occasional law-related story
over the years: Riverview's chief of police, Sterling Opel.

The other man, a Detective Sergeant Mark Samuel, was
only a little overweight. His face was ordinary but nice, rug-
ged. Sabina wondered about the justice in someone with such
sparse hair being dealt a wild cowlick in the few remaining
strands. It leaned and waved as he moved: a lonely palm tree.
His wife, if he had one, should tell him to cut it down.

Their faces, all of them, were a study. Frank Wiley broke an expectant silence by stepping forward and pressing his palms together dramatically, as if he were about to break into an aria.

"People," he said, "there's been another murder." Wiley looked a little pigeon-like himself, but on the scared side. He wasn't taking pleasure in this and Sabina was getting a very bad feeling.

"You don't mind, Frank, I'll take it from here." Sterling Opel literally bumped Wiley's arm with his belly. He planted his feet wide apart and told his story. A twenty-three-year-old auto mechanic by the name of Julie Oleson had been strangled last night at her father's Citgo station. A note found on her body was addressed to Matthew Drum and signed by someone calling himself the "Poet of Pain."

Opel snorted. "Some poet," he said. "Not a rhyme in the whole thing."

"The deal is, he wants the paper to apologize. By which we figure he means that editorial you ran a couple Sundays ago." The Chief turned his bulldog profile toward Matthew Drum. "Your new boss here," he said, contemptuously, "tells me he'll 'take it under advisement.'"

Drum raised his chin and stared back, unperturbed.

Opel continued. "There's a P.S. on the note. It says 'this one's for Albert.' Does that mean somethin' to anyone here?" He paused a moment and then added, "Frank here says his cousin in upstate New York is an Albert, but we don't think that's who this Poet means."

Something in Ed Fountain's face—he looked like he was coming down with the flu—prompted Sabina to ask what they were all thinking anyway. "Is there a connection between this and the other one a couple of weeks ago? The apartment manager?"

Chief Opel recognized the other faces in the room but he

didn't know Sabina and he hesitated. Matthew Drum introduced her: "This is Sabina Shaw. She's helping us with a business plan."

"I'll be honest with you, little lady," Opel said. "We had her ex in custody but now we ain't so sure. He's been hollerin' he didn't do it, and he has a half-ass decent alibi, you'll excuse me."

"But, Mark?" Ella Martinelli by-passed the Belly and directed her question to Detective Mark Samuel. "There was no note with that body. Was there?"

A particular species of smile blinked on and off Mark Samuel's face. God, what was Martinelli's secret? In just three week's acquaintance with her, Sabina had observed that look on how many faces? Kendall Drum, Frank Wiley, Ed Fountain, some droopy-mustached guy in Ella's department named Rudy Parson and now this cop ... all of them suggesting either a shared history with Martinelli, or the desire to start one up. Matthew Drum seemed immune, and so did City Editor Phelps Pascal.

Detective Samuel confirmed that no note had been found in Claire Washington's apartment. Turning to Sabina, he said, politely: "To answer your question, about a connection between that murder and this Oleson girl?" Samuel paused long enough for Chief Opel to stop him if he had a mind to. "It's conjecture at this point," Samuel went on, "but the way we see it, except for the Bogies incident, this is a quiet town. Now two? So they *could* be related. Not saying they are."

The detective seemed content to leave it at that. It was Phelps Pascal who rubbed it in. Shooting his eyes first at Matthew Drum and then back to Samuel, he said, "Both these murders ... they both happened after our editorial."

Samuel nodded. "That's the link we're looking at. If they're connected, you see, then we could have a serial killer here. Technically."

The mantle of guilt; its psychic weight. Sabina studiously avoided looking at Fountain.

Chief Opel glowered at everyone in turn and told them to hold in confidence the little they had learned about the note on Julie Oleson's body. He shoved off toward the door, wearing the pained expression of a spouse at the first marriage counseling session. There he jerked to a stop.

"And you guys got diddly to say about this P.S., this 'Albert'?" He made it sound like one of the *Times* management team had written it.

They blinked back at him, silent, and he and the Detective Sergeant took their leave.

Ella Martinelli was the first to speak. "Jesus," she said.

Matthew Drum gestured to Frank Wiley and they resumed their chairs around the table. Steepling his long fingers together, Drum made a short speech.

"Here's how it is," he said. "The Chief asked me, and I quote, to 'pacify the creep so we can buy more time.' He wants us to capitulate to the killer's demand.

"Do we, or don't we? You're management. I'll be gone inside of six months and you'll stay. So you've got to make a decision now that you can live with. But make it now, and make it once. Because the principles at stake here, what we laid out in the editorial—they haven't changed."

Silence fell. Kendall shifted his weight and his chair groaned. His father swung his head toward him and Kendall studied the wall over the CEO's head.

"I expect all of us to think about it and all of us to contribute an opinion," Matthew Drum said slowly, continuing his laser fix on Kendall. Then he made a sarcastic show of twisting his head around and looking over his own shoulder, as if to say, what is there on this blank wall that should so fascinate my brilliant son? He turned back and gavel-chopped his knuckles on the table.

"Check," he said. *Checkmate.* "We're not about to get any more work done here today. Sabina will continue the meeting, change of topic. Rose is putting in calls now to our advisory board members and I'll be getting their opinions this afternoon and probably on into the weekend."

As he got to his feet, he leaned over Sabina and teased, in a low voice: "How about that, Sabina? Team management, as promised."

Ed Fountain's eyebrow was cocked: "What, you don't get a vote?"

"Oh, sure I do." Drum smiled. "But I've been known to unduly influence my employees, so you'd better make up your minds what you think first."

Drum laid a hand on Sabina's shoulder in passing. "Would you call me tonight? Let me know how it turns out."

Check.

They decided to take the new agenda across the street, to Theo's Bar & G ill. On the way out of the *Times*, Phelps Pascal begged off. "The baby's colicky, Sabina, and my wife'll kill me if I'm late again. Could I just tell you now, my vote is we hang tough."

He said it so easily. Pascal wagged in the tail of Matthew Drum's wind, and Drum had made it pretty clear that he wanted no change in the moratorium policy.

They settled in the familiar back booth. Frank Wiley and Sabina sat opposite Ed Fountain and Ella Martinelli. Kendall Drum pulled up a chair to the open end of the table. They placed side orders of fries, pickles and onion rings.

Wiley ordered nothing. He looked at his watch. "My wife and I have an engagement, I'm afraid."

Martinelli snapped at him. "This is a little more important than the country club, Frank."

"I assure you, Ella, I am not taking this lightly."

"Oh, I know. Sorry. But look at the facts, fellas."

Fellas. This was not the first time Martinelli had subtly shut Sabina out of the discussion; they were not destined to be pals.

"He's already gotten madder," Ella said. "He killed the first one—that black woman?—maybe just in a fit of rage at our editorial, and then he *plans* the second one. The 'Poet of Pain.' You think he's going to stop now? Unless we do what he says?"

"You think he's going to stop even if we do?" Fountain countered quietly.

Ella shuddered, hugged herself and leaned into Fountain.

"I'm on *your* side," Wiley reminded her. "Ed's the one who doesn't want to do it."

"Do what?" asked Fountain, exasperated. "What are we apologizing for? And how? Christ, what are we supposed to write?" He sculpted an imaginary banner headline in the air with one hand. "'Dear Poet, turn yourself in and we will devote an entire issue to your fascinating life.'"

"Noo-o-o," Frank Wiley responded, stringing the word out to demonstrate the end of his patience. "We simply acknowledge the fact of the note, we say that we are complying with the killer's demand for the greater public good."

"You think this sociopath is just going to stop? He'll find something not respectful enough about whatever we publish. Or nothing happens here but he moves away and starts up killing somewhere else. Or someone *else*, somewhere else, gets the idea to push for *his* day in the sun."

"That's somewhere else," Wiley said, shaking his head stubbornly. His voice slid a register higher. "There are limits to our responsibility, Ed." He flattened his index finger on the table. "This community is our responsibility."

Fountain's eyes were almost cranked shut. "Think back

to nineteen ninety-one, Frank. Why were the U.S. hostages finally cut loose? It wasn't because we gave in to the terrorists. It was because we ignored them."

Poor Frank. He had tried to contain the argument to Riverview and Ed exploded it. Wiley rose from the table, fumbling for his suitcoat button. "You have nothing left to lose," he seethed, looking at the ceiling. "And I should remind you, it's my name on the masthead. Over yours." He marched out, taking huge strides.

Wow. Sabina interpreted Wiley's remark to mean that since Fountain had already lost Casey, his daughter, and had no more children, that he didn't give a flip who else died. And the masthead crack—what was that, if not a crass threat that Matthew Drum would move on to his next acquisition but Wiley would remain, and Wiley was Fountain's boss?

Ella erupted. "That asshole!"

Fountain put a different spin on it. "No, no," he said, looking thoughtfully after Wiley. "Listen to what he said. The poor son of a bitch. He actually thinks, if we don't apologize, that he's next on the Poet's list."

"Do you think maybe that's possible?" Kendall Drum spoke, finally. He looked at each of them in turn, ending with Ella.

"How can we get inside a mind like that?" She turned to Ed, laid a fuchsia fingernail on his arm and nibbled on her lower lip. "More likely the Poet would resent you, Ed. You wrote the editorial."

"But he didn't sign it," Kendall reminded her. "My father did."

"That's right," Sabina said. "He's also been on TV, that long interview."

Fountain slapped his palm on the table. "And Drum doesn't want anything to do with this apology bullshit!"

"You don't know that for certain," Ella said, without conviction.

"Oh, come on, honey," Ed said. "Kindergarten primers are harder to read."

Kendall snorted softly—close to a laugh, for him.

"Okay," Sabina said. "It looks to me like your positions are pretty much set, and I've got to call Mr. Drum with your votes. Wiley's gone, but he's a yes, we stick. Phelps is a no, we don't stick, we apologize." She looked at Fountain. "Start with you, Ed?"

"You know what I think." He concentrated on the scarred pit of a cigarette burn on the table, running his finger across it. "No. No apology."

"Okay. Ella?"

She was staring at Fountain. She draped an arm over his shoulder. Her face, acting or not, was a meteorological map. Storms and sunshine blew across it at high speed for all the world to see. Sabina would hate to be that exposed.

"I want to go along with you, sweetie," Ella told Ed. "You know what I thought of Casey, she was ... but I've got two kids and when I picture this effing lunatic out there, you know, who knows what, so I just think that one life is worth more, that we can't risk ... do you know what I mean?" She lowered her head to peer up into his face.

He patted her hand. "Don't worry about it."

"That's a yes, we stick," Sabina said, turning to Kendall. She caught a hungering on his face as he watched the two of them. At her words, it blew away. "How about you?"

"It doesn't matter," he said, quietly.

"You mean, what we do—"

He shook his head and shuffled his feet nervously. "It doesn't matter what we think." And that was all he was going to say on the subject. His mouth closed with the mechanical snap of a ventriloquist's dummy and then he stood abruptly.

"Excuse me," he said, addressing the table top. "I have to make a call." He headed toward the pay phone, digging in his pocket.

"I guess we're finished here," Sabina said to Martinelli and Fountain.

Fountain gave Sabina a we're-in-this-together look. "Except for you."

"I don't get a vote," Sabina said, happy to plead outsider status.

Ed wouldn't have it. "Humor me."

"Okay. I'd vote no apology."

Martinelli made a noise in her throat, a condemning kind of "hmmm."

Sabina waited until Ella looked at her. "Ella, we don't even know that these murders can be linked to the same guy."

"Would your vote change if you knew that? If they were both the Poet, and that the paper did it, ticked him off?"

The principles were the same, regardless. That's what Matthew Drum said, and that's what Sabina believed. She had to repeat it to herself, but she did believe that. "No. I wouldn't."

Ella attacked, in her way. "You don't have any children, do you?" she chirped, as innocent as someone dropping onto a bus seat next to a stranger and simply passing the time.

Sabina knew better, and she was tired. Management consulting was not supposed to be dangerous work. She was not getting paid enough to make life-and-death decisions. Certainly she wasn't paid enough to be insulted by this overblown touchy-feely closet bimbo. Ella's question hung in the air as Sabina threw a few bills on the table and swung her legs to the side. Many unlovely words crowded onto her tongue and she decided to allow herself this small pleasure.

"You know I don't, Ella. You asked me that a while back." She stood and looked down at Ella steadily. "I've taken this motherhood test before. You seem to regard it as a missing chromosome."

Ella clapped both hands to her chest. "Oh, no, listen—"

"It's not your turn." That was nearly a snarl. *Whoa. Down, girl.* "When Wiley told Ed that he had nothing to lose? He was really saying that when Ed lost his daughter, he also lost all capacity to care about other people. You seemed to resent *that* insult."

Ella appeared stricken. Authentic, or an Oscar in the making? Who cared?

Sabina stooped to pick up her briefcase and bid them both a stiff goodnight. An angry ocean roared in her ears as she neared the door, but it wasn't so loud she failed to notice Kendall on the phone. His voice was raised; he was nearly shouting. She pushed through the door and glanced behind her as it closed. Kendall's back was turned to the room and he was hunched over, round-shouldered. He was such a mild-mannered fellow. Who in the world was he yelling at?

Vaguely embarrassed, Ella Martinelli watched Sabina cut like an arrow for the door. "First she's this machine, and then she gets all wounded on me?" Ella turned to Ed Fountain for support. "Was that out of the blue, or what?"

Ed wore his teacher expression. He'd do a slow blink, and when he had her in his sights again it was like, think again, kid.

"Well, really." Ella plucked up a cold French fry and bit off one end. She hadn't been about to eat with Ms. Hoity-Toity Slimbody watching her. She dipped the rest in some catsup and swallowed it. "This pretend vote on what the paper should do—it was a dead and buried deal before we ever sat down. You think?"

Ed didn't answer. His lower lids literally drooped. Ella reached out a hand and covered his. "You're going back to work, aren't you?"

"Yes, little mama," Fountain said, fondly. "It's early."

If his wife couldn't get him to come home, if maybe his wife was one reason he didn't want to go there, then Ella was of two minds about it. At least at the paper he had people around who cared about him. She dug to the bottom of the French fry carton and found a few lukewarm pieces. She took a delicate bite of one and watched Ed as she chewed. "What do you think of her looks?" Ella asked.

"What?"

"Sabina. Do you think she's good-looking?"

"My Lord, but you are a female," Fountain said. He scrubbed his hands up and down his face and laughed. "A cat." He shifted in his seat, preparing to get up.

"But what do you think?"

"Oh, Christ, who cares, Ella?" But he sat back anyway, and gazed off after Sabina. "Classic, I guess."

"Oh, no way," Ella said immediately. "She could never be a model. Age, for starters."

Fountain got up, exasperated. "I didn't say she could, that's not what I meant. Try to get that keen little mind of yours on a higher plane. Okay?"

"'Kay, Teach," she said, impishly. He left with something close to a smile, anyway.

Sometimes Ella thought that a breast reduction was in order. A nursing student friend had told her how maternal instincts were related to big boobs and she believed it. Double-A's probably led orderly lives. Even Ella's husband, her ex, could wring her out with a stunned calf-face he'd turn on her. She was way too easy on people at work, too: like the sales rep who had royally screwed up a major account a few months ago. And her advertising genius, Rudy Parson, who seemed to feel he could come to work whenever he woke up. She'd go in to have talk number hundred and ten about it and he'd wave a hand like, what price brilliance, and pretty soon she'd wind up in the cafeteria with him, trying to fatten him up and suckering for all his questions about how her kids were getting along. Then there was Ed Fountain, so adorable with that little potbelly, which was gone now, come to think of it. Ella had already been a little in love with him and when his daughter died, she would have done anything to comfort him. Offered, in fact. They had been standing right outside Theo's. Ed had blinked quizzically, like he forgot the meaning, what was actually meant, by the word sex.

Ella waved to Theo. She wanted a real drink, a whiskey sour. Both her kids were at friends' houses tonight; she owed herself a little whoopee. Kendall was still on the phone, talking more quietly now. Ella decided to get him drunk, see what more she could find out about Drum Senior and Junior. The way she kept clashing with Matthew Drum, she had an idea her job depended on it.

If she let herself think about losing her job it was like swallowing a carrot whole. Good Christ, it was the fattest salary she ever expected to see and sixteen direct reports! Two kids, a barely-contributing ex-husband, no college degree and no faith in a repeat of the luck that landed her here. In fact, in the seldom-examined corners of Ella Martinelli's soul, she felt like a broad-hipped, acne-scarred fraud hanging on by her fingernails.

She relied on men to get her here and men to keep her here. Men adored her. She figured it was the contrast between her pinky-blond Mother Earth looks and her truck driver mouth. Certain men were particularly easy: like the "hunter," whose dream life would be to sleep every night between a pair of big gazoombas like hers and in his waking hours, hunt down and slay all the threats to the real America: who would be gays, lesbos, immigrants, black skin, yellow skin, liberals ... and skirts who insisted on seats at the corporate table.

Frank Wiley was like that. Ella overheard him on the phone once, sharing his philosophy on hiring women for executive slots. "If you have to sit down to piss, we don't want you." It wasn't for her management potential alone he'd made an exception with her and played at being her mentor. Frank had expected the favors to be returned and he continued to pant after her, in his prissy kind of way, after years of failing to launch his missiles. Ella reasoned she was giving him more pleasure this way. The hunt, forever and ever, amen.

A few men—Kendall's father, more than any other—were so intimidating she had to use her imagination to be at ease with them. She'd think of them in diapers or on the pot or something.

She hadn't needed any mental tricks with Kendall Drum. When they met for the first time about two months ago, he'd slunk into a seat and hunched over a notebook computer on his knees. As she explained the data entry system for classified and subscriptions, he tapped away, his deer eyes riveted on the screen.

Until Ella stood up. "Why don't I walk you through it?" Ella had asked. "You could meet some of my people."

Kendall Drum lifted his eyes at last and they connected with her breasts. A flush suffused his face from collar to sheepdog hair. My God, she had thought. To be that shy, what a handicap! Yet, as she introduced Kendall around the department, instead of the resentful tolerance she had expected to be directed at this symbol of takeover and change, her staff opened up to the guy. He had this bumbling manner and he'd make subtle jokes at his own expense. Ella, a pro herself at drawing people out, felt a reluctant respect, followed by a sense of losing control.

"Oh, damn," Ella had said, making a show of looking at her watch. "Would you look at the time?" She laid her hands on Kendall's arm and back. "Could we get back to my office and finish this up?"

"No problem," Kendall said behind another hit-and-run look. "I've taken up too much of your time already."

"Don't be silly." She squeezed his arm once before leading the way back. His muscles had tensed under her hands. What did that mean? A, he was repulsed because he liked boys. B, he liked girls and her in particular. She decided to find out.

She closed the door and took the chair alongside him. Kendall reached for his laptop on the corner of her desk.

"Would you mind?" Ella leaned forward, head tilted appealingly, and rested her hand on his knee. "Just chatting for a minute, I mean?"

The guy used his laptop like some people groped for cigarettes. He froze, one hand on the keyboard. "About what?"

Ella clapped a hand to her mouth but couldn't keep it in. Her laugh was a distinctive scale-climbing whoop. "My goodness, Mr. Drum, you look like I asked you to stick a wet dick in the light socket!"

Kendall's face flamed. "Perhaps," he said, with no hint of humor, "perhaps if you're going to be talking about my, um, perhaps we could be on a first-name basis."

"I didn't say *your* wet—"

"Right, fine." Kendall charged into the breach. "If you say so. Although I can't see what other, you know, you think I would have access to."

Ella whooped again but stopped abruptly at the look of distaste on his face. "Wasn't that a joke? Or else you shoulda been a lawyer." She patted his knee again, by way of apology. "You gotta understand, I grew up on a farm. I'll take it easy on you, okay?"

She stood and pressed her hands to her lower back, stretching. Kendall hooked his thumbs in his belt loops and stared at the floor. "My folks hardly said a word from morning 'til sundown," she told him. "And they went to bed when the sun did. My English teacher in high school taught us the word 'taciturn,' you know it? Man oh man. That was them." She stared off through the glass, remembering that barren crack in Minnesota, improbably named Blessed Valley.

"No brothers or sisters?" Kendall asked.

She shook her head. "I figured I was adopted." Ella turned back to find him watching her and looking friendlier. He had a nice face, really. "I thought my real father was a boxer from Brooklyn and my mother a Southern belle."

He smiled. "That would fit you."

"Thank you," Ella said, and felt the oddest sensation of tenderness toward him. "What about you?" she asked, and flopped back in her chair. She swiveled to face him, their knees brushing. That should make him squirm.

Kendall shrugged. "Never knew my mother. Raised by my grandparents in the family mansion, in Kansas City. No brothers or sisters. Like you."

"But did they talk to you? Your grandparents?"

"She did, all the time. Pops—that's what I call my grandfa-ther—Pops would mostly grunt, or curse her out."

"Christ," Ella said. "Maybe I was lucky, with the still life." She tilted her head, hoping for a reaction. "You know, like that guy's picture of a farmer and his wife and this pitch-fork? Where you can't tell which one's made of wood?"

Kendall hadn't heard her. He was cranked now. "Pops was different at the plant," he said, brightening. "He liked to say that was where he hung up his soul like other men found a hook for their favorite hat."

"Some kind of manufacturing plant?" Ella asked. "That was his job?"

"A meat processing plant. Drum Meatpacking."

"Aagh. Those are horrible places. I've been in one."

Kendall looked at her, eyes wide. "I guess they are. I remember feeling that way when I was little. It was like walking through a head-on collision. The smell would eat your nose off."

Ella laughed and Kendall looked pleased. "You get used to it. I pretty much grew up there, and Pops ... Pops used to say his manners were better suited to the killing floor than Kansas City society." Ella noticed that Matthew Drum rated no mention at all. But Kendall obviously loved his grandpa.

"Is he still around? Your grandfather, I mean."

"Oh, sure," Kendall said with a lift of surprise, like he hadn't begun to consider that death and old age were acquainted. "He's eighty-four. His hearing's not great but otherwise he's a strong old ox."

"So how come your Dad didn't take the plant over?" Ella asked. "Or yourself?"

"It got sold," Kendall said shortly. "My father called it a 'coup,' but Pops didn't care about money, he wanted the name carried on. My father flies back east and gets famous on Wall Street, and I'm the one who stayed home for two years, hiding bottles from Pops." He thrust his chin out and Ella saw, for the first time, Matthew Drum in his son's face. "Pops spun out. I couldn't take a job, couldn't go to school. I was afraid if I left, my grandparents would kill each other."

Ella had stirred up more than she intended. Kendall closed up his laptop along with his personality, and escaped. She watched him make his way toward the elevator, detouring wide around a cluster of people talking in the aisle. And she remembered, as she watched the computer bump awkwardly against his thigh, being jolted by a second surge of tenderness. He was such a weird duck. He even walked like one.

And here came the duck now, winding his way around the tables to their back booth at Theo's.

"Hey," she said to him, patting the seat next to her. "I got you a beer. Is that okay?"

His face flashed a teensy bit of panic but he was more polite than scared and he sat back down like a good boy. Not next to her, though. He slid the beer to the other side of the booth and settled in front of it.

It took two more beers before Ella could get him to open up like before. She was two sheets to the wind herself and she figured, what the fuck, and just up and asked him: "So what gives with you and your father?"

All she learned was ancient history, but it was a hoot, anyway. Here she was, right off a stupid backwoods chicken farm, and here was Kendall Drum, of *the* Kansas City beef king family, and it turned out he was the illegitimate one! Matthew Drum had knocked up some associate professor at Harvard back in the days when women hardly got jobs like that and they sure didn't keep them by walking around campus behind an illegal bump. So this professor took her bump to Italy on a research sabbatical, she grunted, there was Kendall, and she was all set to toss him to this happy couple in the hills outside of Florence when in came "Pops."

"It was okay with your father?" Ella asked. "Giving you up?"

Kendall twitched a shoulder but it was a lousy bluff; he cared, all right. "They had a fight about it. My father laid down a condition, which was that he got to name me."

Ella had read some story when she was little about an adopted girl who searched and searched for a sign that the mother who had given her up had loved her, and was finally satisfied when the adoption home showed her the home-made foundling clothes she had been wearing and their tiny, precise stitches.

She told Kendall the story. "That showed how much her mother loved her, see? So your stitches are your name."

He gave her a sweet, sad smile. "That's a fairy tale and my family ... isn't. Kendall was my father's older brother's name, who died in Korea. My father blamed my grandfather, I guess because my uncle didn't want to enlist. So Dad named me Kendall to get back at Pops. To be this constant walking-around reminder."

Ella wove her way home shortly after that: alone. And with a renewed determination about Kendall Drum. This, she thought, was one lost soul who was on his own. No goddamn *point* in getting involved with such a powerless duck. He probably didn't have any money of his own, and Matthew Drum had a set of strong teeth, as Ella's own father used to say. Meaning he'd last forever.

CHAPTER EIGHT

ha@dill.drvby.com

Andrew Webster, cruising through his pet newsgroups, swore softly. His only employee was just coming in; he could hear Sojo bumping around in the kitchen, whistling and snapping his raincoat dry. The fourth day of gray drizzle in Washington DC, and Andrew Webster, known to his USENET world as Handy Andy, suffered from cabin fever and a case of grouch. The mood was not improved by the words on his computer screen.

"Sojo? How you doin'?" he called out. Trying to keep it light, he used his Halloween Freddy voice. "Guess what, Sojo? He be baa-a-ck."

"Shakespeer? What his rag now?" Sojo leaned through the doorway, his hands full of coffee makings. He used a forearm to swipe at a drop of water tracing down his cheek.

"Take a look." Webster pushed back in his chair and Sojo bent down next to him to read the screen. "Unscrambled, natch." Webster said. "Some woman disses his top cop show, and look."

Sojo had named the guy Shakespeer after a series of rhyming taunts, some ending with "*I'm watching you,*" had begun appearing in some of the TALK and ALT newsgroups on the

Net. Even when he dropped that sign-off phrase, Shakespeer's messages had a voyeuristic stamp to them. Like this one.

>1997Jun21.088964.311.jr@frat.org>
I'm a SPLIT in the SEam of the skin tight JEans
On the body of the WHORE who dares to DREAM
that WE will hear her 'i obJECT' and 'please reSPECT'
oh PLEASE oh PLEASE oh PLEASE oh PLEASE.
we WILL please this mindless MOUTHless woman
UNdivine
we WILL
We're a KNIFE in the seam of the red wet pants
On the corpse of the SLUT who dared to FANCy
Herself an EEEqual an EEEKqual an EEEEK
a coffin full of screams and dreams UNdreamed

"Man!" Sojo straightened up and looked down at Andrew Webster. "He be buggin' outta control. Where it at?"

"Arts TV. Unmoderated groups, he picks."

"Man," Sojo repeated. "Somethin' new here. He seriously pissed-off."

"A fuckin' loser," Webster said. He spun toward the window and glared at the rain. Sojo stood by silently. One reason he had lasted longer than anyone with Andrew P. Webster, had, in fact, become his friend, was that he knew how to read the weather.

"I knows dis guy, Sojo. Invisible hophead wonderbread *fucker*." Webster looked down at his hands and flexed them open and closed.

"Andy, lissen." Sojo's high forehead was layered in worried gull-wing wrinkles. "You knows how it go. Gots ta put it behin' you, man, or you gonna make you a serious misery—" The look cut him off. So, he'd gone too far. "Right," Sojo said, drifting toward the kitchen. "Sorry, man."

"Forget it."

"Menu done?"

"Yeah."

Webster gripped the arms of his wheelchair and started a series of rapid push-ups, his dark arms densely muscled. He lifted his weight easily, trying to blank out his mind.

Easy for you to say, Sojo.

CHAPTER NINE

The local television and radio stations got hold of the note left on Julie Oleson's body—not the piece of evidence itself, but certain facts like the Poet's threat to kill again if Matthew Drum, through the *Times,* failed to publicly apologize. The story's escalation followed a suspicious pattern of off-the-record attribution. When Chief of Police Sterling Opel was then contacted by reporters for on-the-record confirmation of the leak, he was "forced" to oblige.

The timing also pointed to the cops as the source.

Sabina was in Drum's office Monday morning when he called Opel to officially inform him the *Times* would take a pass on the killer's demand. In the middle of his reasoned explanation—delivered politely if not with the obsequious slurp Opel might prefer—Drum paused. Moved the receiver away from his mouth and regarded it. Hung it up, quietly, and sent Sabina the briefest tic of amused irony.

Opel's backdoor sneak provided him a certain cover. He could withhold what he needed to protect his case, at the same time pointing a finger at the Riverview *Times* to share the blame and dilute scrutiny of the core issue ... that he hadn't a clue who the Poet might be.

Until the leak of the Oleson note, the *Times* had enjoyed

a state of grace for withholding publicity on the Bogies killer. Community groups rallied behind them. An acquaintance of Peg Lindsay's, Carole Forbes-Gwynne, was particularly vocal. Peg thought Carole was driven more by her infatuation with Matthew Drum, but as President of the all-powerful Women's League of Voters, Forbes-Gwynne carried clout. Speakers all around town were bumped to make room for Frank Wiley and Matthew Drum: very hot, very topical. A freelance stringer for a Minneapolis station interviewed Drum and zapped one flattering story to air up there and another version to CNN. Of the three TV stations in Riverview, two ran barebone leaders about the *Times* editorial. The third was Channel 7, the station that the Bogies killer used to broadcast his complaints to millions of people. Channel 7 had the most serious image problem, so they rounded up two of the hostages from that siege and both took to the airwaves in praise of Channel 7's intervention, claiming—and who could argue?—that broadcasting the killer's statements saved their lives. This did not interrupt the ripples of admiration for the local paper and its new owner. Letters and phone calls and advertisers all supported the moratorium policy. It became the politically correct position.

The flurry of attention, nearly all local, had pretty much subsided when Chief Opel or someone doing his bidding pulled the deep throat and leaked the Poet's note. Most of it broke Monday night:

Channel 7: "Our Maria Ferguson has learned that the Riverview *Times* may be implicated, by association, in the murder last Thursday of Julie Oleson. Maria?"

Channel 2: "An anonymous source has informed WJJY that the note found on Julie Oleson's body early last Friday demanded the Riverview *Times* apologize for their June eighth editorial. The implication, neither confirmed nor denied by

Police Chief Sterling Opel, was that the killer will strike again if the paper does not comply ..."

Drum called Sabina before six AM the next morning, Tuesday. He had been tipped about a joint conference Chief Opel had arranged for nine AM at City Hall with Riverview's mayor, Roland August. Sabina watched it in Drum's office, with the CEO and Ed Fountain.

The Mayor wavered between opinions, but did manage to malign the paper's position by calling it an "indulgent luxury." Chief Opel was more direct: "There's nobody respects the U.S. of A's liberal press more than me—excuse me, I meant *free* press, of course. But I got a job to do here, to protect the citizens of this city. This is one helluva credible threat, this Poet. I appeal to Mr. Matthew Drum's sense of civic duty ..."

Opel wouldn't have appealed to Drum at all had he any choice, but sources in the DA's office told Fountain that in a short and stormy meeting, the Chief hadn't received happily his lesson on how the courts interpret the First Amendment, especially since the paper's position was not the right to speak, but the right not to.

So far, no one was officially pinning blame for the first victim, Claire Washington, on the Poet of Pain or on the newspaper by extension. The police could not confirm a fingerprint trail between the Washington murder and Julie Oleson's killer, and a bartender had implicated her ex-husband by reporting a conversation in which he railed about "offing" her.

The *Times* was nevertheless presented with a public relations challenge of massive proportions. "We need a plug-the-dike strategy, fast," Drum said, adding with obvious reluctance, "and I suppose Frank needs to be in on it." Sabina was elected to collect the publisher.

He barely heard her out. "You've proceeded to lead us down the primrose path quite well without me," Wiley huffed. "I believe I'll pass."

So Ed Fountain, Matthew Drum and Sabina put their heads together around Drum's sparkling glass desk.

"It wouldn't hurt to offer a reward," Sabina suggested. "An eight-hundred number for information leading to the Poet's arrest? A full page, maybe—"

"I like it," Drum said. He scanned the internal phone list, dialed an extension and switched to the speaker phone.

"Ella here."

"Mrs. Martinelli, save a half page for tomorrow, display ad. You have someone in Advertising who can string words together decently?"

A long pause. "Rudy's the best," she said slowly. "Who is this? Is this—"

"We've got a job for him," Drum said. "Sabina will be in touch."

Ella broke in before he could hang up. "Mr. Drum! Listen, we've ... I think you should know, I've told Frank ... um, we're losing advertisers? Three cancels already."

"How much?"

"We're checking. One account is a hurt, for sure, it's that big—"

"Call Rose with the totals, Mrs. Martinelli. Keep updating her."

He hung up and turned to Sabina. "Better run whatever this Rudy comes up with past our Boston lawyers, and give the cops a courtesy look."

"Not such a good idea, Matthew," Ed Fountain said. Ed was slumped so far forward on his elbows his head looked like an ornament on Drum's desk. "Having some Advertising guy write this reward offer, I mean. It's not an advertising jingle; it's another chance to state our case."

Drum tipped back in his chair and laced his fingers behind his head. "You wanna have a crack at it?"

Fountain nodded.

"Check." Drum said. "What else you think we should be doing?"

"We've got to look at multiple ways of educating people, fast." Ed lofted his arm in the general direction of the street. "Town's going nuts, rumors are reproducing like mayflies. I think we train any credible breathers and send 'em out there. Start with opinion leaders."

They roughed out a simplified, common message defending the moratorium, and the means of getting the message out. Drum said he'd lean on the advisory board to bring in supportive outside opinion.

They were just about wrapped up when Drum's office door was flung open with such force that the doorknob carved a crater in the plaster wall. Frank Wiley stood there, not a hair out of place, furious. In five strides, the publisher ate up the acre of carpet between the door and Drum's desk, slammed down a piece of paper on the glass surface and fairly spit his words.

"When it rains it pours. Now you've got two leaks for your *management team* to handle."

Sabina didn't know what he was talking about, but she was impressed at his unflinching directness. Wiley usually minced around the CEO.

"Would you care to explain yourself, Frank?" Drum wasn't going to make it any easier on Wiley by reading whatever was on the paper; he kept his seat and stared up at Frank.

It was a little like dream paralysis. Sabina was apprehensive but vaguely entertained as well: Who was going to get drilled, and why? Ed Fountain scrabbled his chair forward a foot and scraped the sheet off Drum's desk. Sabina glanced over and saw boxes and lines ... it looked like an organization chart.

"Let me help," Wiley said bitterly. "The square for publisher?" He snatched it from Fountain and whacked it with the back of his hand. "Empty." He crumpled the paper in his fist and flung it down. It skittered across the desk and into Drum's lap with no effect; his concentration was total.

"In *my* America," Wiley began, "a man faces up to people. A man ..." His bravado was sloughing away with every passing second he looked into Drum's eyes. He appeared *skewered* in place, and then he broke. He turned his back, heading toward the door, and hurled a final salvo.

"I'm not staying around to hear—"

"Get back here, you fucking idiot." Matthew Drum surged to his feet. Wiley pivoted, slow-motion. Beyond him, in the outer office, Rose Malwicki sat stiffly erect in her armless chair, staring straight ahead, her cheeks bright.

Sabina got up quickly to close the door and stayed there, her hands behind her on the doorknob. She was looking over Frank's shoulder at Drum.

"Listen up, you fucking maggot brain. I could have fired your fucking useless ass the first day I walked into this dump. *Fuck* you!" Drum's face was pure loathing. Neither did Sabina recognize the language out of the erudite Harvard graduate. She remembered his chameleon hop into street talk when he needed to persuade the ex-police chief to join the advisory board, but this was no conscious transformation. The words spewed out with the force of nature.

Drum's eyes flickered. He seemed to take in Sabina's presence behind Wiley and it restored some civility.

"Idiot school boy. How about the facts of business for the idiot school boy? *Fact.* Drum Enterprises isn't just me. I report to a board and the board likes to know what I'm going to do with loser properties. *Fact.* The piss-poor Riverview *Times* is a loser property."

Drum was leaning into it on the balls of his feet. Wiley was a statue.

"Another fact. Frank. Who do you suppose the Board would blame for the wasted state of your balance sheets? In a one-newspaper town, yet. Do you wanna take a guess? Go ahead, Frank."

Wiley did not want to take a guess. Every time Drum said *Frank* it dripped with venom, like he slipped an embroidered handkerchief over "you fuck."

Drum leaned against his desk, arms crossed. "Your bloody precious Riverview *Times* was taking a dive, Frank. And it was your fault. Now. I have a reboot schedule with the board. This organization chart went to them, on schedule, to reassure them a strong management team would be in place, on schedule. Why the ... why in the world would I put your name up top?"

Drum waited. Wiley said nothing.

"Do you have a plan to improve earnings, Frank? Now's the time to lay it out. Years late, but I'm listening."

Wiley still had nothing to say. He turned his bullet head and checked out, peripherally, Sabina's position, like he was checking on the obstacles between him and safety.

"That was a dummy chart, Frank. Tell me where you got it."

"It was just there. On my screen. I printed it out."

Drum nodded. "Here's what you do, Frank. You shut up, first, and then find a way to be grateful that I've bought us the time to set things straight. A gift. You're sixty-three, right? Two glory years before you retire."

Something on Wiley's face must have signaled shock because Drum smiled vengefully. "That's right, Frank. The *Times* will be following all Drum Enterprises personnel policies. One of them is mandatory retirement at sixty-five."

Wiley snatched at recovering some dignity and didn't do a half-bad job. "It will be my pleasure," he said. He groped behind him for the door and Sabina helped, stepping up to close it behind him.

The creative mood was gone with the wind of Wiley's exit. Fountain excused himself, icily. Sabina started to do the same until Drum asked her to stay.

When Ed had gone, Drum was silent for a long moment. He lifted his chin and held her eyes. "I don't have any friends here, Sabina." It wasn't a search for sympathy, and she didn't bother refuting it. "I'm forced to choose where to put my trust."

Drum plucked up a glass paperweight and strolled over to the second-story window overlooking Theo's Bar and G ill. Sabina didn't respect his filleting Frank Wiley, but her sympathy was aroused, as Fountain's could not be, by the struggles of running a company—meeting payroll, investor expectations—instead of just working for one. Of course, Linshaw Bicycle Works grossed twelve million dollars its last year and DEI paid fifteen times that in taxes.

"Frank hit one thing on the head," Drum said. "We've got two leaks to worry about now." He propped a foot on the window sill and leaned forward, resting an elbow on his leg. It was a nice move for showing off the stretch of muscle near his ribcage.

"I trust you," Drum continued, "and I trust Rose. As soon as you leave, she'll be in here with all kinds of ideas about how Frank got a copy of that memo and what to do about it. Because there's more where that came from. And it will drive her *crazy* until it's plugged. And that will drive *me* crazy." He straightened and faced her.

"Would you handle this for me, Sabina?" He laughed and ran a hand across his bristly crewcut. "Why don't I just put you on the payroll, you've spent more time here than anyone else."

"How about Kendall?" she suggested. "He seems to know a lot about computers, couldn't he help?"

His face shuttered down, barely perceptible but she had seen the expression before where his son was involved. "Fine," he said carefully. "You're in charge, just get me the result of confidential means confidential."

He returned to his desk. "Rose will know where to start, so check with her." He stroked a button on the intercom and said to Rose: "Back in business here. Give me a rundown on the calls, but first I'd like you to brief Mrs. Shaw on the process," he enunciated the word precisely, "not the content, of our confidential files and correspondence."

Aha, Sabina thought. Trust extended, trust withdrawn. Or at least, qualified.

As she opened the door, Drum suggested she might want to tune in CBS Evening News that night: a low-key aside that was less casual than it sounded and though his eyes were scanning his mail, Sabina thought he looked a little smug. He would no doubt be featured in a story. He wanted an equally low-key but oh-wow response. She ignored the cue and kept on going. He could think of it as a qualified withdrawal.

Sabina spent the rest of the day helping out with moratorium "training" sessions for the staff, then delayed going home for a few more hours. She took in a movie downtown, and stopped off for Chinese. Finally, after 10 PM, she headed home to Melody Lane. She parked, locked the car door and unsnapped her purse. As usual, she couldn't find her stupid house key.

When Jacob moved out, Peg Lindsay considered her daughter unprotected. She presented Sabina with a new key chain and a plea that Sabina separate her car and house keys, and keep the house key in her pocket. Peg reasoned that when the bad guys stole Sabina's purse and lifted her address and other facts of her life, they at least would not be able to stroll unimpeded through the front door of the bungalow.

Sabina had laughed out loud. She told her Jacob had hardly made her safer: He slept so soundly, the only protection he'd provide was his inert form used as a shield. She mocked her mother: "How about I go live in a seamless bubble, on an island somewhere?" Then she dutifully separated the keys, but never could remember to pocket the house key. Now anyone interested in mugging her had all the time in the world as she stood with purse upturned and back to the streetlight.

Distracted by her plunging search, Sabina forgot to step over the loose board at the edge of the wide front porch and as the wood groaned under her weight, something yipped at her from the dark.

"Who is that?" she yelled.

A white slash went vertical. "Don't get all hotted up, y'all."

The porch swing creaked and Olaf Jergensen walked out of the shadows, stretching his skinny little arms over his head.

"Oh, Tootie. God. You little shit."

"Hey! What's up witchew, that's Jake talk."

Y'all. Witchew. The Adorable Toot, as Sabina called him when he wasn't around to hear, was an imitator of first order and for about a year he had been experimenting with the strangest mix of languages.

It took good eyesight to find the adorable parts of him just then. His T-shirt was streaked with grass stains, his light-brown hair was dirty and tangled with pieces of—

"What's this? Forsythia?" Sabina plucked a twiggy growth out of his hair and he backed up a step. Okay. He had been hiding out or sleeping in the bushes alongside his house, before crossing the street to camp out on her porch.

"Look, kid, it's already late, so what's another hour going to hurt? Why don't you hang out with me a while?"

"How about all night?" He posed it with bounce. Let's jam, let's boogie, let's treat this like anything but what it is: Tootie desperate to feel safe because Karl the Jerk Jergensen had slumped home drunk, cuffed Tootie's mother and perhaps taken off after Toot himself. More likely, her smart little friend had rolled quietly out his bedroom window and waited for Daddy's all-clear snores. Sabina's read on it was that the only thing this eighty-five-pound kid could think to do for his mother was at least to stay near, loyally, until Jergensen was finished with her.

Toot stepped out of his shoes and used the rug in the wide front hall as his starting block, crouching down in a rump-high, three-fingered tripod and throwing her a commanding look over his shoulder. Sabina observed his tight little calf muscles and high color: the kid looked healthy enough.

"Bang."

"Aw, come on girl!"

She raised her hand in the air, index finger pointed out. "BANG!"

Toot sprang forward. One leap over a stack of newspapers and magazines, a side-roll jump over the coffee table and onto the couch. He landed on her silk sleep shirt and pulled it out from under him, wiggling his eyebrows in ten-year-old lewd.

"Oh, Toot," she laughed, "it's so great having you here."

It was absolutely so, the presence of another being towards whom she felt affection unmingled with anything else. Tootie's face went blank. He reached for the clicker, kneeled on the couch with his back to the TV and pointed it over his shoulder. "Zap!" He settled down to graze the stations.

"I'm making some coffee," Sabina said. "Want some?"

On Sunday mornings when Toot used to join Jacob and her

for breakfast, he got a kick out of their extending him that offer. He hadn't spent a single Sunday at their house since Jacob moved out. Perhaps, Sabina thought, Toot had finally forgiven her.

"Yah shoor," Toot replied. "Bring on da beans." Now who was he? The lilting Swede part sounded like his father, oh joy.

She stripped off her hose while he was facing the other way and kicked them under the couch. The kitchen—a truly comfortable and rather cock-eyed room with a roiling black-and-white tile floor—was just behind the living room through another wide archway. Sabina liked its cool grittiness under her feet. Summer never felt like summer unless the kitchen floor was a little dirty, a little textured.

Her mind was too much on memories and too little on the familiar motions of coffee-making. When she settled down by the Toot and sipped her coffee, it almost stood her up again.

She had spiked Tootie's with milk and some cocoa but some of the core strength must have seeped through because he was wide-eyed until past two AM, while Sabina buzzed her way through a few months of back-up reading. They hardly spoke, just sat like two old friends, thinking their separate thoughts, together. After Tootie was asleep, curled like a boy-cat in Jacob's old spot next to the lamp, Sabina played with his hair, stroking it lightly and pretending he was hers to keep. She thought she detected a deeper level of sleep in Toot after about fifteen minutes of that, and if he was aware of her messing with him, he gave no sign.

CHAPTER TEN

It was just like Frank Wiley to spread the pain around. Ella had all she could do to keep from chasing after the creep and ripping off his lips. She dialed a buddy in Customer Service, got her voice mail and hung up. Ella spun her chair in a circle and strangled a scream.

Wiley had ricocheted from his run-in yesterday with the big boss and into her office, looking for someone to dump on.

The sleek head cut around the edge of her office door. "You busy, Ella?"

"No, no, come right in, Frank." The weary man collapsed in a chair, his lower lip stuck out like a two-year-old's. He told her about this memo he wasn't supposed to see that showed a reorganization he wasn't part of. Ella wasn't either, *by the way*. The CEO had assured Frank it was just a dummy chart. Frank was not "at liberty to divulge" the reasons for that but not to worry, he wouldn't let anything happen to her.

When he left, his face smooth as a baby's ass, Ella wondered why he clung to a job he didn't need. His dead mama's money, and now DEI's from the buy-out, would save the prick no matter what size rug Matthew Drum pulled out from under him. What the fuck was she supposed to think about a dummy organization chart? Ella gulped a slug of cold coffee and stared unseeing through the glass wall of her office at the rat's maze of metal desks and cheap orange cubicles.

Just as she was thinking she had to talk to someone about this or she'd bust, just as she was thinking, how about Kendall ... who should float into her vision and stand there in that peering school-boy pose, waiting for her to notice him.

"Well, well." Ella waved him in. "Aren't we making progress? In the flesh, yet."

They had what she considered the start of a friendship, but it was a cyberspace thing. On his terminal, he was a regular Cyrano de Balzac—or whatever his name was. Ella began every morning with a quick look and laugh at her e-mail. She'd beep him back whatever she felt like, depending on her mood. He could take her raunchy stuff electronically, even seemed to like it, but no way in person. In person, it was still a teeth-pulling thing. The original Kendall nerd-duck would peep up his shy periscope head, twist it around and then *shoop!* down he'd go.

"We have a problem," Kendall began, looking anything but troubled. He even perched, back straight, at the chair's edge instead of his usual s-curve, sitting on the back of his neck.

"I figured," Ella said bleakly. "You do your socializing on-line."

Kendall started to get up. "This is a bad time. I can—"

"Sit!" He froze in a half-crouch. Ella motioned him all the way down.

She forced a smile. "I'm sorry, sweetie. It's been an awful morning." She walked around her desk for a seat at the small round table next to her aquarium. This was a technique from one of Frank Wiley's bullshit management seminars, sup-posed to make people feel more at ease. Ella just liked this chair better.

"Come on over here, Kendall. Tell me."

It seemed Sabina Shaw had asked Kendall to investigate a hacker in the paper's computer system. Since most of the *Times* data processing work involved subscribers and advertisers, Ella supervised some of DP. They farmed out a lot of their routine stuff.

"Do they know whose files are being messed with?" she asked. "Besides Wiley's?"

"That seems to be it."

"Wrong."

Kendall's eyes shone. His Daddy may call him Director of Marketing, but so far, he'd had diddly squat to do. Here was a job.

"You heard about the cost-cutting memo?" Ella asked.

He stared back, bland as ever. "No."

It looked as if the lines of communication between Kendall and his Papa were not exactly humming. Ella liked that. "Yesterday morning, four of us get this sealed envelope, hand delivered by Rose, which ... you don't know this from me, okay?"

He nodded.

"Okay. It said we've got to cut staff by fifteen percent, and he wants names. In a week." She watched him carefully: still a blank slate. "By *that afternoon* I've got five of my staff huddled in here and they've got the details of the memo exactly right. Oh, and did I add, they're shittin' their pants they're so worried. The contents of that memo—no one got it from *this* little lady." Ella jerked a thumb at her chest. "And even if one of the others spilled it, you know how it works ... they pick someone close to them? That person tells another, it's a slow-tease telephone game and then you start to hear back umpteen different versions?"

"Let me guess," Kendall said. "They get back from lunch, or something, and turn up their screens and it's waiting for them, the memo."

"Bingo. In fact, it *was* right after lunch, you psychic you. Is that how it happened with Wiley?"

"Yes." Kendall's fingers, amputated from his keyboard, twitched over his knees. "Simple e-mail command."

"No, no. This was inserted in their active project files." She frowned at him. "What you said ... that's a good point, Kendall. Why didn't the hacker use e-mail to distribute it?"

He stared down at his shoes. "Hmm. I can only ... hmm. I guess he's showing off. Showing that he knows their passwords."

"So we've got to change the passwords."

Kendall looked alarmed. He blew out his cheeks. "A Band-Aid approach if we don't know how he got them to begin with."

There was a knuckle-rapping on the glass behind them and Ella started. She and Kendall swung around to see Rudy Parson already well inside her office, his arm stretched out for an after-the-fact knock. Parson had thinning blond hair and a sparse Fu Manchu-type mustache that Ella rather liked. He kept food out of it, anyway.

"Hey, Ellie," Rudy said, "sorry to interrupt." He grinned at her and pretty much took over, dropping a paste-up in front of her on the table and leaning over it. "It's this recycling ad, the rush job? We're on deadline."

Ella barely glanced at it; his work was always good and he knew it. "Rudy, have you met Kendall? Kendall Drum, this is Rudy Parson. He's Advertising, like you couldn't have guessed, and handles some of our computer stuff—Mister Jack of all Trades."

Parson crossed one arm over his chest and extended his hand directly in front of Kendall's face. "Just call me Jack," he joked. Kendall wheeled his chair back and shook it.

Ella swept the paste-up off the table. "The ad's fine, I'm

sure. Run it past production. We've got a problem here so I don't have the time for—"

"Yeah, I heard," Parson said, not a bit remorseful for eavesdropping. "You're thinking of changing the passwords, huh? We had to do that at the last place I worked. Maybe I can help?"

Kendall shrugged, so Ella briefed Rudy on the hacker problem and pretty soon, she could have been a smashed bug on the wall for all the attention they paid to her.

"UNIX uses the same conventions as the Net," Kendall said.

"So you're saying it wouldn't have to be someone inside."

"Assuming you've got the software loaded."

"Six months ago the paper changed over, I think it was."

"Then what password system—"

"That's a joke," Rudy Parson said. He slid his superior smile at Ella. "Let me show you, see if Ellie uses the same brilliant system." Parson's knee cracked as he knelt on the floor and bent low to eyeball the base of Ella's monitor. He straightened and groped around the back of the computer near the wall. "Here," he said. "See?" He peeled off a yellow Post-it note where Ella had recorded her password and held it up.

"Clever," Kendall said, straight-faced. The two men smiled and shook their heads.

Ella rolled her eyes. "Excuse me all to hell. But are you saying that all the guy does is creep around the building looking for Post-its, and that's whose computers the memo landed on?"

An astounded look from both of them, like, how low-tech, no way!

"Well, why not?"

They ignored her and started talking gateways and firewalls and sniffer programs. Ella was bored silly. She left to make some phone calls. When she returned, Rudy Parson was gone and Kendall sat patiently, his back to the door, legs crossed and one white hairless ankle jiggling. Brown socks. Blue pants, frayed at the edge.

"You two seemed to hit it off," Ella said cheerily.

No answer. "No?" Ella tried again, curious. Kendall looked miffed.

"Why does he call you 'Ellie'?"

"That's my name. Close enough, anyway."

"It's the way he says it."

"Why, Kendall!" Ella squatted by his side, close enough to let him drink in her perfume, and shook the chair arm playfully. "That wouldn't be jealousy, would it?"

"Certainly not my business," he said stiffly, his face an ugly red. Oops.

"So what did you decide to do?"

"Change the passwords, of course."

My my. He really was miffed.

"Well yes, but how? And how about the hacker?"

"This Rudy," Kendall said, treating Parson's name like a hot cow turd, "says he heard about some free software from a standards institute. The computers generate the passwords automatically."

"We could still leave them lying around. Like I did."

"The computer picks easier ones and they're harder to decode. But we'll have to train people not to do that."

"How about who's doing it?"

"I guess that's my assignment. I don't even know how to start. It could, you know, be someone outside the paper. This gateway is not exactly state-of-the-art."

"Why would someone outside care?"

His shoulder twitched. "My father's empire is a big one."

"Well, major click!" Ella exclaimed. "Shit! He's got to

have some class of enemies out there, with all the buying and firing and such, huh? Serves him right."

Just as she said that, a rustling sounded behind her and Ella slowly stood and turned, the skin on her arms already going prickly. There was Matthew Drum, crisp blue shirt, crisp mean look. She had to learn to close her door.

He talked to Kendall while training his eyes on Ella for a long moment. "Kenny, I need you to drive me to Madison tomorrow afternoon. We've got the *NewsHour* with Jim Lehrer interested in doing a roundtable on the moratorium and that's the nearest city for uplinks."

Kendall didn't respond.

"All right, Kenny?"

"But what's the, I mean, my car isn't—"

"We'll take mine. Mrs. Shaw is coming along and we need to work."

Kendall lifted his chin, a shadow of his father's you-are-a-specimen move. "Chauffeurs can be rented."

"Tempting," he snapped. "But no. Not only is it an unnecessary expenditure, but I have other reasons for asking you and Ms. Martinelli doesn't need to hear them."

He waited. Kendall had no shots left to fire, just his signature one-shoulder shrug. "No problem."

"We leave at noon," Drum said, and was gone.

Ella was discouraged. Every time she screwed up, it had to be in front of that man. Her shoulders folded, her eyes filled. A fat one rolled down her cheek.

"Did he hear me, do you suppose? Why do I have no luck with that man, Kendall? It's like a spell or a jinx or something!" She nodded at the credenza behind him. "Could you hand me a tissue?"

He fumbled the box to the floor, picked it up and thrust it at her.

"Thanks." Ella sniffed and wiped her eyes dry. "Oh, God. I know what's coming. Some heads have to roll around here and mine is going to be one of them."

"No." The single word came out fierce. Kendall stepped closer—hardly clinching distance, Ella thought, but the clinch was there in his eyes. Something that hadn't been there before—a possessive gleam. It restored her.

"You don't be upset," Kendall commanded in a harsh whisper. "This will be my paper someday. If he does that, I'll just hire you back."

"You?" Too late to discipline her tone.

"Why not me?" Instead of shrinking, he asked the question with authority, like he had asked it before of himself and arrived at an answer he liked. Kendall smiled slyly. "Would I be any worse than Frank Wiley?"

Ella's whoop laugh stirred some heads in the department. "Shit, no!" This was more like the e-mail Kendall. "I just meant, you know, how do you know he's going to do that? What if ... well, he could just change his mind or something couldn't he? Unless, do you have it in writing?"

"You sound like Pops. My grandfather." He turned from her, replacing the box of Kleenex. Ella couldn't see his face as he added, simply: "No, he really means it. He promised."

Ella's mouth made the agreeable sounds Kendall expected. Inside, a firm, practical voice said: "*Not bloody likely.* Drum Senior is no way going to turn this over to his kid. A, he doesn't like him any better than he likes *me*. Drum is heavy into humiliating Kendall, that's all. Which means, B, Kendall is heavy into delusion."

CHAPTER ELEVEN

Sabina stretched Jacob's paint-splattered T-shirt to cover her bottom, stooped to retrieve the *Wall Street Journal*, and froze. The left column headline was about Riverview, the small town with the big problem.

Newspaper Baron
In Deadly Showdown
With Serial Killer

————

*Apologize Or Else
Says "Poet of Pain"*

————

Police to Press: Your Civic Duty

————

That Streetcar Named Expire

Oh, boy. Monday, it was the lead news story on local TV channels 5 and 11. Tuesday it hit the Chicago and Minneapolis papers. But now, seeing it in her business bible—now it was official.

She nudged the front door closed with one hip and shook the paper free from its wrapper. Coffee could wait; she backed

up to the wall, slid down to the cool maple floor and devoured the story.

> RIVERVIEW, WI.—A serial killer may be on the
> loose in this quiet Wisconsin town where, until
> a month ago, not a single citizen had been
> murdered in over 35 years. Now three people
> are dead, at least one of them at the hands of a
> killer who pinned a note to the victim demand-
> ing an apology from Matthew Drum, the new
> owner of the morning newspaper.
>
> The Riverview *Times* was purchased in
> March by Drum Enterprises, Inc. (DEI), a fast-
> growing international group of 75 publications.
> Matthew Drum, its CEO, made his financial
> reputation in Wall Street investment firms.
> Now he is engaged in a novel application of
> First Amendment rights: the right *not* to speak;
> not to publish.
>
> This test of wills between murderer and
> publisher began in the early evening hours of
> June 6. Burton W. Warflin, a self-described "as-
> trophysicist"—in reality, an unemployed drifter
> from Cleveland, Ohio—held six hostages at gun-
> point in a Riverview video store. He shot to
> death one patron and threatened more execu-
> tions. Warflin surrendered when authorities al-
> lowed a local television station to comply with
> his demand for a live taped interview. Segments
> of his rambling monologue were aired on net-
> work and cable news shows across the country.
>
> The following Sunday, the Riverview
> *Times* ran a front-page editorial by Matthew

Drum that announced a moratorium policy on news surrounding Warflin's publicized statements, on all biographical details of his life other than his name and the crime for which he was charged, and on future stories of similar crimes, wherever committed, that are deemed by the paper's expert advisory board to be "publicity-inspired."

The editorial read: "We have researched carefully the link between publicity and crime and we're stepping off that streetcar named expire."

Tragically, the editorial itself appears to have inspired another murder in Riverview; perhaps two. Early on June 9, the corpse of Claire Washington, a 44-year-old manager of an apartment complex in a section of Riverview called "the Flats," was discovered in the living room of her apartment. Her head had been caved-in with a garden spade. The coroner calculated she had been dead over 24 hours and may have been killed the same day the *Times'* editorial was published.

Then last Thursday night, June 19, a 23-year-old auto mechanic, Julie Oleson, was strangled while working alone in her father's service garage. Her body was propped on the hood of a car and a note tucked into the top pocket of her coveralls.

The contents were leaked over this past weekend to a Riverview television station. Police are withholding particulars of the note but they confirmed it was signed by "the Poet of Pain," and that it threatened another murder unless Matthew Drum apologizes: presumably, for the paper's editorial.

This industrially-depressed but picturesque community on the bluffs of the Mississippi, which had at first rallied behind the newspaper, is now split by panic: blaming the police, blaming the press, blaming society itself.

In a press conference Tuesday morning at City Hall, Riverview's Mayor and Police Chief both called upon Mr. Drum to consider his "civic duty" and buy investigators more time by responding to the killer's demand.

"So what's supposed to come first here?" said Chief of Police Sterling Opel, 30-year veteran of the Riverview Police Department. "This newspaper's precious rights, or the rights of our citizens to keep on living? This guy Drum is an outsider. Basically, he don't care."

"I don't diminish the sanctity of an individual human life," responded Mr. Drum in an interview with this paper. "But the Chief has an obligation as well to public safety on a grander scale. What we're doing here is acknowledging the media's role in celebrating killers. By considering everything 'news,' we guarantee immortality to the sickest souls in our society and that encourages more killing. That's what we all do, when we read the books, patronize the movies, tune in to the 'true crime' TV shows."

Experts are calling Riverview's Poet of Pain a "special mission" serial killer. According to the FBI ...

Sabina considered not answering the phone but it could be her mother, a news junkie like herself. She reached for it and checked her watch: 6:52.

"Hi, Mom."

"Oh, you little smart aleck," Peg said with a laugh. "Sabina, did you see—"

"I'm reading it."

"Honey, we don't need to meet for brunch today if this means you've got to work."

"No way, Mom, we're still on. Please. My fondest wish would be to have a normal day for a change." *And to keep you out of public places with Matthew Drum.*

She thought of a third wish: to turn back the clock, skip Ed Fountain and his Basset-hound eyes and sad sad story. It wasn't so much guilt over her role in the moratorium and the two dead women who were its byproduct—maybe it should have been—it was Sabina's increasing uneasiness about her mother. The stakes were escalating in this stand-off between Matthew Drum and the Poet. Peg Lindsay, by association, stood with her boyfriend in the crosshairs.

Peg and Sabina met at Entillo's, a new restaurant north of the Bluffs. They licked clean their forks, raised china teacups to their lips, and spoke of blood and urine, stabbings and imprisonment.

Sabina had lugged her daybook to the table and Peg was curious about it so Sabina showed her the system. Peg saw "Mom" on the weekly goal page and pointed to it, acting hurt. "I am one of your goals? You need to log me in?"

Sabina was acutely aware of how her father had driven Peg crazy with his detail obsessing—especially after his early retirement when he didn't have enough to do—and Jacob used to tell Sabina she'd turn out the same way.

"It's a hangover habit," Sabina explained. "From when our company almost plunged into receivership. There just weren't enough hours in the day."

"My goodness, I'm even color-coded." Peg's amusement was of the superior kind, like a zoo visitor. "What does it mean, when you use red?"

"Top priority," Sabina said. "Otherwise the important things don't get done." She looked down at her plate and saw, with growing irritation, that she had wiped it dishwasher clean. She glared at her mother. "If that sounds obsessive, that's too bad."

"Sabina. Sweetheart." Peg's hands crossed prayer-like over her chest. "I am *honored* to be your top priority. Why are you on your high horse over this?"

A dreary Winter morning, three years back. "It's a Jacob memory. He made fun of my to-do lists. He said I obsessed over them. So I stabbed him."

"You *what?*"

"He took my list away from me when I was working on it and wouldn't give it back. He dared me to get through the day without it." Sabina spread the fingers of one hand and pointed to the fleshy area between the thumb and index finger. "This spot here," she said. "I drove a fork into it. Maple syrup and blood on the tablecloth."

Jacob had yelled more than bled. She had been exhilarated; for one moment, at least, she was understood. That may have been her last volatile act within their marriage. She crossed the bridge from vulnerable to unassailable. It was safer there, and it preserved enough energy for working.

"Very uncivilized, I know; I should have talked it out." Sabina played springboard with her spoon on the starched tablecloth.

"What would you have said?"

The waiter refilled their coffee. Sabina held her hand over it until her palm was slippery from the steam. "I guess I wanted to tell him, screw you and your free spirit. And do you think I'd need to make these stupid lists if I had a true partner instead of an arrested hippie?"

Peg reached over and covered Sabina's hand with hers. "My poor baby. You sure had a load on you, didn't you?"

"Except that he was right, Mom. As soon as we got to work, I shut myself up in the office and finished the list. Obsessive-compulsive."

"Utter nonsense," she said sternly. "That's a silly label. When your father and I invested in your company, young lady, we didn't do it to lose money. You know perfectly well what you've accomplished. You made us a good deal of money, don't forget. Do you know what peace of mind that gives me?"

Sabina exhaled on a smile. "Thank you." The waitress laid the check between them and she snatched it.

"Mom? Did you ever stab Dad? Or some equivalent thereof?"

"Some equivalent thereof?" she chided. "Is that how consultants talk?"

"Come on, Mom, you're hiding."

She twisted the wedding ring that now would fit only her pinky finger. Once," she admitted, her cheeks pink, "I emptied the urine bottle in his lap."

"Whoa! How come?"

"Oh, something petty. Our fights are never about what they're really about. Like you and Jacob, you weren't really arguing about the list, were you?"

"So what was yours about? Really."

"About freedom," she said, suddenly glacial. "I promised him, after the first stroke, that he would never go into a nursing home and he was making me live up to it."

By which Sabina understood her to mean her own freedom, not Dad's. Sabina knew the next move was hers, a friend-to-friend prompting. But her Dad was her hero. A bad guy, electing to imprison his wife?

She must have winced visibly, because Peg pointed an admonishing finger at her. "Sweetheart, I don't need you for this. There were so many *good* years. His disease was just a part of marriage, of ... our moral contract." The way she examined Sabina, that judgmental probe, seemed to say that her daughter couldn't possibly understand. And perhaps she was right, Sabina thought, because she had busted up with Jacob for considerably less cause.

"So go ahead and write me down in red, Sabina! I want to spend as much time with you and your brothers and my grandchildren as I possibly can." Peg raised her eyes to the soft green canopy of leaves and sighed big. "I want to *live*."

A half hour later, the odd couples cruised east on Highway 14 to Madison for the taping of *The NewsHour with Jim Lehrer*. Kendall Drum was at the wheel of his father's luxury sedan, Peg Lindsay alongside him. Sabina rode in the back with Matthew. Matthew hadn't been delighted by Peg asking herself along, but she took Kendall's arm and said, "Wouldn't you like to have someone to talk to, dear? Besides," she added, tossing a significant look at Matthew, "I would enjoy a chance to get to know you."

The curving road passed towns with names like Coon Valley, Viroqua, Gotham, Lone Rock. Sabina's job was not to extol the beauty of the Wisconsin countryside, it was to cram into Drum's head a slew of statistics and assorted perspectives on weapons, anti-crime legislation, psychotics and sociopaths. But in lulls while he read her research notes, she stared out tinted windows and rested her mind.

Peg or Kendall had chosen a country music station. Their conversation wound through it, rising and falling like the road beneath them. The pattern of their voices reminded Sabina of musical scores she used to study for fun. The rhythm patterns were peculiar to so many conversations between men and women. Peg's voice started it off: the lilting prelude of a question. There was a whole note rest—Kendall was shy; it would probably be a half or quarter note for other men. A staccato response, flat. Peg accelerated the tempo with another crescendo query and his bass became, *poco a poco*, more sustained and animated. Their voices slowly harmonized in tempo and dynamics ...

Conversation as symphony: Sabina suspected she was experiencing an original thought. She turned to Matthew, inspired to share it, and swallowed her words. His pen was arrested in the middle of a notation and he was bent over it, tight-lipped and scowling.

"Kenny!"

Effective as a pail of cold water, that single word doused the chatter from the front seat.

"Do you mind?" Matthew said harshly. "I've got a lot of material here."

Peg turned around. "Why Matthew! Shame on you! We were only— And we've been talking and playing music the whole trip, what in the world would make you ... if you're going to *yell* at somebody, yell at *me* for pity's sake, I'm the one who's making Kendall talk at *all*. You should be ... well, really."

She sputtered that way when she was quite angry. She subsided, but continued glaring at Matthew. He looked out the window and said, "Sorry, Peg."

She swiveled back to face the road. If it were one of her children she was angry with, Sabina thought, she wouldn't let it go at that. And sure enough, she finished him off quietly. "It's Kendall you should apologize to."

He didn't, of course. Sabina took a few deep breaths to get her stomach unclenched. Peg turned the radio up a notch. Before they reached the outskirts of Madison, Sabina was working with Matthew on summarizing his responses and Peg and Kendall were talking again. But the music of their conversation had vanished.

"Mr. Drum? Stand by, please, ten seconds to Washington." Matthew and Sabina, a phalanx of klieg lights, and a camera operator—a young woman with a blond buzz cut who was wearing, intelligently, as little as she could—were packed into a hot, bright, windowless office the size of a closet. The camera person was being directed from a remote control-room by the Uplink Director. She flashed her fingers in a countdown for Matthew's sake and then he was on. He nodded at the camera; that was all. Sabina guessed that Jim Lehrer or someone was introducing the segment, because she couldn't hear anyone but Matthew.

This was not the glamorous communications hub her mother had anticipated. When Peg was told she couldn't sit in on the taping, her only protest was a woebegone "Oh." She trailed off after the Uplink Director and was back in less than five minutes, gesturing excitedly to Kendall to follow her.

That left Sabina perched uselessly on a stool, watching. She was gaining the impression that the show was going well for Matthew. Four other guests were scheduled for this round-table debate and he seemed to be getting the lion's share of air time. He projected like a pro. Sabina doubted whether Ed Fountain—whose cause this really was, after all—could jerk a listener up by the ears like Matthew Drum.

After ten minutes of sweaty observation, Sabina was considering slipping out to find the control room when Matthew startled her by evoking Casey Fountain's name in a way that would go down poorly with her father, Ed.

It started with another intriguing one-sided snippet. Matthew said, "Oh, come on. You celebrate sleaze because it pays. The president of our own professional society is on record saying that the Achilles' heel of the so-called 'popular' press is that it strives for popularity instead of relevance."

At this point, someone walked on him for awhile. Drum's chin went up and when he saw an opportunity, he waded back in, gloves off.

"You haven't done your research. This moratorium is hardly 'another kind of sensationalism.' You should understand what helped to inspire it. Our editor-in-chief, Ed Fountain, saw his daughter gunned down in Milwaukee a year ago. He lived it, so take up your theory, your abstractions, with him."

Sabina noticed Matthew's memory was selectively faulty: he may have forgotten Ed Fountain's expressed desire to keep Casey's name out of the publicity over the moratorium, yet he didn't let slip who had really written the original *Times* editorial. He was willing enough to take the credit for that.

The interview wound down. At its close, the scantily-clad camera operator raised her fist in a salute to Matthew Drum. "You're good, man," she said, flashing a star-struck smile. "Hang tough!"

Since the news program was taped in the afternoon for airing that night, the odd couples piled back into the car and drove straight back to Riverview so they could catch it in time.

When Sabina turned the key in her front door and pushed, it didn't budge. She reversed the action and the door opened. Just as it dawned on her that it must have been unlocked to begin with, which she never forgot to do, footsteps sounded in the hall. They were coming toward the door and they were easily a hundred pounds heavier than Tootie's.

The most lethal weapon at hand was the door itself. Sabina

kicked it in as hard as she could, spun around to run the other way and heard a huge *"Ow!"* from the intruder. It was wounded surprise, not crazed revenge. Also, she knew the voice.

"Jacob?"

"Ow. *Christ*, Sabina!" He elbowed the door all the way open. He was bent double, gripping his head.

"Jake! Oh, gee, I'm sorry, are you hurt?"

He straightened up, rubbing his temple hard, and Sabina gasped. It felt like the door had slammed into her, instead.

Jacob rushed onto the porch and wrapped his arms around her. "Hey, hey," he was saying. Jacob smell. Hard chest against her breasts. "I'll live, Sabina, come on, what's all this?"

She pushed off and looked again at his face. She couldn't believe she was crying over this, but a runaway truck was loose inside, spilling its load. "Your beard!" The face she fell in love with and married and divorced was no more. The alteration was astounding.

"God, Sabina." He dropped his arms. "I guess I should have known it wasn't concern for *me* that set you off like that."

But it was. It was. True, she wasn't crying because she had hurt him physically; she was stupidly hysterical at her ex-life partner's metamorphosis from the rough-edged, open-range man she loved to this pale-faced corporate type whose shoulders looked too narrow in that dress shirt; whose chin—oh, dear—whose chin was a little on the weak side, now that she saw it for the first time.

After Sabina subsided, they continued to stand half in and half out of the house as Jacob explained he had business in Chicago and thought he'd drive down from Minneapolis so he could settle a dispute at their old bank in the morning.

"I thought you gave me your key," Sabina said.

"I did. I'm the one who picked the hiding place for the spare, remember?"

"Still, Jacob, you don't live here anymore."

"Would you prefer that Toot and I hang around outside all night?"

"Toot's here again?"

"In the kitchen. But Sabina—"

She eased past Jacob.

"He's not exactly in top shape," he called out, and bumped into her when she froze in the kitchen doorway at the sight of Tootie. He was straddling a kitchen chair backwards, his head slumped awkwardly against the curved back, arms hanging straight down and one leg bent unnaturally behind a chair leg.

"Tootie!" As she approached, bending down to see his face, the smell hit her. "He's drunk!" she said in horror.

"Yeah. Upchucked on the porch swing and barely made it to the bathroom. I was just trying to get something in his stomach when I heard you at the door."

"So he can throw it up again?" Sabina looked down at the inert scarecrow, ribs and bony knees, eyes half-closed. "Poor little guy." She ran the backs of her fingers down his cheek.

"Do you think we should take him home?" Jacob looked equally concerned. Without his beard, there was a sweet vulnerability to his profile.

She pictured them carrying Tootie over there and meeting at the door the bigger version of what was propped up in their kitchen. *My* kitchen, she thought. She shook her head. "Mister Mimic here has got to find a better role model than his nasty papa."

They were probably both thinking that Toot had that before they split up, but neither said it. They carried the eighty-five-pound drunk to the bedroom, threw his clothes in the washer and cleaned up the vomit on the porch. Jacob thought Sabina could get into trouble with Karl the Jerk if she didn't notify them, so she made the call and Toot's mother answered. Sabina told her Jake was visiting and they'd take Toot to a movie and have him for an overnight if it was okay with her. Fine, she said, vibrant as a squeezed-dry lemon.

By the time they'd finished with all that, Matthew Drum's TV performance was history. Jacob and Sabina settled on the top step of the porch and she filled him in on the saga of the Poet of Pain. He was intrigued.

"He writes a poem then?"

"No. Nothing like that, according to Chief Opel. He wanted to ask us about the P.S. to Albert. You can't tell anyone about that, by the way. Promise?" Jacob nodded. "My theory is, given the copycat nature of these things, and the victim being strangled, I think he may have meant Albert DeSalvo. The Boston Strangler. There was plenty in our editorial that insulted killers like that, and I would guess this Poet picked Julie Oleson as his revenge."

"His only revenge?" Jacob asked quietly.

"No note on Claire Washington. The cops think maybe her ex-husband killed her." She rolled her shoulder into Jacob's. "Hey Jacob, give you any ideas?"

Jacob didn't laugh. They sat together in suspended peace, listening to screech owls trilling away in the grove of cedars behind the house.

Then Jacob said, "So," and slapped his knees with a forced casualness. Sabina had been expecting this. "It's silly to get a hotel room; I've got business at the bank early. Could I buy you dinner and stay the night? You could crawl in with Tootie," Jacob went on. "It's a big bed. I could take the couch."

"No!"

Oh, God. That was much more vehement than she meant to sound, but she couldn't help it. Jacob recoiled from her side and stood.

"My bag's inside," he said stiffly.

Sabina stayed put, chin in her hands, thinking that no-body was winning here, as usual. She could not bring herself to explain to him the independent island she'd made of that old couch; how it was a survival strategy linked to his new girlfriend, whoever she was. He was apparently prepared to gloss right over all that, pretend she hadn't happened or wasn't still happening.

She wanted to tell Jacob about her mother's view of marriage as a moral contract. It was in the back of her mind all evening to bring that up with him and see where it led. Now it was too late. They bid each other a cold goodnight. Sabina decided, rashly, that if he turned just once to look back at her she'd say something to make him stay, something using her old velvet voice to make it sound like I Love You.

She stood in the shadows of their house—*her* house—rubbing her arms and watching as Jacob entered his car silently and silently drove away without a backward glance.

JR was ready and waiting to watch God the Father spill his propaganda in prime time. A neighbor had asked JR over for dinner so he cleaned up first and stuck a bottle of wine in the refrigerator to take with him. He paced from the window to the TV and back again. He opened the window wide and leaned out. A truck rolled by, a black dog tied to a tire in its open bed. A kid sitting in the passenger seat caught his eye and waved; JR waved back.

It was finally six. JR turned on the television, see-sawed his shoulders to relax them and sat on the edge of the armchair.

The camera pulled back, Bag Eyes turned to his right and there *he* was, looming huge on a screen that everyone else had to look *up* to. Fucking God the Father himself: Matthew Drum.

Bag Eyes asked a question. Other faces and voices chimed in. A forensic psychologist, using phrases like the "rigidity of impulse control training" that washed over JR like white noise. The producer of a TV crime show, losing every round with God the Father. A criminologist who was on Drumbo's advisory board and should have been attached by his lips to the boss's ass. The Chief of the FBI Behavioral Science Unit, his glasses hanging around his neck on a sissy chain, talking about how glorification of killers encourages more killing.

"Uh-uh, buddy," JR said calmly, persuasively, like he was in the TV with them. "One thing to glorify. Something else to insult us. Mess with the truth."

They wrapped it up before 6:30 and JR hurried into the kitchen for the wine, but when he got there, he stared into the open refrigerator trying to remember what he had come for. His thoughts were too full of Matthew Drum. How smug the man had looked, how he shined and glittered in his spotlight like a Fourth of July firecracker.

Oh, yes, yes, yes! JR closed the refrigerator, feeling himself merge with his brothers, feeling the feathery peace in his head. He reached into a drawer for a pen, crossed to the calendar that hung over the kitchen sink, lifted a page, and drew a perfect circle around July 4.

CHAPTER TWELVE

Sabina was in a blue funk. She sat on the window seat in her bathrobe, contemplating the long dateless weekend, and next week the Fourth of July, her favorite holiday, without Jacob. Across the street, Tootie was just emerging from his house. He fished his bike from behind the shrubs and rode off, a trifle wobbly.

Small wonder. He woke up yesterday morning puking again, so sick Sabina thought he'd deposit the lining of his stomach in her toilet. She pressed a cold washcloth to his forehead, useless but comforting. And then she stormed across the street.

After ramming the Jergensen's screen door with her fist and foot, she realized she'd only make trouble for Toot by letting on that he had gotten into the Jerk's booze. So when Daddy Karl opened the door, Sabina lit into him instead about his scuzzy junk car. She lied, telling him she represented a nonexistent neighborhood association and that he would have to tow the eyesore away.

Karl looked down from his advantage of six feet five inches, his mouth slightly ajar. "Or what?" he asked. He licked his pinky finger and stuck it in his ear, digging.

"You're violating a building code ordinance and I can get

the building inspector on you." *You useless drunken childhood-robbing wiener.*

"You do that little old thing, girlie girl." The finger popped out with a wet squeak.

"You're an asshole." It was more an observation than a retort. She really did see him as a black hole of sorts.

He tipped toward her, flexing his hands at his sides.

"Oh, I wish you would," Sabina said. "Then I'd have something real on you." She was amazed to find herself pushing her face into his, like ... what was that favorite word of her father's? A pugilist. But round one was not to be: She wasn't his wife and Karl wasn't, at that moment, drunk.

Sabina was still glaring at Karl's car from the safety of her window seat when the phone rang.

"Hey Sappy Vagina, guess who!"

"Oh, gee, let me think." If she objected to the nickname, Sonny would only use it more. "Pussy Galore?"

"Keeyute. Hey listen, guess who's coming to town for the Fourth."

"You are? Oh, Sonny, thank God. Could we go to the fireworks?"

Pretty subtle. Sonny laughed at her, but in that way she had of complete, sympathetic acceptance. Sonny Ashendorf and Sabina's mother were the only people she knew who had mastered the high art of non-judgmental love. This loving nature of hers was why Sonny had run through so many men. Some of their mutual Riverview "friends" used to call her a slut; Sabina thought of her as a model of evolved humanity.

Sabina was suddenly energized and could think of all manner of things worth doing. When she hung up the phone, her eyes landed again on Karl Jergensen's monument to sloth. A young sugar maple had taken root in a plot of dirt between the hood and windshield and was bravely poking its leaves toward the sun.

City Hall office hours extended to three PM on Saturdays. Sabina decided to file that complaint and get in some exercise at the same time.

As she pedaled up the slab of concrete and crotchety play equipment that passed for a park in her neighborhood, she saw Tootie playing buckets by himself. His dribbling was dispirited and he wasn't setting up right: he would slump to a stop and hurl the ball at the basket.

"Hey!" she called to him. "You want a game of Pig?"

He took a few seconds to turn, resting the ball against one hip. "Nah," he said. The weight of the world was in the kid's voice. His body hung there like it was tethered to the sky by a single frayed string. He turned back to look at the basket, but didn't move.

"Then how about some ice cream?"

That restored some zip. He hopped on his bike and until they reached the busier streets, they rode side by side. Toot would flatten himself over the bike in racing posture and tear ahead a few yards, then coast until she caught up.

He asked her along the way if she thought school "was a big deal."

"You mean getting good grades?"

He shrugged. She waited him out.

"Sorta. And just, gettin' along."

"With the other kids, you mean." A single nod. Sabina slowed down for some railroad tracks; Toot sped up and flew over the rails, his rump jolting high off the seat.

She drew up alongside him. "The people part, making friends? I think that's important. You don't need many real ones, but it does matter."

He was riding upright and easy, hands tucked under his armpits. The crease between his eyebrows was too deeply etched for such a young face; it looked like the imprint of a hot fork. There was much about this boy that was worth loving, and he was smart and fun, too, so Sabina couldn't figure why she never saw him hanging with other kids. She took the leap and asked him.

"If I knew," he snarled, "why'm I askin' you?"

She tried to see Toot with fresh eyes. His public face was often like this, a wall of frowning defense. And those clothes. He had maybe two changes of clothes and they were usually filthy.

"I've got an idea what it might be and you can't get mad at me because I'm trying to help you. Okay?"

"Okay."

They braked for a stop sign and took a left onto a busier street, turning in unison up the first driveway where they could ride together on the sidewalk. "Kids your age are the hardest friends you'll ever have to make because they can be mean and believe it or not," she thought of his father, the meanest man going; oh, well, "believe it or not, many people get nicer as they get older. I think we just get wise to how weak and dumb we can all be, so it gets easier to sympathize with other people."

They stopped at a curb and Sabina grabbed a fistful of his three-day-old T-shirt. "About your clothes," she said. He looked down innocently, like, what's your point? "You don't have to buy anything new, Toot, but you should go around cleaner."

This didn't insult him. He laughed. "That's it? That's all I gotta do?"

Oh, boy. What had she gotten into here? "It may not be that simple. Think of it as a kind of scientific experiment. We'll control for the clothes." He didn't follow all that but he liked the experiment part; it seemed to remove the problem from being his fault.

She pointed toward a side street and they bumped down

the curb. "I know you've got a washer-dryer in your house, I've seen it." His mother must do the washing when she was good and ready and they either couldn't afford more clothes for Toot or didn't notice. "It's the same model as mine. Why don't I just show you how to run it?"

"When?" Oh my, that little upturned face, trying so hard for casual. He probably pictured eight guys on his doorstep in the morning, looking for a shortstop.

"Tonight if you want," she said. "I'll have to cancel all my dates."

"Right, girl!" Toot laughed. "Okay. Then whenever they're dirty I can just come over."

"Well, see, I thought this way, you could just use your own—"

No. It was clear there was some reason, probably associated with the Jerk, why Tootie couldn't do that, so Sabina interrupted herself and said sure, it'd be fun to have him hanging out and she usually didn't have a full load anyway and blah-blah-blah until the fork over his eyes smoothed over.

"That's a boss bike," he commented. "A racer, huh? How much?"

"Twelve hundred retail, but I got a deal, of course." She warmed to the topic: this was lovely home ground. She hadn't talked bikes with anyone for a long time and she let loose with a spiel of technical chatter about frame geometry and butted chrome-moly steel ... until she noticed Toot rolling his eyes.

"We're goin' the same way, right?" he said, incredulous. "Gettin' there at the same time? And my Mom got this second-hand for thirty bucks. Shit, girl!"

Olaf Jergensen, the world's youngest retro-grouch. He was back to examining the bike, asking more questions that led up to a doozy. "You and Jake, you made those, right?"

"Not quite. We were a gizmo shop. You know, the helmets and saddle covers and electronic monitoring stuff, like that. We made some, bought some."

"Oh."

"I know that's not real sexy," she told him. This was not the time for a lecture about competition and profitable niche marketing. "We didn't make the real thing, is what you're thinking?" He shrugged. "That's why I might like this consulting business. You do a good plan for someone and it's like a quality, basic bike frame: it helps the rider last the distance. It's important."

"Making babies is important." He darted a sly look at her. "Why don't you make one of those?"

Sabina nearly barked with surprise. "Geez, Toot, you get right to the personal stuff, don't you?" He pedaled on, awaiting his answer. "A person needs someone else for that. Please tell me you know what I'm talking about."

"You could ask Jake."

"Come on, Toot, you know what divorce is."

"Yeah, but it's just for the baby part."

"Jake ... he wouldn't want to." She couldn't believe she was bouncing this idea back for another round.

"You could pay him!"

Her front tire scraped the curb. "You need two parents to raise a child right. That's what I believe."

He mulled that over. "I count two in my house," he said simply. Sabina knew just what he meant and couldn't think of a single consoling word, except to tell him that childhood didn't last forever.

After they consumed a day's worth of calories at a Dairy Queen she told Toot that she had private business in the courthouse and they parted ways. Sabina tracked down the building inspector, a woman about her age with streaky, cornstalk hair and a sunburn that radiated heat in the air-conditioned office.

Without expression, without commiserating comment, she took down the complaint about Karl Jergensen's junk car.

Sabina left with little hope of retribution for the Jerk and biked home circuitously, meandering around, pretending to be a practiced master at leisure time. She observed Riverview in its yard-tending mode: trimming, planting, pruning. So there was something more to do to a front yard than keep it short and vaguely green. How was it she had no appreciation of shoots and roots? She recalled their disdain as she and Jacob—on bikes or in cars or, for one harrowing year, on a motorcycle—whizzed through neighborhoods like these in Ann Arbor, and then Chicago. They would wonder how people could be sprinkling away precious human hours on their tiny plots of real estate, while a whole world went unexplored. As she turned up her own driveway, Sabina concluded she still felt that way, even though she had sprinkled away fifteen years herself on bicycle accessories.

Two phone messages blinked at her. Sonny again, giving her flight time. And a reporter from *Newsweek* wanted to interview Sabina for a story about the moratorium. He said there was a rush on the article for next week's issue, and could she call him right away?

Butterflies took wing in her stomach. *Newsweek!* She dove for her research and took an hour to cram facts into her head so she wouldn't come off like some woman who had just hung out her management consultant shingle.

He was a personable guy named Berben working on his home computer with a baby cranking away in the back-ground. Sabina pressed the MEMO button on her answering machine to record the interview. If she was misquoted, he was going to hear about it.

There was no way of determining what he'd use and what he'd trash but it sounded like a thorough job anyway: they had already interviewed Matthew Drum, two of the *Times'* Advisory board members, Chief Opel, Detective Samuel and even Julie Oleson's father, Howard, who had been incommunicado since his daughter's murder. Sabina learned from Berben that Howard Oleson had his business on the auction block, the service garage where his daughter had been killed.

After they finished, she rewound the tape and played it back, critiquing herself. Now that she was alone, the spigots of eloquence were cranked wide open and she could think of ten different ways to phrase things, all superior.

For a mortal woman, though, it seemed to be going all right. She trotted to the kitchen and poured herself a glass of wine just as Tootie walked in, carrying an armful of duds topped by a grimy pair of high-top tennis shoes.

Toot asked, "Hey, ain't that your voice? Where's it coming from?"

Who else did she have to show off to? Sabina told him she was going to be in *Newsweek* the next issue and snagged a copy from one of the stacks on the floor to show him.

Toot was impressed. "Oh yeah. We have to read that in school. Hey, Sabina Shaw, famous ... whaddya call yourself?"

"Goddess," she said. She fetched him a soda and they clicked glasses.

It wasn't until Toot's wardrobe was fresh and folded and she had waved him back across the street that Sabina faced up to it. This fame thing. She was getting off on it herself. Criminy, what was the distance between liking it and needing it? And how flawed did you really have to be, to need it so badly that you'd kill for the attention? If she was experiencing a subdued brand of celebrity fever, and she considered herself emotionally stable ... just how flawed did you have to be?

CHAPTER THIRTEEN

Every Fourth of July when Sabina was growing up, the carnival set up at the Vernon County fairgrounds and she and her brothers and every other kid known to them would crunch through fried elephant ears the size of Frisbees and then fling themselves, tongues still seeking powdered sugar from the corners of their mouths, onto rusting carnival rides that knocked them around like bar dice.

No more. As the horizon tipped sickeningly left to right and top to bottom, Sabina Shaw would have paid good money to rent a kid's digestive tract.

Sonny Ashendorf's stomach was tougher than her face, and that was saying something. She'd turned thirty-nine a week earlier and looked ten years older with her sun-torched skin, yet she lounged on Sabina's right, so unaffected that her shrieks were perfunctory.

"This ain't no Magnum XL," Sonny declared in a ho-hum voice. "So, Sabina," she added, conversationally. "A management consultant is someone who manages to consult with anyone who's got the money?"

Sabina could not turn her head.

On Sabina's left side was a real child, the Adorable Toot, who at ten years old surprised Sabina by having a crystal stomach, too. As they spun and spun without end, he was shouting something and it wasn't nice.

"Fuckin' A! Fuckin' A! Fuckin' A!" he yelled, pausing to swallow and starting up again, his eyes rolling in his head.

"Tootie." That was the firmest reprimand Sabina could manage. It was clear he wasn't after shocking them; he was in her sickly condition exactly. She found his choice of words oddly comforting. It's what she wanted to yell out herself.

By the time they jolted to a stop, Sabina and Tootie were gulping desperately. A fellow as brittle as the toothpick stuck to his lip raised the bar and freed them. Sonny pushed off, a jaunty panther, while Sabina gathered Toot in with one arm, as much to lean as to guide, and he let her.

"Nice little ride," Sonny smirked, and made a bow-legged beeline for the beer tent.

She hadn't been riding horses long enough to earn that walk; it was contrived, but funny. Sonny Ashendorf had moved to Wyoming, she once told Sabina, so she could wear blue jeans for the rest of her life. She did look great in them. When they were in junior high, one grade apart, Sonny was a brunette like Sabina until the summer Sonny began the search for a silvery blond dye that would match the mane on Roy Roger's horse. She found it but left her eyebrows alone: dark, thick strokes over brown eyes. The men still found something there worth following around. Before climbing on the Torture Twirl, they had been playing their ancient game, arguing about which one of them was attracting more lewd looks.

Still wearing a patronizing smile, Sonny emerged from the beer tent with foam on her upper lip and a mustard-smeared pretzel in hand. She had passed the acid test with Toot. The first two hours of their carnival wanderings, he'd stuck to the side of Sabina farthest from Sonny, answering her questions after snotty little silences. All that changed after the Torture Twirl.

"You got real horses, huh?" Toot asked, shyly.

Sonny pointed to a tear in her jeans. "Spring fence mending. My favorite for that, her name's Flowers. Appaloosa."

Toot bent to examine the rip over Sonny's calf. Like it was some wondrous artifact, Sabina groused to herself. Here she was, having mastered balance sheets, inventory strategies, benefit plans ... all that was nothing next to straddling twelve hundred pounds of horseflesh.

"Shouldn't we stake out a spot?" Sonny asked, looking up at the darkening sky.

"I hafta piss first," Tootie said. He spotted a Port-a-Potty and swaggered off, perfectly mimicking Sonny's swish-sailor walk. The swish part was so hilarious that Sonny and Sabina bent over, laughing.

Sabina felt extravagantly, unexpectedly alive, having such a great time on her favorite holiday with two of the three people she could count as friends. She should have asked her mother along but couldn't picture Peg Lindsay mucking around the fairgrounds accepting food from people with more tattoos than teeth.

They found a space on the sloping, grassy field where the fireworks were held, and watched the end of the annual Uncle Sam contest. Johnny Rangel was the sole judge—because his station, Channel 7, was the sole sponsor—of a costume contest for kids under twelve. They could wear anything, as long as it was red, white and blue. The winner's gender was a mystery: it looked like a blue pickle with fringe. It squealed when Johnny Rangel lifted it to his shoulders for a victory stroll.

Excellent fireworks weather: no clouds, no moon, no breeze. The sky was their exclusive amphitheater, a great dark wing folded over the expectant audience. Toot's eyes sparkled and his mouth gradually dropped open. Sabina tried not to see his father in his face, but sometimes it was hard. She patted his knee, laid back with her hands behind her head, and gave herself over to the spectacle.

After about forty minutes, they were pitching it all up there. Sabina's father had taught her the names. One was aptly called a whizz-bang. She registered the sound of it before it was run down by a pinwheel, followed by a roman candle and another that looked like a snake, and then the kind, she couldn't remember the name, that spewed out fizzly tentacles. As they faded to black, she tensed, waiting for the loud cracks.

Toot was plugging his ears, his face rapt. They shook him when it was over to get his attention. He looked around, dazed, at the people standing and folding blankets.

To get to the parking lot, hundreds of people squeezed into a narrow alley of cyclone fence set up for crowd control. The air, the bodies, were stifling. Someone stepped on Sabina's bare heel above her sandal. Sonny's arm against hers was moist; they pulled away from each other.

One thing about the Fourth: it didn't have much staying power. The darkness surrounding them felt absolute, as if the great protective wing of dark sky were folding in with crushing intent.

Behind them, some kids set off a burst of illegal firecrackers and exploded themselves in the edgy laughter of alcohol gone down too fast. A little girl alongside Sabina whimpered that she was tired and had to go potty. Her mother whacked her one, which helped a bunch. Her sniffling flared into a grinding wail. Sabina shuffled forward in lock-step, a little sorry for the kid at the same time she twitched in dark sympathy with the mother.

Whoa. She would share that with Toot the next time he advised her to make babies.

Toot stepped in front of her. She ran a finger up his spine and was squeezing the back of his neck when they heard another muffled pop-pop and he wrenched free to look back at the sky. Sabina looked, too, and was nearly knocked off her feet by Sonny lurching sideways into her. Sabina lost her balance and stomped on the foot of the crying kid to her right. The kid let out a yelp of real pain, and as Sabina bent down to apologize, Sonny yelled, "Hey!" in an annoyed way, followed by a wavering climbing scream that cracked Sabina upright. She could only stand there, staring, as Sonny cupped her hands over her mouth and screamed like she'd never stop.

The night was filled with yelling. "Ohmigod! Ohmigod!" from a dozen throats, and "He's been shot! Someone shot him!" Panic spun the crowd away from its center.

A man had fallen against Sonny and was spilled at their feet, one leg bent under him.

Someone said, "It's Johnny Rangel! Oh my God! It's Johnny Rangel!"

Sabina didn't recognize him. She was used to the blow-dried, Pepsodent presence on the Action News. His face was discolored, distorted. He held his neck with both hands and there was blood on his hands and under them. A stars-and-stripes suspender had slipped off one shoulder. Sabina had selected the same design for a line of kids' handlebar tape at Linshaw Bicycle Works. The tape was padded, and they added a luminescent version later that sold even better. The stock number of the tape flashed across her brain.

Johnny Rangel's breath was coming fast and shallow. Sabina dropped to her knees. Sonny knelt on his other side. He lifted his head and said someone's name, "Franny," maybe, but it was gargled. His head fell back and blood splashed out of his mouth.

"Get him an ambulance!" Sabina screamed. But that had to have been done already, she thought. Hadn't it? Hadn't they been here a long time already?

A woman's voice was calling *Johnny? Johnny!* with escalating panic. The circle of shocked, silent people parted for her. Huge, flesh-frame glasses dwarfed a heart-shaped face. Her breath whined in her throat and she fell on him, crying "Oh no oh no oh no." There was a plain silver band on her finger, and on his. Her straight blond hair draped Johnny Rangel's face, hiding it. She covered his face with her kisses and then clamped her mouth to his in a long, last kiss: a resuscitation, a prayer.

She sat back on her heels, looked directly into Sabina's eyes and said, "I walked away from him." The breath whined through her again. "We were arguing and I left him, I walked away!" Her eyes were wide with despair; her cheeks and lips were smeared with his blood. "The last thing I said to him ... the last thing! I said ... oh dear God!"

Sonny closed in on her, held her tight by the shoulders and spoke harshly, past her own tears: "Don't do that! Your life with him is more than the last second! Stop that."

How much time elapsed before they heard the sirens of emergency vehicles? Tootie had sidled over to Sabina. She would have to think later how to help him through this. She put him in charge of gathering the woman's purse and a pillow and a spilled paper bag. He scurried about, the fork marks deep between his eyebrows, darting glances at the dead body. Sabina knew she should get the boy away from there and she knew it was too late.

An amplified voice asked people to disperse. A light from the parking lot shone on the balding head of a man in a suit and Sabina recognized Mark Samuel, leading other suits and uniforms across the trampled straw-grass of the fairgrounds.

The sight of him re-engaged her mind. The Poet? She leaned across the body and spoke to the victim's wife. "Mrs. Rangel?" She tried again. "Franny?" But Franny was in another world, cupping and stroking the top of her husband's head. Sabina plunged her hand into a pocket of Johnny Rangel's khaki pants and her fingers met up with a piece of paper. She drew it out and turned her back to the parking lot, seeking light.

She could make out Matthew Drum's name. Her hand dropped to her knee. She waited for Detective Samuel and the bobbing flashlight beams of his followers. When they had drawn close enough, when the crush of faces were all turned a sickly lemon-white in the artificial light, Sabina looked down again at the Poet of Pain's calling card.

It was short. It said: *Apologize to the fraternity, Drum ... or My Will Be Done!* And: *P.S. This is for Chappie.*

Sabina held it out to Mark Samuel. "Here. This is for you."

CHAPTER FOURTEEN

The joyous Fourth slouched into the distinctly joyless early hours of the following day and Sabina spent them in the mildewed interrogation room and offices of the Riverview Police Department.

She remembered Mark Samuel as a still-waters kind of guy from the meeting at the paper two weeks earlier, when he and Chief Opel asked about the "To Albert" postscript in the Julie Oleson murder note. He was twitchier this night, spinning his chair from side to side and tapping his pen against a coffee cup, but his listening was thorough enough and they plodded through every detail.

Because of Sabina's work for the *Times* and the killer's obsession with Matthew Drum, the detective went beyond just-the-facts-ma'am. He wanted her impressions about the Poet's notes.

"The paper said you've been researching this material so I thought you might be so kind as to share your thoughts with me," Samuel said, business-like.

The man read Sabina's eggshell mood exquisitely. She had not been even vaguely prepared—despite cinematic and evening news exposure at least on a par with any other red-blooded American—to watch a man die suddenly, by violence. It felt like an internal flogging.

"Mrs. Shaw?"

"Yes. I have one idea. The Chappie of this last note? Mark Chapman. He shot John Lennon, remember, and I guess Johnny Rangel is ... was ... enough of a celebrity to make his point. The 'Albert' of the last note: probably Albert DeSalvo, because he strangled most of his victims and that's how Julie Oleson died."

Samuel was nodding. If he already knew that, why did he ask her?

"The 'fraternity' means his buddy killers; his heroes," Samuel said.

"Fraternity?"

"In the note tonight from Johnny Rangel's pocket? I thought you read it."

"Oh, yes." The lights in his office were unbearable. She put a hand over her eyes.

"Sabina, can I get you something else? Another coffee?"

"A painkiller for the brain. Whatever you've got."

"Coming up." He reached in his top middle drawer and patted it down, feeling for the bottle.

"Then, really, Lieutenant, I've got to get home."

"Hey, anything you want if you keep promoting me like that."

"Huh?"

"My rank. It's Detective Sergeant."

Big deal. Under the shade of her hand, she took in the items on his desktop. A shallow dish in the corner held a single sea-green sponge. She lifted the sponge and crushed it. A few drops hit the dish.

"You could maybe get four letters out of this," she said.

"Tops."

Samuel looked at her as if she was a lab experiment gone wrong. "Time to go home," he announced, and pushed to his feet, shaking out first one leg, then the other.

"Isn't this a stamp-licker?" Sabina asked.

"Just a sponge in a dish of water. I use it for my contacts."

"You mean your ... informants, isn't that what they're called?"

He was prying the lid off a bottle of aspirin and he stopped dead, looking at her. "Hay*seuss*, but you are tired! My contact *lenses*." A grin lit his face. "What do you think, I threaten them with a sponge? Like, tell me what you know or by Christ, I'll wipe your face with this?"

His laughing turned hyena-like, in her opinion. She could appreciate that it was funny. From the reverse end of binoculars, she could see that. He handed her two aspirins and she chased them down with lukewarm coffee.

"Come on." He stood alongside her chair. Sabina got to her feet and he took her elbow, saying, "I'll walk you out." She usually felt like a Barbie doll when a man did that, but in the police department at 1:30 AM, the jail on one side and the morgue on the other .... it was not a problem.

The air outside was a welcome slap in the face and Sabina stepped ahead of Samuel to open her car door. He closed it for her and leaned through the open window. "Seems like you think Drum won't budge."

"That's what I think. Nothing's changed in the fundamental reasoning."

"Yeah," Samuel said. There was no mistaking the sarcasm. "This just pumps it, huh? Nice deep line in the sand and the national press'll eat it up."

Sabina turned on the ignition and thought about that. "You know Ed Fountain, don't you? What happened to his daughter? This is no stunt for him. He's dead certain we'd just be contributing to this ... epidemic. 'See-me' crime, he calls it. I think Matthew is behind it for the same reasons."

She didn't actually believe that anymore, about Drum. It

was a loyal consultant thing to say. There was a distant whoosh and the front door to the police station opened for a cop gripping the upper arm of a young woman in a halter top and cut-off jeans.

"How about you, Detective? If you weren't with the police, would you vote we give in? Run some vague apology and the Poet wins? *All* the bullies win?"

Samuel stepped back a pace and played with some keys in his pocket, chin tipped to the night sky. "If I weren't in law enforcement?" he mused, like she had asked him to pretend he hadn't been born. He shrugged and scraped a thumb along his jaw line. "See, I'm beginning to like this town. I don't care as much about big brave messages as I do about the next breather this creep is going to take out."

Sabina had to concentrate to finish the conversation. "You're assuming that if the paper said 'we're sorry' the Poet would cut it out. Let's say that was true: can't the city do something legally? To force Drum's hand?"

"Take forever to get out of the courts and either we'd lose—probably we'd lose, the DA tells me—or the perp would have all that stalking time and it'd be a moot point. We've had the FBI call Drum, the state Attorney General, too, but the man does not pressure easy."

Another whoosh and three more halter-tops walked into the station, chattering loudly. The drunks rescuing the drunk. "I'll talk to him," Sabina told Samuel. "Even though I think we're doing the right thing, you think you are, too."

"Can't ask for more than that," he called after her. She glanced back at him in her rear view mirror. The wind from the jeep swept his cowlick up into a squirrely question mark atop his forehead.

The town square was a tomb. Sabina circled it and drove the fastest route to Melody Lane. She had dreaded going home alone, so after the police finished collecting Sonny's statement, Sabina handed over her house key and asked Sonny to stay over, this once.

Her front door wasn't firmly closed; she pushed it open and found Sonny Ashendorf and Morpheus, fully engaged on the couch. Someone on the shopping network was trying to sell her a tasseled lampshade patterned after one in Dolly Parson's RV but there was no buyer in this room. The cowgirl had stripped down to her underwear and boots, oddly. Her mouth was agape, nuzzling sounds coming from it, mascara under-eye burns. One of her own tough-babe sayings came to mind as Sabina clicked off the lamp: "She was rode hard and put away wet."

Sabina pitched fully clothed onto her bed, praying for oblivion.

A minute later, there came a great pounding. She worked it into her dream but it was relentless. Her eyes ripped open. It wasn't a minute later; it was the next morning. Sonny stood by the bed. She was fresh from the shower, wearing the robe Jacob left behind that Sabina had been unable to de-throne from its hook alongside the tub.

"Rise and shine, Sap Vee. Your boss is on the phone and that ain't all." There was an all-systems-go glitter to Sonny. She ducked away, leaving the bedroom door wide open. The pounding started up again.

"Sonny, that's the front door! Would you get it?"

"If you sa-a-ay so," she trilled. Curious. It sounded more like "you asked for it." Sabina hoisted to a sitting position and picked up the phone.

"Hello."

"Sabina. First, how are you?"

The concern in Drum's voice was her cold-water reminder

of the night before. "Oh, I'm fine. It was ..." She was going to say, inanely, that it was nothing. "I had an easier time of it than Johnny Rangel. Or his wife." She checked the bedside clock; it was not even 9 AM. "How did you—"

"The Mayor paid me a visit last night and my phone and fax have been going non-stop. We're in the fishbowl now. The reason I'm—"

Sabina heard voices from the front of the house—Sonny's and at least two others—and interrupted him. "Matthew, can I call you back? Something's going on here, I just woke up, and there's some kind of commotion in my front—"

"That'll be TV. You're part of the story now, my friend. Look, Sabina, we're fighting back. I've got a press conference on for next Tuesday morning, that's the earliest two of our advisors can get here. Tell the media hawks on your doorstep they'll get all their questions answered then."

Cameras? She stretched the phone cord to cover the few steps to the mirror over the bureau. How pretty: there was her bedspread in miniature bas-relief on one hot cheek.

"So the calls you've been getting?" Sabina asked. "The police released the note?"

"Check. From last night *and* the Oleson murder. The Mayor, county exec, Jaycees president, a school principal, civic groups ... you name it. All my new friends are checking out." His words described a hot seat; his voice was cool, temperate.

Sabina remembered her miniature debate with Mark Samuel. "About the Poet's message," she said cautiously, "what are you going to do?"

"Excuse me? What gives, Sabina? Are you siding with the others? You wanna kiss butt here?"

There was the Jekyll-to-Hyde, Harvard-to-gangster switch. Kiss butt. What a clichéd response to this tangled and bloody standoff. Perhaps Matthew Drum needed to get down on his knees next to one of the Poet's real messages, as Sabina had.

"Listen, Sabina, don't get coy on me. If you've switched sides, I need to know. I'm stacking this deck and I don't need any wild cards in it."

"Have I switched sides," she repeated, almost to herself. He waited. "No," she said finally, watching in the mirror that serious face under the wild curly hair. "No, I guess not."

"Do you understand the momentum behind this now?" Drum said, still angry with her. "We sent out the original editorial over the DEI wire service at headquarters and nearly half of our publications, all over the world, are behind this. On the record, supporting this moratorium." A muted thumping orchestrated his words. Sabina pictured his square capable hands, his square capable jaw.

"I understand, Matthew." She let her own impatience show. "And I said I was behind it. Nothing has changed."

They hung up in an uneasy peace.

Sabina hustled through the mechanics of preparing to meet the public, but her mind was on Momentum. The Big Mo, on both sides. Drum was committed. The Poet was committed.

She saw a mob through her living room windows. It looked like at least three TV cameras, a man and a woman snapping stills, a bunch of radio stations crowding in with their microphones, at least a dozen people she didn't recognize, a gaggle of neighbors ... and Sonny at the apex of the human fan, standing on the bottom porch step with her back to the house. Sabina had been delayed nearly fifteen minutes and why should they wait? Sonny was an eyewitness as well, and her they could get in a bathrobe with a revealing under-arm rip.

When they finished the interview, Sabina watched in dismay as the reporters and cameras surged across the street to surround Tootie and Karl Jergensen. Karl wore a clean shirt, buttoned high, and his hand rested on Tootie's shoulder: a proud, fatherly pose. A curtain in the front room parted and Cindy Jergensen's narrow face was framed there, briefly.

Sonny was remorseful. "They asked who else was with us, I told 'em about Tootie, they said who's he, I pointed over there, I mean, the kid was already out on the porch with his dad."

"It's okay. It'll make Toot a celebrity. Maybe get him some friends."

"How sad."

"No kidding."

Sabina went inside to phone her mother. Peg hadn't called yet, which meant she didn't know. Friday mornings she usually visited Scott Lindsay's grave at the cemetery.

"Mom, before you get all excited by hearing about it somewhere else I want you to know I'm perfectly all right."

"Oh, dear." There was a scraping sound. "I'm sitting down," Peg said, suddenly breathless. "I detest this kind of call."

"That's the point. Better this, saying it's nothing, than one saying it's something, right?"

"Sabina dear, now tell me. *What* is this nothing that was almost something."

Her mother listened and then said all the commiserating, human things Sabina thought Matthew Drum should have said. Overall, she took it pretty calmly and even asked what station would be running Sonny's interview.

"There's something else, Mom." Sabina was using the phone in her front hallway. Sonny settled onto the window seat, her feet propped up, and began scraping off the remnants of toenail polish with a sharp paring knife. "For a while, until they catch this guy? I think it would be a good idea if you kind of stayed clear of Matthew." Silence. "Because he's not going to give in to this guy."

"Nor should he!"

Sabina pulled back. Her mother's voice had that ring, that stentorian clang of principle.

"He's precisely right about this matter, Sabina. It's black-mail and he ... we all ... must not weaken."

"Mom, you sound like Churchill. This is little Riverview, Wisconsin, it isn't a world war—"

"Isn't it?" Clang clang. "Why were *you* so excited about this, then, when you and Ed Fountain first started working together? It is *so* a war, dear, it's a domestic, moral—"

"Oh, Mother, for Heaven's sake! I simply want you to keep yourself safe! At least stay out of public places with him."

Peg subsided. Sabina thought, foolishly, she had won. Then Peg asked, "And you, Sabina? Are you quitting your consulting for the *Times?*" She read her daughter's silence exquisitely and bore down. "The fireworks last night, how private a celebration was that, young lady?"

"Okay, Mom, okay okay. *Touché, olé*, etcetera. I gotta go, but we're going to talk some more about this."

"Yes, dear."

CHAPTER FIFTEEN

"Mama mia gonorrhea," Ella Martinelli breathed as she scrolled through the screen, reading messages posted yesterday on the *Times* internal bulletin board. When she had seen enough she clicked on her mailbox.

>From Ella Tues Jul 8 7:52:12
Check out the BB about this Firecracker murder! Amazing we got a paper out at all yesterday.

>From Kendall Tues Jul 8 7:53:05
P.S. Eliot would be pleased by all the attention.

(P.S. Eliot was a nickname Kendall had dreamed up for the Poet of Pain; Ella loved it. She answered him ...)

>No kidding. Hey K, there's a real bomb in the BB chatter, did you see it?

>The one about the killer was really going for Sabina and missed?

>No. That's silly. A, her friend and that boy were in between, and B, she's a nine-lives type cat. Not that I'd weep big time if someone put a few holes through her, let some of the hot air out, not fatal of course :)

>Speaking of cats :) What bombshell?

>The rumor that your old man, excuse me, our leader,

is bringing in a victim's parent for the press conference. Julie Oleson's father.
>That is a bombshell? Why?
>You really want to know, perhaps Ella will come up there and explain it up close and personal.
>I'm waiting.

She had leaned on the flirt button before with Kendall, mystery son of the Dark Lord. He never answered the door. All she'd get were hang-dog goofy looks or a stuttering change of subjects. So it was with some surprise that Ella found herself, a half hour shy of the all-important press conference, in an astonishing position. Slammed into her backside was the decorative brass knob of Kendall's office door. Slammed against her front side was Kendall Drum, as hard as the doorknob but considerably more interesting. They had been kissing for five minutes. Her mouth was deliciously bruised, her insides a sugar cone. The formidable *achtung* step of Rose Malwicki, Matthew Drum's secretary, sounded too late. Ella and Kendall started to pull apart and then locked in place as Rose pushed through the door, calling Kendall's name.

Trying too hard to suspend her breathing, something squeaked in Ella's throat. Rose said again, "Kenny?" softly, suspiciously. They heard her slow pivot on sensible low-heeled pumps, felt those bifocal eyes cut through the wood.

Ella would never understand just how Malwicki knew who was behind the door with Kendall because the woman never actually stepped the few inches to her left and exposed them. She simply delivered her message and departed as silently as she came, the whip crack of her words echoing in the air: "Kenny. Mr. Drum would like you to videotape the press conference. Mrs. Martinelli can help you. I believe she has no other role today."

Or ever again, Ella thought glumly. The bitch would tattle.

With every paycheck and every encounter with Drum, the focus tightened on that dummy organization chart and the blank space inside the box that used to belong to her.

The press conference was staged in the middle of the newsroom. It put on international display the small-town, messy, under-financed environment where scrappy reporters and editors were taking on their killer Goliath. Matthew Drum assumed a wide-legged boxer stance alongside a podium burdened by microphones of every shape and size. Six people were strung out behind him.

Sabina Shaw, Ed Fountain and Frank Wiley stood in one bunch. A little removed were two Suits from the Advisory Board and next to them, in jeans and an out-of-place yellow V-neck sweater with an undershirt showing beneath, was Howard Oleson. He copied the CEO's stance, legs planted wide, his grease-stained hands clasped in front of him.

Ella felt sad just looking at him. This was what she considered the "bombshell," because if she knew Ed, he wouldn't go along with propping this poor guy up there less than three weeks after he'd lost his daughter. The poor dope was probably still in shock. And because Fountain was in his place on the makeshift podium, it meant to Ella that he was in the dark.

What a cool cucumber Sabina Shaw looked: a willowy sapling in her Pollyanna green silk dress. Frank Wiley was the opposite. His noble brow gleamed with sweat, and not just because the TV lights were hot. He had been whining for Drum to run some kind of front-page apology since before the Firecracker murder; today, he confided to Ella that he and his wife were pushing up their vacation to start on Saturday, even if they had no place to go. Wiley was among those who believed the Poet had meant to kill Sabina Shaw, and that he would march through *Times* targets until he smoked the well-groomed hide of the publisher himself.

The shrink, Lester Malabee, started it off by yakking at them about the Poet's motivations and profile. The only thing that moved were his eyes when they slid up from his notes and peered at his audience. He babbled about "ego-syntonic" murderers who aren't conscious of the desire to kill, but still do it and do it violently. Then he said he didn't think the Poet of Pain was that type. Ella thought, so what the fuck did he tell us for to begin with?

"More likely, we are speaking of an under-controlled rather than an over-controlled personality," Malabee intoned. "A sociopath who displaces his aggression. When he kills, he is usually not sadistic."

Ella couldn't keep from checking out Howard Oleson. He stared at the floor and swayed from heel to toe. It seemed he disagreed. It seemed he thought death by bicycle tire was sadistic enough.

An older man with a fringe of gray hair and a buckskin vest rose in the second row and didn't wait to be recognized. He introduced himself as Bob from *Rolling Stone* and posed his question wearily, in a raspy voice that sounded like old bones hauled across a washboard.

"That's great, doc," he growled, "if this was a textbook, but it's real life, or the taking of it by some asshole who's gettin' his jollies off watching us talk about him. How do you get to the guy?"

Malabee sighted Buckskin Bob down the short length of his upturned nose and told him, with a lousy choice of words, that there should be "prodromal cues" suggesting when the person was ready to kill again.

Buckskin Bob crashed a palm against his forehead. "Let's gloss over the fact you used another fifty-cent word, Doc, and tell us what cues. Cues to who?"

"To his family or coworkers, for example," Malabee said

stiffly. He deliberated carefully before finishing his reply to the half-cocked cowboy. "Behavioral changes like depression. Taking more alcohol or drugs or pills. Physical problems like an upset stomach or hypochondriacal preoccupations." He upended his sheaf of notes, tapping them against the podium. "Is that clear enough, sir?"

Buckskin Bob reeked disgust. "Oh, I'm keepin' up, Doc. Anyone with PMS to a hangover could be the Poet, is what I get out of this. And you want his mother to turn him in."

While the audience tittered and whispered over that, Matthew Drum stepped up alongside the shrink and the man melted away.

"Ladies and gentlemen," Drum said evenly, "any questions about strategies to catch the murderer are more appropriately directed to Chief Sterling Opel when it's his turn." He nodded respectfully in the direction of the Chief. Opel was draped over a computer terminal like it was a Wild West hitching post, the butt of his gun cocked out at an angle from his fat butt.

Drum continued, smiling lightly at Opel. "I can tell you, the Chief will throw the responsibility back on the *Times* doorstep, for he is of the opinion that the person calling himself the Poet of Pain will continue his terrorizing until this paper begs for his forgiveness on page one. He is of the opinion that we are unconcerned about public safety."

Drum shook his head sorrowfully. "Not true. I would ask the Chief, if we can withhold the names of some crime victims to protect those individuals, why can we not withhold certain criminal's names to protect us all?"

He turned back to the audience. Let his upbeat, schoolteacher expression crust over. Ignored the waving hands and shouted questions until silence fell and took on a physical weight.

"Whose job is it to fight crime? Does that belong to the police alone, who have to take cases one at a time? Or do we all own a piece of the problem? Those of us watching from a safe distance, hoping we won't be thrust aboard this runaway crime train someday—don't we have an obligation to look at it, see the entire train from engine to caboose and figure out the best way to stop the *whole-damn-thing* instead of trying to derail one car?"

It was scripted. It was a speech. Ella hated the man ... but goosebumps seized her anyway. The way he played sorrow into anger when he said "the whole damn thing" with that eloquent intensity that Kendall had none of.

"I know there are some of you who question our motives in refusing to give in to the Poet, in taking him on with our silence. I want you to meet a man who is riding this train and can never get off. He wants to tell you why he thinks, as we do, that publicity glorifies and perpetuates the worst kinds of violence in America. Howard Oleson is the father of Julie Oleson, the lovely young woman who was killed June nineteenth. Mr. Oleson is a very brave man to volunteer to speak to you today."

Oleson moved like a zombie, his eyes pinned on Drum until he reached the podium. He bent at the waist, his lips touching a microphone.

"Thanks first for listenin' to me," he boomed. The microphone squealed and he looked to Matthew Drum. Drum put his hand on Oleson's shoulder and told him, audibly, to just stand up straight and pick out one person to talk to.

Ella watched Drum turn and join the others. He chose the space next to Ed Fountain and pivoted confidently. Ed's eyes closed. His chest swelled with a deep breath. Ella started feeling sick.

Howard Oleson tipped toward the microphone, recoiled

just in time to avoid the feedback squeal, and spoke like he'd lose control any second. "First I wanna tell you about my girl, our girl, Julie. My girl was comin' into the business with me. Workin' her fanny off to do good, like she always worked at everthin' she ever done."

Maybe just because her ears were tuned to it, Ella could pick out Ed Fountain's voice, low but distinctly angry. His jaw was thrust inches from Drum's and the CEO was, at last, off balance. The next she knew, Ed was forging the shortest path to the newsroom door, passing a startled Howard Oleson and striding white-faced through two rows of reporters. Ella floated to her feet without will: boneless, empty of thought. At least one light was redirected to shine on Ed, and on Ella behind him, weaving their way through the awesomely silent room. Kendall Drum, standing on a short stepladder with a camcorder on his shoulder, pointed the lens at the two of them.

Just what did she think she was doing? If she thought she was in deep doo-doo with Matthew Drum before, this public side-choosing display would cinch it. Fleeting thoughts of rent payments and dental bills flashed through her head and then they were safe from the electronic eyes and headed for where, Ella hadn't the vaguest.

The Men's Room. Ella stopped herself at the door as it closed behind him. That's what she would have done if she had fucked up like Ed. She'd duck into the Women's Room and scream into a paper towel.

Wait a minute. She *did* fuck up like Ed. Ella took a deep breath, sighed, hugged herself and paced, three to the left, three to the right, then flattened her ear to the door. Ed knew someone was behind him, he had to have heard her heels on the linoleum once they were out of the newsroom. Maybe he didn't know it was her, though.

"Ed?" She pushed the door open a crack. "Ed, are you okay?"

Nothing.

"Look, sweetie, I'm comin' in unless you're whizzing?"

Boom! There he came right at her, still angry and giving her shoulder a good knock as he pushed past. "No goddamn TV in there."

Ella trotted to catch up, holding her arms under her breasts so they wouldn't jiggle. "You thought maybe there would be?"

"Wiley's got one," Ed said.

"I had the idea you weren't real interested in watching this press conference." She checked out his face: hurricane force frown.

"He went too far," Ed said, stonily. "That is one dangerous man." They reached the elevator and Ed's fist lit up the button.

In Wiley's office, Ella and Ed slumped down side-by-side on a white, camel-back sofa and caught the final fifteen minutes of CNN's live coverage of the press conference. Howard Oleson was stumbling through some schtick comparing the moratorium to George Bush's hostage policy—too obviously Matthew Drum's words. Oleson wound down, started to step away and turned back. What he said next wasn't scripted. He spoke from his heart.

"I wanna talk right at the bastard," Oleson said, his head lowered like a bull. "My Julie counted for something. I know why you're pullin' this shit, wanna be a big man! Well, you count for nothin'. We're gonna catch you and we're gonna fry you, and if the world ever gets it right, I pray to God nobody goes to watch! Except the lucky guy that pulls the switch." He pushed a thumb into his chest and his eyes glistened. "I wish to *Christ* it could be me."

There was no way Ella could stand to look at Ed. Sterling Opel was up next in the news conference, but it was a few minutes before Opel could speak, the crowd was applauding that hard, and standing. Reporters!

The Chief didn't have the ideal slot, unless you were a moratorium lover. He made a few stabs at his civic duty arguments and the right to be safe and then was smart enough to take three giant steps back to his hitching post.

"You have to hand it to him," Ed said.

"Opel?"

"Drum."

Sabina Shaw had her moment in the spotlight. She closed the press conference by summarizing expert opinions verifying the impact of publicity on the type and frequency of violent crime. A CNN reporter was wrapping it all up when they heard Ed's name. A big brown-eyed babe on the desk was talking to the field reporter and the question must have been, who was that who walked out, and why?

"That was the paper's editor, and we're told that his own daughter"—the guy looked at his notes—"Casey Fountain, was shot to death in Milwaukee last summer. I'd have to speculate that he just couldn't bear to hear the pain of another victim's relative."

So even Fountain's scorched exit served Drum's purposes. Had no one but Ella seen Ed snarl at Drum before he walked?

Fountain closed his hand around a Princeton Class of '44 coffee mug on the end table. He aimed for the TV and it looked like a good hurl until the mug's owner, Frank Wiley, picked that second to walk through the open door. The mug arced toward Frank's belly and he was all of a sudden a classy wide receiver, catching it in the pocket of his hands and then spoiling the move by dropping it and yelping as the mug bounced off his wingtip and a dark sludge lipped onto the carpet.

"What are you doing?" Wiley yelled, flaring his nose and pointing at the stain like it was a pile of dog barf.

"I beg your pardon, Frank." Those were Fountain's words, anyway. A tissue width behind them was "Back off you asshole." Frank swung his glare to Ella; she scowled right back.

The publisher ignored them and began shoving files and papers into his briefcase. His claws were out, Ella thought: survival mode. She remembered his hot words to Ed Fountain just a month ago at Theo's, when they took their useless vote on the moratorium. *You've got nothing to lose,* he'd said, the first icicles of uneasiness spoiling his Ivy League polite. Now the Poet was way too close and it looked like Wiley wasn't waiting even until tomorrow to start his vacation.

A few *Times* editorial staffers drifted in, then a few more, searching for Ed, but at a loss for what to say. They settled around the room in the few chairs, slumped on the floor, turned their backs to Wiley and perched shoulder-to-shoulder on the edge of his desk.

Briefcase in hand, Wiley squeezed past two more people standing uncertainly in his office door. There were enough bodies in the room now, all feeling that post-event release of tension, to make it more a party than a wake. Someone flipped the TV to a soap and someone else stole the remote and changed the station to Fox, where the President was holding a press conference to push his newest crime bill. A chant went up for the soap.

The decibel level in the room dipped and Ella looked over to the door, where Riverview's mayor was standing. Kendall Drum was right behind him, trying to squeeze past, but too polite to ask Hizzoner to budge.

Mayor Roland August, an alert, fox-faced man, asked a question of the room in general—"Is Frank Wiley around?"— that no one leapt to answer. Ella loved that about reporters. It could be the janitor standing there. Someone stepped up to the Mayor and pointed out the door toward the elevator. The

Mayor turned to go just as a reporter crowding the television set yelled out, "Hey everybody, shut up, it's the President! He's talking about us, about Riverview!"

Roland August whiplashed into the room like a voting lever being slammed into place. There was the famous hoarse voice, and it was praising the "brave little town of Riverview, Wisconsin." A collective whoop drowned the President's next words. The Mayor, his gaze pinned to the broadcast, clapped his hands and shouted for silence.

"We have to fight violence with values," the President was saying. "We've poured resources into prisons and cops and look where it got us." The President was getting worked up. It looked sincere to Ella but you couldn't get a crowd like this to accept anything on face value. Commentary was already starting up. Mayor August had to clap his hands together again.

"This country's heartland is way out ahead," the President said, poking the air with a finger. "This singular town is smart enough to recognize the forces behind one psychopath's actions, and courageous enough to take a stand on it. *For all of us.*"

That busted it open. Everyone was a noise-maker: jabbering or clapping. The Mayor gleamed, like the praise had come to him personally. In the hubbub, Kendall located Ella and hung over the back of the couch, companionably.

"Just exactly what are we celebrating here?" Ella said. She turned to Ed Fountain and found him looking at her, the ghost of his upside-down smile on his face. He patted her knee once and hiked himself up, a slowly reassembled bag of laundry. He was that beat-up looking. No one noticed him leave.

Kendall slipped over the back of the couch and took Ed's place. Ella's eyes were on the air hole that seemed to swallow Ed Fountain. She said, dispiritedly, "Ah, shit, Kendall."

He surprised the hell out of her with an echoing, "Ah, shit, Ella."

Ella socked him on the arm and doubled over, laughing. When she sat back up again, wiping at her eyes, Kendall hadn't moved a muscle. He gave her a deep, sad stare.

"My father just told me to stay away from you," he announced.

Ella ran her tongue across her upper lip and considered his expression carefully. "But you aren't going to," she said, sure of it. She considered his mouth, let herself remember its roughness and let him see her remembering.

"I'm not going to," Kendall repeated.

It was possible he was hypnotized, Ella worried. She didn't want that. The man may have stumbled across free will and it was important he knew it.

"Prove it," she challenged him. "There's a wedding I'm invited to this Saturday. Come with me."

An infinitesimal side-to-side flicker in his eyes; a panic. "It's just that I was supposed to go home this weekend."

Oh sure. Ella shrugged. "Not a problem."

His warm hand closed on her chin and he turned her face back toward him, his battery all revved up. "To hell with that," he said. "I'll take you to that wedding!"

Ella would have laughed at him again, it was such a pitiful breakthrough, except she didn't want to spoil it. She was too happy.

CHAPTER SIXTEEN

Sabina's turn at the press conference podium lasted maybe ten minutes and the afterglow, not much longer. Outside the *Times,* she waded through angry anti-moratorium pickets—many with children—waving signs like SPILL INK, NOT BLOOD and screaming in her face. When she got home, two obscene calls washed the glamour clean away.

There had been the briefest moment of pleasure, seeing her phone answering machine blinking a fat message count. One call came in while she stood there. She screened it.

"This is Andrew Webster," the voice said. "I called you before. You guys don't want to hear what I've got to say that's cool with me." *Click.*

Who the heck was Andrew Webster? Sabina drew her bedroom "office" curtains closed, turned on a lamp and curled up in the desk chair with pen and paper.

Twelve minutes later, the only calls she wanted to return were to Sonny, who wanted "one more golden oldie outing" before she had to fly back to Wyoming, and to the Webster guy. The rest were a mix of irritating, strange, and obscene.

The first obscene call was her ex-husband.

"Hey, kiddo, you're famous!" Jacob's message said. "You're on all the channels up here. Got a joke for ya: Did you hear about the guy they found drowned in a bathtub of milk with a banana stuck in his mouth? They suspect a cereal killer." He paused, making room for her to laugh, and then rang off cheerily.

The malice of this man she had married, telling her a joke like that. More obscene than the message itself was what was behind it, what she heard in his voice and had heard before. He was jealous. Jealous that she was ... what, getting attention? Had a real *special* Fourth of July? Criminy.

The second call was the genuine article. It was a man's voice and surprise, he didn't identify himself. In a gradually slower and louder cadence, his contribution to Sabina's peace of mind went like this: "Hump-pitty Dump-pitty sat on a wall, and Hump-Pussy Dump-Pussy-had-a-great-BIG-fall." Followed by a soft chuckle and a click.

She played it back three times and succeeded in scaring herself thoroughly. The night leered at her through a gap in the curtains. She paper-clipped the two curtain edges tightly together, ceiling to floor. Then she ejected the cassette from the answering machine and threw it in a drawer—an impulse, like saving a threatening letter. This way, when they found her body, they'd have a piece of evidence to start on.

Sabina thought it was time for a drink. She edged into the kitchen, fighting an impulse to slide her back along the wall, and snapped the kitchen lights on and off. They hadn't bothered with kitchen curtains because the windows just looked out onto an overgrown back yard—innocuous until tonight. Leaving the freezer door open a crack, Sabina used its dim light to splash a tower of Jack Daniels over ice.

She'd turned into a yuppie Chardonnay drinker over the years and tonight she hoped it would pay off, that one visit from Jack would induce sleep. In the meantime, she decided to check out Andrew Webster. In his first message on the machine, he claimed to have some information on the Poet's identity, and he didn't sound like a nutcase. She settled down again, jolted back two slugs, and dialed the number in Washington, D.C.

"Mr. Webster? This is Sabina Shaw. I just picked up your message."

He said, "Okay," and strung the word out, obviously irritated, and then waited, like it was she who had first called him. Something rustled, sounding like bedsheets, and Sabina remembered, embarrassed, the time zone difference. It was nearly midnight there.

"Oh, hey, I'm sorry," she said. "It's late here, too, later where you are, I just didn't think."

"Don't sweat it, babe. I was down, not out."

The rustling stopped and his voice shrank into the distance, tinny and remote. He had her on a speaker phone! This was not going well. Sabina hated speaker phones and hated, in nearly every circumstance, being called "babe."

"Must you use a speaker phone?" she asked him, icily.

"Yeah," he snarled. "Yeah, I *must*."

Ever since the Poet of Pain laid his last victim at her feet, Sabina thought she had behaved quite well. That was her last civilized thought. She raised the phone in a death grip over her head and screamed at it.

"God*damn*it I don't need this, who the hell do you think you are I don't need this I don't *need this*! Go to *hell* whoever the hell you are, you ... godforsaken son of a bitch!"

She reared back and pitched the phone straight for the windows. It bounced off the drapes and landed back on her desk, dead. Her breath rasped, oddly centered between her ears, as if it were her brain breathing.

A clucking came from the phone. Andrew Webster hadn't hung up. He was laughing. "You got that right, babe," said the voice. "Hey. D.C. to Riverview, come in, come in."

Sabina took a steadying breath and picked up the receiver just as he yelled into it: "YOU THERE?"

"Geez!" she yelped. "I'm not deaf. At least I wasn't."

"You blasted me pretty good too, girl." His voice was deeply amused.

"Don't hold your breath for me to apologize. And don't call me 'girl' or 'babe,' all right?"

"You want what instead?"

"My name will do just fine."

"That's some weird name. You musta come out sideways, made your Mama mad, for her to hang that one on you."

"So now you want to insult my name for awhile?"

"You gotta admit, babe, Sabina ain't your every day kinda name. For one thing, it rhymes with—"

"Mister Webster. Stop right there." Sabina took a second long pull on uncle Jack. This was going nowhere and taking a long time doing it. "Suppose you tell me what information you have on the Poet."

He came back with a sarcastic "Yes, ma'am, Mizz Shaw," mocking her formality. She could kill this man.

After a sustained silence his voice changed, showed fatigue. Sabina had the impression their word volley had been the highlight of Andrew Webster's day.

"I got your name from a *Newsweek* story," Webster said, "and saw you on TV tonight. Called this Matthew Drum and he won't call me back." There was the unmistakable swoosh-pop of a pair of lips fastening onto and draining a swallow of something. "It's like this. There's this dude, definitely not a dudette, he's been droppin' porn all over the Net, you know the type, a cybercreep no flaming or bozo filters can kill. So a couple weeks back this Shakespeer, that's with a p-e-e-r because he's the stalkin' type, he got real bad, and I caught his address as frat, you know? Like the problem you got, this Poet, I see on the news he been dropping them notes about apologize to the

fraternity? And Shakespeer likes to rhyme his shit, so I put it
together and come up with the chance we might be talkin' to
the same asshole and you could use ALT or some other group to
get him flashin' his real host or domain."

Sabina was stunned.

"You know," he prompted, "flush him out."

A second slurp-pop of his bottle. Something about the
man, Sabina was sure it was a beer. She pictured a long-
necked bottle, dark amber.

"Mr. Webster?"

"I ain't gone nowhere, girl."

"Are you under the impression that I have the slightest
idea what you're talking about? I'm not unfamiliar with the
Internet, but I don't use it except to do research. It's your
jargon that confuses me."

"My jargon. I beg your fuckin' pardon. Over my fuckin'
jargon." She heard a squeaking, followed by the fizz-snap of
a beer can being opened. The bottle a dead soldier already?
This man could drink. His voice returned full strength. With
exaggerated patience, he walked Sabina through the history
of his exposure to a porn-voyeur he nicknamed Shakespeer.

Sabina listened as much to how he talked as to what he
was saying, because she heard an undercurrent of deep outrage that was comforting. She couldn't figure out why, until
she understood that of all the people she'd talked to or worked
with through this escalating mess, only Ed Fountain and
Julie Oleson's father and this long-distance, rude, half-in-the-
bag stranger exhibited an authentically human response—
other than fear—to the murders. It was Webster's *outrage*. Everyone else seemed to regard the murders as either a cash
opportunity, or another True Crimes episode that would float
without imprint through their lives and pass by with the
turn of a page, the switch of a channel.

Webster had stopped talking. "Well? You follow?"

"I follow. You may be onto something." She told him about the postscripts in the Poet's notes and her theory that he was dedicating the killings to other murderers.

"Hey, babe ... Sobeena, whatever." He snorted; he couldn't even say it straight once. It would make his day, to know about the old Sappy Vagina nickname.

"You read these notes yourself?" Webster asked.

"Just the one on the Fourth."

"You see how it was printed up?" Webster asked. "Shakespeer uses a quirky combo of upper and lower case letters, in the middle of words. This Poet do that?"

She closed her eyes, trying to picture the note. "The light was pretty bad. I don't think so. For sure not in his post-script. The top line ... there was a rhyme in it somewhere, but no, nothing like you're describing."

Andrew Webster was not deterred. "Somethin' tells me your poet's my poet, but we gotta know if I'm right about that address, the frat thing."

The long day galloped up behind Sabina. She had to get this guy off the phone. She closed her eyes, swallowed the last of Jack and dropped her head back.

"Mr. Webster, may I summarize your strategy here? Perhaps I don't fully understand it." Her words slurred. She turned the glass upside down on her head. That woke her up, the burn of slush-ice on her scalp.

"This scheme depends on the Poet logging in to the right Newsgroup at the right time, responding to the conversation there, then forking off to deal with you alone in private e-mail. To use your words, even then it's 'suck tit odds' that you'd get his real name. But maybe he uses a real address, and that address needs to be associated with a particular kind of ... what did you call it?"

"A gateway."

"Right, a gateway, that can tell us what computer, where. And if that computer is in some public place where lots of people log onto it, then we also need him to use his right name or initials in *that* address."

Silence at the other end. "Have I got that right?" she asked. "I'm not trying to rain on your parade, I'm just computing the odds."

"Maybe the dude and I hit it off," Webster speculated, "and he gives me his phone number. Or his mail address. How do I know? Or maybe I'll be the chick he was stalkin' when I last picked him up or maybe I'll be both, shit, I don't know! What's *your* plan, babe?"

During that tirade, a furious squeaking accompanied his words. What in the world was that? He probably tortured mice, he was sure angry enough.

"I don't have any idea who you are," Sabina said, too tired to care if she insulted him. "As far as I know, I could be talking to the Poet right now, couldn't I? I mean, why aren't you calling the police with this?"

He crushed his beer can and threw it to the floor. A linoleum floor, from the sound of it.

"No cop in a pea-sized town like yours is gonna know shit about using computers good enough to hunt this guy. Second, I don't do favors for no cops, no way, no time."

She wanted to tell him to shadow box with himself, that she was going to bed. It turned out she just thought about saying it, though, because he was rambling on about the failings of law enforcement.

It was restful. He really had a very nice voice and the ice had melted and was cool trickling through her hair. The computer hummed steadily, an unending whispery exhale.

The next thing Sabina knew she was jerked awake by the pulsing shriek of an unconnected phone. She should call him back to apologize, this Andrew Webster of Washington D.C.

Maybe tomorrow.

Maybe never.

CHAPTER SEVENTEEN

In the dark of the hall closet, Peg Lindsay clutched the heavy folds of Scotty's navy wool sweater and buried her face in it. It still held his shape—especially the pouch at the right elbow, his pipe arm, perpetually bent—but his smell was a memory.

It was no good, using Scott to block out the reality of Matthew Drum. She released the sweater and groped for her new red straw hat on the top shelf.

The past few weeks, there was no mistaking the urgency of Matthew's kisses. Peg was no mannequin herself, by God; she was kissing him back. Beyond that, she had been skittish. Last evening, Matthew had taken her by the shoulders and given her an exasperated shake. It made her feel sixteen years old again. They had exchanged a look, a promise, that Peg could still feel this morning.

She was sixty-two years old, for heaven's sake. A woman whose bureau drawers were filled with neat stacks of white, all-cotton oversized underwear. Who slept with an orthopedic neck pillow and wax-fighting drops of oil in her ears. Who thought of open-mouthed kissing on TV as gratuitous.

At the mirror next to the front door, she tilted her hat first to the left, then to the right. Matthew had called with a

spur-of-the-moment invitation to accompany him, in his private plane no less, to a speech he was delivering in Chicago.
Peg stepped out to her front porch and pinched back her
geraniums. She had time to call Sabina back and clear the air,
but that darn girl. All Sabina had accomplished with her
phone call was to cast a shadow over the day. Peg wanted to
wring her neck.

Mom, really, I wish you would not go.

*Darling, you're sweet to worry, but we've already been through
this.*

*You apparently need to go through it again, then, Mother, since
you don't seem to be thinking clearly. Until the police—*

*You will not use that tone with me, young lady. I am not your
addled old dependent relative, I'll have you know.*

If Dad were alive, he'd be the first one—

*He was my husband, Sabina. I think I know far better than you
what he would say. Do you have the idea we made it through those
years with him telling me what to do at every turn?*

A cold silence. *Fine, Mother. Since I can't finish a thought
without you jumping all over me. Have a nice day.*

Peg had not waited for Sabina to hang up first. "Have a
nice day" was the private shorthand phrase she and her daughter used to sum up the insincere, shallow kinds of things
people say who don't really care about you. It had stung, and
she was sure Sabina meant it to. The snip hadn't called back
to apologize, either.

Though Peg was determined not to spread the gloom, her
resolve vanished before Matthew's plane touched down at
Midway in Chicago and she found herself telling him all
about it. Sabina and she had hardly exchanged a harsh word
since the girl was in college and it nagged at Peg.

"Oh, for Chrissake, how idiotic," was his reaction.

"I take it you're not concerned," Peg replied, drily.

"It's not wishful thinking, understand. Look. According to the FBI profile, I'm a father figure to the Poet and that makes me, and you, safer than anyone in the world. These guys apparently don't have the balls—excuse me—to confront old Dad."

"But there are other opinions, aren't there? Other profiles? Sabina says one of your own advisors calls this man a 'special mission' serial killer. She says his mission is to get you to apologize to his crazy 'fraternity' of famous killers. And she says—"

"Right," Matthew said, with a cynical superiority that Peg usually found annoying but that she welcomed now. "And how does he accomplish this mission if I'm dead? Dead people do lousy *mea culpas.*"

He reached over and tugged on her earlobe. "Believe me, Peggy, we're fine."

Matthew was the keynote speaker at a symposium on "Ethics in Journalism," held at the Omni Hotel on Michigan Avenue. Peg, the only woman at the speaker's table for twelve, found herself between strangers, with Matthew seated across from her. The topic of the day was the *Times* moratorium but Peg was sick to death of it and said as much, so the gentlemen on either side of her talked about baseball, the price of pulp, the latest carcinogen and food allergies. Somewhere in all that, Peg was reminded of something funny one of her grandchildren had said. That reminded someone else of a joke and he told it, a quirky story about a mongoose and the Pope that hit Peg right in the funny bone and she laughed until tears leaked out her eyes.

When Matthew was introduced to a flattering crescendo of applause, he circled the table and paused behind Peg's chair. He leaned over, cupping her chin in his hand. "Tell me," he said softly, "are you at home wherever you go?"

It was too public a gesture. Peg was embarrassed. She faced straight ahead, twisting her napkin in her lap, as Matthew continued on to the dais. It was several minutes before she was able to pay attention to his speech.

Their plan was to hang around Chicago for dinner at the Cricket Club, after Matthew's speech and the awards ceremony, which gave them two hours to kill. They strolled down Michigan Avenue, ducking into stores to avoid a warm, gritty wind blowing off the lake. Peg loved to shop and Matthew endured ... until they wandered into a gadget store. There, in the space of a half hour, he bought a pre-WWI golf club, four shower heads, a data scanning pen, two halogen lamps, a silent electric insect eliminator, a water-resistant cordless phone, a World War II field radio, a pair of nightvision binoculars, and five home peanut-butter makers. With tax, it cost him $2,592.56.

Peg was stunned: at the variety, the speed of the purchases, the size of the bill. "What on earth is all this for?" she asked him.

"Merit gifts, some," Matthew explained. "I like to spring surprise rewards on staff. Some of it's for me."

Matthew collected war paraphernalia, and the old golf club and binoculars were for him, as were the shower heads, for his home in Boston. The rest were gifts.

Matthew held up the data scanning pen. "This is for a young man at the *Times*, name of Rudy Parson. He's been working on our hacker problem, gave me a brilliant presentation on how to beef up security."

"*Five* peanut-butter makers, Matthew?"

"A team at DEI-Munich who brought a big project in under budget," he explained. He cast his eye over the assortment, looking pleased with himself, and tapped the pen on the insect eliminator. "This is for Malwicki, my secretary—well, you know Rose. She has this cottage on the water she says she can't use because of the mosquitoes. This should do it. It'll handle two acres."

Peg imagined an endless whiplash of crunching until she remembered, no; it was all done in antiseptic silence. Ridiculous. A person should stay in the city, then, or at least have to listen to what was happening.

The water-resistant phone was for Matthew's lawyer. "It grows out of his shoulder," Matthew explained. "Now he can go on talking during the three hours a year he floats with the kiddies at their lake in the Catskills." He acted disapproving, but he bought it just the same.

The clerk bustled about, ineptly feigning nonchalance as she closed the huge order. Matthew gave her his Riverview address for Rose Malwicki's and Rudy Parson's gifts. He handed her a different credit card for the rest of the items, and from their exchange about shipping details, Peg understood he was sending it all to his home in Boston.

Peg had not fully acknowledged Matthew's other home. She had been thinking of his private life as transpiring exclusively in the Bluffs of Riverview, Wisconsin. How naive.

His pen poised over the receipt, Matthew turned to her, chagrined. "Hey, Peg, I'm sorry. Look, do you want something?" He waved his arm around the store as if to say, take one; take it all.

She lifted the bag at her side. "I bought it during your frenzy over in Electronics. A three-dimensional jigsaw puzzle, no less."

"Here, let me put in on my card."

"It's *done*, Matthew." She realized she sounded severe, but really. Peg was not eager to be at the receiving end of this particular brand of largesse.

They left the store to a cloudier, colder day, hailed a taxi for the restaurant and climbed in. Halfway there, Matthew turned to her and asked what she'd say to a change of plans. He was mussed-up from the wind and looked as sweet as a little boy.

"I've told you before," Peg said. "I love surprises."

"You should approve this first," he said. "It's not big-city fancy."

"Neither am I."

"Okay." He slid his arm along the back of the seat behind her. "We go home—my home. I make you my shrimp pasta dish, private recipe." He managed to invest "private" with layers of meaning. "Fresh bread, good wine. Jigsaw puzzle by the fire. That's it."

Peg closed her eyes, felt his breath on her cheek. "I think," she murmured, "that would be quite enough."

The pressure was on. Peg's mouth watered and her stomach fluttered in tandem. She was developing an appetite.

The small plane offered touches of luxury: a Persian rug, curtains at the windows, a mini-bar, a small television. Matthew and Peg sat in two of the four wide leather chairs. She kicked off her shoes and he followed suit, stretching his legs. They talked, lazily.

At one point, he tapped her toes with his and asked what she had been like as a girl.

"I wanted to be an Olympic figure skater," Peg said promptly.

"Is that right?" The wintry blue eyes crinkled at the corners. "Triple axels, spins, all that?"

"I'm sure not what you're picturing," she laughed. "I didn't have a coach, and nowhere to practice in the warm months. But I did love it. Scott used to call me poetry on ice." She paused, remembering, and the smile turned rueful. "When I went on skating after I was pregnant, he just called me headstrong."

Scott had been poking along behind her the day she raced across the pond and failed to see the fissure in the ice under a light snow covering. Her tip hit it hard and she was launched. A vision of baby flesh, scattered like pink crockery across the snow, made her cry out before impact and she managed a mid-air contortion, landing on her back. Stewart was born three months later, healthy as a little pig.

"No broken baby," Peg said.

Matthew raised his chin, appraising her as if he could squeeze out through narrowed eyes the twenty-year-old Peg Lindsay. "And no Olympic gold medal."

"Oh, no, I was years past that dream by then." In truth, she had pined for several years over a future only imagined. Peg swiveled in her chair, remembering that girl, and parted the curtains. They flew over popcorn clouds and an indigo horizon. Flying always seemed to Peg both a heavenly and a terminal event.

Matthew seldom volunteered truly personal information but on this short plane ride, he was freer in his speech. Or perhaps Peg was bolder in her questions.

Why no children except Kendall, she asked. His answer shocked her. He told her he had himself fixed, a vasectomy, to spite his father. Matthew called him Ambrose, not Dad or Father.

Peg stared. "To spite *him*?"

"Yeah, I know. Cut off your nose." Matthew dropped his head back and spun the chair, planting his feet high on the upholstered wall of the cabin. "I wouldn't expect anyone to get it. Except him."

"Try me," Peg prompted.

He raised his arms over his head in a casual stretch, but his voice was strained. "Kenny was conceived with a woman twelve years older than me. Not married. Not married to me, either. A professor of mine at Harvard. I made the mistake of telling my mother, and she told Ambrose. He said—excuse me, but you have to hear the exact words of my oh, so cultured father—he said, 'If you won't take responsibility for your dick, then get yourself fixed.'"

"You considered that ... retaliation?"

Matthew got to his feet and crossed to the plane's mini-bar. "I didn't even want one child. But Ambrose did; the last thing he wanted was to have his gene pool interrupted. I'm their only living child. Ellen couldn't keep the kid. I didn't want him." He scooped ice from a pewter bucket. "All the bully could ever talk about was 'no progeny of mine' will ever do this and that. Progeny is the biggest word in his vocabulary."

Matthew's hands stilled and he raised his head, staring at nothing. "You know something? This will sound ... overdone ... but who Ambrose reminds me of most is our Poet of Pain." He nodded crisply, passing judgement on his own opinion. "That's rather perfect. Both of them so desperate for immortality."

He turned and held up a glass. "Get you anything?" She shook her head. Matthew upended a bottle of Jim Beam. "Ambrose had this awful meat-packing business, in Kansas City. His filthy little empire. A badly-run piece of crap held together by so-called gentlemen's agreements between Ambrose and his corrupt cronies. To be honest, his Mob buddies. It was a hell-hole."

He settled back in his chair and took his time getting comfortable, balancing the glass on one knee. "Kenny's mother had the baby in Italy and we were giving him up for adoption when my father chased us down and bribed us to sign the boy over to him." His eyes were locked on hers but now he was looking through her, back in time. "I had a family all picked out," he said. Wistfully? "Sugar beet farmers. A little village at the foot of the Alps. Two other children."

"It wasn't better that Kendall be raised by his grandparents?"

He brought his glass to his lips, watching her over the rim. "Well, Peg, what do you think? Look at us."

Not "look at Kendall," but look at *us*. This desirable, successful man considered himself damaged goods? "What do you mean?" Peg asked. "You've got everything you want. Don't you? And Kendall may not be, well, your average young man but I like him, he's sweet."

Matthew sighed impatiently. "He's a child. At thirty-five, or however old he is, he's a blank slate. Afraid of women, or the right women, anyway. I'd be surprised if he could—" He cut a look at Peg and interrupted himself. "Poetic justice anyway, that Ambrose would have the one grandson and the kid doesn't reproduce." He tossed back half his drink and grimaced; as far as Peg knew, Matthew wasn't much of a boozer. "I know I'm no terrific model here, but Kenny's only deep relationship, for god's sake, is with his monstrous grandfather who he couldn't know or he wouldn't ..."

"Love him?"

"If you want to call it that," he said, sarcastically.

"Matthew. As long as we're on the subject, why did you get so angry at Kendall that time we drove to Madison? I'm reminded of it, because when you ... shouted at him, he was in the middle of telling me about his grandfather. With a great deal of affection."

Matthew nodded. "A great deal of distortion, is more like it. Kenny doesn't understand him."

"But he lived with him all his life, surely he's entitled to his own opinion? I believe people can change. Especially as they get older and closer to dying."

"Oh, Ambrose will never change, believe me." Matthew raised a hand and flicked a ruffled edge of the curtain back and forth. "He's using his money to tie Kenny to him. I took the kid along that day to explain about the buy-out deal with your group, to make a place for him, once and for all. Make him independent from Ambrose."

So that was the reason.

Peg had worked for weeks to put together an investment group to buy the *Times* from Drum Enterprises. Drum sold them on it thoroughly. He said it would be a good long-term investment and then he proved it with an independent valuation that Peg had arranged. He said if they owned the paper, then it couldn't be bought out from under them someday by a corporate bully who would fire the locals and make Riverview's editorial decisions for them from some faraway headquarters.

But his last reason for selling was the one that cinched it for Peg. He had phrased it as a condition: in exchange for a below-market price, they had to agree to a five-year contract with Kendall Drum as publisher, renewable depending on his performance. Kendall's tenure would begin after Frank Wiley's retirement and Matthew assured them Kendall would be prepared for the responsibility by then. "Kenny doesn't have the education," he had said, "and he's not a take-charge type but I think, once you get him going, he'd do fine." When the group was ready to unload the company, they were also contractually obliged to give Kendall Drum first option to purchase.

A loud buzz filled the cabin and the pilot's voice, over an intercom in need of repair, informed them they had begun descent to the Vernon County airport.

Peg buckled her seat belt, feeling uneasy because Matthew looked a little tight; perhaps he regretted opening up to her. "Maybe this will bring you and Kendall closer together," she said.

"Not my objective," was his matter-of-fact response. This was something he had long ago accepted: death and taxes and father-son estrangement.

"And you haven't even told him yet? About his future under the new ownership?"

He set his glass in the bar sink and ran water into it. "The only way I could get him out of Kansas City was to promise him I'd give him the top job at this paper someday, if he liked it. That much he knows, he just doesn't know how we're planning to do it." He wiped his hands on a towel as he returned to his seat. "And now I think he's hanging around the Martinelli woman. She's the town crier. I can't take the chance that he'd tell her and she'd flap her mouth."

Peg felt a lecture building but he wasn't her child, hardly that; so she let herself be distracted by all the busy-ness of the plane's landing and their transfer to the car for the ride home. As well, Matthew was wearing his No Trespass face. He may have opened the curtain a crack but Peg was a long way from backstage.

They fell into an easier silence on the ride home. When the car turned into her driveway, Peg asked what she could contribute to the dinner.

"My treat start to finish," Matthew said. "I'll need to make a run on the grocery store."

"That's silly," she protested. "I have shrimp in the freezer. And salad makings, and apple pie one day old—"

He stopped her with a finger stroke on her lips. "Peggy. Turn off the wife and mother routine, okay? This is no time to be practical." He smiled, teasing her. "You want maybe to split the cost, no obligations?"

She agreed, flustered, but managed to extract a promise from him that he wouldn't stop at the paper. That had happened before, a casual date for dinner at seven that turned into eight or nine o'clock.

"I promise." He lightly touched the back of her hair. "Would you wear that shawl for me? My favorite?" Matthew reached into his pocket and took out a fat ring of keys. He spun them around and extracted one, handing it to Peg. "Just in case," he said.

The key was a tight fit in the lock. Peg eased her head inside, calling Matthew's name to be sure he wasn't home yet. In their three months of dating, Peg had yet to see what Matthew had done to the house. All their at-home socializing had been at Peg's. As she walked through the first floor, she pulled her shawl close around her shoulders. The rooms were dank, smelling more of cellar than an expensive home in the Bluffs. Matthew had stripped the floors of all carpets and then seemingly abandoned his redecorating spurt. The few pieces of furniture were lovely but so spare, literally casting shadows on dusty wood floors under a single overhead fixture. Checkerboard walls showed clean rectangles where the previous owner's art had hung. No photos on tables or mantle, no ashy floor in the fireplace, no magazines, no newspapers— for heaven's sake, where did the man live?

Usually a light burned at the front corner of the second floor. She could see it from the alcove in her kitchen. Peg fervently hoped that Matthew's bedroom, at least, was not so barren. She found herself wondering about his home in Boston, if she'd ever see it, what Boston would be like to live in.

His music system was a mystery. She twiddled and poked until a red bar glowed, but that was it. A glance in the refrigerator and a few cupboards yielded the maintenance fare of a workaholic bachelor.

Before she could begin pacing and feeling ill-used, something thumped against the house and a side door opened into the kitchen. Matthew's arms were full of grocery bags and two bottles of wine, tipped precariously. Peg rescued them and helped unpack the food. It was a repeat of the gadget store: he had bought enough to feed an army. Enough, Peg thought, to feed a motel full of sexed-up senior citizens.

"What's got you looking so perky?" Matthew said, smiling at her.

"Anticipation," Peg said, evasively, "I can't wait to taste what you do with all this."

He turned a grocery bag on its side, crimped the bottom in his fist and jerked it sideways. The contents spilled neatly across the top of the butcher block.

Peg slipped out of her shawl, found an apron and tied it around her waist. "I make a better hostess than guest. Isn't there something ..?"

"Sure." He spun on his heel, considering. "Mind getting your hands fishy?"

In the corner of the kitchen was one of those new-fangled gas fireplaces with a fake stack of wood that ignited via a wall switch. It gave out an old-fashioned warmth, though. Peg dumped the shrimp in a colander and turned on the faucet. Matthew placed a glass of wine at her elbow and disappeared for a minute. The swing piano of Marcus Roberts wafted in from the living room.

While she washed and peeled, Matthew boiled water for the pasta and worked on his sauce. She began cutting vegetables for the salad, sharing the butcher block surface with him. His movements were easy, practiced. It looked simple, and that was best, in Peg's opinion. Yellow bell peppers were roasting under the broiler and Matthew was doing something in a blender that involved cream, cilantro, chives, and freshly ground white pepper.

Her hands stilled as she watched. "Delicious already," she said. He looked up, smiling. His face was utterly relaxed and unguarded.

When Matthew had the sauce underway on the stove, he disappeared into the basement and emerged with a folding

card table. He set it up in front of the wood stove and covered it with a wrinkled navy bed sheet folded in a square. It
was charming, in a way no restaurant could have duplicated.
Peg hoped for a wobble in the table while they ate.

Matthew was lighting candles when the phone rang.

"Ignore that," he said, and held her chair for her. One
ring and the answering machine was triggered. It sat on a
desk just the other side of the archway between kitchen and
living room. His voice on the machine instructed the caller to
leave a message. What followed, they could not ignore.

"Mr. Drum. This is Rose. Again." The woman was hugely
irritated. "If you would provide me with your weekend schedule this would not occur. I am loathe to leave this on the
machine but ..." She dropped the aggrieved tone and turned
businesslike. "We have another leak. It's the old memo file
about the sale. Not DEI to L-S, of course; I mean the MOSS
arrangement. It's on computers all over the building. People
are upset. So. You may call me at home if you wish. Remember
your teleconference call in the morning, eight o'clock our time."

A few seconds of silence. *Beep.*

The MOSS arrangement. That was Peg's investor group, orga-
nized to buy the paper. Matthew had told Peg they could call
themselves anything they liked, so Peg had dreamed up MOSS
as a private joke. It didn't matter *what* the letters stood for—the
whole arrangement stood for Peg's integrity, her reputation.

"God*damn*," Matthew fumed. "So much for the brilliant
Rudy Parson. He should have had the new system installed by
now." He scowled in the direction of the machine, as if the
message was continuing for him alone.

Peg was confused, and more, by Rose Malwicki's message.
She waited in vain for Matthew to explain.

"Matthew! What in the world? Isn't DEI ... isn't that
Drum Enterprises? And how can you be selling the whole ..."

She spread her hands in growing alarm and bumped her glass of wine. On the dark cloth you almost couldn't see the shape of the stain. An apology sidestepped to the edge of Peg's tongue. She bit it back.

Matthew was oblivious to the spill. "Check," he said. "And L-S stands for Langley-Spritz." He calmly picked up a sour-dough roll and broke it open. "They're an information technology conglomerate. You've probably heard of them?"

"Enchilada."

"What?"

"The whole enchilada. The word I was looking for." She waited again. Matthew chewed his bread. His *goddamned* bread, is what Scotty would have said if he were here. Behind that chiseled exterior, Peg had the uncomfortable sensation Matthew was thinking furiously.

"I'm getting a very bad feeling," Peg said slowly. She blotted the wet tablecloth with her napkin, rocking it from side to side and doing her best not to think about the word behind this bad feeling. Failing, of course, to think of anything but: Scam.

"Now you look me in the eye and you tell me." The depth of her anger at last earned his attention. "Is this some sort of scam? You're selling the paper to us, and courting this huge company at the same time? Good heavens, Matthew, every friend I have in this town, those with money anyway, they all put it in when I asked them. Every one!"

"Peg, please. Calm down and I'll try to explain."

The children told her she was cute when she was mad. There was little that could bring Peg to boil more quickly; it seemed they never said it when she was complaining about something trivial. It had become their defense, she supposed, against her rare bouts of real anger. Across Matthew's mouth now, there was just that same watercolor stroke of amusement.

"You'll *try?*" The cane seat of her chair gave a yawning creak as she rose and leaned across the table at him. "Well, I'll try to calm down! Like this!" She reached over and backhanded his wine glass. It skipped right over the butter dish and flew to the floor, shattering.

The humor drained so quickly from his face it seemed an illusion to begin with and Peg felt about an inch high. But she forbid herself retreat. Matthew blinked once. Twice. And then said, with a near absence of expression, "Wow. What I wouldn't give for someone like you in my corner."

That took the spine out of her. Peg slumped back down. "I'm there already, you stupid man! Do you think I formed MOSS because I needed the money?"

Matthew slid a hand toward her across the table. It ended in a hard fist. The emotion in his voice was balled up, too, but it was very real. "And do you think I need a small investor group in Wisconsin to extort Langley-Spritz, or ... or ... push them to make an offer?" He laughed, incredulous, running his hand through his hair. "Jesus, your group would buy it for *under* market value. So just what do you think is going on here?"

"I don't *know* what's going on."

"Here's the important thing," he said, tapping the table gently with his fist and managing to quiet and stimulate her both with his extraordinary eyes. "You are the last person in the entire world I would take advantage of." He laughed again, uncomfortably, and looked around the room as if for escape. "Maybe the only one."

"Well," Peg said. "I would like to believe that." He looked aggrieved. "I do," she added hastily. "I do believe that."

"Thank you." He stood abruptly and didn't so much shrug off his sports coat as strip it off. "You ready to listen, then?" he asked.

I was always ready to listen, Peg thought.

Matthew paced as he talked, showing the strained impatience of a man who rarely explained himself to anyone.

"Okay. When I came to Riverview, I was tired of this industry, the publishing part of it. The game was over. I want to do interactive media next. The way to do it is to take someone over. I've got a group in mind, but they're out of my price range. I can't leverage like I could before, I need a bigger chunk of cash. So I was on the block before I ever met you, do you see?" He threw a look her way and she nodded. "L-S approached me about a year ago; their offer was a joke. I kept in touch with them, played the game." He stopped at the kitchen window with his back to her and stared between two old hickory trees at her house next door. Peg saw she had left more than a few lights burning.

"Then the moratorium strategy comes up. Ed Fountain, the perfect stimulus." He turned his head so she could see his profile. "Do you ever follow DEI on the stock exchange?"

"When you first moved to town."

Matthew nodded. "It's doubled," he said. "All this publicity. Circulation is up at over half the papers, even where superstores are driving off the usual advertisers."

"So it's a seller's market," Peg concluded.

"A seller's market," he repeated. "Check." He turned his head back toward the window and stuffed his hands deep in his pockets. "This leak ... Kenny won't understand. I should call him." He read his watch but made no move to the phone. His blue shirt still showed its dry-cleaner folds; his tie was knotted as high and tight as it had been for his speech. Weariness was only evident in his voice, and that, Peg thought suspiciously, might be irritation at having to tell her what he should have volunteered.

"I suppose I should have let you in on this," Matthew said evenly, no hint of apology. "But Langley-Spritz is real particular about buying ... the whole enchilada. They buy it all, parcel out the different businesses later. They wouldn't understand my making this one deal with you, with MOSS; they'd think they couldn't trust me to leave the other properties alone until the negotiations were wrapped up. And they sure wouldn't understand you guys getting a lower price."

"You couldn't just tell them why you were doing it?" Peg asked. "For Kendall, I mean?"

Matthew turned around to face her, a corner of his mouth quirked up. "It may have escaped your notice, but I haven't exactly got a nice-guy reputation. I plain don't think they'd accept that as my reason. Plus, I didn't know if your group would really raise the capital; these deals happened to come together at the same time." He shrugged. "It's too late now, at any rate."

"In more ways than one," Peg said. He tipped his head, frowning. "I mean the leak that you're selling the *Times* to us, to MOSS," she explained. "Won't this Langley-Spritz get wind of that?"

"Ahh," Matthew said. He passed a hand through his hair again. "It's possible. And the deal is still weeks away from a sure thing." He leaned against the door and gazed up toward the ceiling. "The memo Rose was talking about: it doesn't say anything about my approaching you. It's got to be the documentation of your letter of intent, and it's got to be from early on, before the leak that put a burr in Frank's butt. Because after that, Rose kept all our MOSS business on her laptop computer, off network. The hacker couldn't have cracked that."

"What does all that mean?"

"It means we could salvage this, sell the paper to MOSS, if you and the other investors could make a firm offer right away. Monday if you can, while I'm still in negotiating stages with L-S."

"I'm not in this alone," Peg said. "The others will have to agree."

"I understand." He strolled back to the table and bent to hold one hand over the serving platter of pasta and shrimp. "Still warm." He raised his eyes to hers and said, with a longing that made her smile, "Could we eat? Are we done fighting?"

They tore into the food. It was an elbows-up, bread-dunking kind of meal. Fighting must be good for the appetite and the libido, because the evening was restored to them with all its romantic promise.

Peg felt rather drunk. At some point, Matthew asked her to dance. Or no, he didn't ask, he simply stood and held out a hand and her legs lifted her from the chair and her arms spread to accept him in a single, fluid movement.

He laid the back of his hand on her face. "Your cheeks look like an ice-skater's," he said approvingly. "But hot."

"They get that way in some circumstances," Peg said without thinking.

He turned his hand over and gently pressed his palm to her cheek. He asked, his voice low as if there were other dancing couples who might overhear them, "And what are those circumstances?"

She dropped her eyes. "When I've had too much to drink."

Most of the wine was on the floor or soaked into the tablecloth. Peg's glass on the table remained half-full. She was drunk all right, but it was ninety-proof Matthew Drum. He slowed his steps to half-time and settled Peg's head into the circle of his shoulder and arm. He smelled wonderful. They swayed there together, in a willow-tree embrace, until they weren't moving at all.

"Peg. Peggy."

She felt light all over except at her very center. There was a dense, aching heaviness there that was familiar, and foreign. It was like the shock of running across a picture of herself as a young girl; one she had never seen. She had felt this way before, long ago and many times, but half of the picture was missing, the Scotty half.

Peg was going to cry. Her throat and chest shivered with the effort of holding back from crying.

Suddenly her shoulders were being held. He held her by her shoulders, at arms length, and waited until she looked at him and waited a long moment after that, until she recognized who was holding her.

He said, "Would it help if I asked you to marry me? I am asking. Marry me, Peggy."

Sex was just another ritual. This she thought to herself, or had she spoken it aloud? The idea stirred the air on hummingbird wings, frantic and ghostly visible. Sex.

"It's probably like riding a bicycle," Peg muttered to her image in the mirror. "I'll remember once I start. Once *we* start."

One man she had had, her whole life. Peg shook her head in wonder. Goodness, how she wished Scotty were here to escort her through this haze of "slipping into something more comfortable" and climbing those stairs. Rather unlikely, of course. He'd hardly be taking her where she was going tonight.

Would it help if I asked you to marry me? Would it help.

Above her, she heard faint rustlings and the clump of something dropping to the floor. His shoe. Peg paused with her hand on the doorknob. Only the one?

CHAPTER EIGHTEEN

The call came as Sabina limbered up in her front hall, getting ready for a marathon bike ride. Her watch read just after 9:30 AM.

"Sabina? This is Mark Samuel."

Her heart raced. There was something too formal about him.

"I'm at Matthew Drum's house," the detective said. "It's happened again. I mean, Mr. Drum is dead, murdered."

She closed her eyes. The prayer went something like, *if I don't think it, he won't say it.*

"Now, Sabina. Your mother was with Drum last night—"

"No!" She slammed down the phone and shook her head like a dog out of water, hurling his words against the wall. She felt possessed by a single urgency: go to her. She's all right. She is all right.

Okay. Okay. Now, get your purse. But the car key wasn't in the purse. Where was it? *She's fine. She's in her house, or she's at church where she belongs.* A jacket was looped over the banister post. *This is a mistake.* Sabina's car key, in the pocket. It clattered to the floor. She picked it up, walked out the door. Forgot her purse. Turned back, walked a few steps, turned back again. *You don't need it. Hurry.*

The last thing Sabina said to her mother, in a mean spirit, was "Have a nice day." Not I love you. Not, you're my best friend in the whole world, I love you to absolute pieces. Not even, okay, Mom, go with Matthew, don't worry, have fun. *Have a nice day.*

It was the Fourth of July and she was on her knees alongside Johnny Rangel, looking into his wife's eyes and hearing her wailing lament that her last words to her husband were angry ones.

The Jeep groaned and slowed. She shifted to second. She had reached the steep part of the curving road that climbs to the Bluffs and winds past a par-three golf course and the Catholic cemetery. Her father's grave was in there. They bought twin plots under twin white pines. It was a beautiful spot. So what, is what Sabina always thought. Like her father would care. If he could, he'd rather have been buried somewhere along the seventh fairway, his favorite. Maybe in the bunker, where his buddies would be nervous about wedging up too much sand.

It hit her she would now be visiting both of them under those trees. She couldn't see to drive. She turned through the gates and onto the grass, let go the wheel and pressed the heels of both hands to her eyes, pushing in hard. When she took them away, the world was blurry and she was gazing on a mirage. She swabbed at her eyes in disbelief.

The key ground in the ignition: the engine was already running. She rammed the pedal to the floor and churned up chunks of sod.

She was not going crazy. There was her mother, sitting by Scott Lindsay's grave. On her little collapsible gardening stool, legs primly crossed at the ankles, wearing Sabina's brother's baseball cap and an old, wrinkled shirt with a big tear at the elbow. If this was a dream, Sabina thought, wouldn't she dress better?

Gravel scattered under the wheels. Sabina opened the jeep door, swung partway out and sat there, staring at her, her legs dangling.

"Sabina, there is absolutely *no* reason for your driving behavior." Peg was startled, which made her angrier. "I've tried not to criticize, but this is not a race track, young lady! There are dead people in here!" She broke off and started to rise from her stool, stiffly. "Sabina! Sweetheart! What's wrong?"

God knew what her face looked like, Sabina could only inventory the rest of her. She was Jell-O. "I thought you were dead," Sabina said simply.

"What?"

As Sabina eased out of the Jeep, sobs roiled backwards from her stomach and met with resistance somewhere midway. She was caught up in violent, teary hiccups, noisy exhale-sucks: Wah-*hig*! Wah-*hig*! Wah-*hig*!

"Baby!" Peg's arms were around her. She tried to take Sabina's head on her shoulder but that was ridiculous, Sabina would have to be on her knees, practically.

"I thought you were"—wah-*hig*!—"dead." Her mother's head tucked under her chin in that familiar spot and Sabina luxuriated for as long as she could in the wonderful, radiating warmth of her skull.

Peg pulled back. "Why in the world would you think that?"

Fatigue showed around her eyes but nothing more; no shock. She didn't know. How could Sabina tell her? She made a beginning.

"Mom."

Peg saw it in her daughter's face and leaped to the same conclusion Sabina had when Mark Samuel phone her. Except Peg's intuition was correct.

"It's Matthew?" She waited, helpless, for Sabina to deny it. "He's dead, isn't he?"

"Here, Mom, please." Sabina propped her against the car, ran for the gardening stool, carried it back and lowered her onto it. It was a little canvas job, a cheery yellow. She couldn't think what to say to her mother. It was another shock, a huge quake on top of the smaller ones that were transforming their little town the world had always ignored, and then visited with a vengeance. Peg had no questions, at any rate. Sabina crouched awkwardly in front of her and they held hands. Peg's were liver-spotted, her right index finger a little crooked. They were very cold, and her mother was as still as a slab of granite. Sabina knew when she was ready to go by a kind of internal rearranging, a return to life.

"Mom, where's your car?"

"My purse ..." Peg began, but it was too much for her. Her eyes closed, her face as immobile as before, but tears streaked her cheeks. Sabina helped her into the Jeep and they rode together in silence the half mile to the Bluffs.

Blue strobe lights whirled atop every other vehicle. Officials milled about on Matthew Drum's front lawn—Sabina recognized the Mayor and Police Chief conferring—and Peg Lindsay's neighbors gathered in tight little groups. A yellow POLICE-DO NOT CROSS tape cordoned off her mother's house as well as Matthew's.

As Sabina emerged from the jeep, Mark Samuel trotted towards her. Sabina and the detective were dressed identically in white T-shirts and black sweat pants. One difference: Samuel wore white plastic gloves, which he thoughtfully peeled off. Relief washed over his face when he recognized Peg Lindsay.

"I thought she was dead, " Sabina said, to explain hanging up on him.

"I figured. I'm really sorry, I only meant to tell you she was missing." He peered through the windshield at Peg, who made no move to leave the car.

"I thought we had a kidnapping or worse here," he explained. "Her purse was at Drum's place. Door unlocked. Phone off the hook." The passenger window was open a few inches and Peg could hear them perfectly, if she was hearing anything.

A middle-aged woman under five feet tall appeared at the detective's side. An insignia on her navy nylon jacket read RIVERVIEW ME. Pouchy dark skin rimmed her eyes.

"We done the bedroom, Detective. What else in the place do you need? I mean dustin' and suckin' both." She gestured over her shoulder to Drum's house, where another person in an identical jacket stood in the open doorway, a vacuum cleaner hose slung over his shoulder.

Samuel frowned at the ground, transferred it to Peg. He moved closer to the car and stooped to bring his mouth next to the crack in her window. "Mrs. Lindsay. I assume you were indeed in Mr. Drum's residence last evening?" No answer. "I need to know what rooms you were in." Granite again, Sabina thought. Her mother was probably still in shock, but Sabina read a familiar set to her mouth: *that is none of your concern, young man.*

"It's these first twenty-four hours that are so important, ma'am. I'm sure you want us to get this guy?" Her lips moved, minimally. Samuel turned away, still frowning, and told the technician to cease vacuuming, dust all exterior doors and call it quits. "The Poet's taken to wearing gloves, anyway," he added.

The technician turned to go and he stopped her with a hand on her shoulder. "You bagged his hands?" Samuel asked.

"Gee Mark," she snapped. "Whaddya think?" She clumped away.

"The Poet?" Sabina asked. "So there was another note? Who got the credit this time?"

"I guess I can tell you," he said, looking sour. "Enough

outsiders have seen the thing." He jingled some keys in a pocket. "This one was signed T.S. Eliot. The P.S. dedication was to John Wayne."

Sabina squinted, reading her memory bank of contemporary American killers. "He doesn't mean John Wayne the movie star."

A breeze picked up his lonely cowlick and Samuel flattened it with his hand. "I figured that out, thanks," he said, annoyed.

"I think I remember two John Waynes." Sabina rubbed the back of her neck, trying to dredge it up. "One of them is Gacy, John Wayne Gacy. The other one ... I can't remember the last name, but he was a contract killer, there was this movie about him, Soldiers of Fortune. Or Misfortune."

"No," the Detective said grimly. "It's Gacy he meant."

"How do you know?"

He pulled her a few steps farther away from the car. "Chloroform. That's how Gacy knocked out his boys, remember? A chloroform-soaked rag over their mouths. The Poet drops it in plain sight."

"Matthew was killed by chloroform?"

"No, no. A gun. But he did the chloroform first, we think. The autopsy'll tell us. Came at him from behind, it looks like."

Sabina heard a gasp and turned back to her mother, alarmed that she had overheard, but she stared past them, her hands covering her mouth.

They were carrying out the body. Behind it walked Kendall Drum, Rose Malwicki ... and Ella Martinelli, of all people. Sabina stepped to the right to block her mother's view but it was certainly too late; that snapshot would be forever etched. Matthew was mummified in black plastic—this vital man who had seemed to Sabina like a cross between a Hollywood idol and a four-star general, reduced to evidence in a bag. Her eyes filled. She wanted to ask Mark Samuel if Matthew suffered any, and made several false starts. He guessed what she was after.

"I don't think so," he said. "It was a clean shot to the head. Our Poet's getting to be quite the professional."

"Wait. That's not how Gacy did it," she reminded him. "After the chloroform, he bludgeoned his victims."

"Oh, Christ, I don't know." Samuel pressed his palms together and pushed, then pulled. "So he's not such a professional." A light blinked on in his eyes. "And maybe he knew Mrs. Lindsay was in the house, so he couldn't risk the noise."

"A gun makes no noise?"

"Silencer."

The guy comes ready to mimic John Wayne Gacy but has a gun as backup, *and* a silencer? *Something wrong there*, Sabina thought.

The jeep's door clicked open and Mrs. Magnuson, the neighbor across the street from Peg Lindsay, slipped into the Jeep and reached to hug Peg. The gesture was rejected but she planted herself anyway, patiently. Sabina knew Mrs. Magnuson. It was more likely she wanted to dig dirt than dispense comfort.

"Mark, I've got to help my mother inside."

He stepped into her path, ducking his head so she was looking at the top of his skull, a billiard ball with a goatee.

"Uh, Sabina." More jiggling of change in one pocket. "We need to take her to the station, get a statement. By all rights, I should give her a neuron activation test, too."

"A what?"

"Tells you if someone's fired a gun."

"You're joking." Alarmed, Sabina started past him. He blocked her again, his eyebrows drawn tight. It was easy to forget that this non-threatening cop had worked homicide in Baltimore before retiring to Riverview—for his children's sake, he said.

"Look, Sabina," he growled. "I been a cop over fifteen years now, how about you? You may know all there is to know about serial killers in history, but this is current events and I'm in charge."

"I'm sorry, Mark."

He did the push-pull routine with his hands again. "The reality is, Sabina, this case is a red ball." He jerked his head toward the knot of people on Drum's lawn. "Check it out. Everyone and his cousin with any place in the chain is demanding to stay informed. Mayor's panicked. Chief's paranoid. I can't afford any mistakes."

"Well, I appreciate that, Detective, but what do you think, my mother couldn't work out how to keep this handsome, rich CEO from her door? So she killed a bunch of other people for a cover and then him? I mean, come on."

The fierce scowl again. "How about this, then: You come along with her downtown and she gives us a full statement, and we think about what to do after that."

"How about this, then," Sabina parried. "You come in the house, use a tape recorder if you have to, and we agree not to get Mom's attorney over here."

And so it was settled. Something about Samuel's response made her uneasy, like she'd have been within her rights to just hole up and give her mother time to recover. Oh, well. There was much Sabina didn't know about homicide procedures, and much more she'd rather not know.

Peg Lindsay's had a distinctive smell; Sabina's blood pressure lowered just breathing. Ever the gracious hostess, Peg asked Detective Samuel if he'd like tea or coffee. He declined. Then she insisted on changing out of her gardening duds, which Sabina took as code for giving her time to pull herself together. When her foot hit the first step, she steadied herself with a hand against the wall. Grief had just tackled her again. Sabina started for her but Peg waved her off.

While Peg was upstairs, Mark Samuel filled Sabina in on the morning's events. Matthew had been scheduled to take a teleconference call at 8 AM, Sunday morning. When he didn't answer, the other party phoned Rose Malwicki. Rose drove over, let herself in and canvassed the downstairs, calling his name. She started upstairs but told Samuel it made her uneasy.

"'Something was amiss,' was the way she put it to me," Samuel said. "She also didn't want to snoop around anymore without permission, so she called his son."

Rose followed her instincts and tracked down Kendall at Ella Martinelli's apartment. Ella went along with Kendall to his father's house and they found him on his bedroom floor, naked, a few steps from his bed. They also found the note.

"Kendall mangles the thing," Samuel said, rolling his eyes. "Folds it three or four times, puts his prints all over it."

"Hey, Mark." Sabina was inspired by the memory of the rude voice from Washington DC—what's-his-name, Webster—who thought the Poet and some porn pervert on the Internet were one and the same. "This note. Did it mix up upper-case and lower-case letters? In the middle of a word, sometimes?"

He said, "No." Simply no, but slowly, suspiciously. She had her answer.

"Ah," she said. "But one of them did, right? Julie Oleson's. Had to be, because I saw the note from Johnny Rangel's murder and it was dark, but—"

"Tell me how you knew that."

"Well, sure; I meant to," Sabina said, to no great reception. Samuel's expression suggested maybe she was the one who needed the lawyer.

"To tell you the truth, Mark, I dismissed the guy. It's not as if I was withholding information."

"What guy?"

"Okay. There's been this cybercreep writing porn messages and rhymes in Internet newsgroups and using capital letters in the middle of words. His address is frat-something. It's a fake one, of course, but a guy called me from Washington. When you released the whole note from the firecracker murder, and it said 'apologize to the fraternity'? Well, this Washington guy put it together; he thinks it's the same fellow and he told me about the typeface style."

A quiet tap-tap sounded on Peg's front door and it opened, followed by footsteps. A man in a baseball cap stuck his head around the corner.

"We found something," he told Samuel, while looking pointedly at Sabina.

Samuel waved his hand. "She knows more than we do, anyway, Pete; go ahead."

He chewed, his cheek bulging like a ballplayer's, and looked at her some more. "It's another note," he said.

"What?" Mark and Sabina tied with the word.

Pete brought the rest of his body into the room and delivered a large plastic baggy to Samuel. Inside was a single sheet with multiple creases, opened flat.

"Where did you find it?" Samuel asked.

"The victim's briefcase."

Mark scanned it through the plastic. Before he could finish reading, Pete blurted out, "So old Dan Washington told the truth for a change."

It dawned on Sabina, high speed. "The first murder, you mean? Claire Washington? The Poet killed her, too?"

Pete withered under Samuel's calm, prolonged gaze. "Nice job, Pete," he said. "Now we all appreciate how smart you are."

Pete slunk away. The Detective explained they like to withhold certain information from the public, so that a suspect's disclosures could be verified as first-hand knowledge.

"You might try asking me to keep it confidential," she protested. "I have been known to keep a secret." That sounded a trifle haughty. Sabina was over-compensating for not having gone to Samuel with the Internet tip.

"I accept that, Sabina. It's just that I'm losing control here. Like the others on the scene today—they'll be yakkin' all over town." He had to mean Ella Martinelli. Rose Malwicki wouldn't let a microchip between her lips. Kendall ... Sabina didn't think so.

She plopped down beside Mark on the couch and read over his shoulder as he went over it again. This first murder note was a long one. A salutation to Matthew Drum, a P.S. to "Ted," and no signature. In between Drum's name and the P.S. was a multiple-stanza, neatly-typed poem, using the upper-lower case style the Webster fellow had described. A handwritten scrawl across the bottom said, in all caps, APOLOGIZE. And in tiny writing, the Poet told him how. He demanded his poem be run on the front page of the Riverview *Times*, over the fold. He drew an arrow to the back of the page. Samuel flipped it over. It read: "That lady in the Flats, that was me. Rest assured I mean business."

Samuel summarized the situation, cynicism icing every word. "This means that Drum knew what he had to do to stop the killing. He withheld information to get himself a real good story. To goad the creep into killing again."

She couldn't disagree. Under the circumstances, she couldn't muster the will to defend the slain CEO.

"Mark. Listen, the Poet has to know, from all the press on this, that you guys never got this note. Right? So if he really was willing to stop killing if we met his condition, printed this poem, why didn't he repeat that in one of the other notes?"

His face went blank, thinking it over. "Can't say," he acknowledged. "Maybe he didn't want to stop. Like you've been claiming." He pushed lower in the couch, staring at the note. "Talk about alter egos," he muttered.

The P.S. read, "this one's for Ted." Samuel stuck his thumb next to it and looked at Sabina, inquiringly.

She sucked in her cheeks, thinking. "Oh. Probably ... let's see. The Poet seems to like the real famous—"

"Ted Bundy," Mark interrupted, snapping his fingers. "Sorority girl basher."

"Congratulations." Her head ached. She massaged her temples while re-reading the Poet of Pain's manifesto.

> For the powerLESS to be powerFULL
> We deliver our Word through a gun barRELL
> or knife, bare hands, club and good THINKing
> to show Society the ways it is SINKing.
>
> Whitman, Chapman, Sirhan and Speck.
> These are the MEN who lead us!
> Berkowitz, DeSalvo, Bianchi and Buono.
> Down the path of JUSTice!
>
> Oswald, Ferri, Gilmore and Bundy.
> They live and walk aMONG us!
> Manson, Bremer and J.W. Booth
> and GOD, who killed his SON for us!
>
> We're the Poets of PAIN riding quiet and low
> But the LIARS are louder and in conTROL.
> The FRATERNITY will act as the final WORD.
> We'll speak and speak unTIL we're HEARD.

Sabina read the last stanza aloud, in the whispery sing-song voice it seemed to demand. There they all were, his beloved heroes and fellow fraternity members. His post-script awardees.

"I don't think I was really afraid before," she said. "Not to mention nearly losing my own mother."

The reminder of her mother's part in all this restored the detective to his original objective. "She's been over ten minutes, freshening up," he said. "You think you'd better check on her?"

Sabina nearly ran into Peg in the doorway. She wore a cast-off orange sweater of Sabina's, a long denim skirt and bedroom slippers. She settled into the flowered wing-back chair opposite Samuel and seemed calm enough, but as Sabina watched her answering his questions, she picked up on the pinch of her mouth, the way she pressed her knees together. Her mother was too self-aware. To an unbiased outsider, she might even look guilty. Of something.

It became obvious that Peg had decided she knew best what the police needed to know and what they could do without. She was conducting herself like royalty. It was almost funny. "Yes, I was Mr. Drum's guest for dinner at his residence," she said, with a stiff nod.

Sabina began to fill in an answer for her, to foster the impression of cooperation.

"Butt out," Mark said.

It came to a head when he asked Peg, "When did you last see Mr. Drum?"

She answered promptly. "Around nine p.m. He walked me to my door."

She was lying through her teeth. Everything about her was foreign. Samuel's pen rat-a-tat-tatted on the cover of his steno-style notepad.

"That's a pretty early evening, ma'am," he commented.

"Yes." A pair of eyes in a dense thicket of quills. That's all she said: yes. Sabina couldn't help being proud of her. She had a way of rising to the occasion. She'd fall apart later.

"We found your purse on a kitchen counter," Samuel said.

Peg nodded. "Yes. Thank you."

"Why would you—" the detective began, and was interrupted by Pete returning. A few sharp footfalls and he filled the doorway. Something flowery was bunched up in his right hand and in his left, he held a scrap of bloody-looking toilet tissue between the thumb and index finger.

"You won't believe this," he said excitedly, and then noticed Peg. He nodded to her, "Hey, Mrs. Lindsay."

Her face was changing; she looked sick.

"We got another note, in a manner of speaking." Pete flapped it at us, a flimsy square flag. "Written on toilet paper with lipstick here. See? 'I *can't*,' is all it says."

Peg put a shaky hand to her forehead and shrank a few inches. Sabina crossed to her side, knelt down and rested a hand on her mother's shoulder. "Mom? You okay?"

"Where'd you find this one?" Samuel asked Pete.

Peg answered for him. "I can save you the drama, young man." She faced Detective Samuel. "It's my note. I left it in Mr. Drum's first-floor powder room. And the other object is mine as well. My make-up case."

Yes and no. Sabina recognized that particular violet-and-rose bag as the one her mother took along on trips that required overnight stays.

Peg Lindsay's embarrassment was so pronounced it infected Pete, who shuffled from foot to foot and then left as suddenly as he'd come.

Peg's eyes were closed. She sagged into a corner of the chair.

"Mrs. Lindsay," Samuel said, kindly. "We could have saved you this if you'd just told me what it was you were hiding. I sure knew you were no killer."

"And just what is it you now assume I am, Detective?" she asked him, opening her eyes.

He reached the end of his rope with this particular witness. "Oh, for ... now don't you freeze up on me again, ma'am. I'm doing my job here, and you got a job, too, as a witness in a murder investigation." He let that sink in. "I'm

within my rights to ask were you in the victim's bedroom."
He added, a little more gently, "I really gotta know that."

"No."

He cocked his head at her, suspicious. "'No' you won't
tell me, or 'No'—"

"No, I was not in that room." Her face was open, vulnerable and full of sorrow. This was the truth.

"Did you see anything, hear anything funny?"

Peg grabbed for Sabina's hand but met the detective's eyes
squarely. "I heard something ... clump. Overhead, on the floor."
Her eyes shut again. "I came home right after that. It was
eleven, maybe a minute after."

And maybe seconds in front of the killer, Sabina thought.
Oh, thank you, God.

"Okay," Samuel said. He tucked the bagged Poet letter
into his notepad and got to his feet. "That'll do for now."

Peg's hands floated to a prayer lock under her chin and
she looked up at him. "May I know something?" she asked.
Her entire face quivered. Sabina put an arm around her.

"How did Matthew ..." She couldn't say it.

He showed his experience at delivering this kind of news
in an attitude that was clinical and compassionate, all at
once. "A gun, ma'am. A through-and-through to the head.
I've seen these before, central nervous system, he would have
died right off."

Peg lifted her chin up and down, barely in control. Samuel
withdrew as far as the foyer, then turned around, thoughtfully.

"There's one other thing you could help me with, Mrs.
Lindsay. Were you with Mr. Drum when he let himself into
the house? Because Mrs. Malwicki says a key was right there
in the front door. It doesn't make sense that the Poet had
one, and we can't figure—"

His words were cut off by a keening cry. Sabina had never

heard anything like it from her mother, not even when they buried her father.

"I did that!" she wailed. "He—he—he gave me a key to—to—wait for him and I—I—I— "

"Oh, Mom! Don't!" Sabina enclosed her in her arms and held on tightly.

"Oh, Gawd," Detective Samuel said. The door closed firmly behind him.

Peg told her daughter to go home. Sabina stayed. She told Sabina she couldn't eat a thing. Sabina made her tea and toast with honey. The phone rang and Peg started for it. Sabina unplugged it. Peg was certain she couldn't sleep so Sabina walked her upstairs, covered her with the crocheted daisy afghan and sat beside her while Peg protested she was fine. Just before she dropped off, she took Sabina's hand and said, "I love you, baby."

Sabina was there when Peg woke up. This time, Sabina recognized the woman who said, go home. This time she really did want and need to be alone.

When Sabina dragged into her house mid-afternoon, she couldn't believe the sun was still high in the sky. It felt like midnight. She showered until the hot water heater would pump no more, dressed, and settled onto the deep window seat in her living room with the portable phone. She needed to talk to somebody she could trust, and that would be Sonny Ashendorf. She wanted help working out her conflicted feelings about losing her first client and potential stepfather in a single shot.

A phone rang in the neighbor's house, an electronic chirp-chirp that didn't sound quite right until she realized there was nothing electronic about it. A baby something was perched on the lowest branch of the sugar maple alongside Sabina's front porch—a swollen squat little thing the color of bark that could pass for a tumor in the wood. Its beak stretched wide and skyward and groped the air in the rhythmic, plaintive chirp-chirp that Sabina was picking up through the open window. It seemed a long time the fuzzy lump had to wait; long enough so she started to worry it had been orphaned. A streak of red flashed through the green and a cardinal came home. So the ugly bark tumor was a Baby Cardinal. Amazing. Papa shoved gray-white grubs down baby's throat. Pretty soon Mama Cardinal glided in with her subtle moss green feathers. She flew away and still the plaintive chirp-chirp from the lump. How many grubs could it eat at one sitting?

Just as Sabina was recalling why the phone was in her lap, it rang. This had happened before with Sonny. One would be thinking she'd really like to talk to the other one, and the phone would ring.

Sabina said hello with anticipation. She could sense it was Sonny.

"Well. You sound some better than I figured you would."

"Detective Samuel?"

"You were calling me Mark before."

"I thought it was a friend of mine calling."

"Okay by me, as long as you understand I'm married."

"You know that's not what I meant."

"I know that's not what you meant," he parroted, agreeably.

It would be easy to be his friend, such an easy-going humor. Then she'd have four friends, if she could count Tootie and her mother. Not quite enough for a party, but a start.

"Sabina, we left one piece unfinished. You told me about some guy in Washington, the one who thinks he can connect our Poet of Pain with the Internet snooper? I wanna talk to him."

A dilemma. What's-his-name Webster had said clearly he wouldn't talk to the cops. How should she handle it?

"He won't talk to the cops. That's what he told me, anyway. And you know what, I remember his last name, Webster, but not his first." In an inexplicable impulse of loyalty to the stranger in D.C., she didn't tell Samuel that she had saved the answering machine cassette and could retrieve his name and number.

"Is the guy black?" he asked.

"Huh?"

"Black. African-American."

"I don't know. He could be, I guess. What in the world would make you ask that?"

"There's a long tradition of blacks volunteering nothing to police. They've got their reasons, but it doesn't matter if we can't trace him anyway."

"Suppose he calls me again?" A little disingenuous, since she intended to phone Webster.

"Then get his name, tell him he's got an obligation to help us."

"You didn't talk to this guy. I got the impression he doesn't care about being a good citizen."

"Why'd he call you to start with?"

He had a point.

"Just a minute, Sabina." Samuel covered the phone while he talked to someone else, then came back on to tell her he had to go. "I'm the dartboard for the day around here. Call me if you've got something."

"Mark, just a minute. Could you fax me a copy of that first letter of the Poet's, to Drum? The one with the poem? All the research I've done into his 'fraternity,' maybe I'll get an idea."

He thought it over. "Couldn't hurt, I guess," he said. "God knows I could use some help. Promise me you won't show it to anyone."

That was easy, technically. Half a minute later, the letter cranked out of Sabina's fax machine and a few minutes after that she was reading it to Andrew Webster.

"What did you nickname the guy again?" Sabina asked him.

"Shakespeer," Webster said, absentmindedly.

"Does this sound like him?"

"Yeah."

"He's no dummy, is he?"

"Smart means shit in life," Webster said.

Oh, boy, she thought. Here we go again. She plowed ahead, anyway. "There's a detective here, a pretty decent guy, I think. His name is—"

"Forget it, babe. I told you."

"And I told you, cut the babe crap."

He laughed. "So how'd you get ahold of the poem?"

She told him about Drum's murder. It was hot news, not even on the national circuit yet, but Andrew Webster barely reacted.

"You don't seem surprised."

"People gettin' popped every day," he said, bitterly. "This one counts, is all. Great white publisher."

Sabina had nothing to lose, dealing with the Master of Rude, so she just up and asked him. "Are you black?"

This seemed to genuinely amuse Webster; his laugh lost its bite. "Yo babe, I is, 'jus black wit some cream messin' it up. How dat, you hear it now?"

The change was remarkable. Two different people.

"Dude's ass be black," he went on, changed suddenly; angry. "You forgot to ax, where dat black ass at? I be tellin' you, dat ass ridin' a wheelchair."

He hung there until she had to fill the silence. "I can't think what to say. Except I'm sorry. That's probably the last thing you want to hear."

"You'd be correct, girl."

The ice had broken a little and they had something resembling a conversation. Webster took a "drive-by bullet" in the back while he was carrying a bag of groceries to his mother's apartment. (Sabina couldn't summon the gall to ask if the shot were intended for him. A freak accident, she supposed, would be even harder to live with.) He had always had a way in the kitchen so he opened Handy Andy's catering service—Handy a black-humor play on handicapped—and it started to catch on as a noontime and business-meeting service to respectable businesses in respectable neighborhoods. After training himself to 'talk white' by mimicking the news anchors on television, sales picked up considerably.

"They never see me, just our menus on their computers every morning. Now I got too much business."

"So expand."

"Tell it to the banks," he snarled. "Who don't make loans to vets of the wrong color."

Consulting advice was not what Andrew Webster needed. He just needed someone to hurt and it wasn't going to be her. She told him she had to go.

"Just a sec," he said. Squeaking came over the line again and now Sabina knew the source: his wheelchair. "Why don't you gimme the name of that cop and his number? Don't mean I'm gonna use it, just to have it."

She gave it to him.

"I did what I said I would," Webster added. "Floated three messages on the Net, where I think Shakespeer hangs. Sounds like he been a busy boy, though. Maybe no bites."

"If you get one, you'll call Mark Samuel, right? Because I think the legal thing for me to do here is to give him your name."

Webster's voice went nasal and high: "I think the legal thing to do here," he mocked. "I thought you bought into my condition, babe. I'll tell you straight, if they call *me*, I ain't talkin' and I won't start up with them, neither. So you tell your fuzz-buddy from me, he wants cooperation, he waits for me to call him. Or I'll check in with you."

Oh joy. She and her phone pal were building a future.

CHAPTER NINETEEN

Sabina knew she had toiled too long in the corporate world when she conjured up a pie graph as a metaphor for Matthew Drum's death: one slice devoted to grieving, the rest for deciphering and distributing the CEO's complex litter of holdings.

It didn't help that he had been cutting two secret deals and trying to hide them from the elusive computer hacker who had twice struck the *Times*.

A small cadre of Boston-DEI folk was working with the New York law firm of Brakken & Farley on Langley-Spritz's purchase offer for DEI. No computer link existed between Riverview and Boston on these negotiations, though Rose Malwicki knew about the talks. Conversely, until the computer break-in on the day of Drum's murder, Rose was the only inside person privy to a separate sale of the *Times* being arranged by Matthew to a mystery group known as MOSS. After the first break-in flashed a dummy reorganization chart around the building, she prepared all MOSS sale documents off the network. Rose told Sabina, with a flicker of distress, that she had failed to excise two early memos-to-file on MOSS. It was one of these the hacker had discovered and routed, again, to computers throughout the organization.

Kendall Drum was more in the dark than anyone.

He certainly had cause to feel overwhelmed. First, he had to find out with everyone else—via the filched computer file—that his father was selling the paper to this MOSS group. The next morning he found his father murdered. He endured three hours of police questioning that same day, and from the cops (who listened to Drum's answering machine and talked to his attorney), he also had to learn that his father was close to selling all of Drum Enterprises, Inc., to Langley-Spritz.

It was a little harder for Sabina to accept that Kendall was equally ambushed by the fact of his own inheritance. But unless it was acting worthy of an Oscar, no other conclusion was possible.

He called her Monday afternoon, stuttering between embarrassment and panic.

"This lawyer just called me, what time was it, just a half hour ago. I never heard of the guy, his name, wh-what was his name—"

"It doesn't matter, Kendall." She tried for soothing but it came out patronizing. "Concentrate on one thing at a time. Tell me what he said."

"He said Dad left it all to me!"

One of Sonny Ashendorf's more memorable homemade aphorisms went something like: that's hardly a sack of snake shit. Where was the snake shit here? Considering DEI's worth, it looked like a nine-hundred-million-dollar problem. If Kendall didn't know what to do with it, he certainly would have the funds to hire someone who did.

"You didn't expect that?" Sabina asked. "You're his only child, aren't you?"

"But he thought I was a fuck-up!" he said. "His words. Why would he leave it to me?"

What a lot of displaced emotion she was hearing, but what and why? It occurred to Sabina that this boy-man might just be scared to death of everything. It also occurred to her that maybe Matthew Drum did not, indeed, mean to leave it all to Kendall. More likely it was by default. He expected to live at least to a reasonable age, so he was getting by with a boiler-plate will.

"Kendall, is that what you want me to help you with? The will?"

"No, no, sorry. This lawyer ..." He took a deep breath and continued more calmly. "He said he's the administrator of Dad's estate. He's telling me we have to sell to this Langley-Spritz right away because the value of the whole deal is sinking fast. Because there's no ... my father ..." This time it wasn't a reined-in stutter; Kendall simply couldn't apply the word dead to his larger-than-life absentee father.

"Sabina, I don't know what to do. The attorney wants to go over it all tomorrow morning and he's the only attorney I know; the ones that Pops, my grandfather, would recommend ... well, they'd either be dead or maybe not too straight up. I don't want to ask Wiley and Ed Fountain is holding this whole place together ... would you come in, sit in on the call? Didn't you sell your own business, that bike company?"

"Pretty minor league, compared to this, Kendall." He blew out air; no arguing her into it, just a wasted exhale. "But okay, sure. Why not?"

Matthew's lawyer's name was Duncan Farley, senior partner and co-founder of the Boston law firm Brakken & Farley. Farley explained it was his job as estate administrator to maintain the value of all assets and so it was his duty to warn Kendall, the heir, of the quick depreciation that DEI would undergo as time went on without anyone competent at the helm. He said it just that way. Kendall didn't twitch, simply closed his eyes and tee-peed his fingers against his lips. His skin was chalky, puffy. His usually shiny flop of hair looked dull.

"So if Kendall okays the sale to this Langley-Spritz, can you just do it?" Sabina asked Duncan Farley.

Not so easy. Kendall was sole inheritor in the will but until the court declared that the assets had passed to him legally, they would be frozen for the year or longer it took to probate the estate. Unless, Farley said, dangling the word out dramatically. Unless the heir gave consent to sell an asset and the court gave permission.

"In Wisconsin," Farley said, "that's a circuit court judge, probate branch. I've got the name. We'd need to request an immediate hearing."

Sabina gave Kendall a moment to respond but when he didn't, she said to Farley, "Let's assume you go ahead and do that. Right Kendall?" He nodded. "He agrees," she told Farley.

"Then we've got another problem," Farley said. "Something I didn't know when we talked yesterday, Kendall." He waited, to no avail, and went on. "They're re-thinking the price. That's an exact quote. They smell blood, of course."

Sabina had been tracking the publishing industry since taking the *Times* job and a synapse connected. "Couldn't you tell them if they stand behind the original offer, we'll agree not to open up the sale to other bidders? There was that Texas chain not so long ago, where Gannett and Fox were out-bid by fifty-five million dollars, remember? The point being once it goes to auction you never can tell."

"That's a risk," Farley said. "It could go the other way on us, they could come back with a lower offer."

A risk. Wasn't that just like a lawyer. Sabina asked Kendall what he thought of the strategy. He nodded and she translated for Farley. "Try it. Kendall agrees."

There was silence. Farley said, suspiciously, "Is he still there?"

"Yes, Mr. Farley," Kendall put in with sudden dignity, perhaps trying on the mantle, however brief, of CEO of Drum Enterprises. "You are authorized to proceed."

Silence again. Then Farley said: "Thank you, Mr. Drum." And ended the call. Sabina couldn't decide if his words cloaked sarcasm or sorrow.

"Kendall, what about you? What do you want? This lawyer works for you now, you know. He can help you try to get whatever you want."

"All I want is to get rid of everything. I don't know how Dad stood it, owning all that."

Made sense to her, and it seemed in keeping with Kendall's nature.

"But what will become of you?" she asked again. "What will you do?"

He stared.

He hadn't gotten to that point yet?

She smiled at him gently. "You could buy any business you want, you know. You'll certainly have the money."

"I could buy this paper back," he said slowly, in a low-boil enthusiasm. He blinked once and it subsided. "Oh, but that'd be a long time off, what'd the lawyer say, a year or so before the estate is clear."

What a cherub. "Um, Kendall. If I could suggest, it would be hard to find a bank that wouldn't loan you whatever you need, on your collateral. Criminy, they'd fall all over themselves to get to you."

That reminded Sabina of the mystery MOSS suitors for the paper and she asked him what Duncan Farley had had to say about them, about how to treat that piece of business in light of the bigger sale of DEI.

"I didn't tell him," Kendall said. He picked up a pen and doodled on the desk blotter. "I wanted to wait to talk to your mother." His eyes lifted to the wall clock. "She's coming in an hour."

"What has my mother to do with this?"

He lifted his pen mid-doodle. "What do you mean? She's MOSS."

Sabina could only return the same wide-eyed blank look. Kendall told her that MOSS was Peg Lindsay and some other deep pockets in town who had been working with Matthew Drum to buy the Riverview *Times* from DEI for nine million dollars.

So that's why Matthew Drum was courting her mother, she thought. She didn't like it, but it explained a lot.

That evening, Peg Lindsay called to ask if Sabina would join her on the screen porch for a lemonade and a story. She said the story was about a group of senior citizens in Riverview who almost became owners of the local newspaper. "There isn't much to tell," Peg said, "but Kendall wants you up to speed because you're helping him through all this, bless you, baby. So come on over whenever you've a mind to, I'm squeezing the lemons now."

When Sabina arrived four minutes later, Peg was still squeezing. She pointed to a jacketed folder on the kitchen table and told Sabina to sit and read and she'd understand. It was the offer of purchase from MOSS for the *Times*, complete but for signatures, and included the proviso for Kendall to have a shot at the top job, and at owning the paper.

Her mother was right about there not being much else to say. With Matthew dead, and the paper part of the whole estate entanglement, and Kendall Drum provided for in much grander scale than Matthew's attempt via MOSS ... there wasn't any point in going ahead.

Sabina talked her into spiking both lemonades with a little rum. When Peg turned to do it, robot-like, it hit Sabina that her mother was the single slice of grieving in Matthew Drum's pie. However unworthy his motivations may have been, Peg was missing him.

"So why did you have a meeting with Kendall?" Sabina asked as they settled in the cool cloak of dark and sipped at their rum-lemonades.

"I wanted him to understand that Matthew really did care for him, in his way. He was trying to make Kendall secure here."

"Did he accept that?"

She was in the hammock. She didn't answer right away but pushed off with one foot. It made a rusty noise as it rocked. Cicadas thrummed in the forested bluffs below the porch, where Sabina spent summers building forts with her brothers. She heard kids pitching stones into the Mississippi and laughing high and wild. She heard her mother crying.

"Mom? Mom, what's wrong?"

"Kendall cried," she said, choking. "When I told him what his father was trying to do for him."

Well, well. So he had been in the dark about that, too.

She let her mother be; why shouldn't she cry if she needed to? They listened to the night and after a long while, Peg's sniffles turned to snores.

Sabina bent over the hammock and poked her. "You look awful."

"Thank you, dear."

"I mean, why don't you get some sleep?"

"I believe I was."

"In bed. It's getting cold out here."

Peg trudged into the house, obedient as a played-out third-grader. Sabina hugged her goodnight at the front door.

"So Mom? What does MOSS mean, anyway? Or is that another secret?"

Peg tipped her face up. "No secret. It's an acronym." There was enough life left in the woman to leak out around a satisfied smile. "Mother of Sabina Shaw."

CHAPTER TWENTY

Toot and Sabina swayed lazily on her porch swing, using their bare toes to march the pegs around an over-sized cribbage board at their feet. It was long after dinner, ninety-seven degrees and holding, still so humid that each breath was a face plunge into a hot wet towel.

"Ooh, what's that stink?" he asked, scrunching up his nose.

"In your dreams, kid. There's no skunk in sight here, we're on First Street for heaven's sake."

"Fifteen for two," Toot said, knocking her foot out of his way. "Eat my dust, woman." He picked that up from Jacob. Sabina felt no twinge, hearing it again.

They looked up at the sound of a horn down the street. It had to be a heat-inspired mirage: a cool blue convertible cruised sedately down Melody Lane. As it drew closer, Sabina recognized Mark Samuel behind the wheel, tootling his fingers at her. She thought it an unlikely car for the rumpled, steady cop-father. Tootie was off the porch in a heartbeat, cards scattered every which way.

Mark eased to a stop and flattened his cowlick with one slap of his palm. The setting sun cut through a gap in the neighbors' row of arbor vitae and shone full on his smile of cocky pride.

"Like it, kid?" he asked.

Toot thrust both hands into the back pockets of his fall-down pants, thumbs hanging out, and deliberated. "Pretty nice." His thumbs twitched. "Corvette?"

Samuel nodded. "'Fifty-six."

Toot knocked his toe against a tire. "Work on it yourself?"

"Yep. Want a ride?"

"Wow! Yeah!" Tootie body-rolled over the side and settled in, spreading his fingers wide over white leather seats.

Mark gave Sabina a wink and they were off. Halfway down the block, had to be at Tootie's request, the car surged from a staid twenty MPH to god knows what.

A few games of solitaire later, headlamps swung into Tootie's driveway. Their two heads were close together, consulting about something on the dashboard. Sabina heard Toot, in a stage whisper: "Awesome!" It was easy to read his mind. The last thing he wanted was for his father Karl to hear them and stumble down the steps.

Something was not quite right at the Jergensen's house. Sabina stared until it hit her, with a delicious kick, that in the war of Sabina Shaw vs. Karl the Jerk, she had won a battle. No silhouette hulk of rusting Buick remained in their yard. She was so accustomed to its sentient presence she almost felt badly about it, like an ancient beast had been slain and dragged off by its predators. All that remained was a dead-grass sink hole and the faint depression of tow-truck tires on the lawn.

A car door clicked shut and Mark Samuel backed his work of art out of Jergensen's driveway and into hers. Tootie waved goodbye and disappeared on the far side of his house to hoist himself in through his bedroom window.

"How about a beer?" Sabina offered as Mark climbed the steps.

"Why not," he said with a careless flip of the hand. The convertible had roused the devil in him. He tested his weight

on the porch railing and settled there, leaning against a wooden
upright and facing in the direction of his car. He didn't trust
her neighborhood; it looked like he'd be on theft watch
while they talked.

Sabina grabbed two St. Pauli Girls from the fridge and
returned to the porch, pressing the moist glass to her forehead.

"So this is a social call, huh, Detective?"

"Not quite," he said, his eyes glancing off her halter top
and cutoffs and returning safely to Corvette sentry duty. "I
mean, I'm off duty but I'm on the job. If you follow."

"Say again?"

Samuel tipped back his head and finished half the beer,
neatly. "I need to talk about the case and there's nobody I
wanna do that with at the station. Who can help me, I
mean." He screwed up his face, considering how that sounded.
"It's a small department, homicide."

"Yes," she agreed. "You're it."

"Unless you count the Chief."

"Like I said."

She stepped over the spilled cards and got comfortable on
the porch swing. "Why me?"

"That MTV show," he said, with a slight mocking smile.
"Another worshipper at the feet of the research guru."

Samuel hadn't invented that, so she had to bear it. Sabina
had been one of many interviewed on-camera for a program
called "Why They Kill: Riverview's Serial Nightmare." The
voice-over introduction hung the Research Guru title on her,
though she had asked them for Management Consultant.
Mainstream respect wasn't in MTV's mission statement and
maybe they didn't have time. Her sound bite lasted exactly
twenty-three seconds.

"You've heard of the prepared mind theory?" Mark asked.

"Sure. When facts merge with instinct and you get something original. It works in research and strategic planning, too.

I take it you mean if you and I rehearse what we know about the Poet, you might get some flash of who he is. Like that?"

"Well, let's pretend," Mark said. "Speculate. Let's speculate that Matthew Drum maybe wasn't murdered by the Poet."

"What?"

He propped an elbow on one fist and tapped his thumb against a front tooth. Detective speculation pose. "Or that he was, but the Poet's not so zoned after all; maybe he was after Drum from the beginning and Julie Oleson and Claire Washington and Johnny Rangel were just diversions."

"But why? If he wanted Drum from the beginning, why not just kill him, and just him? How does being the Poet help him, as a cover?"

"It gets us concentrating on someone foreign, that's how. See? Some unknown psychopath."

"How does this killer know that Matthew's going to take up the gauntlet by pocketing that first letter? How does he know he and Drum are going to fall into this ... gruesome contest ... to begin with?"

He tucked his chin into his chest, thinking. "Like this, maybe. If I'm right, if the Poet knows Drum he knows he'd never roll over and do what the killer wants, especially publicly. And remember the demand in that first note, the one Drum hid from us? It said to run the poem above the fold. How many people would use that phrase? I say Drum's killer is in the business."

"Okay," Sabina said. "I'm hooked." She grabbed a pillow from the end of the swing and sailed it to him. "Here. You look uncomfortable." He threw it on the porch floor and flopped down, hands crossed behind his head. He had a view of her dead spider plant and the right rear fender of his baby.

Sabina started it off. "Frank Wiley, candidate number one: He and Drum had a huge fight a few weeks back, in front of Fountain and me. Matthew was going to force Wiley into early retirement."

"What for?"

"I think, part general incompetence and part Drum just couldn't stand him. But Wiley has a physical alibi; he's been on vacation since last Thursday, right after—"

"Nope," Mark said. "Vacation from the paper, yes, but he never left town. I saw him dash in and out of the PDQ myself, early Saturday." Mark rolled to his side and propped his head on one hand, looking up at her. "Funny thing, too. He looked like he didn't want to be seen. Had an old hat pulled down low, sunglasses."

She could not feature tight-assed, loose-lipped Frank Wiley wielding anything stronger than a pink slip. "He was hiding, all right, but not because he's the Poet. He was scared silly the Poet would get him next."

Sabina ran a fingernail up the wet St. Pauli girl label and split her in ragged halves. "You want another beer?"

"I need to make room for it."

She showed him to the bathroom, herding him through her disastrous living room. She snagged two more bottles and a hunk of cheddar and waited for him outside, gnawing on the cheese. The drapes were closed at Toot's house: unusual. She listened for Karl's bellow, but all was quiet.

This prepared-mind game was beginning to give Sabina the creeps. When Mark reappeared, she said, "Your turn."

"Okay." He eased himself back down to prone position. "How about Ed Fountain?"

Now she truly didn't want to play. "That's ridiculous."

"The word at the paper is that Ed was beginning to think that Drum had his own little game going with this publicity standoff. That's why he marched out of the press conference, they say."

Sabina began pacing, stepping over Mark's body and reaching the end of the porch in five barefoot strides. "Ed Fountain is not a murderer. Period. Not of one person and certainly not four. No."

Mark stared at the porch ceiling, his foot jiggling. "How do you read Ella Martinelli?"

She bit back her first response, a catty one, and tried for objectivity. "Not Matthew Drum's most favorite staff member—they had a little to-do at one of our meetings—but hardly a murderer." She stepped over him, heading to the other end of the porch.

"No more or less than Fountain or Wiley, anyway."

"What do you mean?" she asked, intrigued.

"Would you land somewhere, please?"

Sabina took his old spot on the porch railing and looked down at him.

"She's hiding something," Samuel said. Uncomfortable with her towering over him, he threw the pillow against the house, fluffed it up, then did a double-take and laid his palm against the wood siding.

"Is this place ... pink?"

She sighed. "Salmon."

He whacked the pillow again. "Ella hasn't been what I'd call generous with information. She talked like she was telling me everything. How she didn't like Drum; how she did like his boy, Kendall; that they had started going out. But she's holding back and it doesn't take a genius. Kendall is an only child and his daddy's rich. Daddy dies, Kendall inherits, Ella marries Kendall."

"But she has a good-paying job," Sabina said, inanely. A salary versus a fortune?

"And two kids," Samuel countered. "And an empty box on Matthew Drum's reorganization charter, so Frank Wiley tells me."

"I didn't know that."

Samuel pushed his fingers through the hair over his ears and frowned. "The Ella I know lets it all out, chatty and cozy and just ... Ella. It's bad enough she talked up the details of our physical case, spread the murder scene stuff all over the paper. Then she holds something back." He shook his head sorrowfully, disappointed with his Ella. "But she's like a snappy poodle with no bite, just likes to parade. She didn't do the murder. So what's she hiding? Who's she protecting?"

He answered his own question. "Kendall, obviously. If the paper gets sold, there goes his future. Maybe their future, because papa Drum isn't going to die of natural causes for a long time."

Ah, Sabina thought. Now he came to it. This is what Mark Samuel wanted to talk about from the beginning. To hell with Wiley and Fountain and Martinelli. "You think Kendall would kill his own father?"

"I know whenever we talk, he's thinking through his answers super careful-like."

A screen door slammed next door and the neighbor's kid, Artie, leapt from the top step of his porch to the ground. There was a low whistle. Mark got to his knees in a fluid bird-dog motion and watched Artie circle the Corvette, watched until the kid hopped his Harley and roared off. Mark sank back down, a smile lingering.

He picked up where he left off. "So everyone knows that father and son got along like shit. Then someone leaks the news that Papa's selling the paper to a local group. There goes little Kenny's future, right?"

"But Matthew had arranged a job for Kendall in that sale," Sabina blurted out.

"And didn't tell Kendall," Mark shot back.

"You knew?" she asked. "Kendall *told* you he didn't know Matthew had made this provision for him?"

"He did. And your mother confirmed it."

"Why would he do that? Admit he had a motive to kill his father?"

"Because of something else in the MOSS deal. If he knew about the publisher's job being his, then he'd have to admit he also knew about the other half of that agreement, the performance clause. Kendall had to measure up within five years or he'd be out. My theory? That little baby was the part that stuck in his craw."

"Hold on." Sabina climbed off her perch on the rail and sat down cross-legged, facing Mark. "I'm a little stupid on a couple of beers. I don't get it."

"Okay. You get access to certain facts when you got a homicide. First you go down the money trail."

"And?"

"And I say Kendall saw a big squeeze coming. He stands to inherit a lot of money from his grandfather, this old coot in Kansas City, Ambrose Drum, who was old enough to die yesterday. But the old coot has written into his will that his millions will not go to his only grandson until said heir is fifty years old. Fourteen years away. Okay? But his father, Matthew Drum, is worth even more money. All of Drum Enterprises International. Kendall could buy a couple hundred Riverview papers with that dough, and it wouldn't depend on some performance clause, either."

It was her turn to dish out the surprise. "Are you sure Kendall knew he was gong to inherit DEI?"

"Of course he knew. Assumed, anyway."

"I don't think so." Sabina told him about Kendall's call on Monday and how genuinely surprised and unhappy he sounded to have just learned he was heir to all of Drum Enterprises, Inc.

"He was *unhappy* about it?" Mark asked, pushing off from the wall and looking intent. "Think. Is that the best word for it?"

She thought. "Not exactly. More like shocked. Overwhelmed."

"How about guilty?" For the first time during their prepared-mind experiment, cynicism hung on his words.

Sabina thought about it again, hard. "It was just an impression over the phone. This kind of speculation isn't fair."

"Guilty," Samuel repeated, rolling the word around in his mouth like an exotic appetizer. He relaxed again and his face moved into the shadows. "We'll look at it your way: His father promised him he'd get to take over the *Times* after it was running profitably again. Kendall thought he'd never inherit DEI. Knew he had to wait until he was fifty to get his granddad's money. So our little paper is his only shot. Kid didn't even finish tech school, much less Harvard, like his Daddy. Then he learns Matthew is dealing on the sly, planning to sell the paper to this mystery MOSS group and not telling anyone about it, especially Kendall. Let's accept he's telling the truth and he doesn't know about the arrangement keeping his spot secure. Or he does, but the performance clause eats at him: he doesn't think he can cut it.

"How does our man feel?" Mark went on, relentlessly. "Feels double-crossed, don't you think? He pops Matthew. Then when he learns his old man left it all to him, *then* what's the operative word? Guilty. He's got a drop of conscience left, and he feels guilty. Dad didn't deserve to die."

Neither spoke for a few minutes. It was so quiet that when the Detective yawned and mowed his face with both hands, Sabina heard the whiskery rasp. He heaved himself to his feet and put his hand out to help her up. They were both tired of the game.

He trotted down the steps and said, "See you tomorrow."

Matthew's funeral was the next day. That must be why Mark wanted his mind prepared, Sabina thought. All those suspects, herded together in a single pen.

She didn't want to dwell on the image of Matthew Drum's formaldehyde-injected body in its coffin, so she turned a golden-oldie radio station up loud and spent two hours in a frenzy of cleaning until she was tired enough to sleep. She pushed through the tooth-brushing and house shut-down routine, stripped off her shorts and top and fell on the couch in her bra and panties.

Sabina's mind was still racing, evading sleep, when something outside creaked. A branch in the wind? She was intimately acquainted with the sound of the board at the edge of the porch and it wasn't that. She stared at the flickering shadow patterns on the ceiling, listening hard, and then turned her head. All three windows were wide open over the windowseat. There was a man's figure there, stooped over and looking in at her.

She jerked upright and screamed, "Get away from there!"

The shadow unfolded fast as a switchblade and was at her door, pounding so hard on the wood she thought the triple-paned glass above would bust for sure. He was yelling; no, bellowing. It was Karl the Jerk, blind drunk and bull mad.

Well, so was she. Sabina stomped to the front door. He was hollering that she messed in his business and he was going to mess with her face. He called her unpretty names at the top of his lungs. Spitting and hacking while he did it, but making a few of them clear enough.

"Goddamn tattle-tale! No goddamn city inspector gonna protect your ass from my ... my *vengeance*, you hear me!"

"I hear you, you *asshole loser* and you get off my property *this minute*."

What was she doing trading insults with this ape? She stepped back and plucked up the phone to dial 911. Glass shattered. The top pane of her beautiful 1920s front door was spider-cracked out from a finely-pulverized center the size of the Jerk's fist. Somehow, it held.

She leaped back to the door, put her palms against it and raised on tiptoe. "You are breaking your way into prison you awful piece of *shit* Jergensen, now get away from there! I'm calling the police!"

He stopped the pounding. He didn't stop the screaming.

"Slimy whore!" he yelled. "Lemme in there you better clear out the back door you slimy bitchin piece a"—hack-hack, thwock-pitouee. It took it out of him. "Piece a snaky-assed fuckin' bitch," he finished, but he was losing steam. Whatever he was drinking tonight, he drank again in a great inhaling sniff that had Sabina swallowing convulsively. God, what a turd, she thought. How *could* he have fathered that neat little boy?

By hopping in the air, she caught glimpses of the Jerk's retreat. She turned on the porch light and he wafted away like a bad smell, shaking his fist and muttering.

Sabina sagged against the door. She was really scared. She just didn't know it until then, and she didn't know what to do. If she called the cops, they'd go roust the Jerk and upset Tootie and his mom. If she let him get away with it ... well, then he would get away with it.

Like he'd even remember by tomorrow, Sabina thought. Oh, boy. She turned off the porch light, closed and locked the windows, and collapsed on the couch. The more she thought about what a mucky pit of waste was Karl Jergensen— to be honest, the more she thought about the names he called her—the madder she got. Sleep would not come. She'd just about decided to file a report on him when the creak came again.

No, this time it was a groan, the top plank on the porch. Sabina slipped to the floor, crawling fast into the hallway so the Jerk couldn't peer in at her again. Trembling radiated from the pit of her stomach. It could be fear but it felt like a hot coal of mad.

The doorknob jiggled—not as if he were twisting it, but a minute shiver, like he was picking the lock. So it was stealthy he was being this time. She swiveled her head in the dark, wanting to lay hands on a heavy object that could do a man real damage and finding nothing.

A memory saved her—a memory of Jacob's last visit. Sabina duck-walked to the door and ever so slowly and silently turned the lock. She would make it easier for him. It took Karl a few drunken seconds to try the door again but she was lucky; he did. It opened real slow and careful. His arm in a dark sleeve—nice burglar touch, Karl—was the first part of him to snake through the open space.

She didn't wait for the rest of him. She hurled all of her weight against the door.

It was a grinding thrusting swearing screaming assault, Sabina on the door and the door on Karl. He tried to insert the rest of his body and she tried to stop him and she won. Sabina didn't know how long it lasted but she meant to hurt him, all right. For sure, his arm would not soon recover.

Sabina didn't have to make a call-the-cop decision this time—the neighbors did it for her. She persuaded the nice young officer that Karl was going nowhere; they could take him in the morning and spare the family.

It was nearly dawn when she finally fell asleep, back in her own bedroom where she belonged and behind a locked door. She dropped off with an odd memory. All the screaming that filled the night air during Karl's last visit had been hers. Not a peep from the hugely drunk and blasphemous Jerk. Karl Jergensen had been perfectly silent.

CHAPTER TWENTY-ONE

Ambrose Drum was accordioned into a gadget-laden wheel-chair, his knees swaying to one side. Though he assured Sabina and Peg that he was able to walk, for his son's funeral he chose to motor in under his own power. He waved off a St. Raphael's usher and cruised jerkily down the aisle of the church, looking eerily like a pull toy as he tracked the erect figure of his wife Lucille. His head in its red leather racing cap thrust forward and a fat, unlit cigar rose at a jaunty FDR-angle from the corner of his mouth. A cane was mounted in an aluminum sheath on the back of the chair. A portable phone in its black leather case was slung below his right arm, the cover folded back and dangling, as if he expected a call at any moment; as if he'd take it, in the middle of services for his only son.

When Kendall Drum told Peg Lindsay that his grandfather was infirm, she offered to put him and his wife up for the night in the first-floor rooms that had been remodeled for Scott Lindsay's illness. The Drums accepted, but not for an overnight. They flew in early from Kansas City on a private plane and Ambrose Drum rested while Lucille and Kendall visited the church and tended to a few remaining details of the funeral service. Then the Drums took Peg and Sabina out for lunch at Angie's House of Angus.

The tension between the Drums was as thick as the choker slab of beef Ambrose Drum ordered. Kendall and his grandfather—"Pops"—had a mutual-admiration society going which effectively excommunicated Lucille Drum. And Ambrose and Lucille's dislike for each other was a polished, prehistoric *thing*, so vividly alive they should have set a place for it at the table.

Lucille Drum was an artfully refined old dame with an amazing hour-glass figure and pride like a stiff collar holding her head high. Yet her anguish over Matthew's death broke through the façade. She picked at her meal. Her hunger was for news of her son, for personal anecdotes of his time in Riverview. That was what Peg wanted, too—to talk about Matthew—and those two remarkably different women huddled together in private conversation.

Ambrose Drum exuded an oddball charm. He called Sabina "Missy," with a light of fun in his diamond-bright eyes that were so like Matthew's that Peg literally gasped on meeting him. And like Matthew, Ambrose had his own force field of energy: an absorbing appetite for life that appeared undefeated by an osteoporotic spine, prostate cancer, eight-five years of life ... and the death of his last child.

There the resemblance between Matthew and Ambrose ended. He had none of his son's grace or subtlety. His great knuckled hands and big feet were the fading caricature strokes of a hulking bull of a man. His cap covered hair as sparse as Matthew's was dense. It failed to cover a bony knob high over one eye that looked like the asymmetrical stub of a rhinoceros horn.

It was Lucille Drum who reminded Sabina of Matthew. Her regal bearing, and her hands ... the same strength; even the same flexible double-jointed thumb. Take away the nail polish, age spots, a gargantuan emerald ring: Matthew's hands.

They arrived at St. Raphael's nearly an hour early but it was already filling up. The funeral was a social gotta-do. Detective Sergeant Mark Samuel was positioned against the back wall, looking miserable in a black suit too heavy for the weather.

Ambrose Drum invited them to sit with the family in the front. Lucille clearly disapproved and Peg Lindsay was a great deal less inclined. She had to get pretty firm with Ambrose.

"Then I'll have you at my side in the reception line," Ambrose Drum announced and spun his chair away, case closed.

That would be a lot of handshaking. Sabina thought her mother's eyes and cheeks were over-bright already. Peg led the way, selecting seats on the side aisle farthest from the front doors. Peg detested sympathy when she was close to tears; she wanted to barricade herself from tsk-tsking friends.

The thick limestone walls of St. Raphael were covered with images of Christ in one or another stage of suffering and persecution. As a teenager, Sabina left church feeling guiltier than when she came, despite a few Saturday nights custom-designed for confession. The organ started up a Chopin Waltz, the C sharp minor. It wasn't the usual funeral dirge but had a lovely, lyrical melancholy. The organist was playing it heavy-handed and too fast.

Kendall sat between his grandparents in the front pew, his head like a clean, alert sheep dog's smack next to Ambrose, leaving space enough for another body between Kendall and Lucille. Ambrose's wheelchair was parked empty in the aisle: so, he could walk, or at least pivot. From a distance, it was easy to read bereft into the stillness with which they faced the gleaming mahogany coffin resting five feet in front of them. A single strand of white hair had pulled free of Lucille Drum's French twist. Sabina imagined her doing her hair that morning, arms raised in a familiar routine to begin a day unlike any other.

Matthew's body was going next to Kansas City for a full mass service and burial. A few days later, a memorial service was planned in Boston. That would be the big one, with DEI employees from all over the world paying their respects.

Mr. and Mrs. Frank Wiley streamed up the aisle toward one of the front pews. His wife, her arm linked through his, waited with a sunless smile as Frank stopped here and there to press a shoulder, shake a hand. Rose Malwicki was one of the people Frank stooped to address. He whispered something to her and as he moved on, she raised a gloved hand to swipe at her ear.

A woman entered the church swathed in black from head to toe. She was short and a little dumpy. She walked head down with unexpectedly long strides to a seat two pews in front of Sabina and Peg.

"Who is that, Mom, do you know?" All Sabina could make out through the woman's veil was an ordinary face, two chins, and a chic, short hairstyle.

"No idea," Peg whispered. "An out-of-towner, by the looks of her."

Lucille Drum had elected not to use St. Raphael's choir for the funeral and a gaggle of them arrived together, spotted their fellow choir member Peg Lindsay and crossed to the side aisle. One by one they filed past, some of them stretching across Sabina to touch her mother's shoulder. The last one slipped a single yellow rose into Peg's lap.

Ella Martinelli made, for her, a quiet entrance, walking into the church on Ed Fountain's arm. That must indeed be a bad marriage, Sabina thought, if Ed's wife wouldn't even accompany him to the funeral. A few other faces from the newspaper were familiar to Sabina. Phelps Pascal and his wife; she looked like a runner, too. Rudy Parson, the FuManchu mustache from Advertising, who slipped into a seat behind Fountain and Martinelli and poked his head between them to say something. For Sabina's money, Parson wasn't half so smart as Ella thought he was. Sabina had passed the hacker problem over to Kendall, he had bowed out to this Parson, and the *Times* network was hit again the day of Drum's murder.

Matthew's words echoed in her brain. That day of the first leak, alone with him in his office after the scene with Frank Wiley. *You're in charge, Sabina. Handle this for me.* And she was blaming Rudy Parson and Kendall? Sabina remembered, sadly, something else Matthew said that day: *I don't have any friends here, Sabina.*

Ella was transformed by mourning attire: Las Vegas to Peoria in one wardrobe change. She'd tamed her bottled-sun hair with a clip at the nape of her neck and a modest-brimmed hat. By all rights, her breasts were too large to pout but she managed that sexual magic act anyway. She wore a plain, classy gray dress and the pout was subdued; she was subdued all over.

Sabina was still looking her way when Ella turned her head and their eyes met. She mouthed something Sabina couldn't make out, then raised her watch hand and tapped the watch, a question on her face. Sabina took it to mean, later. She gave Martinelli an okay sign, reluctantly. The woman had been treating her like an airborne TB germ and now she wanted to talk.

Here and there, people were whispering, laughing, hopping up and down to talk to friends. It was only after Father Madigan began the service that Sabina realized what was off. The mood of the congregation was too festive. Relieved. Most everyone in town thought that now Matthew Drum was dead, the Poet had exacted his ultimate revenge and would kill no more. Sabina didn't agree, and neither did Ed Fountain. They feared this latest and greatest act would mainline fame so urgently into his psyche that they'd need a stake through his heart to stop him.

Peg and Sabina stood together outside one arched entrance to the church basement. Peg was dreading the reception line. She smoothed her knit skirt with her hands, her lips a thin line of tension.

Across the wide vestibule behind them came the ker-chunk! of the heavy outside door opening. Sunlight slashed across their shoes and they turned to see Kendall Drum maneuvering his grandfather's wheelchair through the open door, Lucille holding it wide. The babble of voices floating down the steps grew louder. On Father Madigan's request, people were holding off for a few minutes to give the Drums time to take their places.

The Drums disappeared through a twin arched doorway and Sabina turned to her mother. "We don't have to do this, you know."

Peg fiddled with the perfectly aligned cuffs of her checked jacket. "We said we would."

Sabina reached out and held her hands still. "We promised nothing. He didn't exactly *ask* us. And after all, you weren't related to Matthew."

"No," she said distantly. She opened her mouth as if she wanted to say more. Closed it. Then looked up at Sabina in mute appeal. "I need to fix my face, dear, would you go ahead?"

Sabina understood. She could spare her mother the chore of explaining to the Drums that she wanted to sit this one out.

She passed through the doorway and it all became a whiff more bearable, thanks to the St. Raphael Funeral Society. All morning and the night before, they'd been cooking for the record-breaking crowd expected today. The room was wall-to-wall white-covered tables. Six along the back wall held the buffet. Urn-shaped vases of flowers or plants anchored every table.

Lucille and Father Madigan were talking a few feet removed from Kendall and his grandfather. Sabina bent down to make it easier for Ambrose.

"Mr. Drum, my mother won't be joining you in greeting the guests. She is not up to it." Sabina threw it out with a touch of belligerence, expecting resistance from the tough old bird.

Ambrose reached out his gnarled, freckled hand and she took it. It was cold, hard, huge. "Does her credit," he said plainly. His bright eyes took a slow vacation over her face. "Your place is with her, Missy," he said. His mouth quirked to one side. "Do an old stallion a favor? Save me a spot wherever you plant it."

By 'it,' she assumed he meant her butt. The wadded-up stud from the turn of the century was flirting with her. "I'll beat 'em off with a stick," Sabina said, and smiled at him. She had to exert some pressure to retrieve her hand. As she turned to go, she caught a glimpse of Kendall's averted, pained face. He must think his grandfather's behavior unseemly.

Well, she wouldn't help Ambrose behave poorly. She set her purse on a chair at the closest table and tipped three metal chairs against its edge, reserving places for all of them.

After Peg joined Sabina, they sat watching as people offered the Drums their rehearsed words of sorrow. Nobody in town knew Ambrose or Lucille, and few people knew Matthew or Kendall. So the crowd was nothing more than groupies, of a sort. Fountain had called them star fuckers. Who was the star, though? Matthew, or the Poet of Pain?

Sabina spotted the black-veiled woman, holding up a wall, and nudged her mother. "Mom, look at that. Isn't she acting a little weird?"

The woman almost ritualistically lifted her veil. Her face was unremarkable. The hair was her glory: a fashionable blunt cut of a pewter gray, as thick and smooth as a tongue-washed cat. She stared at the Drums with a nervous intensity that went beyond groupie, clutching a large handbag to her stomach as if it contained the crown jewels.

Sabina and Peg clutched at each other at the same time and with the same irrational thought.

"What if—" Peg started.

"A gun?" Sabina breathed.

She jumped to her feet and Peg hauled her back down. The woman in black unclasped her bag, reached in and emerged with ... a piece of Kleenex. She blotted her lipstick and checked it in a small mirror attached to the flap of her purse.

"Oh, my," Peg gasped, holding both hands against her cheeks. Sabina fought a surge of hysterical laughter. She was relieved when a coalition of Peg's friends swarmed around.

Sabina eavesdropped for a time, glad to hear their talk steering clear of the murders, and then wandered away. She accepted coffee from a roaming Funeral Society-ette and landed on another chair at another empty table.

Kendall had positioned himself behind his grandfather's wheelchair—protected by it or protecting Ambrose?—and only rarely did he step around it to awkwardly accept someone's hand. Because of his osteoporotic spine and his seated position, it was physically difficult for Ambrose Drum to meet someone's eyes and increasingly, as Sabina watched, he wasn't bothering. He turned his head to the side, hands dead on his lap. As for Lucille, she levered her hand at people like a wax museum mannequin. Small wonder the reception line was moving rapidly. People turned away from greeting the Drums with an airless look of mass exhalation. Father Madigan must have picked up on it because he was moving down the line of people and gesturing at the buffet tables.

"Sabina?"

Mark Samuel, weighed down by two huge plates of food,

was a welcome sight. She smiled gratefully and they got right to work, not much needing the ritual of chit-chat after their marathon talk of the night before.

"My favorite kind of food," Sabina told him after half was devoured. He pointed the corner of his napkin at her mouth. She swiped at it and licked her finger. "I love big sloppy globs of cafeteria-type stuff like this. Macaroni and cheese and runny lasagna and mystery pastas. Good bread to mop it up with."

"Must be nice," he said, half resentful. "The kind of metabolism lets you have it all and still—" He gestured at her with his fork.

"Still what, Mark?" she asked, feigning innocence. It had been too long since a man got personal with her; he could at least finish the compliment.

"But that's right," he said. "You run a lot, don't you?"

"Bike."

He shrugged. "Same diff."

"I don't bike that much anymore." Jacob and Sabina used to race, picking out three or four finish lines in a string of spontaneous challenges that would keep them out until their lungs were in flames.

"Sabina." An undercurrent of business in his voice shot her back to how he sounded the morning Matthew was killed, when she thought her mother had been, too.

She looked at him warily. "What?"

"I heard about that trouble you had last night."

Was that all. It was sweet of him to look so concerned. "Remember that kid you rode around in your convertible?" she said. "His old man was who was bothering me and believe me, it's nothing. He's nothing."

Mark continued fixing her with the worry frown.

"I *saw* him, Mark. Karl Jergensen. He was right there, on my porch."

"The first time," Samuel said. "He was there the first time. Not the second."

"Not the second?"

"Officer Bertram found Jergensen at Terrell's Tap. Bertie stopped in there just ten minutes after leaving your place. Jergensen had been holding down that stool for two solid hours."

"Oh, I don't believe—"

"Witnesses, Sabina. A bar full. Plus the guy was too drunk to get off the stool, much less ram your house."

"Well, then ... who?" Her face went numb. Drum's killer? The Poet had been to her house? Had wanted to ... God.

In a blink, she was into denial. "Oh I don't *think* so." She felt a smile lift the corners of her mouth, painted there by the reasonable woman she heard arguing her point. "No way. I mean, look, Mark, I crunched the guy a few times with my own front door and he runs off? Does that make sense? Really. Some killer!"

Samuel stared at her steadily. "So what's your theory?"

Again, that sheltering kindness behind his words. She pressed her fingertips to her temples and focused on a potato salad stain on the table cloth. "What's yours?" she asked, surrendering.

"You've been on the tube, in *Newsweek*. Something you said pissed him off. Just like the *Times* editorial got him started on Drum."

"So now you *do* think Drum's murderer was the Poet?"

He dismissed it as beside the point. Sabina tried to think what she may have said to incite the sicko but could only concentrate on the amputated sensation of a two-inch thick slab of oak pinning the arm of a man who wanted her dead.

A Funeral Society-ette cleared their plates. Sabina's chest fluttered. "This food doesn't feel right," she told Mark. "What I already ate."

He was a father with hands-on experience, it was clear. He scanned the table for something for her to throw up into. The sight of him lunging for the potted plant was comical; it dissolved the airy lump in her throat.

"It's okay. I'll be fine. It was just ... unexpected."

"Sabina, you cannot stay in that house alone."

"You know, I really think I scared him off for good." *Criminy, who said that?* she thought. She didn't mean a word of it.

"Now how the hell would you know that?" Mark sneered.

Before she could answer, they were interrupted by a tall, silver-haired man with heavy black-framed glasses. He introduced himself as Matthew Drum's lawyer, Duncan Farley, and said he had to catch his plane in a half hour and hated to interrupt, but.

Mark sent Sabina a get-thee-to-a-nunnery look and excused himself. She turned her diluted attention to Duncan Farley. He didn't demand much: he said their strategy had worked and Langley-Spritz had come up with full price for DEI, Inc., as well as agreeing to sell the *Times* back to Kendall. Sabina said, that's nice. It was clear he expected more. He left abruptly and so did she, heading for the restroom, a cry of *sanctuary, sanctuary* running through her head. She wanted to run cool water over her wrists and take ten minutes to close down her ears and her brain.

It was not to be. In the stall next to hers, Sabina spied a pair of sensible black heels, so she didn't know enough to cower in there. As she was rinsing her hands, the subdued version of Ella Martinelli emerged. Their eyes met in the mirror. Ella froze, one hand in a fist against her chest and the other clutching it.

"Sabina, you've gotta help me, I've gotta spill my guts to somebody, I don't know what to *do!*" This erupted like oil from a resuscitated duck. It wasn't melodramatic because she wasn't acting.

She was, in fact, crying suddenly, and crying hard. Sabina locked the bathroom door. She had tissues stuffed in her pocket for her mother, who hadn't used any. She unlocked Ella's hands and gave her the wad. "Take these. Take your time."

Ella honked a good one into the sea green tissues, balled them up and leaned into the mirror, swabbing at the streaked mascara under her eyes.

There was nothing to sit on but toilet seats so they perched on the vanity, on either side of the sink. Ella regained some control but the distress showed in the blurred, red-tipped wings she made of her hands as she talked. Sabina could tell they'd be in there a while. She interrupted Ella to borrow the piece of gum she was talking around, scrawled *Out of Order* on a paper towel and stuck it to the restroom door.

Ella said her relationship with Kendall "might be the real thing; it might be l-o-v-e with a capital L"—so Sabina would understand why she was talking to her and not the cops.

"About what?"

New tears leaked from her eyes. "Sabina, I'm scared shitless Kendall offed his own father!"

She gave Sabina the rest of the story with a brand of uninhibited honesty that was a little like being caught on the highway of her brain at rush hour.

Kendall and Ella had had their first real date the night Matthew Drum was killed. She took him to her friend Isabel's wedding.

"He's more *normal* acting than what he's been before, and he's laying some moves on me. So we go back to my place, my kids are tucked in two floors below us at my sitter's, by pre-arrangement, see, I was thinking big. Kendall's like an animal, it's *great*, you coulda wrung me out. And then whoppo!

the guy shrinks like a violet, in more ways than one if you catch my drift. Maybe I did something to shut him down, I'm clueless. All I know is I don't wanna give up a night's sleep worrying about it with this guy curled up against my backside, but he's makin' no noises about leaving. I'll tell you straight, he's acting like he *had* sex. Amazing. So I set him up on the couch and I go to bed by myself."

Aha. "What time was that?" Sabina asked her.

Ella gave her a level, agonized look and said, "Time enough to get over to his dad's and do the business. I know from Mark Samuel what time the coroner says he bought the farm. It was around eleven o'clock, give or take."

"But just because Kendall has no alibi, you—"

Ella stopped her with a woeful shake of her head. "I wish," she said. "You gotta let me finish. So the next morning I get this urgent call from The Fraulein—that's what we call her, Malwicki. Is Kendall there she goes, and I say yeah and she says, would he get to the Bluffs pronto, she thinks something's wrong at his dad's house.

"Kenny wants me to go along. We get there, we get up the stairs, we're into the door and Kenny screams." Ella closed her eyes, apparently picturing the scene. "The Fraulein yells what's wrong. Should she come up, the chickenshit. Kendall's blocking my way. I think he's trying to protect me, and maybe he is, but here's what I can't forget. I see there's a note by ... by the body. Like the Poet would do. Kendall's standing there going oh my god oh my god."

She picked up the ball of used tissue and started in tearing it apart, looking down. "So I step around him and pluck up the note. And before I know it, Kenny's at my shoulder and he grabs it from me and folds it over and turns his back and stuffs it into his pocket. He goes into a fresh bunch of ohmygodding. And I'm right with him."

Ella bit her generous lower lip, remembering. "He's so quiet."

"Kendall?"

She shook her head. She meant Matthew. The corpse.

"I gotta finish this, so you get it. What I saw on the Poet's note. I saw the signature, and it's something only Kendall and me knew about." She turned wide, tragic eyes on Sabina. "It's our private name for the Poet. We call him P.S. Eliot, because he calls himself the poet, and because of this post-script trademark of his? Ha ha." Bits of tissue were raining on her lap. "He'd actually signed the note that way."

Sabina leaned forward, reading her lips. "Did you say P? P as in ... persimmon?"

Ella rolled her eyes. "There's the difference between you and me," she said. "I woulda said P as in piss."

Sabina grinned at her. "Believe it or not, that's the first word I thought of. I just didn't say it. So we're not so different."

Ella wouldn't buy that. "I wouldn't dream of x-rating piss outta my vocabulary. And persimmon?" She laughed. "Would not exactly be next on my list."

"Well, excuse me for my upbringing." Sabina concentrated on this problem of the signature. Ella had it wrong. Mark Samuel had described to Sabina the note left with Drum's body, and he said it was signed T.S. Eliot. Kendall must have pulled it away from Ella before she could see it clearly. Samuel would not approve of Sabina telling this to Ella, however.

She stalled. "Listen, Ella. If Kendall was trying to hide the note from you, why did he take you there in the first place, and why in the world would he sign the note with P.S. Eliot? This private name the two of you had, that you would tell to the police?"

"Except I didn't," she said guiltily. She locked her hands under her legs and banged her heels against the vanity doors.

"You mean you think Kendall is giving you some kind of test?"

She straightened up, pulled the elastic band from her hair and inched her fingers up her scalp from nape to crown, scratching and sighing gustily.

"Or maybe he's asking for help. Like you said, in that MTV show? When you were laying out what the FBI says. That's why I'm spilling this to you, Sabina. This is your shtick. What do you think? Is he, like, begging me to turn him in? Deep down, I mean?" She closed her eyes. "I'm already personally in a shitload of trouble for not tellin' Mark about this. I know it. I plain don't know what to do. I feel like a wet old rag without a bucket to drip in."

Sabina slid off the vanity and stretched her arms to the ceiling, thinking, *you shouldn't do this*, and then going ahead anyway. "Look, Ella," she said with an inward sigh, "you've got it wrong." Hope shimmered across Martinelli's face. "You can't tell anyone this, and that includes Kendall. Do you promise?"

A vigorous nodding.

"It was signed T.S. Eliot," Sabina continued. "Not P.S. Mark told me, and he studied the thing. So it's just a coincidence. Don't go around talking about it at all, okay?"

"Okay," she said slowly, thinking it over. "But listen, Sabina, then why did Kendall snatch it away from me like that?"

"Well, I can think of two reasons." Sabina smiled slyly. "First, he made the same mistake you did, thought it said P.S. Eliot and that *you* killed Matthew."

"Hey, not funny!"

"More likely, he had time to see the rest of the note and it wasn't pretty. He just wanted to spare you seeing it, I would guess."

"Yeah!" Ella declared, and the sun broke through. She arched her back in a lazy cat stretch and sang out, "Thank you Lord!"

They fussed around in front of the mirror for a few minutes, getting ready to rejoin the fun. The cloud of gloom lifted off Ella with the speed of light and she was all of a sudden a make-up expert, dispensing advice.

"Coloring like yours," she said, with a discriminating squint, "cries out for the Toast of New York." She held out her tube of lipstick and Sabina tried it. She was right.

As they returned to the reception, Ella squeezed Sabina's arm. "Listen, Sabina, you took a load off my mind. And I've been kinda bitchy around you."

When Sabina didn't answer, Ella wrinkled her nose. "Hey, don't trample me down arguing."

Sabina laughed. "The cheering up goes both ways." Ella had certainly distracted her from thoughts of her early-morning visitor.

Ella steered them away from a group of people standing in the doorway. "So I wanna tell you, A, I owe you a favor. And B, you're not such a bad broad. And C," she added, lamely. "If I can do anything for you."

"Actually, Ella, you can." Sabina had decided to take Mark's advice, and she could hardly worry her mother over this; she'd insist on knowing why.

Ella didn't flinch. "Name it."

"A place to stay. I need one. Tonight, anyway. Maybe a few nights."

"Ah," she said sagely. "Boyfriend trouble."

"More like ... a gentleman caller who's gotten a little persistent."

"A gentleman caller," Ella said, rolling her eyes again. "Persimmon."

Back inside the hall, Sabina saw that Peg Lindsay's friends were still clustered around her, and there was Ambrose Drum at her side. He was telling some story that had the whole group laughing. To Sabina's experienced eye, her mother's smile was forced. She was exhausted. Time for home.

It took them ten minutes to weasel away. They had to promise Ambrose they'd visit him next time they were in Kansas City.

"None of this next time crap," he said to Sabina. His chin was up, a la Matthew. "You, Missy. Young Kendall tells me you're hot stuff. You come with Peg here. Red carpet treatment. I got friends not dead yet. Get you some customers. There's a bunch lookin' to pass on their business to the kids ..." He broke off, waving his hand. "Never used to hold much stock in outside consultant crap. Maybe I should have." He chopped his hand in the air again, dismissing them.

From charmer to curmudgeon in a single, short and one-sided conversation. Oh, well. At his age, and considering the occasion, what was normal?

Sabina dropped her mother off and stopped at Melody Lane to collect enough clothes to see her through the weekend. She wasn't exactly looking forward to a slumber party with Ella and her urchins. She would probably have to share a bottom bunk with one of them. Ella looked like a cat person. Multiple cats, probably.

Sabina was leaving a note for Tootie on her front door, telling him they'd have to skip laundry night, when she thought to check her answering machine.

There was a single message on it, from Andrew Webster.

"Hey, babe. Handy Andy here. Now I hope you're sittin' down, 'cause my main news ain't pretty. I got a fat nibble from Shakespeer. The Poet to you. I got his host system, like the mailbox where he gets his mail, and it's inside your little paper there. Do you copy that? He's broadcasting from somewhere inside the Riverview *Times*. Now you call me, babe. Anytime, and quick, 'cause Andy gots a plan."

CHAPTER TWENTY-TWO

Handy Andy sniffed out this Shakespeer-maybe-Poet by thinking like him. He concocted the persona of a maddened ex-firefighter who had been injured on duty and blamed the incompetence of a female firefighter. 'Flint,' as Andy called himself on-line, cruised the .alt newsgroups where Shakespeer had posted his most vitriolic verses. Then he worked at standing out even in that crowd. He advanced a theory that black men deserved their negative images on TV; that they shot off guns and shot up crack as compensation for sexual inadequacy. (His on-line language was less academic.)

As he had hoped, his words attracted some serious flaming and several anonymous cowboys who rode to his defense. One of them was Shakespeer. Andy identified him by the slashing depth of his obscenities and by one posting where Shakespeer reverted to his familiar upper-lower case style.

They "talked" after midnight for two days, Shakespeer probably using a computer from his home. Andy was unable to glean any intelligence out of the electronic return address except for "JR" as a user name. The breakthrough came last Friday morning, the day of Matthew's funeral. Shakespeer posted a comment with a different return slug—a complicated Gateway address that revealed the Riverview *Times* as the domain but ran gobbledygook for the portion that was normally the computer user's name. Flint responded, continuing his strategy of flattery and emulation. Eventually, Shakespeer asked for a real-time computer talk over the weekend. 'Flint' said he'd be out of town and tried for Monday afternoon around four o'clock, when Andy figured Shakespeer might be at the paper no matter what shift he worked. Shakespeer agreed.

"But he don't want me contacting him first," Andy told Sabina. "I wait for him to start it up. That's when we execute my plan. We finger the fuckhead."

"Who's 'we'?"

"That would be you plus me, babe."

All she had to do, Andy said, was tap in a single command: *Finger@rivtimes.com*. That would show which computers were in active use. Andy would call her when and if they started up and talk her through the rest of it.

"We isolate the computer and then you call in your police pals. Let them wrassle around with Shakespeer, see if they can turn him into your Poet. Simple."

This simple plan made Sabina jumpy. On Saturday morning of her weekend stay at Ella's, she found herself sharing the whole scheme as she and Ella sipped boiled coffee on the tiny balcony of Martinelli's apartment.

"Finger?" Ella asked. "Like, up yours?"

"More like ... where are you. Pointing the finger. What computer is being used in this communication with Andrew Webster, and who's using it."

"So we have to, like, walk *by* this murdering asshole?" Ella asked. "While he's on-line with your friend, to see who it is?"

Sabina heard the *we* of Ella's question with some relief. It was kind of Ella to assume a helping role and not make a big deal of it. "Not like that," she told her. "When we run this finger program inside the paper, it should pop up with the real names, or initials or nicknames, of the people who are registered to that particular machine. We make a printout and call Detective Samuel."

"Why not tell Mark what we're doing from the start?" Ella asked.

"Andy won't do it. He thinks the cops are computer stupid. And besides, we aren't absolutely sure that Shakespeer is the Poet. Not in a way the cops would buy."

Ella shook up a bottle of lilac fingernail polish and propped a bare foot on the iron rail of the balcony, spreading her toes. "How come he doesn't trust the cops?"

"Oh ... it's a long story."

"Hey, honey," Ella said with her rock-and-roll laugh. "One thing there's shitloads of this weekend is time. Kendall went home with his folks. His grandparents, I mean. My other boyfriends are stuck at the White House."

So Sabina explained the rest of it, except for Mark Samuel's suspicions about Kendall Drum. With no computer or office at the *Times* to call her own, Sabina was going to need Ella.

What sounded like high-tech, breezy heroism in the Saturday morning sunshine—Sabina and Ella's Big Adventure—definitely lost its glitter on D-Day. The chatter over Monday morning breakfast was provided entirely by Ella's kids. Ella bolted for work, dropping the kids at the sitter downstairs. Sabina dawdled over the paper, made all the beds, and when she finally got behind the wheel, she dawdled there, too.

The *Times* had her on indefinite retainer to help Frank Wiley and Kendall with all the details of change of ownership but she knew she'd be useless today. Her attention was thrown ahead to four o'clock. Everyone at the paper would be moping around in a post-funeral, pre-acquisition funk. She even dreaded the tired old building itself: The clanking wheeze of window air-conditioners; stuttering fluorescent lights; tiles half-removed from a lobby renovation that Matthew Drum had in the works before he ran out of time.

Sabina had to pass through Rose Malwicki's office to get to Kendall, who was working now out of his father's quarters. Rose wasn't in yet; Sabina wondered if she had an attitude about working for Drum Junior. Kendall was hardly one to strike fear into her heart.

Kendall was lying in wait. He bid her good morning, twisting in his father's chair from side to side and watching her with a barely suppressed ... something. He had been through the wringer since his father's murder. Sabina had seen several moods but never cheery, never self-confident.

"Guess what?" he said. "Langley-Spritz made an offer and Duncan's advice is, take it. So DEI is off my back and I'll be buying the *Times* back from them."

"I know. Farley told me at the funeral. Congratulations."

He jumped up. "Now we can concentrate on fixing this place." He strode to the round table and reached for a grease board leaning against the wall behind it. He had to put some weight into dragging it out. "Look what I bought!"

Sabina couldn't help laughing. "Kendall. You've just inherited enough money to sustain an entire third world country, and you're showing off this purchase like, like—"

"Like it's important?" he said, with that odd pent-up energy. "It is!" He crouched in front of the shiny white surface and uncapped a grease pencil. "I don't know who to call to get this mounted on the wall, so ..." He wrote *Goals* across one side of the board, as he had seen her do in their first strategic session with the *Times* management. On the other side, he scrawled a big *How*.

"You stay where you can see and I'll kneel here and off we go."

"Off we go where? What are we doing?"

Kendall turned his limpid brown eyes on hers as if she was the one wearing the new personality. "Planning. This paper is dying. There's so much to do. I've got ideas"—he smacked his head—"like a bomb inside my head, but I need your help organizing, and figuring out what comes first."

He had the ideas, all right. He talked about electronic information business ... maximizing advertising dollars ... interactive selling ... something called RBOCs which he had to explain to her ... computerized databases—they spent an hour on that alone. It was a measure of Matthew Drum's inhibiting power over his son that Kendall could have sat dumb through their long strategic planning sessions, simmering these plans of his and doodling on his yellow pad like the village idiot.

By the time he launched into the need for special-interest zoned sections, the greaseboard was full of his cramped writing and it was way past lunch. Kendall finally sat back on his heels and rested. He'd kept his sports coat on and the heavy shock of hair over his eyes was stringy with sweat.

"Do you think," he said uncertainly, "that we could ask Mrs. Malwicki to transcribe what we've done here? So we can keep going?"

"I certainly think *you* could."

Kendall could record this himself, warp speed. Sabina suspected he was intuitively flexing his power muscles. Screwing up his courage, he poked his head into Malwicki's hive, but the queen bee was not home. He turned back, covering. "I forgot, she asked for some vacation days. Or just one, I forget."

"I can copy this down, Kendall."

"No, no," he said, faintly alarmed. "It'll take me five minutes." He settled behind the glass desk and clicked open his laptop.

As Sabina watched him slope-shouldered over his keyboard—his profile, the heavy hair falling over his eyes—a rare intuition seized her.

"Kendall? At your father's funeral, did you meet a woman who was dressed all in black, kind of short and wide; she was in the church—"

Kendall's fingers curled up into his palms. He stopped typing and looked up with a proud, shy smile.

"That was my mother."

Sabina's jaw dropped.

He ducked his head, smiling more broadly. "That's just how I felt." He pushed the keyboard to one side and leaned on his elbows, studying his hands. "Her name is Ellen. We're getting together in New York, next month. She wanted to know all about me."

"Well, of course she did. How wonderful, to meet her for ... the first time?"

"Do you know, she's a professor emeritus at *Harvard*?" He looked out the window, obviously remembering the meeting with pleasure. "She's smart. Real nice. Her field is anthropology. Harvard, where my father went to school, is where they met. My grandfather wouldn't let me go there, he calls it a breeding ground for snobs. But not her."

He looked at Sabina sideways, tentatively. "Can I tell you, I mean, are you interested?"

Mark Samuel thought this was a killer? He made Sabina want to push the hair off his forehead and hide notes in his lunchbox. "Of course, I am. Criminy, Kendall, this is a big deal."

He told her more about Ellen, and about his two half-sisters and what they did and where they lived. Then he was talking about Matthew, about his father, and it all changed. He was again consumed by the peculiar, agitated energy.

"I asked her about how she met Dad and all. She said he

was kind of an outcast at Harvard, who she took pity on. She called him self-centered." He paused for a beat and added: "A self-centered bastard."

This ivy league professor, just reunited with her son, could she have used those words? Or was Kendall embellishing on her theme?

"She must have felt more than pity for him," Sabina said. "You don't get pregnant from pity. And we're all self-centered at that age."

Kendall glowered. "You don't know anything about him," he said, bitterly. He drew an imaginary box in the air, like he was making a television. "You want a picture of the real Matthew Drum?"

She didn't answer. Kendall leaned back in his chair, face turned to the ceiling.

"Picture this. Man has a son he never bothers to see until the boy is ... oh, about seven. Then man takes him for a week on a cruise with man's wife. Ignores him. Pays a lifeguard to teach kid to swim. Three years pass. Man marries again. Takes son on a trip to South America with latest wife. The boy has asthma and is scared of everything down there, but especially worms that are three feet long. The boy has nightmares. Man sends in new wife to see why son is screaming. Then the boy gets a case of serious fleas and the remedy is, scrub him down with lemon. He pays another stranger, a hotel maid, I think, to do it."

Kendall glanced at her mildly, as if the subject of this story were truly unknown to him. "Not a fun bath. It stings like crazy." He turned his eyes back to the ceiling.

"The son cries and cries. The father stands watching. Cold as ice. When it's over, the man, the *father*, says, 'I wish the old man could see you now!'"

It was a chilling tale all right. For its own sake, and for the intense feeling Kendall managed too well to contain.

Sabina jumped on the first available excuse to break off the session and Kendall didn't object. She grabbed a late lunch at Theo's and then simply wandered around the *Times* trying to look like she was on her way somewhere important. With a half hour to go before the four PM "fingering," she finally gave it up. There was one person in the building who had to be equally antsy, and that was Ella Martinelli.

As Sabina waited for the elevator to take her to Ella's office on the second floor, something sharp jabbed dead center in her back. The backs of her knees tingled and she swayed into the wall.

"Hey hey hey!" Ed Fountain held her around the waist for a second and then stepped back. "Sabina, I'm sorry, I didn't mean to startle you."

"Oh, Ed," she breathed. "That's okay."

When she offered no explanation for the jitters, Ed reached across her and punched the button again. "All the sensitivity seminars I've taken," he joked, "advise that if you've got to touch the women you work with, never touch the good-looking ones."

The elevator dinged its arrival and they stepped on, facing each other obliquely.

"So who were you expecting?" Ed said lightly. "The Poet of Pain?"

"That's it, Ed. Death by elevator."

"Except I'm on board with you. Not too smart of me, is it?"

"You've got to make a mistake sometime," she countered. She tried to match his repartee tone but it didn't work, quite, and Ed gave her another curious look, not so good-humored, as she got off on the second floor.

Ella wasn't in, and then she was, after how long Sabina didn't know except it *still* wasn't four o'clock. They talked a little, about her kids and then about their ex-husbands. Then they ran out of things to say and simply waited until 3:55.

"Five minutes to go, Sabina. We might as well get the screen up?"

"Okay. Let's do it."

Sabina typed what Handy Andy told her: finger@rivtimes.com. The screen blinked, then columns of data scrolled into view. It meant nothing to her; they wouldn't know what to look for until Andy established a connection with Shakespeer and phoned them.

Ella drew closed the hunter green blinds on the glass wall of her office. There were no blinds to cover her office door or the two narrow glass panels on either side of it but Sabina didn't know who they were hiding from; the gesture fit their cloak-and-dagger mood. It was quiet out there, anyway. Most of Editorial came on at 2 PM, on another floor, and Ella's staff left at 3:30 PM. The union printers weren't due until five o'clock.

"Son of a bitch but I'm nervous!" Ella exploded, and followed with a hearty laugh, her lilac-painted fingernails spread against her throat. "There's not a damn thing to be goosebumped about, is there, Sabina? It's just gonna be the screen and the phone and you and me, and then ..."

"Right," Sabina nodded. "And then we see."

"Tell me again, what are they doing?"

"It's a 'talk' program. They're connected only to each other and their screens go blank with a dotted line across the middle. So when one of them is typing to the other, it appears real-time on that person's half of the screen and the other can read it immediately, or interrupt real-time. Just like we talk."

When the phone rang, of all things that should have made Sabina leap out of her skin, it didn't. She reached for it calmly.

"Andrew Webster for Sabina Shaw."

"I'm here, Andy. It's me."

"Okay, babe, I got the sick turd. We're doin' it now and you should see the shit he's puttin' up." He paused. "Just a sec, gotta answer the asshole." The clicking of his own keyboard came across the wire, faintly.

"So you got the program up?" Andy said.

"Yes."

"These things is different, people dick with 'em, so you tell me what you see."

She read him the column headings.

"Stop. Now check the length. A status bar? Should tell you how many pages."

Sabina pulled down a menu to find the status bar command, suppressing a ludicrous desire to laugh. The memory of an old movie was ratcheting across her mind: She was a terrified passenger, taking over the controls of a plummeting 707 and being talked down through a radio headset by her suave fiancé.

"Okay, Andy. It says six pages."

"That's manageable. Hold." He turned back to his screen, humming a little as he composed God knew what to keep Shakespeer on-line.

Ella bumped Sabina's shoulder. "What're they saying to each other?" she whispered.

Sabina passed it on. "What's he saying to you, Andy?"

"You really wanna know?"

Ella heard that and nodded. Sabina said, "No."

"Okay now," Andy went on. "Scroll through those pages, watching the Idle column. Tell me when you get to any that show, oh ... under thirty seconds."

The screen rolled past their eyes. Ella jabbed a fingernail at it and Sabina stopped. "Here's one. Sixteen seconds."

"Okay, watch it," Andy said. Click click. "Now: did it change?"

"No."

"Move on."

The very next one was it. "Here's another," Sabina said. "Watch it ... should change ... now!"

"It did!" Ella squealed.

"Hey! Who's there!"

"A friend," Sabina told Andy, feeling Ella's breath on her bare arm. They looked at each other. Ella was ablaze with the excitement of the hunt and Sabina guessed she looked the same. "I couldn't do this without her, Andy."

He grunted. "Double-check here, when's the log-in time for that column?"

"It reads, Mon sixteen-oh-four."

"Okay, babe. That's the man. What's the name?"

"It just says 'JR.' It says that about ... six times." Ella reached across her and hit a key to print the screen.

"That's his open screens, babe. Wait a minute, he's rappin' at me again." Tap tap tap. "The rat-ass is Shakespeer certain. Remember I told you? He used JR as a user name when he was workin' from home. So now you gotta find out who JR is and what computer he uses."

Sabina heard paper ripping off a perforation from Ella's ancient printer and told Andy to hold on. She put the phone on the desk and rubbed her neck.

"Ella, who is JR? Do we have a JR here?"

Ella frowned at the printout, twisting a strand of hair around one finger. "I can't think ..." she began and then went electric with an idea. "That's what a postmaster's for," she said, waving the paper at Sabina triumphantly and heading for the door. "There are so many dumb codes. I'll be right back!"

Sabina picked up the phone. "Andy? Ella's gone off to check a postmaster list. We should know then."

"Jesus, woman, that's no *list*, a postmaster's a *person*. You best watch yourself there."

She couldn't agree more. This was exactly what they were *not* going to do: wander around the building playing detective. Sabina put the phone on the desk and charged after Ella.

Advertising and Circulation was a narrow bullpen area with standard black metal desks. Along an inside wall, a row of head-high fabric partitions formed semi-private offices. There went Ella, big blond hair turning into an orange cubicle about twenty yards away.

Sabina decided against screaming her name and kicked off her shoes to make time. From a distance, she heard Ella say, "You're still here! Rudy sweetie, I need your help. What employee uses JR as a user name?"

When Sabina turned the corner of the cubicle, Ella was standing behind his desk and at the shoulder of Rudy Parson, the blond man with the Fu Manchu mustache. A gooseneck lamp burned over a tilted artboard in the corner, but Parson was working at his computer. Ella leaned over the printout she had spread in front of him, her finger poised on a line. Parson gave it a nearsighted squint, his long, rather mournful nose nearly touching the paper. He started a little as Sabina silently invaded his space, raising only his eyes. His mouth twitched in a smile that was gone as fast as it came and he continued his bow-shouldered examination of the printout. The way he huddled there, head thrust out, hands locked in his lap, reminded Sabina of Ambrose Drum's turtle-shell posture in his wheelchair.

He rocked back in his chair and then crouched forward again. "You've been running a finger," he said.

"Yeah," Ella told him. "Can I explain later? We just really really need to know who this JR is. You've got records of this stuff, right?"

Parson covered his mouth with one hand and stroked the wings of his mustache. What took so much thought? He had the records, or he didn't. Ella threw Sabina an exasperated grimace but waited quietly.

"The files are not adequate," Rudy said. His eyes squeezed shut. "But I have excellent recall. Hold it. I'm remembering ..."

"Kendall Drum," he announced and the eyelids shuttered up. "He asked for JR because there were two Drums. JR for junior, I presume."

Ella gasped. She cradled her arms together, looking at Sabina imploringly. "I don't believe it."

"Wait a minute," Sabina said. "I think ... didn't I see Kendall's name on the first screen? I mean, the first page there?" She moved to the edge of Parson's desk. "It would be one page earlier, Rudy, can you flip it over? I'll show you."

He was motionless except for his head, shaking stubbornly from side to side. "He wanted two user names," Rudy said. "I recall that. I recall wondering why, at the time."

"Can I just see?" Sabina persisted, reaching for the printout to find Kendall's name for her own satisfaction. Rudy planted his right arm across the printout. He turned to Ella with wounded dignity. "Ellie. I am the postmaster, am I not? Is my word in question here?"

Sabina's heart floated free in her chest. It was such an unexpected, violent physical response that it interfered with thought. Ella said something soothing to Rudy. She patted him on the back and reached for the printout, tugging it out from under his arm. Sabina recovered enough to apologize and a small voice in her head praised her, saying, that was smart, Sabina. She took two steps backward and turned, willing herself to walk away normally. Ella caught up with her.

"Oh, Sabina!" Ella said, low and passionate. "I don't ... I can't *bear* ... oh, *fuck*!" She stopped three feet from her office door, covering her face with her hands. Over her shoulder, Rudy Parson's head topped his cubicle wall and he watched them. Sabina propelled Ella around the corner of her office, closing the door behind them.

As soon as they were out of his sight, her heart left the dock again. She bent over so the blood would run to her head and pivoted, hands on her knees, to see if Ella's door had a lock on it. Thank God, yes. Sabina turned it.

A tinny warbling came from Ella's desk. Handy Andy had hung in there and was trying to rouse them.

"Ella," Sabina said. "Shush. Kendall is not this JR. He's not the Poet."

Her eyes were twin swamps. "Not? Then who ... oh, Sabina, get real! It's not Rudy." She sighed big as the arrow of accusation, in her estimation, swung back to her Kendall. "Listen," she said, "Rudy's just sensitive, an artist type."

Sabina's legs wanted to run far away; her head told her to stay. "Tell me why he calls you Ellie."

"Christ, Sabina, not a biggie. It's a version of Ella, is all. He said—" She broke off, then gave out with a diminutive "Oh." Her blue eyes grew large. "He said he liked the sound. The ... the rhyme. Ellie Martinelli."

Sabina tipped open a slat of the window blinds and peered out. At least Parson wasn't still standing there like a bug-eyed ostrich. Andrew Webster squawked on the desk.

Ella's voice was barely audible. "He said, did I know my name was a poem."

They stared at each other. Tiny spiked heels marched up Sabina's back and arms.

"It's also the way he was sitting," Sabina said. "Hunched over, hands in his lap."

"Like he was hiding something," Ella agreed.

"He was. Short sleeves, and his suitcoat hung on the back of his chair. Remember, the Poet ... my house ..."

"Oh, God," Ella groaned. "We need help."

"No shit."

They continued staring at each other, fear feeding fear. The phone, silent for a few moments, yelped again and the trance was broken. Sabina picked it up and waited for a space in the rhythm of Andrew Webster's calling her name. "Andy, Andy, shh! I'm back."

A flat, tense command. "You-get-the-fuck-out-of-there-*now!* He knows, Sabina, he *knows.*"

"Calm down, Andy, I know he does, we were just with him, but we've got time because he thinks we think that JR is someone else."

"No no no no no you stupid idiot! He sent me a message said, 'a finger up yours, you're dead, Charlie, and so are your angels'! He got me made, he got you made, get your asses out!"

There was a rap on the glass. Ella whimpered. Sabina's lungs were punched flat again. She looked up slowly, already panting for breath. Rudy Parson stood there, visible behind the glass panel, with one hand on the doorknob and the other poised and ready to rap again. He was smiling in an ordinary way. The skin on his raised arm, his left arm, was a mottled, bruised blue.

"Andy?" Sabina said. To her own ears, she sounded prissy and formal, like an old-fashioned schoolteacher. "Would you please call the police? Our man is at the door and I'm hanging up now."

Still locked in a staredown with Rudy the Poet, Sabina kept the phone pressed to her ear and used her thumb to disconnect the call. She was going to try 911 and she had the idea that if Rudy noticed her starting a new call, he'd snap.

His voice came clearly through the glass. "May I come in, please?" He jiggled the knob.

Out of the side of her mouth, Ella said, "It might be safer, Sabina. Maybe we can talk him down."

"Like hell." Sabina heard three distinct tones but it didn't ring. They were going to die because she had no tactile memory for the phone keypad. She moved the receiver an inch away and stole a glance. Goddammit! The lowest number was the pound sign, not the nine. She punched it, then one and one, and looked back to the door. He was gone. The number rang once as Rudy reappeared. His pale face had gone blood red. He was hoisting a heavy brass lamp, the shade stripped off.

"Sabina!" Ella rushed her and ripped the phone from her hand. "Speed dial Kendall!" She touched a number. Glass splintered and a shard spun past them. Ella screamed. The phone skittered off the desk's edge and hung there by its cord, spinning.

Ella stood with her back to Parson, rote screaming "Help help help help help!" Both her hands churned the air, loose at the wrists like a kid who had just let go of a hot stove burner. Sabina was aware of an hysterical logic. Ella would press on, a broken recording, until Kendall picked up his line.

At least she was doing something.

Rudy reached through the hole he made and groped for the doorknob. He couldn't quite reach it and cut his arm. Breath whistled through his teeth. He made no other sound but the extra volt of rage was visible in an engorged neck vein. He picked up the lamp base again, holding it like a spear.

It dawned on Sabina it was not a spear; it was a lamp. At the moment he crumpled a second basketball-sized hole in the glass, she moved. She raced for Ella's tall oak coat rack and backed up, holding it parallel to the floor.

It wasn't much, but action gave her the illusion of control and Ella, seeing her assault the coat rack, snapped into an alert silence.

"If he had a gun," Sabina hollered, "he'd have used it by now so grab something, get yourself a weapon!"

"Yes!" she shrieked, whirling around. "There's two of us!"

Rudy was rotating the lamp like a monster swizzle stick, reaming out a larger hole, glass splintering everywhere. Sabina watched this at a remove and grew still, every cell in her body going into a deep crouch. Patiently, she awaited the right moment. She couldn't impale him on a coat rack but she intended to use it like a cow catcher and herd him away long enough for help to come. Or something.

Just as his head and chest poked into striking distance, a jungle shriek curdled Sabina's blood and Ella stumbled past with her arms cranked around her bulky goldfish aquarium. She doused him with the water first—the single large goldfish sailed out and slapped into his chest—and then she twisted her body into a really marvelous shot-putting pose and heaved the whole aquarium, electric cord trailing, at his head.

She decked him. He fell on his butt in the aisle outside Ella's office, sitting with both hands behind him for support and looking stunned. Blood gushed from his nose and a cut over one eye.

"Quick, Ella, unlock the door! Then get behind me, get hold of this thing!"

Ella scuttled to the door and swung it wide and Sabina churned forward. Rudy rolled, folding his knees under him and preparing to stand. The coat rack twisted in Sabina's hands as Ella got purchase. Wordlessly, they charged.

Sabina aimed for his head. Ella made an adjustment—she seemed to be targeting the man's balls. They ended up striking him in the collar bone and pressed on, knocking him down again. The base of the coat rack was four wooden legs fastened to a circular metal band and they caught the side of his head in that circle and bore down with all their might. He twisted and pulled with his hands to get free but the coat rack spun in place until one of the legs flattened his nose a second time and he screamed—a raging, maddened scream that convinced Sabina he'd killed every one of Riverview's victims.

The sound of his scream had a heat that melted her muscles and Sabina recoiled, just enough. Parson pumped his legs, running horizontally on the floor until his feet met the side of the nearest desk. He planted them, pushed off powerfully and wrenched his head and shoulders free.

He scrambled to his feet and was nearly vertical when they hit him again but this time Parson blocked the assault with his hands and clung to one end of their makeshift battering ram. His mouth and stringy mustache were covered in blood. He roared again, opening a black void in all that red, and thrust the coat rack away. Sabina lost her balance, stumbled. His hands clamped around her throat. His thumbs stabbed at her windpipe. She closed her eyes against the awful sight of him. The world was shrinking with amazing speed, all her senses shutting down.

An air-splitting screech scorched her ears: Ella the earth mother. Sabina's eyes jammed open again to see sharp nails rake across Rudy Parson's flesh and turn it red, fresh red. There was more hollering, new voices, footsteps pounding the carpeted aisle from the elevators. The cavalry had come.

CHAPTER TWENTY-THREE

Bluff Road used to be the ultimate bike or sled run. It still was, with snow cover, but the city had too long ignored the potholes and now it was coast, brake and swerve. Sabina had been looking forward to a wilder bike ride, to letting the wind wash her clean.

The Channel 7 van passed her, going up. Behind her helmet and sunglasses disguise, Sabina smiled. They were heading to her mother's house, where she spent the night and where they would not find her. Even if she were there, fetal-curled under her old dotted Swiss bedspread, she could count on her little mother to bar the door.

Sabina's brain was a playback machine repeatedly scanning their fumbling escape from the Poet of Pain. Its favorite footage was the first taste of unconsciousness, when his hands closed on her throat, the world slurred, and she understood how desperately she loved life.

Sabina passed under the wishing limb, a branch of a century-old silver maple that dipped like a giant's elbow across Bluff Road, so low you could touch it from the back of a pickup. Just ahead was a sharp bend that pulled the road around the cliff and away from the Mississippi. The wishing limb was the marker spot for a game of chicken she and her brothers played when they were kids, until their father found out about it and shut them down. Swearing off the brakes, they used to steam through the curve, trying to cleave to the safe side of the center line. Centrifugal force usually put them a foot into the oncoming traffic lane as they rounded the cliff. Their sole defense was to cock sharp ears for engines gearing down to climb the hill, but Sabina remembered a few times they also relied upon the reaction time of startled drivers.

Just last October she had hurtled joyfully through this curve. Now she stopped, one foot on the pavement, nervously clicking her brake levers. There could be a car she couldn't hear through her helmet. Or maybe she'd run into a silent deer leaping across the road.

Sabina forced herself to push off, gathered speed ... and pumped the brakes, hugging the cliff.

For heaven's sake. It wasn't as if she were a battered soldier, returning from war with shrapnel wounds or a missing leg; she had endured only a glancing consideration of death. Yet her sense of immortality was forever gone. Loving life because you almost lost it was probably a wiser way to live, but it saddened Sabina. Rudy Parson, among other things, was a thief.

And a fish killer. Ella Martinelli leveled that charge at him yesterday and now, remembering it, Sabina laughed aloud.

Parson had been cuffed and Mirandized. As Mark Samuel and another cop got their prisoner to his feet and started moving him toward the elevator, Ella saw her goldfish. In all the commotion, the poor thing had skidded under a desk, gills heaving, and had given it up.

"Oh, no!" Ella cried out. "Fergie!" The cops spun around to see where Ella was pointing—dreading, perhaps, a victim somehow overlooked.

She stooped and pinched Fergie's tail. "That's it," Ella declared, and grimly stalked toward Parson, flopping the fat fish at him like an admonishing finger. "Look what you've done! He was almost eighteen years old! You can just consider *this* added to the charges against you, mister!"

It was an inappropriate, whacked-out reaction. They were all in various stages of shock. Sabina didn't know how many minutes they had with the Poet before Mark and the uniforms got there, but it was enough for the four of them—Ed Fountain, Kendall Drum, Ella and Sabina—to peer into the twisted psyche of Rudy Parson.

Hannibal Lecter he wasn't. When Ella's nails met up with his face, Parson backed up, covering one eye with both hands and squealing *ow-ow-ow-fuck-ow*. Ed Fountain reared up behind him, locked his hands together and straight-arm hammered Parson across the back of his neck. He went down silently, and silently curled into a ball. He expected to be kicked, but Ed bent over him, head bowed and panting, one hand resting on Parson's ribcage. Sabina was a still-life with her hands pressed to the hot skin of her neck where Parson's had been, and Kendall and Ella were hugging each other.

"Cut that out!" Sabina screamed at them. "We've got to contain him!" In a wild panic, she patted her hands across the nearest desk, a blind woman searching for rope or twine ... an Uzi would have been nice. She looked up to see Kendall lurching bug-eyed under the weight of a heavy glass coffee table and making hernias with every step. The table had a small wood base and four, thick, curved legs meant to suggest elephant tusks. Kendall landed the table near Parson's feet, reached under it and threaded him through by the ankles until he was covered from shoulder to knees by the table. Parson stared up at them obliquely, his damaged eye clenched shut.

"Tie him!" Ella yelled. She jerked at a cable on the back of a computer and the rest of them got the idea. They soon had Parson splayed out, his arms bound to separate table legs.

Fountain waited until Parson was secure and then asked, "What the hell is going on?" He and Kendall had jumped Parson on faith that Ella and Sabina wouldn't be coat-rack jousting for frivolous reasons.

"He's the Poet." Ella said. Her words ran together in her excitement. "Unfuckin' believable but he is. It's so hard ... well look at his arm, the left one? He tried to kill Sabina last Friday and she ... and then we were doing this finger thing with a guy in D.C. and Rudy tried to say it was Kendall who was JR instead of ..." She turned her big cushiony eyes on Kendall and reached for his hand. "Oh, Kendall. He killed your father."

Kendall leaned toward her as if to read her lips. Fountain moved to stand over Parson, interrogation posture.

"What's your name. We talked at the funeral but ... what's your name?"

Parson leveled his good eye at the ceiling and a beatific smile lit his face. "Charles Whitman, Junior."

Ella snorted. "Oh for chrissake, it is not; your name"—she lifted her eyes to Ed—"his name is Rudy Parson."

"Charles Whitman Junior," Parson insisted, calmly.

"Do you mean ... the Texas Tower Charles Whitman?" Sabina said. "Who killed all those students back in—"

"Nineteen sixty-six," he gloated. "August one. The little boy was born from his dead mother's belly. Delivered by bayonet."

Oh my dear God, what a crazy squirrel this is, Sabina thought. Charles Whitman bayoneted his wife, all right, but there were no children. Best not to argue with him. "So that's why you're JR on the Internet?" she asked.

He smiled his enlightened Buddha smile. "JR has many identities. They live in him."

His fraternity buddies. Those noble colleagues he evoked

in committing the Riverview murders: Ted Bundy and Albert DeSalvo and Mark Chapman and John Wayne Gacy.

Ella took a turn and it was out before Sabina could stop her. "What about this T.S. Eliot? How you signed the note we found on Mr. Drum?"

The cops had been holding that back, one of the rare elements of their crime scene that hadn't been tramped on, pawed over or otherwise released through the gossip and media mill. Too late now.

Rudy closed his eyes and rocked his head from side to side. "T.S. Eliot," he repeated. "The Waste Land." The good eye drifted open and dreamily drank in Ella's face. "Perfection? Matthew Drum needed redemption. JR delivered."

In two strides, Kendall had appropriated Ed's spot alongside Parson's head. He nudged it with the toe of his shoe. "You killed my father?" he asked. Sabina tensed. Kendall sounded tame and that was the problem. She had a vision of him drawing back his foot and driving it into the Poet's temple.

Parson struggled to inch away from Kendall. His wounded eye twitched violently, setting in motion one side of his blood-encrusted face. "He was warned," Parson said querulously. "He had his chance. I had my orders."

"Holy Jesus," Ed Fountain said. "I suppose God himself talks to you, is that it? Is that it, you *ass*hole?" Ed was balanced on the balls of his feet, fists shoved deep in his pockets, his breath still coming hard. Kendall cupped a hand on his shoulder.

"Yes," Parson acknowledged, pleased to be understood. "God. Using my brother's voices, but God behind it."

Inspired, Parson fanned his own flame. "I have a responsibility to history. To help the powerless become the powerful in an unjust society. With each death, the fraternity is reborn, one by one, to live on. In me!"

As he ranted on, his scratched eye gradually opened and filled with moisture he did not blink away. His words had a rhythmic, transfixing quality. It took a minute for Sabina to realize he was reciting his poem.

"For the powerLESS to be powerFULL we deliver our Word through a gun barRELL ..."

Ed Fountain broke the spell. "He's fucking enjoying this!" Fountain was a man approaching Heartbreak Hill, his breath ragged and harsh. He loomed over Parson and screamed at him to shut up.

Parson's tongue slowly snaked between his lips and touched his revolting string of a mustache, tasting blood. He looked into Sabina's eyes and smirked. He said: "Hump pussy dump pussy."

Ed Fountain's knees buckled and he fell onto the man's head. For a split second Sabina was afraid Ed had literally collapsed, a heart attack or something, but no. He was coordinated dead weight and he ground both knees into Parson's already broken nose and lacerated eye.

That's how the police found them: Ed mashing the face of a sobbing, cursing Rudy Parson; Kendall Drum, Ella Martinelli and Sabina Shaw standing faithfully by.

Sabina rode hard, until every muscle begged for mercy. She found herself twelve miles from the Bluffs and her mother's house. They were long ones, pedaling back. To divert herself, she thought about ways to make up to Mark Samuel. The detective had been furious with her and the "stupid Lone Ranger game" she played with Andrew Webster.

She wasn't sorry she cooperated with Webster in fingering the Poet. Andy would never have gone through with it otherwise. It did bother her that she withheld solid information from Mark, as well as a few irksome thoughts that weren't in the same category but that she thought Mark would want to hear. As she wobbled down Bluff Road, coming full circle back to her mother's, Sabina decided confession was the only way to make amends.

Peg had left the front door open but the screen door locked. The woman was learning. She materialized in the darkened hallway, startling Sabina.

"Geez, Mom. Don't lurk like that."

"One cannot lurk in one's own house." She thumbed open the lock.

"We're going on vacation," Peg declared, defiantly, as Sabina sank to the floor and wrenched off her shoes. "Ambrose Drum called. He tried to get you at home and then called here. He asked us to visit them in Kansas City for a few days and I accepted."

She steamrolled ahead, ticking off the reasons. One, Sabina needed a break from this town—hadn't she done enough; hadn't she delivered the killer? Two, Peg felt sorry for the old couple. Ambrose, she said, phrased it like this: "Won't you come see this ailing old fart before he's a footnote in history?" Three, what better time to take off, Sabina was between jobs, wasn't she? And Ambrose wanted to help; he had scheduled two meetings for Sabina with his friends in the food service business.

"He's scheduled them, Mom? Is that what he said? Before talking to me?"

Peg shut down, sensing resistance to the trip where Sabina was only expressing incredulity at the man's ego, at the way he arranged other people's lives to suit his purposes.

Once in a while, Sabina could figure out the right thing to say at the right time. "You left out another reason," she told her mother. "Nobody needs a break more than you do, and we've never taken a vacation together, have we? As friends? So let's do it."

Peg's mouth trembled and she turned away. As Sabina watched her lift a potted fern from the pine shelf next to the door and buff the wood with her sleeve, she understood how much her mother was grieving the loss of Matthew Drum.

"I'll check out flights, Mom."

Peg replaced the fern and cuffed the sides of some magazines until they lined up properly. "We leave on Thursday morning. I got you a window seat."

Sabina changed into a white silk blouse, borrowed Peg's genuine pearl earrings, and tamed her hair with two faux pearl barrettes. That's as far as she could take this conciliatory business with Mark Samuel. The blouse was tucked into wrinkled wash jeans and she had only the one pair of black biking shoes at her mother's house.

She drove downtown, thinking through various opening lines that would banish Mark's resentment of her playing cop. None of them featured an insult, yet that was what came out.

"What a pit!" Sabina said cheerfully, leaning the well-dressed half of her body around his office door.

Mark was fiddling with his window air-conditioner unit—trying to turn it down, Sabina hoped, because the place was freezing. He looked over his shoulder and said, without missing a beat, "So's your house."

"My house?" That was a solar plexus hit. "How can you compare this"—Sabina stepped in, wrinkling her nose—"this old deli drawer, with my house?" She persisted, trying to get him to distinguish between a good mess and a bad one. "Do you mean the piles of magazines, and papers? That's not bad housekeeping. That's my reading system."

Mark walked back to his desk. "I see," he said seriously. "I would have called them fire code violations."

The tug of war was going nowhere but it was friendly,

anyway. Sabina dropped uninvited into an orange plastic chair and smiled. "I could do this all day, you know. Two older brothers."

"Ah," he said. He sat down in his luxury chair, a worn plaid relic with most of the stuffing plucked out of one arm. "What brings you here?"

She wondered whether to start with the fluff or the biggies, and recalled a lecture she had heard Ed Fountain deliver to a reporter intern about an inverted pyramid: Get the important stuff up front, while you've got their interest.

"You're not going to like me much, but Ella told me something the day of Drum's funeral that I plumb forgot about until this morning."

Mark narrowed his eyes. "You plumb forgot, huh? People start talking out of character like that, Sabina, and I figure they're lying."

Lying. Boy, did she hate that word. She didn't owe him this; he was the detective. Sabina rested one foot across her knee and jiggled it, biting back her first hot words. "Okay, there is a lie in there," she said, unapologetically, "but a white one. I didn't feel I should violate Ella's confidence.

"So. What she said was that when Kendall and she were together on that Saturday—remember, his alibi? That Kendall was sleeping on the couch in the living room and she was in the bedroom, right around the time Matthew was being murdered?"

Mark's eyebrows skimmed high.

"And there's something else," Sabina continued. "Maybe one of the others told you this, but if they didn't you should know that before you and the troops got to us yesterday, Ella spilled the beans to Rudy Parson about the last note. She asked him why he had signed it T.S. Eliot. I know you were trying to hold that back."

"What a stupid shit," the detective said after a moment.

That was going a little far. Sabina thought Ella had behaved wonderfully in their battle with the Poet. "She was just excited. It's not every day—"

"Not her. Kendall. He's with Martinelli, late at night, alone ... and he sleeps on the *couch*?"

Oh, criminy. "I won't dignify that."

"Yeah, yeah," Mark said. The rusty sophomoric leer faded as he thought over what she had told him. He propped his right elbow on the back of his left hand and leaned into the torn chair arm, his fingers busily digging at the stuffing. Sabina wondered what kind of shape the chair was in when Mark first inherited the Poet of Pain case.

"I'm of a different mind about Kendall at this point," Mark said, bringing his faraway look around to her. "But thanks for telling me." He slapped both palms on the chair arms and scooted forward, unmistakably her cue to leave.

She was miffed. "That's it? You can't tell me why?"

He read his watch. "I promised my kids ... okay, I guess I've got a few minutes." He plunged an index finger into the stuffing and twanged away at it. "It's the timing," Mark said. "If Kendall's reason to kill his father was because Matthew broke his promise to him—or seemed to be—by selling the paper, and that information is leaked out on Saturday morning? Kendall was at the paper all day and with Ella at night, no gun registered to him that we know of and none of the dealers around here sold one to him that day. He just didn't have time to plan this thing, alibi or no alibi." He planted his palms on the desk.

She didn't cooperate. Something was wrong. "He just 'didn't have time'? You already knew that. When we talked last Thursday? You knew about the leak on the MOSS sale, you knew Kendall was in the dark about the purchase contract giving him a shot at the top job, you knew his whereabouts on Saturday, the day Matthew was killed ... what's different now? Especially with me telling you there's a hole in his alibi?"

Mark looked at her like she was a crazy woman. "Rudy Parson is what's different. He confessed to this murder, and to three others, remember?" He stood up and shrugged into his suitcoat, tugging at the shirt cuffs. "It was like hunting a deer from sunup to sundown, you finally close in, and it dies of natural causes at your feet. I gotta tell you it was disappointing. This Parson poured it out, we could hardly get a question in edgewise."

"God, Mark, isn't that the point? I have to remind *you* that this guy thinks his body is some kind of reincarnation vessel for all his psychopathic fraternity members? For pity's sake, he'd confess to killing Santa Claus if you asked him."

Samuel leaned stiff-armed on his desk, all good will drained from his face. "And do I have to remind you," he said, low and tight, "that the chief, and the mayor, and the governor, and the fucking U.S. Attorney General, for Chrissake, have all been on TV hip-hip-hooraying the end to these murders? The case is down, Miz Shaw, and yours truly is not gonna officially or unofficially suggest we don't have the guy that did 'em locked up and halfway to justice. Do you understand?"

"I understand that isn't a question," she threw back at him. She also understood that Mark Samuel was more complicated than her first impression of a good-natured guy just trying to break the back of crime. He had his own pressures, his own agenda.

"I'm disappointed," she told him frankly. "I thought you were more ... intellectually courageous."

Mark straightened up and turned his face aside. "Oh, little girl," he said softly. "Come on. I'll walk you out."

As Sabina turned to the door, she saw the whole back

wall of his office was devoted to the Poet of Pain case: victim and scene photos, maps, computer printouts, memos ... and blow-ups of the Poet's notes. Before Mark could herd her out the door, Sabina nosed up against the neatly aligned and chronologically-ordered notes. Left to right, from Claire Washington to Matthew Drum. Handwriting on the first only. Laser-printed, all of them. Two different typefaces. No, three. Drum's note used helvetica.

"Mark, look. Here's something else that's bothered me. Can I just tell you?" She waved him over. "Humor me. I can't seem to help myself."

"I feel like Dr. Frankenstein," he moaned.

She pointed to the Poet's first note that he sent to Matthew Drum after he busted in Claire Washington's head. "In his poem the paper was supposed to print? Do you see John Wayne Gacy's name there?"

"Don't go rhetorical on me, Sabina. I don't have time."

"Okay. All his other P.S. heroes were in his original poem, but not John Wayne Gacy. Not the P.S. from the note left with Matthew's body."

It was clear he wasn't buying.

"It doesn't fit, Mark. It stands out."

"You do realize," he said, "that you're talking about this fraternity like it's a real thing, ivy-covered walls and membership rites?"

"But surely patterns mean something. It isn't consistent that the Poet would have named an outsider."

Mark's lips twitched. "So the Poet has standards on who he'll let into his fraternity?"

"Why not?" she said, with a bravado she didn't feel. "Is that any crazier than making one up to begin with? How do you catch people in lies, anyway? Don't you look for inconsistencies like this?"

Mark whacked the note with the side of his hand. "What makes you think this list of brothers is complete? It's just some rhymes thrown together. Poetic license, what to put in or leave out."

She was only half listening. She studied the wall of facts, going over all the names ... Sirhan and Speck, Berkowitz, Oswald, Manson and Bremer, J.W. Booth ...

"Maybe ... How about this? Nobody here killed children, like Gacy did." She turned to Samuel. "Maybe that's it. Remember Wayne Williams, the Atlanta child murders? He's not in the fraternity, either."

Mark stared at the board, rubbing his jaw. "Charles Manson," he said, touching the name in the poem. "There was an unborn baby in that one."

He had her there. He didn't stop to gloat, just checked his watch again and patted her arm. "Douse the lights when you go, Sabina."

Sabina studied the notes a little longer and got nowhere. She turned off the lights and closed his door and wondered, walking up the stairs to the main entrance of the police station, why she was hunting for meat on this cleaned-up bone. It would give her no pleasure to pin Matthew Drum's murder on his son.

"But what about Ella?" she muttered to herself as she took the wheel of the jeep. It would be nice to know for sure that she wasn't giving her heart to a murderer.

Another idea was snuffling around the corners of her mind; another what if? When it emerged full blown, she swerved against the curb and turned off the car.

Samuel's comment about Kendall not having time to plan the murders ... what if Kendall learned about his father selling the paper *before* Saturday? As a matter of fact, why had they been assuming that Rudy Parson was the Riverview *Times'* computer hacker? What if that hacker was Kendall, and he had a lot more time to build up his anger against his father, however misinformed? Time to plan the murder, time to plan his alibi?

There was one person Kendall Drum would confide in, one person he had a lifelong habit of turning to, and that was his grandfather, his Pops. Ambrose Drum. In two days, Peg and Sabina were going to see the Drums. It shouldn't be too tough to find out if Kendall called Ambrose about the *Times* sale, and when. He told the police he learned about it on that Saturday morning, along with everyone else. If Kendall was lying about that, there could only be one reason why.

CHAPTER TWENTY-FOUR

They caught a two-prop to Madison, to catch a bigger plane to fly to Milwaukee, to transfer to a bigger plane to fly them to Kansas City. Sabina could have driven to Missouri in about the same time and then they'd have had a car to tour around in. Peg said taxis would do fine and as to the prospect of traveling 450 miles with Sabina at the wheel, she'd just as soon go directly to the cemetery and fall in.

She was full of cracks like that during the flight and was, in general, chattering too much. During quiet spells, she bent her head to a book opened flat on her meal tray but rarely turned the pages.

They came close several times to talking about Matthew. Sabina would change the subject. Her mother was supposed to be getting away from all that. When Peg introduced it again—"Did I tell you about the fancy private plane Matthew and I took to Chicago, that Saturday?"—it finally sank in. This was part of the mourning process.

"We haven't talked about that day at all," Sabina said. "If you're up for it, I'd like to hear ... anything. I didn't get to know him, really."

Peg stared past her daughter at the clouds and talked, in fits and starts, for nearly an hour: about Matthew's life or what she knew of it, about their Chicago shopping trip, and even about the night he was killed.

An announcement from the pilot was the first interruption: Kansas City was just ahead and he was describing the landmarks to watch for. Peg fell silent.

"Mom. You really loved Matthew, didn't you?"

"It was a beginning," she sighed. "He loved life. He lived so ... exuberantly. No one should have it ripped away like that."

"Amen," Sabina said, fervently.

Peg covered her daughter's hand. "He asked me to marry him that night."

"What?" It was a shout-whisper, the kind that announced juicy stuff and got heads swiveling their way.

"Do you think it impossible that I could be attractive to a man like Matthew?" Peg asked, reprovingly.

That was exactly what Sabina *had* thought. "He was so unlike Dad," she offered, lamely.

"My, yes. I thought I liked that. I did, except ... That last night, your father was there with me."

With great forbearance, Sabina let the seconds tick by and then could stand it no longer. "*What*, Mom? Dad was there how? Do you mean, your conscience wouldn't let you ... you know. Decades of faithfulness, like that?"

"Heavens no, dear," she said, amused. "No, your father would want me to be happy, I'm sure, however I went about it." She was wearing a cheerful red-and-white striped blouse with a big bow at the neck and she played with it self-consciously. "I think Scotty kept me from going up those stairs to Matthew's bedroom." She set her jaw pugnaciously, daring Sabina to puncture the idea of her father, Guardian Angel.

"Hey," Sabina shrugged, "don't look at me for an argument, Mom. I know when to get analytical and when to just accept something." The questions she really wanted to ask would have shut her down for sure: Did the lights flicker on and off? Maybe a cold spot at the foot of the stairs?

"So would you have, Mom? Would you have married Matthew?"

She thought it over, running a finger along the edge of her tray. "I'm not sure. To be honest, I didn't like the way he asked me." Her eyes flashed the old Irish fire. "It was romantic ... but not a decent proposal. It seemed to come out of him in the heat of the moment. Because ... well."

"It's okay. I think I get it."

Sabina thought it far more likely that her mother's pride or old-fashioned virtue—not the ghost of Scotty Shaw—were what kept her from Matthew's bed, and saved her life.

The flight attendant locked Peg's food tray in place and asked Sabina if her seat was in its full and upright position. Apparently not. Sabina obliged while peering through scratched glass at Kansas City rushing up at them. The two rivers, the Missouri and the Kansas, twisted together in the heart of the downtown. It was 4:30 in the afternoon, rush hour, and the expressways and numerous bridges were glittering tails of start-and-stop traffic.

The taxi driver they drew was a wiry redhead of indeterminate age wearing a Kansas City Royals jacket. She hoisted their luggage into the trunk and they were off to Hyde Park, where Lucille and Ambrose lived in her family's original home.

"We'll see where Matthew grew up," Peg said, her voice falsely bright again. She was nervous about their hosts. So was Sabina, and more so because she was plotting to manipulate Ambrose into a conversation meant to reveal whether or not his grandson was a killer. It was the Riverview version of Watergate: what did he know and when did he know it.

Their driver—Mavis, it said on her license—was a chatty sort who took them on a choppy verbal tour of the city in between her breakneck threading in and out of traffic. Sabina gripped the armrest, while Peg was the picture of serenity. How, Sabina thought, can she complain about my driving and then bask through this like it was a hot air balloon ride?

"If we went west here," Mavis said, "instead of East like we got to, to get to Hyde Park? You could see some super buildings, the old KC stockyards, and Kemper sports arena is there, and a little—"

"The stockyards?" Peg interrupted her. "I imagine that's where the Drum's meat processing plant was?" She turned to Sabina. "It was in the family for years. Father to son, father to son."

"My uncle was there," Mavis said, a piece of hard candy clattering against her teeth. "Bad business, them closing it down like that. So many men, see, and no two-income families those days, or else both sides of the couple worked there."

"When was that?" Sabina asked. "Was it losing money or something?"

Mavis whacked the candy from one cheek to the other, thinking. "The year I graduated. That would be nineteen eighty-three. I dunno why they done it. It was a beef cattle and hog processing plant, see, and Uncle Conrad says, hell he's still sayin' it, that they had the market by the tits. He's still hot as green fire he lost that job."

Peg inched forward on her seat. "I heard the Mob was involved in that business," she asked Mavis. "Is that true?"

"Well, it's sure no secret in this town," Mavis said. "Not just that plant, neither." Her radio squawked. She spit the candy into the palm of her hand and plucked up the mike, telling the dispatcher she was twenty minutes from being free.

"Who told you that, Mom? Did Matthew?"

She nodded and pushed back in her seat, looking out the window.

It wasn't hard to picture Ambrose Drum as comfortable in the company of gun-toting friends. It was very hard to fit Matthew into that scene, or Kendall. Maybe that's why Matthew had sold the operation out from under his father.

They left the expressway and drove through a heavy industrialized zone. They must have been near Independence because Mavis asked if they wanted to take in Harry Truman's home. "Two bucks more is all it'll go ya," she said.

"I don't want to worry the Drums," Peg said. "You'd better take us directly there, Mavis." Mavis grinned at Sabina in the mirror. Her license was posted in plain view but no one actually *used* her name.

"Well," Mavis said, her eyes disappearing in crescent slits, "we gotta go by there anyhow, to get where you folks wanna go. No charge."

"I should think *not*," Peg said, folding her hands over her purse.

The Truman house was modest: a pretty, welcoming two-story white clapboard with scalloped trim around the roof and a fat man in a uniform standing guard alongside a tall iron gate. Sabina twisted in her seat and watched it disappear. For two dollars, perhaps Mavis would have slowed down.

"Lucille told me that her home has been nominated for the National Historic Registry," Peg said. "It should be something to see."

And so it was, in a way. The taxi's tires swooshed against the curb and utter stillness enveloped the interior of the cab as they all stared in awe at a three-story mansion and attached round tower of chipped, mustardy brick. The tower, formidable as a gallows, had a separate peaked roof and dark narrow windows taller than a man.

Sabina shuddered. "Forget the historic register. I'd enter it in a contest of Halloween Houses I Have Hated." Mavis smacked her head on the front seat, cackling merrily. Fine for her; she didn't have to go in there.

After wrestling the bags from the trunk, Mavis pressed her business card on them. "Call any time," she said earnestly. "I take the phone into the can; trust me, if you want Mavis you can find her."

The taxi roared off and they stood alone alongside their bags on the sidewalk. In a small voice, Peg wished she had booked rooms at the Ritz-Carlton.

It sounded good to Sabina. "We could make up an excuse. Your back? We could say you need a special mattress." She repeated it, practicing. "Yes. You require a mattress with a board."

Peg sighed. "I think, Sabina, this is the kind of house where all the mattresses are hard enough." She squared her purse on her shoulder. "I tried to tell Ambrose I'd rather stay at a hotel, but it's impossible to talk to him on the phone, he keeps repeating after you and he's got it all wrong. It's 'what what what' until you're screaming at him." She dipped her head at their luggage—"Can you get those, dear?"and started forward.

Sabina was rooted, feet of cement. Peg walked several paces before turning around, inquiringly. "Sabina?"

"What did you say, Mom? About the phone call?"

"What?" she asked, confused. "Ambrose, you mean?"

Sabina flapped her hands. "Shhhh! Come here!"

Peg hustled back. "What in the world? Sabina, what *is* the matter?"

Sabina's mind was a Rolodex gone amok, flipping forward and backward in time. "Your friend Ethel, Mom, isn't that her name? The one with the hearing aid, didn't you tell me she's always getting her consonants mixed up?"

Peg repeated, "What in the world?" and reached for Sabina's forehead in the ancient mother-gesture, laying the back of her hand against it. "What does Ethel's hearing aid have to do with the price of eggs?"

Sabina's mind scrambled for something, some believable cover-up for her mother's sake, when they heard Lucille Drum's voice calling down to them.

"Is that you? Mrs. Lindsay? Sabina? Are you coming?"

They jumped like thieves. "Never mind," Sabina said. They turned toward the backbone of endless, shallow stone steps that led up and into the home of Lucille and Ambrose Drum. She thought: *let the vacation begin.*

Lucille Drum admitted them with a meager smile. Their invitation, it would appear, issued primarily from her husband, and Ambrose was sequestered with his physical therapist.

"The therapist fights the arthritis," Lucille explained dryly, "and Ambrose fights with the therapist."

Sabina and Peg stood like immigrants, luggage in hand, making empty conversation about the trip. Sabina was wondering if Lucille would let them past the entryway when Peg removed her hat, casually hung it on one of six ornate hooks that framed a beveled-glass mirror and fluffed her hair. She touched the mirror: "This is Victorian, isn't it? It's a work of art."

Lucille thawed a degree and asked if they would enjoy a tour.

"Oh, yes," was Peg's prompt reply, and it was genuine enough; she did love antiques.

Thanks to a pile-up of questions from Peg, the tour lasted nearly an hour. Nothing was required of Sabina except to choreograph her movements to theirs. She was grateful. It gave her time to prepare herself.

The Drum mansion wasn't the mausoleum advertised on the outside but neither was it a place Sabina or Peg would call home. It was all Lucille, or her parents and grandparents and great-grandparents. *Her* treasures, *her* heritage. She might have been a lifelong spinster, for all the notice she took of Ambrose in her precise monologue about the things in her life.

The woman was a terrible snob. Peg's questions grew increasingly mechanical; she was revising her sympathies toward Lucille, and regretting her choice of vacation spots. When Lucille walked them through the guest suite they were to share and expertly lowered a Murphy bed sized for pygmies from its niche in a wall—"This is not to sleep on, of course"— Peg pressed the unyielding corner of a mattress on one twin bed and cast Sabina a desperate, I-told-you-so moue. The thing looked like concrete under a slippery, beige silk bedspread.

"Would you enjoy a drink, ladies?" Lucille finally asked. Sabina brightened noticeably and Lucille's hooded eyes blinked in studied dismay. "Oh, you poor girl," she exclaimed. "Both of you, how remiss of me!"

Remiss, hell, Sabina thought, as they followed the old dame's erect figure into the third-floor elevator. They earned this drink and Lucille Drum knew it. The elevator gave a clanking jerk and began its slow descent.

"Where are Ambrose's rooms?" Sabina asked, too late aware of the implication that husband and wife did not share the same quarters.

"In the tower," Lucille said matter-of-factly, tilting her head in that direction. "There's no entrance from the main stairwell."

Who was walled off from whom? Of all men, Ambrose would have been the type not to suffer from lack of sexual outlets. Is that why his tower had a separate entrance? So his women guests would not set foot in Lucille's landmark?

"That must have been a challenge," Peg said. "Decorating in the round."

The elevator stopped abruptly. Lucille pulled a large rubber-tipped lever to the right and the doors took over, sliding silently apart.

"It's worse than that," she said, stepping off first and turning to wait. "The space, geometrically, is half a circle joined to half of a hexagon." Her hands were loosely clasped at her waist: a perfectly-trained docent. She had given this tour many times before. She led them into the parlor, speaking over her shoulder. "We have been forced to renovate the area due to Mr. Drum's disability. The results are hideous. I believe that is the reason for the committee's recalcitrance to add us to the Registry."

Ah. The all-important Historic Registry of Haunted Houses committee. Peg made a weakly commiserating sound but Sabina was full up with this self-absorbed, supercilious piece of history who asked what flavor tea they would like when Sabina was hoping for a good stiff shot of Jack Daniels.

Lucille withdrew, elegantly, to the kitchen. Like one of those farces where someone flees through one door in a long hall of doors at the moment a pursuer bounds through another, the sound of Ambrose's voice swelled as Lucille's footsteps receded and then he was upon them, booming hello, whirring toward them in his chair, his eyes shadowed by the red leather racing cap.

He cruised up to Peg and wrapped his hands around hers. "My dear Mrs. Lindsay," he said, "you do me an honor in accepting my invitation. You look beautiful, my dear."

"Thank you," Peg said, loud and clear.

Ambrose winced and pointed to his right ear. He wore a flesh-colored hearing aid, the power variety that wraps around the ear like eyeglass frames. "I got my orders," he said. "Don't need to shout."

Peg smiled. "I'm sorry. But what happened to Peg?"

"Hah! Peg it is," Ambrose boomed. "It's this blasted parlor, makes you put on the airs; I've told that woman I'd rather greet our guests in a meat locker." He turned to Sabina, the ghost of a grin on his lips, and motored over to her chair. He sandwiched her hand in his and examined her.

"And how are you, Missy?"

"I'm fine, Mr. Drum."

"Hold on!" he protested, squeezing down with those cold hands. "None of this mister crap, we already went over those rules, right, Peg? Now! What can I get you Wisconsin dames to drink?"

He slapped at the controls on his chair and spun backward until he was parked beside a tall, dark cabinet. He wiggled a small gold key in a lock and a door dropped down. A small spotlight was triggered over a bountiful supply of spirits.

"I'll take anything amber," Sabina said.

"That's my girl." Ambrose's hand circled the neck of a tall crystal decanter. "You, Peg? You gonna let us out ahead of you?"

"Lucille is bringing tea."

"Tea schmee," Ambrose grunted. "Damn teetotaler, she is. C'mon, what'll it be, sherry is right next to tea if that'll make you feel better."

"Scotch on the rocks," she said, with alacrity.

"Hah!" Ambrose saluted her and worked with some difficulty to remove the corked stopper. He finally wrenched it off with his teeth.

When Lucille returned, trailed by a maid in full uniform bearing a tray of china and silver and tall, frosted glasses, Ambrose was launched into a story about his father's prohibition-day antics. If he was aware of her standing behind him, he didn't show it. Lucille gestured for the maid to set the tray down. She lifted one glass and joined them, sitting a little apart, her slim legs crossed at the ankles and an expression of hostess attentiveness on her face. Sabina wondered, all those years with Kendall and Ambrose shutting her out, was it like this for her? Nose pressed to the window?

Dinner was served precisely at 8:30 PM in the richly-paneled dining room. It went on and on; it lasted half their lives.

The Drums never broke out into open clashes—that would have been a relief. Peg resorted, finally, to the most unimaginative of excuses. When Ambrose suggested finishing with a cognac in the parlor, she pleaded a sinus headache.

"I'll get you both settled in," Lucille said, getting too quickly to her feet.

Ambrose swung his head to Sabina. "How about you, Missy? You got a sinus headache, or could I ply you with liquor in my private rooms?"

The lewdness was contrived. When she said yes, he showed a wary surprise.

"Fine," he said. "Follow me, separate elevator down the hall." Sabina kissed her mother and promised to come to bed soon.

Ambrose buzzed down a short hallway and through a large kitchen with institutional-sized appliances, where he asked the maid to bring a bottle of Glenlivet and two glasses to his rooms.

His private elevator was cramped. The ride was short and wordless. When they reached his room, Ambrose whished away toward a door Sabina presumed to be the bath. He flipped a switch on a gold-plated intercom built into the wall at wheelchair-level and said: "John? I'm ready." He maneuvered the chair to face her. "That's my man. I've been trapped in this blasted chair too long and I need to go to bed. Don't worry, I'll wear a dressing gown."

"I'm not worried." Sabina had not consciously wanted to insult him but saw her words did just that. He backed through the bathroom door and kicked it closed.

John startled Sabina by walking through the wall. Night air wisped at her ankles. The curved door he used was papered over like the rest of the room and on the other side of it, she made out the landing of a winding metal staircase. On seeing her,

John stuttered to a stop, then nodded and continued to the bathroom where he rapped perfunctorily and let himself in.

While the two of them were closeted together, the maid arrived on the elevator and wordlessly crossed to Ambrose's king-size bed. She transferred a decanter and two glasses to his bedside table, actually curtsied in Sabina's direction, and left silently.

It would be a stretch to call the space decorated. No Historic Registry members toured this room; it was a utilitarian hodgepodge. A flat-screen TV dominated an entertainment center that itself filled one of the walls of the semi-hexagon. A wheeled cart on the other side of Ambrose's bed overflowed with videotapes, remote controls, books, an ice bucket, soiled glasses and paper cups, newspapers, empty cartons of Oreo cookies. A stainless-steel exercise triangle dangled above his pillow. Its hoist bar was covered with adhesive tape heavily soiled by use. A full-size refrigerator was built into one wall. The "gallows" windows they had seen from the street were set into the semi-circle portion of this space and were uncovered, but too black with night for Sabina to see the view Ambrose would have from his bed, or from the single chair, a patchwork recliner. A good-sized oak table with claw feet dominated the middle of the room and it was piled high with more papers, magazines and, oddly, the mounted and stuffed head of a black bear, snout up.

The bathroom door opened. John pushed Ambrose over to the bed and stooped to lift the footrests of the wheelchair. Ambrose slapped at his hands.

"I'll take it from here," he said gruffly.

John looked like a summer hire, raw and scared. By his hesitation, Sabina concluded that Ambrose was not in the habit of doing for himself at this stage; this was for her benefit.

"I said vamoose you ... get out!"

There was plenty of power left in that voice; it acted like a shotgun at John's backside. The door snicked shut behind him and then blew open again. They heard John flying down the metal steps and an airy "god*damn*" floated up behind him.

A nervous laugh escaped Sabina. Ambrose looked pleased, whether at her enjoyment or the young man's distress, she couldn't tell. He snagged a walker and locked his chair, then heaved to his feet, pivoted, and backed up to the bed. She forced herself to watch him since that's what the man apparently wanted: Was he after making her uncomfortable, giving himself an edge? She would not oblige. She stood impassively, making herself relax. His eyes darted at her. He lifted his legs into bed and covered them with an ugly brown-gold afghan. As he squirmed around, getting comfortable, he was scowling in annoyance.

"You gonna get that door or you expect me to?" he snarled.

When Sabina turned around from closing the door, he had removed his ubiquitous leather cap. Lamplight gleamed off the smooth skin of his high forehead, and the raised welt or bump that had reminded her on their first meeting of a hacked-off rhinoceros horn.

Ambrose worked a control at his side and the bottom of the bed ground until his knees were propped up. "I didn't expect company," he said angrily.

"You invited me."

"Hah! Didn't think you'd come!" He made a stab at flirtation. "Unchaperoned ladies ..." The energy dribbled away and the old man tossed his head as if to say, enough with the games. "Why did you?" he asked.

"I thought we should talk."

Ambrose raised his chin. "I'm taking this drink," he declared. "You?"

Why not. "I'll get it," she told him. From another part of the house, water whooshed through pipes. Sabina poured them a half tumbler each.

Ambrose's hand trembled as he accepted his glass. "Goddamn old age."

"I didn't notice it earlier." This sounded cooler than Sabina felt. "Maybe something else is making you shake."

Ambrose's neck was so immobile that looking up at her was an effort. He gave it up and swallowed a big gulp of Glenlivet. It burned just to watch. When he spoke again, it was with the old command.

"Siddown over there," he ordered, the liquor sloshing onto his knuckles as he gestured at the multicolored recliner near the foot of his bed.

Sabina moved instead to the cluttered table. She stacked loose magazines into a pile and perched on the cleaned space, gazing down into the open, snarling snout of the stuffed bear. Its incisor looked sharp. She tested it with her thumb and then said, her heart pogo-sticking, "I thought we should talk about Matthew's murder."

His answer ambushed her. He said, "Me, too," and he chuckled. "You're not as smart as you think you are, Missy, because that's exactly why you're here." He massaged the bridge of his nose and stared at the drink in his other hand. "You got it all figured out, I see. Kendall killed his father."

Sabina lowered her palm over the tip of the wide yellow tooth, tracing a light, tickling circle. It wouldn't be a simple thing, to puncture flesh without the bear's cooperation, without the torque of live jaws scissoring together.

"No," she answered him. She lifted her eyes and waited for him to cease worshipping his booze. "No. I think you killed Matthew."

The old man's lower lip relaxed against a line-up of small

brown teeth. That, and silence, was the extent of visible surprise from the old meat king.

"I'm not wrong," Sabina said. "You had it done."

He nodded, and raised his glass to her.

"You're admitting it?" She had expected a fabrication. Surely Ambrose knew this bedroom *tête-à-tête* was no social occasion.

"Hell, yes, why not," he snapped, surly as ever. "Didn't I say that's why I got you here? You're my witness. My grandson's insurance policy."

Sabina needed to lean against something. She picked up her glass and crossed to the recliner.

"Tell me," Ambrose said, eyes shut prayerfully. "You alone in this? Do the cops think Matthew's murderer was someone different?"

"So far they accept the Poet's confession—Rudy Parson—for all the murders." She thought of Mark Samuel. "There's one who suspected Kendall. Now, I'm not so sure."

Ambrose smiled, satisfied. "That's the one Kendall told me about. After this Parson was arrested, *then* the boy tells me about this detective nosin' around him. Hah! Kenny couldn't kill a mosquito if it wore a malaria sign around its neck." He spun his glass between the palms of his hands. "So," Ambrose summarized. "Good I got you here then. If suspicion ever does fall on Kendall, I want someone to know the truth. Enough to create what they call reasonable doubt. This Poet may not hold to his story, or that cop might get curious again, find some evidence that looks funny. I can't have them screwing Kenny with this. Can't have it."

He rummaged through a bedside drawer and came up with a half-chewed cigar, tongued it, and stuck it in his mouth. "Now tell me how you know it was me," he said, with a suggestion of anticipation. Read me a story, mommy.

He still wore the putty-colored hearing aid curled like a fat worm behind one ear. "I could show you," Sabina said. "Turn the volume down on that hearing aid. Like you do when you take a phone call?"

Ambrose started to reach for it, then returned his hand to his lap. "Blasted thing squeals," he confirmed. "What's your point?"

This was the guesswork part. "Kendall told you about a nickname for the killer. Remember?" She deliberately lowered her voice. "P.S. Eliot."

"Yeah," Ambrose said. "T.S. Eliot. What I specified they should use on the note. So what? They bought it, didn't they?" He clamped down on the cigar.

"I said P as in persimmon, Mr. Drum. *Pee* S Eliot, because of the P.S. dedications in the Poet's notes. *Pee* S Eliot was a *private* joke between Kendall and Ella Martinelli. It was too much of a coincidence, that the Poet would sign his last note T.S. Eliot. And people hard of hearing have big problems with the phone. You heard wrong."

The cigar shifted from side to side. "Wait a minute," he said. His hand fluttered up to the rhino knob. She began to hope it was a tumor, and malignant. "Kendall's the one found that note, so when you say, coincidence ... does the boy think that I ... does he think I ..."

"What's wrong, Ambrose? You can do it, but you can't say it? God." She considered her half-empty glass of Scotch, considered the source, and set it on the floor.

"Kendall has sure been covering for you," Sabina said. "He's sure been acting guilty. For you."

It was easy now to put herself in Kendall's shoes and see how it all fit. He wasn't just covering up his own minor crime of busting into the file that disclosed the MOSS sale memorandum. He was far more desperate—after reading the botched signature on the death note—to hide the fact that his beloved Pops had sufficient time and resources to plot Matthew Drum's murder. Kendall dredged up every bad memory he could of his father to make bearable his knowledge of who the murderer really was. Perhaps even to help him excuse Ambrose for the act.

"If you want to know for sure if Kendall suspected you ... after Matthew was murdered, how long did it take Kendall to call you?"

Ambrose tugged at an ear, thinking. "He didn't," he said, distressed. "He never did, I saw it on the news." He pointed at the looming TV screen. "The boy never did tell us himself, we had to call him. But he buys it now," Ambrose exulted after a moment. "When this Parson fella was caught, Kendall called me right up. Sounded more like himself." Ambrose raised his glass in a toast. "My boy Kendall. What a loyal boy."

She leaned forward, elbows on her knees. "Your boy Kendall," she said, repulsed.

"What?" Ambrose asked. He dialed up the volume on his hearing aid.

"Your boy Matthew! What about your boy Matthew, you sick old freak!"

Sabina was coiled at the edge of the chair, shivering from the inside out. Ambrose Drum showed her indifference; nothing else. He lifted his chin and regarded her down his nose.

"What do you know about families, my dear girl? About dynasties, and dreams." He pulled the cigar from his mouth and laid it on the bed. "Call me whatever, heard it all before. Egomaniac. So be it. What do you think Matthew was?"

She felt cleaned out of words. If he wanted to share the tale of injustice done him, he'd have to do it without any wheedling from her.

After a long silence, he did.

Kendall called his grandfather on Monday night, five days before Matthew was murdered, to tell Ambrose that Matthew was selling the paper and breaking his promise to Kendall. What was Kendall to do now, he asked his grandfather. Where would he go.

"The boy cried," Ambrose said, somewhere between pity and disgust. "His father ... this was one more in a string of goddamn betrayals, and the last one, by God!"

To provide Kendall an alibi for the murder, Ambrose made his grandson promise he'd come home for the weekend. It was Kendall's regular weekend visit, once a month, and he had never failed, but this time Kendall broke that promise when Ella Martinelli made him a better offer.

"I've been prayin' for years the boy would put it to some young thing," Ambrose said. "Didn't think he could get it up! Hah! He picks that weekend to do it!"

The son of a bitch shook his head like, isn't that just my luck, to have it rain on my golf date. He went on to relate what must have been, in his mind, the most egregious of Matthew's betrayals; one their cab driver, Mavis, had alluded to. In 1982, Ambrose asked Matthew to come back into the family business. He needed his son's help in raising money to upgrade the plant and Matthew had worked in investment firms during the heyday of leveraged buy-outs. Matthew succeeded in getting all the money Ambrose needed, and more, in the form of an acquisition offer for the business.

"Against my will!" Ambrose yelled, pounding his old freckled fist on the bed. "Without my knowledge! The goddamn yellow snake." He was gripped by a bitterness so profound even murder could not, apparently, appease it.

Ambrose sent the buyer packing. So Matthew made another run at the business, in secret. A real estate conglomerate owned major stock in the Drum Meatpacking Company and

Matthew quietly bought up those shares, increasing his ownership stake and diminishing that of his parent's shares. Ambrose—without Lucille—sued Matthew for breach of fiduciary duty. Matthew sued back. It was settled by the courts with Matthew buying them out, after which he made a few "face-lifting" improvements.

"And sold it to a stranger!" Ambrose raged. "To a stranger! Who tore it into pieces and sold it again. My grandson's birthright, what I built, what my father built, what *his* father built!"

Vengeance is mine, saith the Lord. His rage was so fresh, so savage, it was as if it had all happened yesterday and Ambrose had been waiting mere moments, instead of years, for his payback excuse.

He thrust a thumb at the controls and the bed bucked in the middle. He swore and punched again, lowering the head of the bed to a forty-five degree angle. His face was pink. If Ambrose Drum was going to have a heart attack, now was the time. Sabina wouldn't mind watching.

"I heard that Benedict Arnold once on the phone, before I cleared out of there," Ambrose said. "Heard him braggin' to his lawyer, another hoity-toity Harvard piece a shit." He licked his lips. "He was talkin' about Kenny and me, the boy had been workin' at the plant for three years and was doing good. Called my company an 'ancient, crumbling kingdom'. Said it was his job to save us. To save *us*." He raised his glass to his lips, found it empty, and brushed it off the bed.

"I'm curious, Ambrose. You're so into protecting Kendall. Why does your will deny him any money from your estate until he turns fifty?"

"Money!" Ambrose snorted. He stared fiercely at the ceiling. "Money doesn't last, your reputation lasts! What you build. I knew money would ruin the boy like it did his father. Matthew had no idea, *no idea* what it means to stay and face your problems. No idea about loyalty, about living by a man's code of honor! I believe in consequences, in accepting responsibility. Not my son! Fuckin' parasite. He got his riches, he got his fame, he paid no dues."

"What a bunch of crap," Sabina said. "God! What a lie! Kendall has all of DEI now— Who did you think would inherit it when Matthew died? That's money beyond your wildest imaginings. No. No, you King of Nothing, here's why you killed. Because Matthew took away your little piece of immortality—twice, didn't he? My mother told me Matthew got himself fixed right after Kendall was born. Goodbye to your progeny. Goodbye to the family business. And you think Kendall is not quite right with the ladies, so the great Ambrose Drum, he gets no monument at all, made of bricks or made of flesh. Isn't that it? That's why you had your son killed. It just took you a while to build up enough hate, and to find some other reason to justify it to yourself."

On target. The breath whistled in and out of those wafer-thin nostrils.

"I say, thank the Lord there won't be another Ambrose Drum in this world!" Sabina wrapped her arms around herself and struggled to steady her voice. "Now I'd like to lay a little story of loyalty on you. Something you should know about your son's awful betrayal of Kendall."

She told him of the pains Matthew had taken to form a local investor group so that Langley-Spritz wouldn't control the *Times*. How he had written into the sale contract a stipulation that Kendall be given the top position. "On *trial*, Ambrose. So he'd earn it."

She stared holes in that wasted face, waiting for some hint of comprehension, of guilt. His mouth pushed in and out, sucking on the information. It took him no time at all to compensate.

"Delayed payment," he said. "Delayed payment for all he did to Kenny and to me." The lips, in and out. "He was a monster. I made the monster and I can unmake him."

What was the point, Sabina wondered, in the face of such massive, exquisitely rehearsed self-denial. "Why do you think I won't tell the police what you've told me?"

"What for? I won't be alive by the time it got to court and I don't know the name of whoever did it. Christ, I didn't even need a professional, I coulda probably got a hundred of the laid-off guys from the plant to do it. What was hard, was getting the cash and a way for the go-between to come collect it and do the Poet note for me without Lucille catching on. I'm a prisoner in this bloody tower, it'll take an act of God to get me out of it."

"Let's all pray for that."

He snorted.

"Okay," she said. "Then why would I implicate myself as an accessory?"

"You don't have to." He jerked a thumb at his bedside table. "Top drawer. There's a dozen blank pieces of stationery in there with my John Hancock. You tell this story, if it comes to that, after I'm six foot under. Mail it anonymous from Chicago. We had three different law firms workin' for us there. The cops can figure it was one of them sent it, on my direction."

"You could get an attorney to do it, for that matter."

"Don't trust the bastards. I'm not writing anything down until there's no option."

"Then Kendall. Why shouldn't I tell him?"

He had an answer for that, too. Elastic as a rubber band he came back at her and smiled, a Machiavellian puppeteer who knew his little assistant oh, so well. "Break his heart for nothin'. Why hurt the boy? He's been hurt enough. So has your dear mother, I'd wager."

The bastard.

"I could tell Lucille, then. She has a right to know."

He showed his small brown teeth. "Hah! Scandal. She wouldn't say a word, just make my life more a livin' hell than she's doin' already."

That was a consoling thought, anyway. "And if something happens to me, what then?"

"God, woman, you shoulda been a lawyer yourself! I can't plan it out through all time. I'm eighty-five. I'm tired."

Her legs started her toward the bedside table. She found the sheets of stationery, folded them twice, envelope-size ... for all the world like a woman who had made up her mind to go along.

"I don't know," she said, thinking it over.

"Oh, you'll do it, honey," came Drum's voice from the bed. He stared up at her face, reading it, his eyes dull. "Everyone does what I want."

And then Sabina was reading him back. Suddenly, it was easy.

"And you don't really like that, do you, King of Nothing? You don't respect it, and you don't love what you can't respect.

"There is the one person," she continued slowly, tapping the stationery sheets against her hand. "One person who didn't do what you wanted him to. One person you really loved in this world. Who fought you every step of the way."

Ambrose's eyes were shuttered. He rubbed at the rhinoceros stub.

"You killed the only thing you loved." Tap tap. "No one else will ever be as much like you. Not ever."

The old lungs wheezed. "Get out!"

She stepped closer. His lips were shut over a jaw dropped wide behind them, locked in a phantom scream. A macabre face; the work of a novice mortician.

"Mr. Drum. Shall I tell you what you look like now? Yes? You look exactly as you will when you're laid in your coffin."

Sabina decided to take the outside stairs. She could use the air. At the door, she looked back. His head was turned on the pillow, watching her.

"With any luck," she said, nice and loud, "with any justice, that'll be real soon."

EPILOGUE

Justice took its sweet time. Another nine months were to pass before Ambrose Drum died.

He lived long enough to see his only descendent marry, finally, at the age of thirty-seven. Two weeks later, Ambrose was gone. In Sabina's opinion, it wasn't old age alone that killed him.

Ella Martinelli and Kendall Drum were joined in the holy bonds on Valentine's Day. It was a suitable date, for they were much in love. Sabina stood up for Ella, and Kendall's mother Ellen was his best man. Ella was allergic to flowers so she tossed Sabina a wax banana—her Toast of New York lips smiling suggestively—before ducking into the limo beside her groom.

Sabina happened to know, because Ella insisted on telling her, that Kendall Drum was a stud. "He's ready all the time, Sabina, I tell you, I've never known anyone like him! Now that he's got that sweet thing cranked up, by Christ but he can keep it going!"

By the time Ella shared that insider information they were pretty fast friends—close enough so Sabina wasn't too jealous. They sat around more than a few times, building up their capture of Rudy Parson until they were performing luminous acts of heroism. Sabina's fantasies tended toward the intellectual, Ella's were more acrobatic. At some point, one of them would begin their ping-pong toast:

"We are woman."

"Hear us roar."

She was a glowing bride. Kendall bankrolled a splashy, day-long wedding the likes of which Riverview had never seen and would not soon forget. Not that it was their plan, but it was a great start to Kendall's reign as publisher of the Riverview *Times*. The wedding brought in multiplier dollars to rival a trade show at Chicago's McCormick Center. Riverview merchants would be demonstrating their gratitude with advertising dollars for years to come.

Sabina grew more and more confident than she'd never have to save Kendall from the law. Rudy Parson's confession details held, even though he started owning up to every murder that came down the pike. No one officially questioned whether or not he had applied a similar me-me-me to Matthew Drum's murder.

Chief Sterling Opel, Mayor Roland August, even Frank Wiley all preened so thoroughly and publicly about the brave little town of Riverview facing down the Poet of Pain, the symbolic scourge of America, that nobody but nobody was going to reopen it. The case was down, the rights sold, the witnesses paid. Chief Opel used his earnings to retire from the force. Three months after the Poet's arrest, he moved to Florida and began a second career earning healthy fees for crime-fighting speeches.

Before the Langley-Spritz purchase contract for DEI was complete, Kendall Drum insisted on an amendment. It required the new owner to continue the moratorium for a minimum of three years. The nauseating biography of Rudy Parson, dragged into public view by all-the-facts style journalism, never saw the light of day in the pages of former DEI papers, nor in thirty-five other publications that boycotted the story in sympathy.

Thanks, perversely, to all the publicity on the Riverview standoff, suppression of a criminal's propaganda became a cause célèbre. It was referred to as The Poet Pledge. Proponents called it an important tool in the arsenal of activist journalism. Opponents were quick to point out that the Poet was caught, in part, *because* his notes were published.

At Rudy Parson's apartment, authorities found a scrapbook full of clippings about his fellow fraternity members, personal correspondence with some of them, and the odd photo Parson had taken whenever he could get away to hang out at some hero's trial. When Sabina heard about the scrapbook, she asked Detective Samuel if John Wayne Gacy was in it. They were having lunch at a hamburger joint and his mouth was full. He chewed with great thoroughness, swallowed, said "No."

She later learned, from a gossipy police reporter at the *Times*, that Mark Samuel left his career job in Baltimore for an ugly reason. He accidentally put a bullet through the neck of an eight-year-old kid who was playing drug lord in his mother's car. When Sabina understood that about Samuel, she thought she also knew why he didn't want to rock the boat in Riverview. And why he informally adopted Tootie.

Mark began dropping by her place on Melody Lane and Tootie, seeing the convertible parked there, would mosey on over. The detective's wife didn't like him spending so much time at Sabina's, so she started coming along. Pretty soon they felt sorry for Tootie's mother, Cindy Jergensen, and lured her out. (Karl the Jerk had abandoned her over the Christmas holidays and Sabina tried convincing Cindy he could not have bought her a better present. It wasn't easy.) Throw in Sabina's mother, Ed Fountain, plus Kendall and

Ella ... and it was a quirky new set of friends Sabina acquired. Ages ten to sixty-three and not a bike rider among them. They were all recovering from something. Tootie was often the center of attention. He adored it, in a gruff kind of way. He was pretty busy with friends his own age but he continued to toss his grunge outfits in Sabina's washing machine, saying it brought him luck. His mother promised to get him a puppy and he planned to name it Maytag.

Sometimes an entire week could pass without Sabina thinking of Jacob and it was a good thing, because he was remarrying. His bride wasn't a biker. She baked.

"I understand, Jacob," Sabina said when he told her. "Who needs to tour around France, when you can stay home and punch up a nice slab of sour dough, right?"

"Very funny," Jacob had said, grumpily. "*You* certainly sound chipper."

As Ambrose Drum would say: Hah.

Handy Andy Webster would have been a colorful long-distance addition to Sabina's new society of friends, but he retreated so thoroughly Sabina couldn't even get him on the phone. She called right off to thank him for sending in the cavalry on the day they captured the Poet. A man named Sojo answered. He put the phone against his chest, came back on and said, "Andy says you're welcome, babe. *He* said the babe part."

"No kidding," she said. "There's something else. Tell him we're being pestered to give the details of how we tracked down the Poet and it's no story without him."

"Uh-huh."

"Would you ask him that? He's the real hero here."

"Ask him what."

"Should we give his name to the reporters?"

For this, Sojo put the phone down but was back in short order. "Says, he don't care about being no dead hero."

Made sense to her. It plain hadn't occurred to Sabina that Ella and she might be tempting targets for the next Poet. They consequently avoided all the publicity they could without cheating the legal process. (Rudy Parson made it a lot easier by pleading guilty.) To outsiders, their silence looked like they were either heroically modest, or cleaving to the principles of the moratorium. Not exactly.

As for the management consulting profession ... Sabina grew to like it, most of the time. A former parts supplier for Linshaw Bicycle Works put her on a one-year retainer and she picked up two jobs from a Rotary speech.

Naturally, she refused Ambrose Drum's help.

That last morning in Kansas City, her mother swung her legs over the side of the bed at dawn, her cheek creased from sleep, and declared they had to get out of that house.

"I really cannot face another meal with those people, Sabina. What is that song?" She scratched a foot, trying to remember. "'Who should you call,' it goes."

Sabina laughed. "Who you gonna call ... Ghostbusters!" And there was the answer lying lonely on the dresser between their beds. "Hey, we don't need ghostbusters, we've got Mavis!"

They caught Mavis—as she had predicted they might—in her bathroom, and were rescued and gone by 6 AM, leaving behind a note of weak excuses for Lucille. The beds at the Ritz-Carlton were wide and soft and with Mavis as their personal escort, Sabina and Peg had a good deal more fun than the average tourist.

Sabina thought about Ambrose frequently in the weeks after their visit, and she wrestled with her silence; her compliance to his wishes. A conversation with Kendall Drum helped her come to peace with it. It was more of a monologue than a conversation. Kendall was excited about all his modernization plans for the business and even more excited that Ella had agreed to marry him. When Sabina asked if his grand-parents were coming to the wedding, and his newfound mother ... the floodgates opened.

"I've been thinking a lot about my family," Kendall said. "Trying to figure out what went so awfully wrong. The way I work it out, is it all started with Kendall—my uncle Kendall, he would have been—getting killed in the Korean War.

"Grandmother blamed Pops for forcing Uncle Kendall to enlist, and he blamed her for denying him *his* shot at being a World War II hero. He used to say she deliberately got pregnant with my father to keep him home. When Kendall the First was killed, it seemed like Grandmother's lifelong campaign was to make sure that my Dad didn't turn into another Ambrose. And to train him to hate Pops, too.

"You know how I got my name, don't you? Dad's one condition before he'd let Pops adopt me was that my name be Kendall. He wanted to rub Pop's nose in it, make me a permanent reminder of the first Kendall. I always thought my father didn't care a thing about me ever, not even when I was a baby, but your mother told me a story about how he searched for just the right adoptive parents, and interviewed a bunch of them, and had picked out this home for me in Italy where I would have had a good life.

"Maybe Pops should have left me alone. Maybe I would have been better off as Antonio Salvatore or whatever. I sure wouldn't have ended up a thirty-six-year-old virgin! In Italy, that's probably against the law.

"But Pops was capable of love. He loved me. Grandmother once told me that she thought my father was jealous about that. Jealous of me!

"I ran away from home once. I hid in the woods for two whole days. When Pops got hold of me again I thought I'd really get it but instead ... he cried! He said, everyone I get close to betrays me. Promise me you won't ever betray me. He was shaking me and crying at the same time; I was scared to death. I promised him.

"After I ran away that time, I was only nine or so, his tirades were never at me anymore. I could watch them and they didn't scare me anymore, they didn't move me one way or another. Pops liked that, I think. He always liked people who could stand up to him but I wasn't doing that, it's just that he had declared me off limits.

"I'm beginning to understand my father, now that it's too late. He must have been a battleground for the hate between my grandparents. He hated them both, that's how he survived. He took from both of them what he needed: money for Harvard and graduate school, some of grandmother's family's connections for early help in his career.

"Geez, what a screwed-up family. Can you understand why I wouldn't want kids of my own? Ella's two have already turned out good. I'm happy with that.

"Pops is a natural bully. He's bigger than life. But the men in the plant loved him. I was proud to be his grandson. Everything that scared me, he'd flick off like dead flies. He was a bulldozer. My own father, too. Both of them knew how to go after what they wanted in life, even if the things they wanted were kind of detestable. That gene skipped me.

"But look what I've got now. I've got Ella Martinelli to love me! Pops is still hanging in there, to see all this. And this newspaper, I can't tell you what it means to me, to have a place where I can do something important. I'm going to make this the best place to work that anyone has ever seen! People are going to love coming to work here. I don't want anything else in life: just Ella and her two kids and this. My mother is talking about coming to live here, boy that would be great. That's enough, don't you think?"

Yes, she did. And as Sabina listened to the sweet-natured man who had fallen blissfully far from the twisted Drum family tree, she completed her pact with Ambrose. For what purpose would she snuff out Kendall's long-postponed joy? There was no prospect of finding the real killer. The good of seeing Ambrose punished could not outweigh the bad of laying more ancestral pain on his grandson.

On Valentine's Day, her decision was reinforced. Lucille Drum would suffice as a tool of torture. The wedding lasted two hours, the reception rocked on and on until nearly midnight, and Lucille and Ambrose Drum stuck to the end.

For Ambrose, it was a bitter end.

The old man had dropped weight from an already spare frame. His knuckles and ear lobes and nose were huge, everything else sunken. His tuxedo stood out an inch from his neck. His skin looked strange—splotchy and dark, like the tobacco from a thousand of his unlit cigars had been rubbed into it.

A new attendant with powerful sloping shoulders and a short forehead haunted his wheelchair and when Ambrose needed to get up some stairs or go through a difficult doorway, he picked him up and tipped the frail body against his chest like a string of jointed sticks. For the proud old meatpacking king, it was humiliating. He would turn his face into the man's chest, and endure.

Sabina learned early the reason for his glowering silence. He couldn't make out what people were saying to him and so they stopped trying. Lucille had his hearing aid in the pocket of her navy silk suit. It fell out in church, when Lucille was fishing around for her glasses.

Ambrose was still without it at the reception, until very late in the evening. Guests had been taking their leave, stopping by to drop final good wishes on the bride and groom. Sabina was sitting with Kendall and Ella and Ella's two children at a table in the center of the room when Lucille approached.

"Ella, dear?" she said, laying a hand on Ella's shoulder. "My husband would like to meet your children, would you bring them over?" Ambrose sat alone at a table in the corner, his head tipped to one side and a hand raised to his ear. Lucille had returned his hearing aid to him and he was adjusting it.

Ella had been intimidated by Matthew Drum but his parents were in another league entirely. She surged to her feet, electrified, and clutched at her children's hands. Those two, Emeline and Jocko, were turned out like a magazine ad when the wedding began but now they were tired, cranky, and wearing cake on their clothes. The five of them, Kendall trailing, moved in tight formation over to Ambrose Drum. Sabina heard a whine from Jocko and his mother's sharp response, then silence. Just as they reached the old man, the band started up one of its last dispirited tunes. Sabina couldn't hear a thing; she could only watch.

Lucille stood a little apart, arms crossed over her chest. Ella pushed each child forward. Ambrose barely looked at them. He reached out a hand for Ella and she took it. A moment later, he dropped her hand, flung it from him. Kendall stepped forward and put his arm around Ella. He turned her toward him, said something to his grandfather over his shoulder, and the new family moved away in a bloc. Ambrose watched them go. He held his fists to his chest and a tremor ran through him. When he swung his head around to look up at Lucille ... she smiled.

Sabina didn't talk to Ella again until after she and Kendall returned from their Las Vegas honeymoon. Ella said "that old fart" came close to spoiling the wedding for her until Kendall calmed her down.

"His grandfather wanted to know when we were going to start a family. I said, here's our family. He blew them away, Jocko and Em. Kendall, the sweetie, he said, as firm as I've ever heard him, 'this is my family, Pops.' That old asshole looks at me, he says, 'what's the matter with you, you can't give my grandson what he really wants?' Then Kendall said, still being so sweet to the bastard, he says, 'Pops, I'm adopting these children. This is my family. I think you should apologize to Ella.'

"Well, of course, the old fart didn't. He just reaches up and turns off that hearing aid, just tunes us out and then slumps in his chair like I've stabbed him through the heart or something."

"How did Lucille act?" Sabina asked. "Did she say anything?"

"No, and she should have. I mean, she knew what our plans were. She even brought it up, while I was getting ready for the ceremony. She said, in that snooty way she has, 'Kendall tells me you have elected not to have more children, my dear.' I told her, I should say so. I told her I got my tubes tied when Emeline was born, so it wasn't like I could change my mind even if I wanted to.

"I mean, the old bitch knew that. So that little scene with her husband, what was that all about?"

To borrow Ambrose's favorite word and turn it on him: Hah. Sabina could hear him plain as a bell ... until the memory was run down by another, by Matthew's voice.

In her head, in her heart, it said: *Checkmate.*